7-2014

W9-AHR-511

JUST 18 SUMMERS

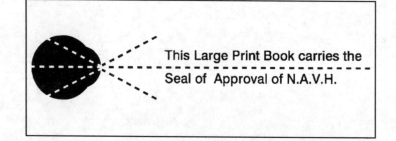

This Large Print Book carries the
Seal of Approval of N.A.V.H.

JUST 18 SUMMERS

RENE GUTTERIDGE
& MICHELLE COX

*Based on the screenplay by
Marshal Younger, Michelle Cox,
and Torry Martin*

THORNDIKE PRESS
A part of Gale, Cengage Learning

 **GALE**
CENGAGE Learning·

Farmington Hills, Mich • San Francisco • New York • Waterville, Maine
Meriden, Conn • Mason, Ohio • Chicago

GALE
CENGAGE Learning®

LIBRARY OF CONGRESS CATALOGING-IN-PUBLICATION DATA

Gutteridge, Rene.
    Just 18 summers / by Rene Gutteridge & Michelle Cox. — Large print edition.
        pages ; cm. — (Thorndike Press large print Christian fiction)
    ISBN 978-1-4104-6925-0 (hardcover) — ISBN 1-4104-6925-5 (hardcover)
    1. Wives—Death—Fiction. 2. Family vacations—Fiction. 3. Parenthood—Fiction. 4. Child rearing—Fiction. 5. Large type books. 6. Domestic fiction. I. Cox, Michelle. II. Title. III. Title: Just eighteen summers.
    PS3557.U887J87 2014b
    813'.54—dc23   2014006579

Published in 2014 by arrangement with Tyndale House Publishers, Inc.

Printed in the United States of America
1 2 3 4 5 6 7 18 17 16 15 14

For John and Cate

— R. G.

For Jeremy, Tim, and Jason
The summers didn't last long enough.

— M. C.

CHAPTER 1
BUTCH

Used to be, in the "olden days," as his father-in-law called them, the seasons were predictable. Winter ushered in a chill that stayed in the bones until spring thawed the snow and ice and brought in comfortable temperatures, gradually warming day by day into summer, when stifling heat had to be endured only for a little while because fall was around the corner.

But that was before global warming, or as Butch Browning liked to describe it, before seasons became irrelevant. Now there were tornadoes in winter and heat waves in May.

The kind of sweat induced by both heat and extreme boredom dropped from his brow onto the face of his watch as he checked it for the fourth time in ten minutes. He tugged at the collar of the only starched shirt he owned and listened to a young woman, introduced by the principal as Madison Buckley, read from the dictionary during her valedictorian speech. She was literally reading, word for word, all the definitions of *success*. For the price of valedictoriandom, he thought she might be able to come up with one on her own, but it didn't look like it.

Butch endured this graduation ceremony at the football stadium, during record-breaking heat on a virtually windless day, only for his nephew. Jenny's nephew, to be exact. But this morning when he was thinking of skipping the ceremony and mailing the gift, he'd heard her displeasure, in the form of guilt, like a wave rolling him right out of his bed. She placed a lot of importance on family. Always had. When he'd had a falling-out with his father years ago, it was Jenny who worked to get them set right.

It wasn't Butch's thing, though.

He was soaking straight through his only good shirt, listening to an eighteen-year-old lecture other eighteen-year-olds on how to succeed in life. *Yeah, well, life has a way of making sure you don't see what's coming.* That's what he'd say if he were up there.

He glanced down at Ava sitting next to him, her hip touching his. Now that Jenny was gone, she never sat by him without touching him. It was something he'd had to grow used to. He was a man who cherished

8

personal space.

He'd been a lot of things before, with no clue as to what he should be now. Every day was like wandering into a dark forest with no map, no compass, and a flashlight that had pulled nearly all the juice from its nine-volt battery.

Ava tugged at the neck of her shirt. Sweater, to be exact. Christmas sweater, to be more exact. It had Rudolph on the front, with a bright-red blinky nose that had actually worked before Butch accidentally washed the battery pack he was supposed to know to remove. But it was the only thing he could find that was clean this morning, as they'd overslept and he'd rushed to get them both ready. He didn't turn on the news to hear the meteorologist's prediction of unseasonably warm weather. But who was he kidding? A sweater like this shouldn't be worn past February — any idiot would know that.

His daughter's cheeks were bright red and her bangs had curled into a wet mess on her forehead, but she sat upright, not complaining, focused on the young blonde woman at the podium who droned on and on about her vast achievements. Ava's little mouth moved as she unconsciously repeated the words to herself. It broke Butch's heart.

Jenny used to do the same thing when she was intently focused on a conversation.

Finally, at the point that his deodorant had failed its commercial claim of lasting for twenty-four hours in the Sahara, they got around to calling out the names of the graduates.

"Nathan Anderson," said the monotone voice over the loudspeaker. Cheers erupted and Butch clapped loudly and whistled through his fingers.

Ava, a sweaty mess of heat and charm, grinned at him. "You gotta teach me how to do that whistle thing."

"Okay," he said. At least once a day she asked him to teach her something. He hadn't gotten around to any of it yet. He was still teaching himself how to do laundry. He'd almost gone broke buying them new packages of underwear every week for the first eight weeks after Jenny died. Now he could do the basics of throwing in a load with all the right colors, at the right temperature, with the right detergent — when he had the time.

He remembered a moment three weeks after they were married — Jenny holding up a white shirt that had ended up smeared with pink, thanks to the lipstick she'd left in a pocket. *That laugh.* He missed it. He craved it.

Suddenly hats shot high into the sky on the football field and the band started playing something triumphant. Time flies when you're lost in thoughts of days before you had to learn to do laundry.

Like an avalanche, the crowd rolled down the bleachers and onto the field to find their graduates.

"Hey, Ava, stay right by my —" Butch looked down, but she was gone. "Ava?"

He barely caught the top of her little head bobbing between people as she raced to find her aunt Beth. Maybe he should worry about her more, but sometimes it seemed his little girl knew how to take care of herself better than he did.

With the back of his sleeve, he wiped his forehead as he made his way down the bleachers. The field was so crowded he was actually locked in place by a couple of families, unable to move anywhere. All he could do was stand there and wait for someone to step aside. Jenny used to tell him he should be more assertive, but he could only assert himself in the place he felt most comfortable — a construction site. So he just stood.

But then his gaze wandered to the place he'd tried not to look the entire time he'd been at the football stadium. Across the field were the home team's bleachers. And eight rows up, in the center section, was the place he'd first seen Jenny. He'd transferred over from his old school and been backup quarterback his junior year. It wasn't until his senior year that he even had the courage to talk to her. She sat in the same place every home game, cheering and holding up some kind of poster she'd made. He'd heard she used to be a cheerleader but blew out a knee her sophomore year. She was voted "most liked" their senior year. Four days before they graduated, he asked her out.

"Madison! Beautifully done!" a woman said. Butch snapped his attention back to the field. A striking and severe-looking blonde woman embraced the valedictorian. She swept the girl's hair out of her face and smoothed her gown. "I thought you were going to get your bangs trimmed."

He imagined what Jenny would say to Ava if she were valedictorian. Probably nothing about her bangs.

A man, presumably the girl's father, shook her hand and nodded in agreement like they'd just signed a binding contract. The whole family seemed very pulled together, dressed correctly for the weather and weirdly sweat-proof.

Finally the sea of people moved and Butch was able to make it to Nathan, who he swore had grown a foot since he last saw him. He was now taller than his father, but still an inch short of Butch.

"Congratulations, Nathan," Butch said. He handed him the small box he'd been clutching for two and a half hours. The paper was red, the corners crisp, the tape invisible. The silver bow sparkled in the sunlight.

"Thanks, Uncle Butch." Nathan took the box.

"Yeah, good job," Ava said, tugging at Nathan's gown.

Nathan ruffled her hair and said, "Thanks, Ava." Was it just him, or had this kid's voice dropped four octaves?

Beth was now by Butch's side, looking adoringly — not at Nathan and not at Ava, but at the package. "Wow, look at that, would you? So well wrapped!"

"Oh, Jenny wrapped it before she . . . Well, obviously it was Jenny. She'd been eager to give this to Nathan for months."

He expected Beth's expression to fade into the same one everybody wore around him these days, bobbing her head steadily as she tried to find words to change the subject without looking too obvious. If he'd seen it once, he'd seen it hundreds of times. The guys at the site were just now starting to look him in the eye, and only if it was more awkward not to.

But Beth didn't do that. She smiled at him, met his eyes, just like old times.

They all watched Nathan unwrap the gift. He dropped the paper to the ground and opened the box, pulling out the small, brushed-silver pocket watch.

Beth stepped forward, touching it lightly with her fingertips. "I recognize this."

"Yeah, it was her father's . . ." Butch cleared his throat and tried a warm smile toward Beth. "Your father's, too. There's an inscription inside."

Attention shifted back to Nathan as he opened the watch and read it. " 'Psalm 90:12. "So teach us to number our days, that we may apply our hearts unto wisdom." ' "

"Beautiful," Beth said, patting her heart while simultaneously taking Butch by the arm, leading him to turf a few feet away.

Beth had a warmth about her that reminded him of Jenny. The sisters didn't look alike, but they cared alike. Beth was just slightly nosier. Her hand was on his shoulder now. "Are you okay?"

He tried to appreciate the gesture. "Yeah.

I'm fine, Beth. We're making it."

"Are you sure?"

"Absolutely."

"Because Ava's wearing a Christmas sweater during a heat wave in May."

"Oh . . . that . . ." Butch sheepishly glanced his daughter's way. Even while she was shaking the sweater to try to create a breeze on the inside, she still managed to look poised and carry on conversations. She was Jenny's Mini-Me. "I couldn't find anything else that was clean."

As soon as he said it, he wished he hadn't, because that kind of statement caused a woman like Beth to believe it was her moment to be a superhero. By indicating there might be a need in his household, he'd just handed her a cape and permission to dominate. He should've said something about misreading the weather report — thought there was a chance of snow.

". . . come over and do some laundry? I have to work tomorrow. Starting to sell a new line of party products. So far it's beating my Tupperware stint. But I could definitely come over in the evening and even set up a system to —"

"No, I can do laundry."

"Oh." She sniffed. "Do you need a meal?"

"We're fine."

"I know Ava has a couple weeks of school left. Can I give her a ride?"

"I can do that."

Butch could almost hear the hiss of air leaking from Beth, like she was about to collapse right into the grass. Even her hair looked to be wilting.

"Butch . . ." She dabbed her wrist against each eye. "I promised Jenny I'd help out with you guys if something ever . . ." Beth placed a gentle hand over her mouth, pausing as the tears rested against the rims of her eyes. "Let me live up to that promise."

Butch nodded, fully understanding the burden that came with not being able to lend a hand. Beth had a good heart.

"You can. I promise. At some point. But right now, I've got this new life. I need to get used to it."

For once they seemed to understand each other. Beth inflated with a smile, a warm hug, and a whispered thank-you. She came away a little wetter, but they'd had a moment Butch knew she needed.

"You know we pray for you every day," Beth said as she stepped back.

"Yep. Thanks."

Then he felt a hard punch on his arm. He turned to find Tippy standing next to him, grinning like a ten-year-old. "Butch."

16

"Hey, Tippy. Hi, Daphne." Butch assumed Daphne had come to support Beth, but he knew there were a thousand other things Tippy would've rather been doing. Butch could relate.

Daphne, however, seemed fully engulfed in something else. It wasn't immediately clear what that was. Since she'd gotten pregnant, Tippy had lamented on the job site every day about what was happening to his wife. "She's lost her mind," he would whisper, almost like she might be somewhere close enough to hear him make the confession. Last week he'd described her sudden need to clean everything in the house — and not just clean, but scrub "till the germs scream and run." But she seemed fine to Butch when they worked on the company's books, so it was hard to know.

"Are you two coming to the party?" Beth asked them.

Tippy nodded just as Daphne answered, "Oh, we can't. The book says I need to synchronize my sleep schedule with when I want the baby to sleep. I'm already six minutes late for my nap."

"Yeah, what was up with Madison's speech? I think the polar ice caps melted during point number seven," Tippy said.

"Shhh!" Daphne subtly pointed over her

shoulder in a way that said, *Don't look.* Naturally Butch looked.

Oooooh. He was putting it together. Madison's mom was Helen, a lady Jenny used to scrapbook with. They were neighbors with Beth and Larry. He'd thought they looked vaguely familiar in a neighborhood-barbecue sort of way.

Daphne rubbed her belly with both hands, circles in opposite directions like the "wax on, wax off" scene from *The Karate Kid.* "Beth, I'll see you at scrapbooking," she said.

Butch glanced at Tippy, who looked weary just thinking about what was ahead for him at home. "See you at work tomorrow, buddy," Butch said.

"Save me," Tippy mouthed as Daphne pulled him along. They disappeared into the crowd.

Butch wished he could offer Tippy some advice, but the truth was, he wasn't around much when Jenny was pregnant with Ava. He was consumed with work, trying to make enough money to support this kid he was bringing into the world. He'd worked long hours and weekends, too. Before he knew it, the pregnancy was over and Ava had arrived.

The conversation moved on to other

things and Butch was left alone for a moment. He observed Ava chatting with the adults like she was one of them. When he was eight, he couldn't have carried on a conversation with an adult if his life depended on it.

He was about to grab Ava and leave when he once again found himself within earshot of Helen. He tried to remember her husband's name. Jenny had talked about them, said they were the kind of people she had a hard time relating to. But Jenny always found the best in everyone. She had faith in people even when they didn't deserve it. She believed every person had a good side.

He took a couple of steps back, just for eavesdropping purposes, and turned slightly to observe as he heard the father ask if Madison was ready for her gift.

Diamond earrings, Butch guessed. That's what he would want to get Ava for her graduation gift, even though he'd have to save for months.

He noticed no one was holding any kind of gift. Instead the father took Madison by the shoulders and turned her toward the parking lot. "Right there," he said, pointing.

Helen and Madison were both looking the direction he pointed, as was Butch. They all saw it at the same time: a brand-new black

Mustang with a big yellow bow on it. The father handed Madison the keys and she squealed, jumping up and down, hugging everyone around her, then running toward the car, two younger siblings trailing in delight.

Butch stared at the car in disbelief. He'd wanted a Mustang his whole life.

"Can we really afford that, Charles?" Helen asked.

Charles. Right. That was his name. Jenny said she'd met him only a couple of times but that he seemed to be an uptight kind of fellow. He and Helen looked to be in their early forties, but their stuffy ways — and late-generation names — suggested they were older.

"Oh yes," Charles said. He didn't appear that uptight. He'd bought a car without his wife knowing and seemed extremely sure it was okay.

"Do you know something about our budget that I don't?" Helen asked.

Butch was in a full-blown stare now. She *really* didn't have a clue that Charles had bought a car, and by the strained look on her face and the way her eyebrows were almost touching her hairline, Butch realized this could get ugly very fast. At least there was something interesting to listen to on this football field.

Charles turned toward his wife and took her hands. "Well . . . I was going to wait until after the party to tell you this, but since you asked . . . I got a promotion!"

Helen jumped into his arms. It felt a bit like *Christmas Vacation,* when Clark announced they were getting a pool, until she abruptly stopped the hug and adjusted herself from the top down.

"It's a big one, too!" Charles said.

But the squealing was apparently over. Butch sighed and turned away from the glee. He observed Ava for a moment and wondered if diamond earrings would be the last thing on earth she'd want. Was he that out of touch? Didn't every girl want diamond earrings?

No. Every girl wanted a sports car. How was he going to be able to afford a car for her? At best, it'd be an old clunker, the kind with half the paint stripped off that you could hear coming a mile away.

Just then Larry, Beth's husband, gathered everyone around and turned to Nathan. "We got you a present!"

"What?" Nathan asked.

"Here you go!" And with great dramatic flair, he held out keys.

Butch shifted his attention to Nathan,

expecting him to howl with excitement. He didn't.

"These are the keys to the car I already own," Nathan said flatly.

"I know. I filled it up with gas."

"Oh. Awesome." Nathan, good kid that he was, was trying awfully hard to look enthusiastic, but his shineless eyes weren't cooperating.

Larry smiled and patted him on the back. "And there might be a check on the driver's seat."

Nathan grinned and started trotting toward the car.

Family wasn't his thing, but Butch knew there was a reason he liked Jenny's so much. They were grounded, for one. And as he watched Ava cling to Beth's waist, he knew no matter what, he had to keep them in her life, even if it meant having Beth come do his laundry once a month.

He just hoped his little girl could endure a life full of disappointments. He wasn't going to be able to give her what Jenny had given her. Jenny had almost a magical way about her, like she was born to be a mom and had superpowers to prove it.

Butch, on the other hand, knew how to draw a paycheck and keep up on the mortgage. That was it.

There was no fairy dust. Just sawdust.

"Come on, Ava," Butch said, taking her hand. "Time to go."

"Are we going to the party?" she asked. Beth slid an arm around her shoulder. A hopeful expression grew on both their faces.

"Well, um . . . yeah, maybe we'll stop by. We've got things to do. Laundry and whatnot. We'll see."

Ava began walking, glancing back at Beth. "That's a no, if you're wondering."

Butch waved and they walked to the truck together. Maybe he should take Ava to do something fun today. A trip to the park. He opened the door and she climbed into the front seat, where Jenny would've never let her ride, but where she'd been riding since the day Jenny died.

Once inside the truck, he turned on the air conditioner full blast. Her hair blew backward like she had stepped into the path of a hurricane. It looked like she was riding the wind. The seat nearly swallowed her whole, though. Sometimes, with all her wisdom and maturity, he had to be reminded of how small she was.

As he managed his way out of the crowded parking lot, Butch knew the truth was that he didn't really know how to talk to his daughter. He knew he should talk more.

Mostly they watched TV together and let other people do the talking for them.

"Cool enough?" he asked over the noise of the air conditioner.

Ava nodded. Her cheeks were returning to their normal color.

"Hey, listen, sorry about the sweater thing. I don't know what I was thinking."

"That's okay." Just like her mom, she always forgave. Always.

He reached for the radio. "Mind if I put on the game?"

"Go ahead."

He smiled at her because above all things, he loved to see her smile.

And on cue, she did. "Go Chiefs." She pumped her fist.

"Red Sox."

"Football?"

"Baseball. It's baseball season now."

"Oh. Got it. Go Red Sox."

"You betcha. They're going to be good this year."

"That's good."

"Yep."

"Pizza tonight again?"

"You want hot wings instead?"

"Pizza's okay. Hot wings are usually just for adults."

"You're sure?"

"I'm sure."

He smiled and drove on, but he knew something — he'd never really understood women, and he certainly didn't understand them in pint size.

CHAPTER 2
BETH

"Thank you so much for coming!" From the door of her home, Beth waved graciously at the final guests to leave the party. They were church friends whose daughter used to babysit Nathan. That sweet, mature teenager was now an attorney with two kids of her own. How was that possible?

Inside, she heard the commotion of her family still buzzing with the excitement of the party. She stood with her back against the door, observing streamers scattered across the wood floor, balloons deflating on the table, a half-eaten cake with clumps of icing on her finest silver cake server.

She could still remember Nathan's first taste of cake, on his first birthday — a small version of the big cake they'd served to family. He'd gobbled it down without even a second thought. Robin, her eldest, had taken an entirely different approach to her first piece of cake. She gently stuck her finger into the icing, prodding it as if testing to see if it was alive. With great hesitation, she licked a very small piece of icing off that finger, eyed the slice suspiciously, then pointed to a spoon. Once she had a utensil in hand, she went forward, eating the cake with the other hand, holding the spoon in the air the entire time. Chip wouldn't touch his cake and to this day had a strong aversion toward icing that nobody could really explain. Beth thought it might be due to the cupcake binge she'd gone on three days before he was born.

Now, in a few short weeks, Nathan would be off to college. Robin was home for the summer. She'd been away at college, getting her basics, undecided in her life goals, but Beth tried not to push. A couple of months ago Robin had talked about taking some summer classes. They'd have to discuss that soon. After that, only Chip would be left at home, and if Beth wasn't careful, in the blink of an eye he'd be gone . . . grown. He was already taller than she, passing her by two inches in the spring.

Beth stepped toward the cake table, taking the knife and wiping the icing off with a napkin. What was happening to her life? When had motherhood begun to flee? It was the only thing she knew. She could barely remember life before kids. What did she do with all her time?

Cupping her hand, she began dusting the crumbs off the table into the other hand. Behind her, echoes of the family all together, all under the same roof, gave her peace.

Soon she went to join them in the living room, smiling through the pain of realizing that come August, they were going to lose Nathan. Not lose him like he was a set of keys, but lose him from the safe haven of the only place he'd called home. He'd gotten a scholarship to Ohio State. It was a fifteen-hour-and-thirty-two-minute trip by car, if you averaged Google Maps with MapQuest. She'd checked it three times.

Beth paused just inside the room, listening to Nathan laugh. His voice was so deep. He was, after all, eighteen, but she could still see that boyish charm in those big, beautiful eyes, now shadowed by a strong brow, just like his father's. Robin giggled the same way she had since she was two. Beth watched them all as they relived the "worst valedictorian speech ever," with Chip, fourteen going on twelve, imitating Madison as she kept flipping her hair with her fingers while she spoke. "Shhh!" Beth said. The Buckleys were their neighbors, and though she was certain a great deal of space and building materials separated the two homes, Helen was nosy enough to render walls useless.

"You did great, honey," Larry said, walking to Beth and bringing her to his side. "That cake was amazing! Glad we have some left." He pecked her cheek and grabbed the remote to turn on the TV. She marveled at how he didn't seem at all bothered by the "lasts" that were taking place right in front of their eyes.

Nathan, engrossed in his phone, lightly punched her on the arm as he walked by. "Yeah. Good party, Mom."

She mustered a smile while remembering him standing in that very spot, holding his diaper in one hand and a wipe in another, having decided at the age of eighteen months that he was perfectly capable of changing himself. Then he wet the floor. It had been such an inconvenience . . . they were late for church and she had a big mess to clean up. But what she wouldn't give to be able to hold him in his diaper again.

"I'm going to bed," she said, starting to head upstairs.

"What? So soon?" Larry asked. "*Cake Boss* is on."

"I'm all graduated out. . . ." She smiled like she meant it, but a lot was changing.

This wasn't her first time to have a child move out. Yet she was taking it much worse than she had imagined. Why? She'd always had great plans for that middle bedroom upstairs. It had its own bathroom . . . perfect for a guest bedroom, she thought. She'd reimagined it a hundred different ways thanks to all the home-decorating shows. Now she'd give anything to keep the Star Wars sheets on the bed.

"Good call," Larry said. "I'll DVR it for you."

"Okay," Beth said lightly. Upstairs, she grabbed her pajamas and went into the bathroom to change. But once she closed the door, the tears she'd been holding in all day caught up to her. She leaned on the bathroom counter and tried to compose herself, but they kept coming. Closing the toilet lid, she sat down and rested her head in her hands, elbows on her knees.

"Jenny . . . ," she sobbed. This would be a time when she would normally call her sister, drive over in her pajamas, and they'd eat ice cream while Jenny somehow found the bright side to it all. Now Beth had to find the bright side all by herself. She'd spent every day of her life praying for her children and her family and her marriage. God had always been there, easy to talk to.

But tonight her prayers were like hollow, empty echoes against the cold bathroom tile.

Beth wiped her eyes when she heard Larry come into the bedroom. He rummaged through his closet. She sniffed the last of her emotions up and away and quickly changed into her pajamas. She scrubbed her face and teeth and then opened the bathroom door. Larry was at the foot of the bed untying his shoes.

"Robin is back!" Beth sang. "That's what I'm going to focus on. Robin is back for the summer, and God knew I needed all three here for a little bit with Nathan leaving."

"Are you okay?" Larry's eyes were wide.

"I just came into the room telling you my positive thoughts."

"I know. But you look terrified."

"I do?"

"A little. In the eyes."

Beth dropped to the bed, falling backward and resting with her arms flung open against the comforter. "I'm just trying to not fall apart, I guess."

"Me too."

Beth looked at him. "What do you mean? You seem fine."

Larry shrugged and said nothing. He took his pajamas and went to the bathroom, quietly closing the door.

Larry was fine. He was always fine. He was a rock. She had to be strong too. That's what Jenny would've told her — to be strong and find the good.

CHAPTER 3
LARRY

Larry stood as Gerald shook his hand. "Great job, Larry. These sales numbers are impressive. I usually dread the board meetings, but not tonight. You've done an amazing job turning all this around."

"Thanks, Gerald. Let me know how the evening goes."

"You want to join us afterward for dinner? Don Huffman will be there, and it never hurts to rub shoulders with him."

"Nah. Going home tonight. Nathan's leaving for college in the fall, so I want to . . ."

But Gerald had lost interest as his phone dinged with a text. Larry smiled to himself. Right now Gerald's kids were still in junior high, so maybe he couldn't relate. One day he'd know.

Larry got himself some coffee and went to his desk. He tried to focus on work, but his mind was captured with ideas about what he and Nathan could do together this summer. Maybe catch a Chiefs game. Or go see the Grand Canyon. Do a *Diners, Drive-Ins and Dives* tour.

An hour sped past, interrupted by his office phone buzzing and his secretary's voice coming through crackled and irritated, which was nothing new. Carol was the kind of person nearly every other person feared becoming when they got old. Two more years and she'd be retired. He didn't want young and flirty for her replacement. He just wanted stable and flexible and not chained to nicotine. Carol had finally switched over to the new vapor cigarettes. Every time he walked by, she was sucking on those things like a baby with a pacifier. She had nearly every flavor they made, but they didn't seem to make her less cranky.

"Larry, your daughter is here to see you."

"My daughter?"

"That's what I said. She has her boyfriend with her."

"Her . . . her what?"

"Send them on down or what?"

"Um, yes. Please."

Larry stood and opened his office door. What was Robin doing here? She never came to his work. He wouldn't have even thought she knew how to get to his office. His heart filled with dread. This couldn't be good, whatever the reason was.

Robin breezed down the hallway in a yellow sundress. Behind her was a guy he recognized, a friend of hers, dressed a little slouchy for Larry's taste — flip-flops, jeans that dragged on the ground, and hair past his chin, cut exactly how Beth had worn hers when Robin was tiny.

"Dad!" She wrapped her arms around him.

"Hi, spumpkin," he said, using the nickname he called her as much as possible. She never cared when he said it in public. "What are you doing here?"

"Can we sit down?" she asked.

Larry looked at the kid behind her, who was grinning, his hands in his pockets, his plaid shirt buttoned slightly askew.

"You remember Marvin, right?"

They shook hands. "Marvin, yes. How are you? You're Robin's friend from college, right?"

"Well, I live near the college, but yeah . . ."

Larry shut the door behind them and offered the only two seats in his office, mismatched chairs that needed to be recovered. But he didn't really have that many visitors outside company personnel.

"So what's going on?" Larry asked as he sat back down behind his desk. He punched

35

his desk phone to silent, a feature he'd actually never used before.

"Well," Robin said, a huge grin stretched across her face, creating dimples in each of her cheeks. "Marvin has something to ask you."

Larry rested easier. Marvin probably wanted some business advice or perhaps thought Larry could get him an interview at the company. Larry's first advice would be to tuck his shirt in and get a haircut, but he reminded himself to keep the horse before the cart.

"Mr. Anderson," Marvin began. Larry noticed the kid was trembling.

"Yes?"

"I wanted to . . . I wanted to ask . . ."

"Yes?"

"For your daughter's hand in marriage." Marvin reached over and literally grabbed Robin's hand.

Larry grasped the edge of his desk, suddenly feeling like he was falling. "You, uh . . . what?"

"Marriage," Marvin said plainly, loudly, like perhaps he'd mumbled it the first time.

"Robin?"

"Yes."

"Dad?" Robin leaned forward. "Are you okay?"

"This is just . . . so . . . shocking. I mean . . . shouldn't you date first?"

"Dad!" Robin giggled. "We *have* been dating. For four months. We started out as friends — you know, like you and Mom. And then we decided we really liked one another and now we're getting married!"

Larry grabbed his chest where it felt like his heart broke. "But . . . aren't you *asking* for my permission here?"

Marvin cleared his throat. "Yes, sir. I believe in trying to keep the older folks' traditions, you know, and I told Robin that was, like, a sign of respect I needed to do."

Larry thought Marvin might benefit from an English class or two, but that was the least of his concerns now. Here this kid was asking permission in front of his daughter, more as a token gesture than a rite of passage.

"See? That's the kind of heart Marvin has," Robin said, filling in the long gap of silence.

"Um, sure, but . . ."

Marvin held up a finger. "Babe, why don't you go out to the waiting room for a bit and let me talk to your pops."

Pops?

Robin pecked him on the cheek, wistfully smiled at Larry, and left.

"You can just call me Larry."

"Oh, okay. Pops is what I call my . . . Anyway."

Larry folded his hands atop his desk to keep them from shaking. His knuckles were white and his stomach cramped. "Marvin, listen, I have some concerns, to be perfectly honest with you. We don't know you at all."

"I get that. I really do. If I had a little rug rat who came to me all stoked about marrying a pizza man, I'd be wondering. I would definitely be wondering."

"A, uh . . . pizza . . . Yeah. I am wondering. About a lot of things."

"First of all," Marvin said, sweeping the hair out of his eyes, "I have a job. I know that matters. I work."

"Managing a pizza place?"

"Someday, sir. It's a dream of mine. You should also know I'm an outdoor enthusiast. I love rock climbing, skydiving. I learned early on that passion takes money, and money means a job. I've worked since I was fourteen. I can make a buck go a long way. I bought state-of-the-art climbing gear for 75 percent off, just using patience and intuitiveness."

Larry hated to be so shallow and was grasping at any kind of straw here, but he was thankful the kid could use a word with multiple syllables.

Marvin was still rambling. "A few things about me that I'd want to know about me if I were marrying me or if my daughter were marrying me. I mean, I don't have a daughter — I'm just trying to provide an example . . ." Marvin took a deep breath. "I have my GED. Won't lie to you, there was a time when I didn't think high school was important, but then I came back and aced that sucker. I work extra shifts all week so I can have my weekends to play. And that's where Robin and I have really connected, you know. We climb together. She's really athletic. I taught her to kayak last weekend and she picked it up just like that. And you should've seen her the first time she sky-dived —"

"What?"

"Tandem, of course. I had her all the way down."

Larry waved his hands, trying to get the image out of his head. "Marvin, please . . . just . . . wait. This is a lot to take in. We didn't even know you two were dating. I mean, Robin has mentioned you a few times, but we just didn't realize . . ."

"Us either, us either. But then one night under the stars in the backwoods, *bam!* It was like something clicked with us, and we realized how much we loved hanging out and being with each other." Marvin scooted forward in his seat. "I really love your daughter, sir," he said with the kind of genuineness that caused Larry's guard to drop for a second. Larry slumped a little watching him. "I promise to take care of her. I know she will take care of me. We're really good for each other." His voice softened. "She's such a great person, Larry. She's kind and loving and has a real heart for God."

"We've raised her in the Christian faith."

"Me too, sir. I feel really connected to God and all that when I'm up on those mountaintops and up in the air. Nothing like it."

"So . . . you're a Christian?"

"I explain it this way: Jesus is my parachute in life. He keeps me from crashing. He takes me on the wind and gently puts my feet on the ground." Marvin smiled. "Am I right?"

"Uh, yeah. And also saved us from our sins."

"Yep, that too. That and so much more. People just stay there, you know? Don't stay there, I say. *Live* in your freedom."

Just then the door opened and Robin hopped in, her whole face bundled up with

hope. She clasped her hands together. "So
. . . ?"

"We've had a good talk," Marvin said.
"Yeah, Larry?"

"Uh, yeah, but . . ."

"So that's a yes?" Robin asked, glancing
between Marvin and her father.

Larry looked down, trying to think, then
back up.

Robin apparently took that as a nodding
of the head and squealed. "Thank you,
Daddy! Thank you! I'm so happy!"

Marvin stood and offered Larry a knuckle
bump. Then he and Robin hugged and
kissed. Larry turned to stare at his paper
bin.

"Okay, Daddy, we gotta go. We'll make
the announcement to the family tomorrow
night!" Robin let go of Marvin, walked
around the desk, and wrapped her arms
around her father. She kissed him lightly on
the cheek, just like she had since she was a
year old. "I love you."

Tears welled in Larry's eyes. He closed
them and held her tight until she let go and
rushed back into Marvin's arms.

They began to leave, but Robin turned.

"Daddy?"

"Yeah?"

"Don't tell Mom, okay? I want her to be

surprised."

He nodded. *Don't tell Beth?* How in the world *could* he tell her? As shocked as he was, this was going to be too much for Beth. Nathan leaving, Robin getting married to a kid they hardly knew, all on top of losing her sister and closest friend? He was actually glad to be the one *not* to tell her.

He watched Robin walk down the hallway, hand in hand with Marvin.

Carol was suddenly in his doorway.

"What's the matter with you?" she said, her scratchy voice a scrambled mess of damaged vocal cords.

"Nothing. What do you need?" Larry sat down in his chair.

"Chatted with your daughter out there. Said she was getting married."

"That's right."

Carol stepped in and closed the door. "You okay?"

"Why wouldn't I be okay?" Larry asked, even as he could still feel the moisture in his eyes.

She plopped down and took a drag off her vapor pipe, or whatever it was called. "Let me tell you a story. My husband is a butcher. He can chop up bovine all day long. He once got lost in the wilderness and had to survive on skunk."

Larry just blinked.

"What I'm saying is, he ain't no sissy. When our daughter eloped and returned to tell us she was married, do you know what he did?"

"Does it involve an ax?"

"He dropped to his knees and cried like a baby, right there on a rug made of a bear he killed with a bow and arrow. It does something to a daddy's heart." Carol took another drag, then held out her vapor pipe, which today smelled like lemon pie. "Need a puff?"

CHAPTER 4
BUTCH

Butch loved days like this, when the sun beat him out of bed by just a few minutes. The morning air was cool, but by lunchtime it was warm and bordering on hot. The smell of construction might as well have been a big, fat, juicy steak. It meant things were getting done, men were being employed, structures were rising, and business was good. Those things alone could get him through a day, no matter the challenges that a construction site could bring.

But now he had other worries. Jenny used to do all the worrying, enough for the both of them. Now it was up to him. It was just that he wasn't exactly sure what he should and shouldn't be worried about.

Tippy had listened to him complain all morning, and now they were on the topic of Ava's movie-viewing habits.

"It was called *The Glitter Ponies.*"

"Was it about what it sounds like it was

about?" Tippy asked as he heaved another sack of concrete out of the truck and onto a pallet.

"Exactly. It was a movie about ponies covered in glitter."

"What did they do? Fight crime?"

"No. They helped other animals that don't have glitter."

"Did the glitter give them special powers?"

"As far as I could tell, the glitter was only aesthetic."

"Did they come from a special glitter planet?"

"Unclear. Truthfully, the whole story line was hard to follow. And I think that's because there was no story line at all. There was no purpose for this movie other than to sell Glitter Pony dolls." Butch sighed. "But Ava loved it." He paused for a moment, stretching his back out. They still had a dozen more bags to unload. His muscles ached, but it was his mind that was bent. "I think I'm going to rent some World War I and II DVDs. She needs to know about Winston Churchill. Is *Schindler's List* too hard to follow for her age?"

"Probably too disturbing."

"Oh. Sure."

"You should ease into it. She's at the bottom with glitter animals, so maybe next you should try *Secretariat,* then *Where the Red Fern Grows,* and then *Of Mice and Men.* Maybe throw *Charlotte's Web* in there."

"Sure. She makes it through those and then we're right at *Band of Brothers.*"

"I don't think she could do the whole boxed set in a weekend. Maybe one DVD every Saturday or something."

"That makes sense. She just needs to know that there are no Glitter Ponies, and I don't think she knows that."

"Well, she is young. I had imaginary friends when I was young."

"Really? You don't seem like you have an imagination," Butch said.

"Well, they weren't friends so much as talking tools. My hammer and saw didn't get along."

"They still don't," Butch said, cracking a grin.

"Funny. You're never going to let that go, are you?"

"Probably not."

"Anyway, that's how I got my nickname, Tippy."

"I thought it was because you're always knocking over people's stuff."

"Common misperception. But in my imaginary world, my hammer couldn't speak very well, so instead of calling me Timothy, it called me Tippy. Then my brothers started calling me that and it stuck."

From the other side of the pickup, one of the guys walked by with a wheelbarrow. Butch tapped the top of his own head and pointed to him. "Hey! Jake! Where's your hat? You wanna pay my insurance premiums when you get hit in the head with a steel beam?"

"Sorry," he said and hurried off.

"It's Jack," Tippy said, pulling another cement sack out of the truck.

"What?"

"His name is Jack. Not Jake."

"Oh." Butch scratched his head. "That's weird. I've called him Jake since he got here. He's never said a word."

"You're not the easiest guy to approach, you know."

"Whatever. I'm as gentle as a Glitter Pony."

Tippy laughed, and they finished pulling the rest of the bags onto the pallet. Once they were done, they leaned against the side of the truck, and Butch pulled off his gloves and wiped his brow.

"How am I gonna raise this kid, Tippy?" he said, staring at the busy site, listening to

47

the drone of the tools and machines. "We have nothing in common. And what about when she starts asking about . . . you know . . . underwear stuff?"

"Get a book. They got a book on everything. Daphne bought about fifty books on pregnancy and child care." His shoulders slumped. "She's making me read them all too. I won't lie to you — it makes Glitter Ponies sound appealing. Right now I'm on a chapter that describes bowel movements and when you should be alarmed by them. I can't admit to her that all poop, no matter the color, alarms me."

Butch groaned. "I'm not walking into a store and getting a book about children's underwear. They'll put me on a watch list."

"I'm no expert, but to me every parenting question can be answered with duct tape and Ritalin."

"When she asks about underwear, I'm not handing her a roll of duct tape."

"Yeah. That'd probably put you on a watch list too."

Butch put his hard hat back on. "This is going to be a long ten years, Tippy. Maybe nine if I can get her off to college early." He felt a crushing grief swell over him. It came and went — not as often as right after she died, but he still never knew when the waves might hit. "I miss Jenny."

Tippy nodded, pulling down the brim of his hat. He gave Butch a firm pat on the shoulder. "Butch, you know, you don't have to be here. You can go home and figure stuff out. I can handle things here. It's my job." Tippy glanced at him — one of the few people who could still look Butch in the eye. "After Jenny died, you didn't even take time off."

Butch returned Tippy's affection with a hearty back slap. "Are you kidding? This is the only part of my life that I understand anymore."

"Okay, then. We better get on it. Unless, of course, we're expecting a shipment of glitter."

Butch laughed as Tippy walked away toward the site. He looked at his watch. He had to pick Ava up from school in less than three hours. Then he was going to have to explain that Glitter Ponies had no value and that maybe they should watch a PBS science show. Maybe he wasn't the best dad, but he thought that early on she should at least know there were no such things as fairy tales and happy endings.

He supposed she already knew that, first-hand.

CHAPTER 5
BETH

Beth whisked the Alfredo sauce, trying to keep it from burning, as Chip watched.

"You know, baby boy, I should've done this more often — cooked from scratch. I know how to do these things, you know. I'm a good cook. It's just that I run out of time and . . ." She checked the pasta. "Anyway, I think I'll do this more."

"What's the occasion?" Chip asked.

"Why does there have to be an occasion?"

"Because that's the only time you cook like this."

"I would cook more if I weren't running my children to every activity under the sun." She glanced at Chip. "I'm assuming you're planning on playing summer ball?"

Chip shrugged. "Thinking about it. I have until Thursday to decide. So what's the occasion again?"

"There's no occasion, sweetie. Robin asked if we were going to be home tonight.

I said yes. Then I realized you'd be home, and Nathan, too, and I thought it'd be nice to have a big family dinner. Robin's bringing a friend but that's okay. The more the merrier." Beth's phone dinged with a text. "Can you read that to me? It's your dad. I texted him about dinner."

Chip grabbed her phone. "He said 7 p.m. is fine for dinner. He'll be here right at seven."

"Your dad must be swamped at work. He never works until seven. He was late last night, too." And acting weird. She asked him what was wrong, but he'd said he was just tired. She knew he'd been working hard to try to get the sales numbers up in his division, so maybe that was it. Or maybe he was more ripped up about Nathan leaving than he cared to admit.

Beth put the green beans in the oven to roast and began shredding more parmesan cheese to pass at the table. "You know," she said as Chip watched, "this is your aunt Jenny's recipe."

"Cool."

"She was a really good cook. I told her she should start a blog about cooking when Ava got older. All of her recipes are her own. She was really good at making up recipes." Beth shook her head. "Not me. I have to follow them exactly. But Aunt Jenny, she loved to experiment."

"Maybe we should go buy Ava some summer clothes. I don't think she has any."

"She's fine. Butch just . . ." She sighed, stirring the sauce, peppering it periodically. "He just has some adjustments to make."

"Man, Mom, if you died, Dad wouldn't know what to do."

"Your dad would be fine," Beth said with a small smile.

"No, he wouldn't. The time you and Aunt Jenny went on that weekend trip, he nearly killed Robin trying to put her hair up in a ponytail."

"How could you remember that? You were like three."

"I remember the screams."

"Hey, why don't you go set the table really quick for me, okay?"

"Okay."

Affable Chip, always willing to help.

Despite her breakdown over graduation, Beth was actually feeling good today. When Robin called this morning to see if she could bring her friend for dinner, Beth realized again what a true blessing it was to have Robin home for a while. God knew. He always did. And Beth was glad. She and Robin had drifted apart a bit while she was off at college. Robin seemed restless, ready to explore the world, and Beth tried to let her. Now they could reconnect.

A car pulled into the driveway and Chip went to the front window. "Robin and that guy are here."

"His name is Marvin. You've met him before, remember? A couple of months ago?"

"Yeah, he was cool. Funny."

The door opened and Robin came in, her hair curled, wearing one of the prettiest blue dresses Beth had ever seen. "Hi, Mom," she said, hugging her warmly.

"Hi, Mrs. Anderson," Marvin said.

Robin elbowed him. "Call her Beth."

Marvin laughed. "Okay, hi, Beth. Thanks for having me over for dinner."

"Mom! What are you making? It smells amazing!"

"Alfredo," Marvin said. "I'd know that anywhere. One of the pizza places I work at makes an amazing Alfredo pizza."

"From scratch," Beth said. "It's Aunt Jenny's recipe."

"Aunt Jenny's the one who died a couple of months ago," Robin said.

"Sorry for your loss," Marvin said, looking at Beth.

"Thanks, sweetie. Well, dinner is almost

53

ready. Have a seat at the table if you want. Drinks are in the fridge."

Larry was home right at seven, as he promised, and the food was waiting on the table. Beth greeted him at the door. "Our whole family together for dinner!" she said.

"Plus one," Larry said, casting a look toward the table.

"You okay?" Beth asked. "You look pale." And he had a small line of sweat at his hairline.

"I'm fine, just hungry." He set his briefcase down by the door and went straight to the table.

Dinner was as delightful as Beth could've hoped for, and she realized just then that her life was in complete order. Maybe it hadn't been for years, with chaotic schedules including her side jobs, Larry's work, and the kids' activities, but tonight, right at this moment, life was good, all the way down to what had to be the most perfect meal she'd ever cooked. Everyone commented about it. And they hadn't even tried dessert yet!

Beth decided to clear some dishes before bringing out the cobbler. She stood and gathered her plate and utensils, but Robin said, "Wait."

"I'm just getting some dishes out of the

way to make room for the dessert."

"Before you do that, I need to tell you something."

Beth set the dishes down, remembering another time Robin uttered those same words. She was fifteen and by the grace of God had been filled with remorse for lying to them about where she'd been on Friday night. She was twenty-one now. By the delight on Robin's face, Beth knew it was going to be something good this time. All kinds of possibilities flashed through her mind. She'd decided to go to med school? She'd started training for a marathon? Unbeknownst to them she'd invested in Apple stock?

"What is it?" Beth asked. She glanced at Larry, who must've been remembering the lying incident too because he was the picture of dread.

Robin gestured that Beth should sit, and then she stood, clasping her hands together as if she were about to make a speech to a large crowd. Chip glanced around. Larry was holding his knife like he was about to stab something. Nathan was texting or doing something with his thumbs and his phone. Beth kept her attention on Robin and every minute expression on her precious face.

"Well," Robin said, swaying back and forth with her hands now clasped behind her back, "I've actually been holding on to this news for a couple of days because I wanted Nathan to have his time to shine. . . ."

Nathan looked up at the mention of his name.

"But . . . ," Beth said, gushing more than she intended. She was just really eager for some good news.

"I'm getting married!" Robin's arms shot into the air like somebody had scored a touchdown. The only one clapping was Chip.

"To . . . ?" Beth couldn't finish her sentence because her mouth wouldn't close.

"To Marvin," Larry said, looking at his plate.

"Of course to Marvin! Who else do you think it would be?"

Marvin stood and wrapped his arm around her waist.

If Beth didn't have such an aversion to awkward silence, she would've still been frozen in a state of shock, but Robin's hyper-gleeful expression was dropping by the second, so Beth did what she could to fill in the gap. "Oh!" she proclaimed, though it was so unspecific that Larry glanced down like he might've stepped on her toe. She forced a smile. "Oh, oh, oh!" She was going to have to move on to another letter of the alphabet, but she was still so stuck, so confused, so horrified. Weren't they just friends?

Larry took Beth's hand and said, "Great!"

Robin's expression dialed back up as she glanced between them.

"So great. So, so great. That's the word I was looking for." Beth held tightly to Larry. "When is the big day? To Marvin? To marry?"

"August!"

"Ahhhh . . . gust." She thought it came out like a wheeze, but it was hard to tell because Robin was happy-screaming. Now she was holding out her hand, wiggling her ring finger.

"Where's the ring?" Nathan asked.

Robin frowned. "Right there!" She wiggled her finger again. They all leaned in for a better look. Beth still couldn't see it until Larry pointed out what looked like a string around her finger. Upon leaning in closer, she could tell it was metal, but she wasn't sure it would survive a high five.

"August . . . ," Beth said again. "That's two months away."

"I know this is kind of a shock. But Marvin and I have been good friends for a while and decided to take it to the next level and then realized we wanted to take it to the *next* level."

Beth was covering her mouth, hoping it looked like delighted shock. "We didn't . . . we didn't even know . . . you were dating." Robin had brought Marvin home a couple of times, but it seemed more like a casual friendship. Robin hadn't talked of love or anything close to it.

"Good job holding our secret, Larry," Marvin said with a wink.

Beth's mouth hung open as she looked at Larry. "You . . . you knew?"

"No! I mean, not really. I mean, they dropped by my office and broke the news . . ."

"Like the gentleman he is, Marvin asked for Dad's permission."

"And you said . . . ?" *Yes?* "Yes, yes, yes . . ." Beth clapped lightly while pulling away from Larry.

Robin shrieked again with delight and then started telling the story of how Marvin proposed.

Beth said, "This definitely deserves dessert! Let me go get it!"

In the kitchen, Beth held a dish towel to her mouth. She wanted to scream, but it was the kind that should only be done facedown in a pillow.

Practically in a trance, she grabbed some dessert forks, forgot the dessert and circled back, then returned to the table.

"I have more news." Robin grinned, but it was the kind that came with the edges of the mouth trembling a little.

Beth sank into the empty chair at the far end of the table, the one nobody ever used.

"I'm taking a break from college too."

The faint sounds of video game explosions filtered underneath the closed bedroom door. Beth and Larry had said their normal good nights to their children, but nothing was normal.

Larry was in bed beside her, tucked under the covers, wearing the lightweight flannel pajamas Beth's mother had gotten him for Christmas. Those hadn't seen the light of day since they were opened Christmas morning.

"Why the flannel?" Beth asked — not as flatly as she intended — as she clutched the sheets.

"The what?"

"The flannel. You're wearing your flannel pajamas. In a heat wave."

"I am?" Larry looked down, rubbing his

chest to double-check. "Oh."

Beth rolled to her side and stared at her husband, who was staring at the ceiling.

"I didn't see this one coming," he said.

"You saw it coming before I did. I can't believe you didn't tell me."

"They wanted to surprise you."

"Well, count me surprised out of my everlasting mind. Larry, she's getting *married.* Three days ago she was in a car seat. And why is she dropping out of college?"

"It's like we lost two kids in one week," Larry said. Beth noticed he was still wearing his watch, which he usually took off before bed. She heard the ticking, not with her ears but with her heart. Time, it seemed, had always been a blatant enemy of the human race, but now it was her own personal foe, and she never saw it sneak up on her.

"She assured me after dinner that she was just taking a break," Larry said. "She and Marvin want to work with inner-city kids or something — I don't know. . . ."

"How did we get here?" Beth breathed. "And Marvin? What do we know about this boy? He delivers pizza. He needs a haircut. That's it. Were they really that serious? Did I miss something?"

"He didn't even ask my permission." The slight warble in his voice was the only hint at that deep wound. "I mean, he did, but they were already planning to get married. Maybe it's no disrespect. It's the generation . . . the no-permission-needed generation."

Beth sighed. "That's what you're worried about, Larry? We hardly know this boy. *She* hardly knows this boy."

"I would've said no."

"Really?"

"I don't know. Maybe not. He's kind of likable."

"Kind of clueless, at least from what I can tell." Beth rolled to her back. "Is this really what Robin wants for her life? To be married to a pizza man?"

Larry took her hand. "Well, if I remember right, when we married, I was tossing newspapers. And not even real newspapers. Advertising newspapers that had lame coupons."

Beth tried to smile. "Yeah. But you didn't *like* it. Marvin doesn't seem to have any life goals besides pizza."

"He took her skydiving."

"No. Robin is terrified of heights."

"It's true. That's his other passion."

Beth flopped her arms over her face, trying to block the image of her little girl barreling through the air toward the ground.

How could she have missed the signs? She didn't dislike Marvin. In fact, she had actually liked him a lot the few times she'd met him, when she believed he was just a friend. She'd always pegged Robin's future husband as someone like a dentist or an architect or a handsome man related to Steve Jobs. What could she possibly see in a guy whose name hit the height of popularity in 1922? "Every day of her life, as she walked out that door, I prayed over her little head — that she would be okay, that her feelings wouldn't get hurt, that God would be by her side and take care of her in every way. Since her very first crush, I prayed for her soul mate."

Larry stared vacantly ahead. "It does something to a man, to know he has someone to take care of. Maybe Marvin's testosterone will kick up a notch."

"Marvin isn't the one."

"He isn't?"

"Her soul mate, Larry. He can't be, right? A boy named Marvin Hood who sells pizza. That's not her destiny."

"And she'll be . . . ," Larry started. He shook his head as if the words were too large to come out of his mouth. The next were whispered. "Robin Hood."

That fact alone caused a wash of nausea

Beth hadn't felt since she was pregnant.

They lay in silence for a while. Beth replayed the dinner conversation over and over again in her head, hoping she'd misinterpreted something. Maybe buried under the joyous screams were subtle clues that Robin truly wasn't happy about it. Beth had more gold in her fake china than was in that ring. Surely Robin had a bit of shallowness somewhere deep down inside her that made her wonder if she really could be happy with a string ring and a guy who smelled like pepperoni five days a week.

"Come August," Larry said, "we'll be down to one child."

Beth had left the room. Not physically, but she was gone, retracing every important conversation she'd ever had with her daughter, burrowing into the words, wondering where she'd accidentally misguided her. Had they ordered pizza too much over the years?

Beside her, Larry grabbed the aspirin bottle from his nightstand, the one they kept there in case of a heart attack. He popped one in his mouth. Maybe he was taking preventative measures.

Beth sank lower into the bed, pulling the covers higher up her body. "I don't think she knows about dryer sheets," she said.

Larry gulped the day-old water next to his bed. "Dryer sheets? I thought we were worried she was marrying the wrong guy."

"Yes, that. It's all so clear, Larry. Don't you see? She's not ready for marriage to anybody, pizza man or banker." Beth grabbed a pen and paper from her table. "She doesn't know about bleach! She can't sew on a button. She doesn't know at what temperature a chicken breast can kill you."

"She's got to get a degree. We're going to have to insist on that." Larry ripped the covers off and sat on the edge of the bed, his back to her.

Beth ignored him, hurriedly writing down everything she'd failed to teach her daughter. She'd thought she had time. Robin was just a kid, right? "She's just a kid . . ."

"What are our kids going to remember about us after they're out of the house?" Larry said to the bedroom wall they'd been promising to paint for five years. "The TV shows we watched together?"

"I need to show her about résumés and how to balance a checkbook. I also never taught her how to make an omelet."

"I haven't done enough stuff with them."

"Marvin should know this about her. Does he even know she can't cook?"

"I have to make some memories."

"The omelet is essential, especially when you're broke. It's cheap. It's protein. You can vary the ingredients and it feels like you're having a different meal every time."

"We're gonna do some stuff. Our family. Starting now." Larry rose.

Beth glanced up from her notes. "Like right now? It's late."

"It's never too late. That's what Dr. Phil says." He glanced at his watch. "Oh. Wow. It is late. But now I'm hungry." He walked to her side of the bed, sat down, and took the paper and pen from her. "Now you've got me thinking about omelets."

Beth felt tired, but she could never resist that smile of his. "I thought you hated my omelets."

"I haven't eaten one since the day I told you that if I had to eat one more, I was gonna puke."

"Because we ate them too much, not because they tasted bad."

"Yes. But time has passed and now it sounds good again."

"I should brush up, pay attention to my steps so I can show Robin."

"Perfect."

"You get the eggs out. I'll be down in a second." She cast him a mildly amused look and a little wink, trying to hold down the hysteria she felt building inside her. Larry, she knew, was incapable of feeling hysteria. He barely worried, which was medically provable by blood pressure numbers that rivaled men half his age.

Beth, on the other hand, had worried plenty over the years. But maybe she had worried in all the wrong places, about all the wrong things. She had worried about stains. And bills. And report cards. And all the things she thought she should — all the things the parenting magazines paid experts to write about. She'd bought books about how and what to pray over her children. It surprised her to find prayers about things like their attitude on personal hygiene. She'd never even considered that, but she prayed about it all.

But she never thought to pray about a pizza boy named Marvin. She never saw it coming. How could she have seen that coming? Now her firstborn had ambitions to be a wife. And didn't know a single way to make an egg.

Beth burst into tears.

Chapter 6
Daphne

Daphne awoke to the sounds of screaming. She sat straight up, glancing toward the open window, where a perfect breeze lifted and lowered the thin drapes she'd sewn herself three weeks ago. More screaming. This time it wasn't a dream. She'd been having bad dreams, a lot of them lately. Some friends told her it was pregnancy hormones. She thought maybe she just missed Jenny. Whatever the case, she now had a real-life, pint-size nightmare on her hands.

She angry-mumbled as she sat up on the edge of the bed. This wasn't plain old everyday screaming. It was high-pitched screaming, the kind that caused heart attacks in old women and labor pains in pregnant women.

Daphne grabbed her belly and sighed. Just Braxton-Hicks, but they were uncomfortable. How was she supposed to get any rest with these stupid false contractions and those kids running around like the world was ending?

Poking her feet into her furry slippers, she stood and shuffled to the window, whipped the drapes back, and watched the four children running in the backyard of the house next to theirs. Lily, a precocious five-year-old whose pigtails resembled horns more often than not, kept screaming and running, screaming and running. The other kids giggled, but not Lily.

Daphne got Lily's attention by waving her hands.

"Lily. Yes, you. Lily. Come here for a minute. I'd like a word with you."

Lily stood with her arms dangling by her sides, her eyes wide and searching. "I'm not supposed to talk to strangers."

"I'm not a stranger. I'm your neighbor. I've known you since you were born."

Now Lily had her arms crossed. "That's not what my mom said."

"Your mom said I haven't known you since you were born?"

"No. She said you were stranger. Stranger than our other neighbors."

Daphne crossed her own arms. "Is that so?"

Lily was beginning to look terrified, so

Daphne tried a lighthearted laugh. It failed on nearly every level. Lily looked ready to run inside.

"Listen, Lily, I just want to talk to you about all the noise you're making."

Lily took a few timid steps toward the open window that Daphne hung out of. "What about it?"

"It's just that — and maybe your mommy never told you this — but you should be using your outdoor voice."

Lily cocked her head. "Huh?"

"There's an indoor voice and an outdoor voice. See how I'm using my indoor voice right now?"

"But you're outdoors."

Technically, yes, she was, but she tried to keep on point. "And then there's an outdoor voice. An outdoor voice is slightly louder than your indoor voice. It's designed to be heard over things like the wind and maybe the rumble of trash trucks."

Lily was gawking now.

"Then there's the voice you're using."

"What's that called?" Her hands rested on her tiny hips.

"It's more the kind of voice you'd expect to hear during the apocalypse."

"The what?"

"It reminds me of the screaming you'd

hear in a zombie movie."

"I'm not allowed to watch those."

"I see." Daphne thought for a moment. "If I all of a sudden started screaming right now, what would you do?"

"Cry."

"Why?"

"Because you'd be having a baby out the window and that doesn't seem like how it should happen."

Daphne sighed. Maybe she should be more direct. "Yes, see, I'm pregnant. And pregnant girls . . . ladies . . . need naps. So that's my point — I'm trying to nap but I can't because you're screaming."

"I hate naps."

"I bet you get cranky without one, though, right?"

"My mommy calls it 'mood-challenged.' " But Lily seemed to be thinking about this. "Is that why you're like the way you are? Because you're mood-challenged? Because you don't get your naps?"

Daphne shook her head but said yes at the same time. "If you could just keep that in mind during the afternoon, I would be so grateful."

Lily nodded and left to rejoin her friends. They all started screaming.

Daphne sighed again, checked her watch,

and walked out of the bedroom. Tippy must be home. She could smell the construction site like it'd walked in her front door.

"Honey, you really have to shower when you come home from work. I can't be inhaling fumes. You know that."

Tippy made a grand, sweeping gesture around the room. Daphne smiled, clapping her hands together. "I knew this would work! And it's so cost-effective, isn't it? I should post this on Pinterest."

All around the living room, on everything that had a corner, Tippy had secured pool noodles, cut to spec. No matter where the baby fell, he or she would be completely safe and she and Tippy would stay on budget. Maybe it was a ridiculous sight. It did mess with her Pottery Barn sensibilities. But her perspective had changed so drastically lately. It seemed danger lurked around every corner ... literally around the corners, but also in food preservatives, shampoo dyes, cleaning chemicals, solar bursts, rainwater ... The list went on. She'd filled half a journal documenting everything she was supposed to stay away from while pregnant.

But today they'd conquered one issue: corners. Daphne fell into the sofa, lifting her swollen ankles onto the injury-proof coffee table.

"You okay? You look tired. Didn't you take a nap?" Tippy asked. "Butch is giving you half days off so you can rest."

"Believe me, I tried. I finished the books around noon. But Lily next door insists on playing at a decibel typically reserved for a rock concert. Doesn't she understand that even with the amniotic fluid, our baby is at risk for tinnitus?"

"She's just a kid," Tippy laughed. "They have no volume control."

"Promise me, Tippy, that we won't be those parents."

"What parents?"

"The kind whose kid throws a fit in a grocery store while they do nothing about it. We live in a cul-de-sac, not a jungle. Lily should take into consideration that there are other people living within earshot. That's all I'm saying."

"Well, I for one love to hear kids laugh and play outside. It seems the world is right when they do."

"You realize our children won't be playing in the front yard until they're sixteen."

Tippy nodded. "Of course."

From nearby, Daphne grabbed the new parenting book she'd ordered off Amazon. She was halfway through it, and it contained some of the most valuable information she'd acquired to date. The title was *Fighting Infant Obesity in the First Thirty Weeks*.

"Did you read the chapter I marked last night?" she asked Tippy, eyeing him over the book.

"Yes, I did," he said proudly over his shoulder as he tried to open a cabinet. "Why won't this open?"

"You installed that thing."

"I know, but an adult is supposed to be able to open it."

"Try to push that tab harder."

"I'm pushing it as hard as I can."

"Well, I'm comforted knowing there is no way our baby can get in there."

"It's not like it's a knife collection. It's just some junk and old board games."

"Tippy," Daphne said, lowering the book, "that might as well be a pit of vipers. Board games have tiny pieces that could choke our baby."

"True," Tippy sighed. "But all I need is some tape. If I could just get in here!"

"So back to the questions for the day. At two months, how much breast milk per feeding?"

"Five to six ounces. I'm literally going to have to take this thing off at the hinges."

"And how many feedings per twenty-four hours?"

"Eight to ten."

Daphne gasped, causing Tippy to turn around. "What?"

"Are you trying to make our child obese?"

"Sorry! Five to six. Five to six. Don't know what I was thinking. At eight to ten, I might as well feed him a cheesecake."

"Or her." Daphne smiled.

"Listen, sweetie, do you think we need to triple-proof these cabinets *now*? It's going to be months before the baby can even reach up here."

"You want our baby to be obese *and* dead?"

Tippy bit his lip. Daphne took a deep breath, trying to dial it back a notch. She knew her hormones often made it hard for her to think like a man. But she had to get Tippy to understand just how important all of this stuff was. She'd read five times the amount of literature that he'd read. The baby was coming soon and he still didn't understand the need for organic cotton burp rags. He was so behind.

"Got it," Tippy said, finally pulling the cabinet open. "Looks like you have to push down, pull with your thumb, then twist with your pinkie."

Daphne put the book down. "Tippy, our little one is going to be here soon. I know this all feels extreme, but you and I are getting ready to be in charge of a life. We have to protect this child from dust mites and bedbugs. From illiteracy and attention disorders. All before kindergarten. And those are just the tangibles. What about the intangibles? What about our child's spirituality and his or her life philosophy? We really need to plant deep-seated ambitions early on, like at six months, or our kid is going to be one of those people who deliver pizza well into their forties. You don't want that, do you?"

"It'd mean free pizza for life, right?" Tippy's grin dropped off his face. "No. Right. Obviously. Probably should have him stay away from the entire food industry to avoid obesity in general." He wiped his brow. "I gotta run to the hardware store to get some stuff to build the support beam under the crib that you wanted."

"All right. But don't stay long." She'd noticed Tippy seemed to want to linger away from home more. She'd send him out for kale and he'd return home two hours later.

Daphne wandered into the kitchen for some coconut water. Maybe he was just as stressed-out as she was. He put on a good front, acting like sending off for SAT help books now was too early, but she could feel it. He was sharing the same terror that kept her up at night, pacing the hall, wondering why they hadn't started a college fund for their child when they were first married.

Well, none of that mattered. She couldn't dwell on the past. The baby would be here soon and they had to get things in order, including the water filters he'd yet to install in the bathtub or the kitchen sink. Later she would show him the article she found on amoebas in drinking water, but for now there were other matters to attend to.

She blew out a tight-lipped sigh. The most important thing for her to remember was to stay calm, to not stress. Jenny had talked about that when Daphne first got pregnant, when they'd taken Ava to the park. "You're going to start feeling a lot of fear, but you've got to stay calm. Do a lot of praying about whatever is bothering you."

Daphne noticed that the voice mail light was flashing on her home phone. Someone must've called when she was napping. She picked up the receiver and punched in the code.

"Hi, Daphne. This is Carrie from Dr. Petree's office. Listen, just wanted to alert you that your group B streptococcus screening came back flagged. Nothing to worry about at this point, okay? It just means we'll need to treat you with antibiotics during delivery so the baby won't contract the infection at birth. See you at your next appointment. Call if you have any questions."

Daphne dropped the phone back into the charger. A wave of nausea passed over her as she slumped against the counter. Nothing to worry about? Strep B was the leading cause of life-threatening infections in newborns. It could cause mental retardation, impaired vision, hearing loss . . .

Daphne trembled, trying to remember to pray. *Breathe. Breathe and pray.* How could this happen? She'd been so careful about everything. *Everything!*

Next door, Lily screamed.

CHAPTER 7
BETH

It couldn't have been nicer weather for a Saturday in early summer. Beth stood in the kitchen stirring the lemonade. Next to her a stack of *Good Housekeeping* and *Better Homes and Gardens* magazines loomed like a skyscraper over a smaller city. She'd been a year behind until last night, when she stayed up to go through every single one. Neither she nor Larry had slept well lately. Larry plotted out their "Summer of Intense Fun" while Beth marveled at how far she was from actually doing anything worthy of these magazines.

She flipped from page to page, noticing how moms had designed entire rooms for their children's benefit, complete with DIY chalkboard walls and hidden reading nooks. She marveled at homemade cookies sitting on handmade ceramic platters in the middle of spotless kitchens. Real fruit was clustered in the bowls on the magazine counters. The bananas were actually yellow, not brown. And the kids were actually eating the fruit.

She'd had plans like these, to make memories worthy of magazine covers. But something happened along the way. She still wasn't sure what. Life, perhaps. But who doesn't life happen to? What kind of excuse was that?

She stared down at the linoleum floor under her feet. They'd vowed that the new century would not arrive before they put in tile. But here it was, green and dull and curling up at the edges.

Jenny would've never let her house go like this. She'd been the DIY queen. Of course, it helped that her husband was a contractor. But everything in her house always looked . . . perfect. Maybe if Beth had paid attention to the details, Robin wouldn't be so quick to want to run off and get married.

Larry walked in, carrying a stack of rectangular boxes. "Found them! They were buried at the back of the attic, behind the VHS boxes." He peered over the stack. "What's that?"

"Lemonade."

"What's it for?"

"To drink."

"Don't we usually drink soda?"

"Usually," she said, smiling, "but not

today. Today begins a new era for us. And it's fresh, too. I squeezed a dozen lemons by hand. My thumb is still cramped."

Larry looked impressed. "Nice."

"We really should've taught our kids not to drink soda."

"Whose plates are those?" Larry asked, setting the boxes of board games on the counter.

"Ours."

"Those aren't ours."

"They are. I bought them at Target for when we went on picnics. They're plastic and durable and cute with the little ants, don't you think?"

"But we never went on a picnic."

"I know. And it's a shame, isn't it? So today we're using these. I've got chips and salsa and lemonade. What a great family day, right?"

Larry grinned. "That's the spirit! Pour me a glass. I want to be the first taste tester. And also eat chips for breakfast."

"Can it. They're late sleepers." Beth took one of the plastic cups that had come with the picnic set, filled it with ice, and poured the lemonade for him, watching with delight as Larry took a big gulp.

He grabbed his face and yelped.

"What?" Beth gasped.

"Did you put sugar in this?"

"Well, yes."

Larry's face was turning red. "Not enough, sweetie. Not enough."

They stood there taste testing for ten minutes, Beth adding one tablespoon of sugar at a time. Finally Larry grabbed the sack and dumped the rest of it in. A poof of sugar smoke rose from the pitcher.

"You've now reduced this to a health hazard," Beth growled.

Larry poured another small glass and smiled. "Maybe. But it tastes amazing! Way better than soda. Here."

Beth took a sip. "Wow. That's nice."

Larry lowered his voice. "And that's the key here, sweetie. We've got to pack almost two decades of memories into a summer. We can't risk something like sour lemonade. Every time one of our kids looks at a lemon from now on, they'll remember the ecstasy of that first sip, the sugar coma that followed, and remember us."

"I hope they remember these plates. They're cute, aren't they?" As Larry started to walk off, Beth grabbed his arm. "Was Robin up yet?"

"Not yet."

"Do you think today's a good day for me to talk to her?"

"About what?"

"About *what*? About her upcoming wedding and marriage and all that."

"Beth," Larry said, "she's twenty-one years old. You can't talk someone that age out of something they want."

"Are you not the least bit worried?"

"Of course I'm worried. But trying to convince her not to marry Marvin will only drive you two further apart."

Beth's arms fell to her sides. "What do you mean, further apart?"

Larry looked regretful. "I didn't mean it exactly like that."

"Then what did you mean? Are we not close?" Beth glanced down. "Never mind. I know what you mean."

"Look, we're kind of scrambling here. Both of us. The last few years I've been chained to my desk at work. I've missed more dinners. Worked on the weekends sometimes. Robin's been off to college, and so naturally there's been a separation between the two of you. It's expected."

Beth felt herself tearing up. "I just don't understand why she didn't tell us about Marvin . . . that they were serious, in love. . . . She just sort of dropped this on us."

"Then let's make the most of our time,

okay?" Larry smiled and slipped out the front door toward the porch. Beth stood there for a moment, not thinking about him or the boys or Marvin or Robin.

She thought about Jenny — how she had been robbed of all the time in front of her. In a split second, she was gone from the earth and didn't have as much as a minute to say good-bye. And here Beth stood, with time to be had. What was she going to do with it?

She could stew about Marvin, or she could dive in and make plans with her daughter. Dress shopping. Picking out flowers and invitations and wedding themes.

Beth smiled at the thought. She tried to imagine Marvin in a tux. That was more difficult. Then she was back to plotting how to convince Robin that Marvin wasn't the one.

She grabbed the pitcher and walked out to the front porch. As Nathan and Chip gathered around, she set out the snacks and lemonade on the wicker table that looked about to fall apart though it had never been used. The *porch* really hadn't been used, not like she'd hoped when they first moved in.

For three weeks in 2007 it housed a floral couch that they'd tried to donate to charity but nobody wanted. Their neighbor Helen finally called the police to complain, so they decided to burn it in the backyard and have a bonfire. The smoke got too thick and then another neighbor called the fire department. To this day Beth still found small scraps of floral material buried in the soil of their yard.

Other than that, the porch just sat here, serving as the bottom lip of the house, having nothing to say. They walked in and out of the house and never gave it a second thought, but it was nice. A fresh coat of paint would make it look magazine worthy. It needed a good sweeping, too.

"Is this urine?" Chip asked, gawking at the lemonade.

Beth sighed, tearing her gaze from the old swing that drifted slightly in the wind. The rope was frayed like she imagined her nerves had been a few times through the years. "It's freshly squeezed lemonade, Chip."

"I thought we were having soda. You said snacks and drinks. That's why I got out of bed."

"Your mom worked very hard to make the lemonade. We're all drinking the lemonade," Larry said.

Robin opened the front door and stepped out, looking surprised they were all there.

Larry slapped his hands together in excitement. "Robin! Just in time. We're reinstituting Anderson Family Game Night."

"It's morning," Nathan yawned.

"What's that?" Robin asked.

"Don't you remember? We used to do it all the time. I mean, at least sometimes. At least once, on that snow day in '99?"

Robin smiled and patted him on the back. "Aw. That sounds fun, Dad. But I can't. Marvin and I are registering for gifts."

"Oh, come on, just one game," Beth said. "It's been forever since we played. You used to beat us all, remember? Plus, I murdered a dozen lemons for our pleasure." Beth gestured, more toward the ant plates than the lemonade. She wanted Robin to see the whole picture.

Just then Marvin pulled into the driveway, honking and waving. A pizza sign, like a shark fin, was secured to the top of his car.

Larry was trying to persuade Robin to stay for the games. "Invite Marvin!" he said. And while they chatted about that, Beth slid off the porch and toward Marvin's car.

"Hi." Beth smiled.

"Mrs. Anderson. Beth. Hello." Marvin was ducking to see her out the passenger window.

"Marvin. Hi. How are you?"

"Had to work late every night this week. Summer hits and pizza sales spike."

"Well," Beth said, leaning down to look at him through the window. "I feel as if we hardly know you." She let those words linger, though Marvin seemed unaffected. "Let's have you over for dinner again soon."

"I would love that," he said with a smile.

"Also, you do know that . . ." Beth glanced over her shoulder. Robin was still on the porch. "That she can't cook."

Again, he just smiled and blinked, waiting for her to go on.

Suddenly there was a peck on Beth's cheek. "Gotta go, Mom."

Beth straightened, stepping aside. Robin opened the car door, which creaked like it could've worked as a sound effect in a horror movie. "Hey, Robin. Do you want me to come with you?"

Robin was snapping her seat belt. "To register for gifts? That's kind of our deal, what the couple does together."

"Oh yes. Of course. Well, maybe we can look at . . . Have you thought of invitations? Or I know a nice cake lady three houses down."

Robin smiled. Not the kind of smile that had delight in it, but the kind that held pity. "Sure, Mom. But I gotta run."

"You're not staying for game day?"

"What's that?" Marvin asked. "That sounds fun."

"I'll tell you later. We gotta go, babe."

Beth sighed, backed away from the car, and watched them drive off, a sick feeling settling in as they disappeared out of sight. Not that long ago her little girl, hair in pigtails, hands sticky from taffy, hopped her Candy Land piece from purple to purple, across the bridge, squealing and clapping and then throwing little fits when she didn't get to the end.

August.

She returned to the porch and poured herself a glass of lemonade. Nathan rubbed his hands together and grinned. "Nothing like a game of Scrabble to separate the smart people from the average."

Larry was wearing the excitement of a man who'd scored Super Bowl tickets. His eyes were wide with anticipation as he made room on the wicker table. "You guys know that I used to dominate this game when we played as a family."

"The last time we played, I knew eight words," Chip said.

Larry had always been competitive. When he beat Robin four times straight at Chutes and Ladders, Beth had to suggest to him that he might let her win once.

Larry grabbed the box on top and with his hand swiped away the thick layer of dust that confirmed it had been a very long while since they played board games.

Beth leaned in to look. "That's not Scrabble. That's Candy Land."

Nathan groaned and threw his head back, staring at nothing. "Awesome."

Larry looked pained as he hurriedly sifted through the rest of the boxes. Chutes and Ladders. Connect Four. Battleship, the nonelectronic version.

Chip was holding Candy Land. "Hey, the good news is that Nathan only has to know his colors for this."

"Hilarious," Nathan said. "Do we really have to play Candy Land? It's kind of lame. It also makes me hungry."

The magazine moment was quickly slipping through the cracks in the porch. Beth handed him the lemonade she poured. "Here. There's a cup of sugar per glass. You should be fine."

"Are you guys kidding me?" Larry said. "Where's your spirit of competition?"

"This is a game featuring mountains made of gumdrops. It doesn't sound all that cutthroat to me," Nathan said.

Chip gargled his lemonade and then

gulped it down, punctuating it all with a burp. "Let's just toss that thing. Nobody wants to play Candy Land."

Beth grabbed the game off the table. "No! I mean . . . no. I want to keep it." She held the box against her chest.

Larry stood nearby, his hands on his hips, looking like he'd just lost at a board game. This day was not turning out how they'd planned, but that's how life had gone for most of their time as a family. Good intentions always seemed to get derailed. Yet . . . a smile emerged on Larry's face.

"Since when has this family ever played by the real rules of board games? I say we make up our own," he said.

Nathan and Chip glanced at each other.

"Ladies and gentlemen," Larry said, as charming and enthused as Tom Bergeron announcing a dance number, "Welcome to . . . Full. Contact. Candy Land!"

Chip's arms shot up, his fists punching through the air.

Nathan smirked. "Seriously, Dad?"

Beth smiled and handed the game over. Somehow, Larry always knew how to save the day. As her boys came up with game rules, including acquiring cherries and whipped cream from the fridge, Beth noticed Helen walking out her front door, dressed like it was the most important day of her life. But that's how she always dressed. Beth was mostly all baggy jeans and sweatshirts, but Helen looked tailored, as if her clothes were made specifically for her body.

"Hannah, don't forget your tiara!" Helen waited on her front porch, a designer bag dangling off her arm.

"Oh no!" Chip said. Beth's attention returned to her boys.

"What did you get?" Nathan asked as Chip held up the Candy Land card.

"Queen Frostine!"

"Get him!" Larry and Nathan shouted, and yelling like banshees, they all poured off the porch and onto the lawn.

Nathan, with his long legs, caught Chip before he made it to the sidewalk, tackling him to the ground. For a moment all that could be seen were arms and legs rolling over the grass.

"Beth!" Larry called, pointing to the whipped cream can. "Hurry!"

Beth jumped off the porch and ran toward the chaos, her hamstring reminding her that jumping and running, particularly at the same time, had consequences that required ice packs. But at the moment she didn't care.

Nathan held down Chip, who was giggling so hard he was barely fighting it. Beth sprayed a crown of whipped cream on his head as Larry simultaneously dropped cherries on top.

The giggling was suddenly undone by a loud, pointed clearing of the throat. Helen now stood at the fence. Queen Frostine in the flesh.

Beth dropped the can into Larry's hand as the chaos continued, then walked over to the property line, wiping the cream from her fingers onto her jeans. "Hi, Helen."

"What are you doing?" Helen's eyes widened by the second as she observed the boys tumbling around the front yard.

"Playing Candy Land!" Larry shouted as he whizzed past. Beth marveled at his speed. When was the last time he chased the boys around?

Beth turned her attention back to Helen, who motioned for her kids to hurry into their car, as if shielding them from witnessing the aftermath of a car wreck. With her children safely inside their sedan, Helen began eyeing the weeds by Beth's porch. It had been a while since she'd weeded the area — or planted anything significant, for that matter. It was just a bunch of dirt, a few random rocks that used to serve as accent pieces, and weeds that would never pass for exotic plants like she'd once hoped.

"Excellent use of your time," Helen said, her narrow eyes cutting back to Beth.

"Well, you know, we've just realized the kids are growing up so fast and we were going to play a board game, but then . . ." Squeals broke her concentration. Chip was on the ground again. This time his belly button was getting whipped. "Anyway, one of those moments where you —"

"I see. Well, at least this mess won't stick around like that TP fiasco a couple of years ago. I don't mean to be rude, but there was a moment, six months into it, when I wondered if *anybody* was going to climb into that tree and get the rest of that mess. Exterior toilet paper really does bring down the value of the home and all the homes nearby."

Beth sighed, nodding. They'd been particularly busy that season. They were hardly home, grabbing food on the go, occupying the house only to sleep in their beds.

"Where are you off to?" Beth tried a smile, even as the flatulent sound of the emptying whipped cream can broke the brief moment of cordial exchange.

"Taking Madison to gymnastics. Hannah has pageant practice. Cory has a soccer game." Her voice was low and her words clipped, as if it were a sin to show any kind of a drawl. Then her tone lowered even further. "It wouldn't hurt to get your kids in some summer activities. Keeping kids busy prevents things like —" she gazed toward the boys — "spontaneous childishness. After all, Nathan is eighteen now. Shouldn't he be — ?"

A horrible sound, like a pig rooting around in mush, cut Helen off. She gasped and guarded her pearls with her free hand. But it was only Nathan, attempting to eat the whipped cream off Chip's cheek.

Helen raised an eyebrow. "Shouldn't he be looking into packing for that college he got into?"

And then it happened, so fast and intense that it took both of them by surprise. It was so . . . abrupt . . . that Beth actually looked up because although the day was bright blue and cloudless, she thought it had started raining.

But no. She had started crying.

To look at Helen, one would've thought Beth's clothes had turned to dust and she was now standing stark-naked.

"I'm sorry," Beth said, swiping the tears as fast as she could. "This is such a hard time. The kids are growing up so fast, and . . ." She shook her head, not wanting to ramble and not wanting to get into Robin's upcoming wedding.

Helen reached into her purse, the kind with a metal closure and sturdy, well-supported sides. Beth thought she was going to pull a tissue out, but instead she held a small business card toward Beth, as discreetly as if she'd just passed her a hygiene product.

"What's this?" Beth asked.

Helen's voice was so hushed that if the wind had blown by at that moment, Beth would not have been able to hear her. "His name is Dr. Reynolds. He's a therapist."

"A thera—"

"Shh. He mostly counsels women after botched plastic surgeries, but I've found him to be quite helpful with delicate situations."

"Like crying . . . ?"

"You should invest in waterproof mascara. That's one tip. But call him. He might be able to help you." Helen reached out as if she was going to touch Beth but stopped a few inches short. Perhaps it was the warmest she could be. "I know it's been difficult losing Jenny." Helen tilted her head like she was trying to view Beth in another light, then sashayed toward the car, her hips swinging from side to side like a pendulum. Her platform shoes made her a good three inches taller than she really was, but Beth always felt she was a towering presence anyway. Her hair was white-blonde, the kind that nobody in their forties comes by naturally, but it was shiny and pretty and a far cry from Beth's frumpy ponytail.

It had been Jenny's idea to invite Helen to scrapbooking one day after meeting her at Beth's fence line.

"She seems like she needs friends," Jenny had said.

Beth had moaned. "Must you love every stray dog?"

"I must." Jenny had grinned, and by the next week, Helen began coming to scrapbooking. And as Jenny had predicted, she never skipped a single week.

Larry was suddenly by Beth's side.

"What this time? Our front door creaks in a way she disapproves of?"

"Larry . . ."

"What? She's awful. She always has been. Don't know how you spend time with her. Remember how she dogged us about the toilet paper stuck in our tree?"

"Well, it was an entire roll."

"It was a few pieces. Nothing more."

"She was just wondering what we were

doing with whipped cream and cherries and all that."

Larry punched his hands in the air. "See? How fun was that? Totally off the top of my head, too. This is going to be a summer to remember!"

"Where are the boys?"

Larry glanced behind him. The lawn was quiet and empty, except for a small trail of whipped cream that was sinking into the grass. "Oh. Well, um, they probably wanted some Xbox time." He looked at his watch. "I mean, fifteen minutes is a long time to run around the yard. Plus we ran out of whipped cream." He resumed glancing around the yard as though they might be there. "I'm going to see if I can lure them to the zoo. Remember how much they loved the zoo?"

"That was me. They begged to go home every time."

"Really? I don't remember that."

"Larry," Beth said as he started to walk toward the house, "aren't you . . . sad?"

"About what?"

"Robin. Nathan. The whole idea that we're losing two kids in one year."

"I know! That's why we're planning the Summer of Fun! Intense Fun! Right? Am I right?"

Beth tried a smile. "Sure."

Larry cupped her shoulder and gave her a thatta-girl shake. "I'm just diving in, Beth!" He hurried inside.

She turned and watched Helen back out of the driveway in a sedan that gleamed like the sun had given the car its celestial blessing.

Beth stood all alone. Even the birds stopped chirping.

Chapter 8
Butch

Butch loved the feeling after a long, hard day at work of coming home to Jenny, sinking into the couch, kicking up his feet, and watching sports highlights. Before Jenny died, the rest of what made it perfect was the smell of food being cooked in the kitchen and Ava running around the house with her toys. There was a lot of laughter. A lot of peace.

Now it was different. Ava sat on the couch next to him, curled up against his rib cage. It wasn't comfortable, but he tried not to move. Her attention wasn't on him, though. It was on the TV. Instead of ESPN highlights, they were watching the Food Network. It was like Ava was in a trance.

"Sweetie? You okay?"

She nodded.

"Bet you're hungry."

She didn't even blink. "I miss food."

"Food? We've got —" The doorbell rang.

98

"See? Pizza's here!"

He hopped up, hoping Ava wasn't super hungry because he was pretty sure he could eat the whole thing by himself. He grabbed the wad of cash on the table and opened the front door.

"Hey, Marvin." He took the box and handed over the cash. "Congratulations. Heard the good news."

"Thanks."

"I'm sure you and Robin will be very happy together." Butch tried a smile. Not the thing he was best at, but people were uncomfortable around him these days. Nobody liked to bring up marriage or love or spouses or anything that might trigger a memory of Jenny. The thing was, she was still always on his mind, whether they did or not. "Very happy."

"Oh yeah. We are. I just got a Wii."

"Ah. Sure. That should help."

"See you tomorrow, Mr. Browning." Marvin started to walk off but then turned around. "By the way, seeing that you order every night from us, I can just put it in as a standing order, and that way you don't have to bother calling."

"Oh."

"Just a thought."

"Well, sure, that would make sense . . ."

Butch stepped outside, out of earshot of Ava. "It's just that Ava feels better when she sees that I'm able to take care of her. I know it sounds stupid, but I think her knowing that I know how to feed us by calling brings her a lot of comfort. Make sense?"

Marvin was shaking his head. "No offense, Mr. Browning. I don't understand a lot of things. I mean, people want to make it complicated, but the way I see it, it's about loving the person you're with. You felt that way about Mrs. Browning, didn't you?"

Butch nodded, casting his gaze away. "Yeah. I did."

"Yeah. So, I mean, I don't know anything about child rearing and that stuff, but I bet Ava doesn't care that you don't cook. Robin doesn't cook. But she loves pizza, so it all works out that way."

"It's just that Jenny used to cook."

Marvin looked concerned. "Do you think I should be worried that Robin doesn't?"

Butch laughed under his breath. Yes, there'd been a time that he, too, was so self-absorbed he missed the point to a lot of conversations.

"No, man. It's fine. She's lucky to be able to have pizza at a moment's notice."

Marvin's face lit up. "Exactly, right?"

"Yep."

"Hey, um, can I ask you something?"

Butch glanced inside. Ava was glued to the TV. "Sure."

"Listen, I'm . . . I don't think . . . I guess what I'm trying to say is . . ."

"Yeah?"

"I'm not fitting in very well with Robin's family."

"Oh."

"I don't mean this to be awkward. I know you're kin and all that. But I'm trying, you know? I just thought you might have some, like, tips. What can I do to help them like me more?"

"What makes you think they don't like you?"

"I read body language pretty well. It helps in the pizza business."

Butch cleared his throat. "Well, um, I don't know. It's gotta be hard to know your daughter's marrying — I mean, getting married, so maybe that's what you're sensing."

"I don't think so."

"Okay. Well, my advice is . . ." Butch stopped for a moment. What advice did he have? He searched the corners of his mind for any tidbit of anything that resembled advice. Then he remembered a conversation he'd overheard Jenny and Ava having when Ava was around four. She'd come home

101

from a birthday party crying that nobody would play with her or talk with her. Jenny had stooped down, taken her little hands, and given her a five-minute talk, probably an eternity to a four-year-old.

Butch looked at Marvin. "My advice to you is to be yourself, you know? God created you the way you are, just exactly like you're supposed to be. They'll come around eventually and see what a great kid you are." He swallowed. "Man, I mean."

Marvin looked engrossed. "Wow. Yeah. Deep."

"Then I'll see you tomorrow?" Butch asked.

"See you then." Marvin smiled and left.

Butch shut the door and took the pizza into the living room, where Ava was still absorbed in the TV show. He grimaced. "What *is* that?"

"It's calamari, Dad. Before they cut it up and fry it. That's squid, you know."

"Oh. Yeah. Well, good thing they fry it. They serve it with marinara, right? Speaking of marinara . . ." He gestured formally to the pizza box.

Ava flipped the lid open, pulled out a piece, set it on her lap, and began picking the pepperoni off.

"You don't like pepperoni?"

"Not really."

"I've ordered pepperoni pizza every night this week. Why didn't you say something?"

"I just take it off."

"Do you like cheese?"

"Yeah."

"Then I'll have them make it half-cheese tomorrow."

"Okay. Also, this is the time that you should tell me not to put my pizza in my lap."

"Oh . . ."

"Because it leaves grease stains."

"Right. Yeah, need to buy some paper plates. Sorry."

"We have regular plates, you know."

He did know. But he hadn't opened a cabinet since Jenny died. He remembered the day she found the dishes, 80 percent off, on clearance. It was as if she'd struck gold. She was so proud to have matching plates. Finally.

Ava was back to watching her show. Some cooking contest, with the contestants being very dramatic about how they served their food. Such formality. For squid?

Butch walked to the kitchen, his appetite suddenly waning. He stood there a moment, catching his breath, trying to separate Jenny from the dishes. At some point he was going to have to use those dishes. But that meant washing them too. He hadn't loaded or unloaded a dishwasher since the day he married that wonderful woman.

With one big, deep breath, he opened the cabinet and took out a plate. As he walked toward the living room, he got a little idea. It reminded him of what Jenny would do. She was good at capturing the awe of children. She was like the pied piper. Kids flocked to her, and she loved being around them.

On his way out of the kitchen, Butch snatched the dishrag. He flipped it over his arm and put his nose in the air as he rounded the couch.

"Madam, your plate." It was the worst British accent ever attempted.

Ava smiled. "Daddy, what are you doing?"

"For your pizza, madam."

She took the plate and grinned. "I would also like some water, please, sir. The fancy kind of water in the fancy kind of glass." She sounded perfectly aristocratic.

"It would be a pleasure." He laughed all the way back to the kitchen, grabbing the nicer glasses from the back of the cabinet. Last he'd heard, Ava wasn't allowed to use them, but he didn't really care about preserving the crystal. When he returned with the stemware, Ava looked truly impressed.

She sipped the water carefully, her pinkie floating away from the glass like any proper princess. "Very fine water. Thank you. Also, I am old enough to use a knife."

"Don't push it," Butch said with a wink.

She sighed but still looked delighted. *That* was what he hadn't seen on her face in a very long time — delight.

They ate in peace for a while and Butch found himself weirdly interested in the cooking show. He had no idea that the cooking world was so competitive.

As Ava was finishing her pizza, she said, "Oh, I have to make cupcakes for Thursday."

"Wha . . . ?" His pizza slice, on its way to his mouth, fell limp like it had fainted. He set it down. "What do you mean?"

"It's the last treat day of the year, and it's my turn."

"Well, we've got those Little Debbie —"

"No."

"No?" Butch's heart had that funny little tickle that turned out never to be funny. "We have to *make* them?"

"Yeah, nobody likes the store-bought kind."

"I do."

"If I show up with store-bought cupcakes

on treat day, you may as well give me head
lice, too."

"Really?"

"Just ask Payton Carter. She brought in
celery with peanut butter one time. No
one's heard from her since."

"But —"

"Also, Jacob Farrell is allergic to anything
synthetic, plus all preservatives and most of
the dyes. Makes him really hyper. His mom
sent a note about it."

Butch swallowed. He'd met Jacob's
mother. He didn't want trouble from her.

"All right, I'll make some tonight." Cupcakes. How hard could that be?

"Thanks."

"Sure."

"Also, Saturday's my graduation."

"From what?"

"Second grade. Last day of school is
Friday. Ceremony is Saturday. I need a
dress."

Butch waited for her to slap him on the
shoulder and declare it a joke, but she just
stared at him.

"They're . . . they're actually having a
ceremony?"

"None of my nice dresses fit me anymore.
I thought the black one might, but it was
short and I looked like one of those girls

106

Mom told me I shouldn't ever look like."

"O . . . kay. Where do we go for that kind of a thing?" He tried to think. Did they have dresses at Dollar General?

"The mall."

"The mall. Great. We'll go sometime this week."

With that, Ava looked satisfied and ate happily in silence.

CHAPTER 9
BETH

"Another tissue?"

"No thank you."

"Are you sure?"

"Yes."

"It's just that your first tissue has been . . . incapacitated."

Beth looked down. As she opened her right hand to see what he was talking about, the tissue fell to the floor like dandelion dust.

She glanced toward the man sitting across from her, a notebook in his lap and a coffee mug next to his shiny, stoic leather chair. Dr. Reynolds's dark, bushy mustache twitched with concern. He was tall, African American, with beautiful light-brown eyes and a voice that sounded like he should be making Allstate commercials. But he was sort of an intimidating presence. It was that mustache — black and dense and all-knowing — that made her squirm in her seat.

"I'm *so* sorry," Beth said. Her eyes were watering and her hair was hanging over half her face. Until this point, she'd managed to seem like the kind of person who makes a psychologist question why they've come for help. *She seems so pulled together,* she hoped he thought. But by the look on his face, it became clear that her five minutes of girdled normalism were gone. The seams had busted and she was hanging out all over the place.

She grabbed a new tissue as she took in the office. She hadn't really noticed it when she came in, too intent on making the impression that she was here out of choice, not desperation. It was a nice office. Cozy, with a good view of the parking lot. She liked the lamps, which painted the room in golden light. No fluorescents to be found. That was comforting because she did *not* look good under fluorescents.

"What was I saying?" she asked, dabbing the corners of her eyes.

"Well, I introduced myself and shared my credentials."

"Uh-huh."

"And then you introduced yourself and told me about your family."

"Right."

"And then you burst into tears."

"Oh."

"So you're in the right place," Dr. Reynolds said with a gentle smile, "but I still don't know why you're here."

"Okay. Well, I probably started crying when I said Robin."

"Robin. I thought it was Marvin."

"Oh, maybe that's right. Maybe I said Robin and then Marvin and then burst into tears."

"That seems correct. Well, let's take it from the beginning."

"Sure. From when I started feeling bad about myself as a mom?"

"Okay."

"It was probably when Robin, at the age of three, refused to potty train and I was crying myself to sleep at night. I decided to take a weekend with my girlfriends."

"That sounds healthy."

"And the next thing I know, she doesn't know how to cook. I never taught her to make an omelet. I abandoned her at the most crucial and private time in her life — potty training — and now she doesn't know how to pretreat a stain or deal with difficult people or fry chicken."

"How old is she?"

"Twenty-one. She's making the biggest decision of her life — who to marry — and

I've completely failed!"

"I'm to assume Marvin is the man she is going to marry?"

"Yes," Beth sniffled.

"And Marvin is disappointed that Robin can't cook?"

"No. No, it's not that."

"He likes eggs?"

"He likes pizza."

Dr. Reynolds picked up his coffee and sipped it without taking his eyes off Beth. She dabbed her face but the tears didn't seem like they were going to stop.

"I'm sorry. I know this is confusing. I'm making no sense and shredding tissue like it's cheese." She laughed, but it didn't sound natural, even to her. "Then again, we keep you in business, don't we?"

Dr. Reynolds slowly set his coffee mug down, placing it just right on the coaster. She saw that his mug read, *I have CDO. It's like OCD, but all the letters are in alphabetical order as they should be.*

She then noticed an entire shelf filled with various mugs.

"I collect them. It's a tradition of sorts. Whenever it is time for a client to leave me, I ask that they buy me a mug to remember them by." She was so thankful at that moment that he didn't say *patient.* He picked up his pen. "Now, back to you. You were saying?"

"I don't know what I'm trying to say. I'm just all messed up, Dr. Reynolds."

"I believe what you were trying to say is that your daughter has grown up and you feel like you've missed some crucial years. Now she's marrying a man named Marvin and doesn't know how to make an omelet, so how can she know if this is the right man? You're wondering if it's too late to make up for lost time or if it's too late to talk some sense into her."

Beth nodded, her eyes wide.

"Your other children are Nathan, who is eighteen, and Chip, who is fourteen." He glanced at his notes. "And then there's Marvin, whom your daughter is about to marry."

Beth nodded again.

"And he likes pizza."

Beth blotted her eyes. "He doesn't just like it. He delivers it."

His poker face blipped for a second, noticeable only by the mustache dropping a quarter of an inch. He seemed to understand, as if it would be his worst nightmare too for his daughter to marry a pizza deliveryman.

But then his mustache twitched and it was back to business. "All right, Beth. I want to assure you that you're going to get through this. Transition is hard. I also want to tell you this."

"What?" Beth felt a swell of hope because his mustache looked poised to deliver good news.

"I used to deliver pizza. For a while between high school and college, I didn't really know what I wanted to do with my life. I couldn't decide what my passion was. But I found my way, and now I do what I love. Nobody wants to deliver pizza his whole life. Marvin will find his passion. In fact, he probably already knows what it is, and perhaps he needs a wife to show him that he's got it in him."

Beth sank deeper into the overstuffed yellow chair, relief cradling her on every side. "I see." She nodded and smiled. "You know, Dr. Reynolds, you don't seem like the kind of doctor who would be interested in counseling women about plastic surgery."

A small, wise smile emerged from beneath the 'stache. "I'm not. But I have one patient who believes that since it was her issue, it is probably every other woman's issue too. Word got around that I was a guru in this field, and suddenly 30 percent of my clientele are botched plastic surgery victims. But mostly I'm just a Christian counselor."

"Well, do you think you can help me figure out how to talk Robin out of marrying Marvin?"

"My suggestion to you would be to let Robin make her own decisions about life, and we'll help you accept them."

"She's twenty-one. We're not talking about whether she should wear the white or black dress to prom. This is a life-altering decision."

"Most are when you get to be an adult. One decision can affect everything and everyone around us. But it's her life."

Beth crossed her arms. "And I suppose next you're going to tell me I shouldn't teach her how to make an omelet."

"Don't you think that if Robin wanted to learn, she would ask you?" Dr. Reynolds set his notebook aside. "Beth, did you work outside of the home?"

"Kind of. I was the lady who always got talked into selling the product of the parties I was invited to. Scented candles one year. Cute bags and purses the next. I've done makeup and pantry organizers and casserole mixes and bath towels and on and on. I've tried to bring in extra money as much as I can."

"Because the kind of guilt you're experiencing usually comes from full-time working moms I see."

"I was there every day of their little lives. But somehow I got sidetracked."

"How?"

"I don't know. I can't name it, see? I mean, I went wrong somewhere. Somehow. But with what? PTA? Maybe. What was the point of all that time on the PTA? I could've been teaching Robin to cook. Maybe if I'd stopped and played Barbies with her more, I could've been Ken and shown her what kind of husband Barbie was looking for. Instead she played by herself while I tried to keep up with the laundry, and somewhere along the way Ken became a pizza delivery boy and that was the dream. And now Nathan is leaving for college and it just went by so fast. They're almost gone, all of them. You blink and someone you've seen every day of your life is . . . gone."

"Not gone. Just away."

Beth looked at the clock. Their time was up.

She hated time. Jenny was not "just away." She was gone. And because of that, Beth had to pay a man with a mustache eighty dollars an hour so she would have someone to talk to.

115

CHAPTER 10
BUTCH

Butch had been trying to remember what Ava's bedtime was. He'd apparently been getting it wrong for weeks. A month ago her second-grade teacher, Mrs. Murdock, had called to say she was falling asleep in class.

"I see." Butch had tried to think of a question Jenny might ask. "Is she sleeping during her nap time?"

Long pause. "Well, um, Mr. Browning, we don't have nap time in second grade."

"Oh, right. Of course. Sorry. It's just that Jenny used to handle these things."

"I understand," Mrs. Murdock said. "You know, if you ever need any . . . advice . . . I'd be happy to help."

He didn't know if she meant that or not, and he didn't know if she understood how much help he really needed or the kind of help either. So he just said a polite thank-you and tried to get Ava to bed at a decent hour from then on.

She'd finished her bath and brushed her teeth. Now he stood outside her door and listened. It was quiet. He didn't know if that was a good or bad sign. But he knew, undoubtedly, that she needed to be tucked in, that he needed to kiss her forehead, kiss her stuffed bunny, and remember the stuffed bunny's name.

Mobee?

Mopsy?

No, Mobsy . . . wait . . .

He was halfway into the room when he realized Ava was kneeling by her bed, hands clasped, staring at him.

"Oh. I'm sorry."

"That's okay. You want to pray with me?"

Dread kept a smile at bay. No, he did not. But that was the equivalent of telling a kid you didn't believe in God. He did believe in God. He suspected that God did not believe in him. And he really didn't have very much to say to God anyway.

"That was . . ." He took four steps backward. "That was kind of your and your mom's thing and —"

"You can say hi to her if you want."

If only he could. If he could just talk to her one more time. He'd give anything. But he understood Ava's need to do this, to talk to the ceiling like she talked to her stuffed

117

bunny. She could imagine her mommy talking back to her. Butch couldn't. He glanced from the floor to Ava. Her eyes were round and full of hope.

"Well . . ." There didn't seem to be a good excuse coming, which was strange because typically he had a full arsenal of them for nearly any occasion.

"Come on." She beckoned him like she was the parent trying to coax a little kid into doing something he didn't want to do.

His steps were tentative, as if he were avoiding land mines. He finally reached the bed and sat down, folding his hands in his lap.

"You have to get on your knees."

"Oh. Really?"

"In this house, yes. Everybody has their way of doing things."

"Right. Okay." He knelt, his left knee popping from an old football injury. Then his back spasmed for half a second. But finally he got there.

Ava smiled triumphantly. "Dear God, thank You for a beautiful day."

"Amen."

"I'm not done."

"Sorry. Go ahead."

"Help Catelyn. She was sick today."

Silence. Butch peeked to see what she was

doing. Her eyes were squeezed shut and she looked totally focused. Butch wondered if he should say something. Was she waiting on him? This was getting awkward.

Then, "Tell my mommy that I drew a picture of a tree today and my teacher really liked it. Ariel Forrester said hers was better, but mine had glitter and I can color between the lines. Ariel's looked like a green cotton ball. I drew in the leaves like Mommy showed me."

Butch felt the lump in his throat, the one that never went away with a swallow and that had rarely left since Jenny died. He remembered the drawing lesson Ava spoke of. It had been last year. Ariel, then a bossy, sassy first grader in class with Ava, liked to put Ava down and tell her how badly she drew. Ava, the ever-determined kid she was, worked all through the summer to improve her drawing so she could one-up Ariel Forrester.

Ava's run-in with Ariel had been the first time he'd seen Jenny so up in arms. Usually Jenny was the peacemaker. She tried to get both parties to see things from the other person's perspective. When Ava first came home and complained about Ariel, Jenny said, "Well, maybe she doesn't have a mommy and daddy who take time to look at her pictures." But as the year wore on and it was clear that Ariel was just a spoiled-rotten kid, Jenny had finally had enough. One night as they lay in bed, she suddenly said, "I'm going to set that little scaly mermaid straight!"

Butch had been so startled he almost fell out of bed. He thought she was asleep.

"A mermaid's cute till it comes up against a shark. Then it's just a singing fish."

Butch couldn't help but laugh. Jenny's face was turnip red. She didn't find his amusement funny.

"Honey," Butch said. "You can't go stomping into the school to set a first grader straight. That's how you get on the evening news."

"True." She sighed and rolled over to face him. "I just hate how it makes Ava doubt herself."

He stroked her hair. "If I know you, you'll find a way to help Ava figure this out."

Butch blinked and the memory was gone. Ava, however, was still praying. "The teacher put it up on the wall. Tell her tomorrow if you can . . ."

Butch shut his eyes and tried not to cry.

"I know there are probably a lot of people up there, but my mommy's the one with the long hair and really pretty . . ."

Butch put a hand on Ava's shoulder. "Ava, God knows who your mom is."

"You're right. She's the one always singing, and God likes singers."

He nodded, keeping his eyes closed. Of course God knew her. Because Jenny knew God, and that was just how it was. Maybe Butch couldn't offer much wisdom, but he knew there was no doubt God knew Jenny Browning. Butch had witnessed her spend every morning with Him since the day they were married.

"Tell her Daddy said hi too . . ."

He hadn't spoken to Jenny since she died, and that was how it was supposed to be. Maybe heaven was there. If it was, she was in it, but there was a gulf the size of the universe between them, so what was the point?

"And, Jesus, also please help Daddy become a better cook."

Butch looked up and found her peeking out one eye at him.

"Sorry, Daddy. It's not your fault. It's just that Mom told me whenever I had a trouble, I should talk to Jesus about it. I'm not mad at you. I'm just worried that I'm not eating the rainbow."

"I can't cook, that is true. But I definitely can't cook a rainbow."

She smiled. "It means eating all the colors using vegetables and fruits."

"Oh." When was the last time he'd bought a fruit?

"Amen." Ava rose and slid into bed, pulling the covers to her chin.

Butch sat on the edge of the bed. "You drew a picture of a tree?"

"It was really a fish. But Mrs. Murdock thought it was a tree. I drew scales the way Mommy taught me to draw leaves and, anyway, it worked out because of the glitter."

"Well, I'd like to see it."

"They'll send everything home the last day of school, so you can see it Friday."

"Okay."

Ava held out her bunny to be kissed.

"Good night . . . um, Moo . . . Mo . . . Mu . . ."

"Macey."

"Good night, Macey." He kissed Ava. "And good night, Ava."

"Good night, Daddy."

"And, Ava?"

"Yeah?"

"If you ever punch Ariel in the nose, you won't be in trouble with me, okay?"

"I don't know how to punch."

"Then I think we have our weekend

project cut out for us."

"I don't think Mommy would approve."

"You might be surprised."

A small smile emerged on her lips, and her eyes grew distant, like she was imagining herself in a fistfight. Her expression twisted suddenly. In her mind's eye, she was giving someone a black eye and happy about it. But then the expression faded and she looked at Butch.

"Maybe I should pray for her instead."

"A girl like that doesn't deserve your time, you know."

Ava shrugged and rolled to her side, her eyes blinking slowly and heavily. "Good night, Daddy."

"Good night, Ava." He walked to the door and was about to slide out when she turned toward him again.

"Daddy, can I ask you something?"

"It's late, sweetie . . ." He checked his watch. Well, not that late. He decided to walk back in. He was going to have to start tolerating these inconveniences, deal in patience with her. She probably wanted to know what the weather would be like tomorrow — a stall tactic, he knew, but he could afford at least one. "Yes, Ava?"

She rose to an elbow, looking intently at him. "I want you to tell me what happened to you that day."

"What day?"

"The day that Mommy died."

Butch's heart thudded with alarm. He was not expecting that question at all. He didn't even know how to answer it or what she was really asking. He slowly sat on the edge of her bed. She struggled to loosen the blanket underneath him.

"I'm not sure I understand what you're asking."

"I remember that you came to school and got me, and when we got home, you told me Mommy had died in a car wreck."

Tears stung his eyes. It was the hardest thing he'd ever had to do. "That's right. That's what happened."

"But what happened to you that day?"

He touched her arm. "I guess I don't understand what you mean."

"Were you at work?"

"Yes, I was at work. At a construction site."

"So how did you find out about Mommy's wreck?"

Butch tried to gather himself, tried to answer as straightforwardly as he could. But he wasn't even sure this was a good idea. "I got a call from a police officer on my cell phone."

"How did he know your number?"

"I'm not sure how they knew. Maybe they looked in Mommy's phone."

"What did the police officer say?"

"He said that I should go to the hospital, that Jenny — Mommy — was in a wreck."

"Were you scared?"

"I was scared, yes. Tippy drove me to the hospital."

"And then what happened?"

Butch pushed hair out of her eyes. "Ava, why do you want to know this? What are all these questions about?"

She shrugged. "I just want to know."

"You don't need to know this stuff."

"Yes, I do."

Butch stared at the floor. What was he supposed to do here? He glanced at Ava. Her eyes were wide, searching him.

"Well, it was at the hospital that the doctor came out to the waiting room and told me that she didn't . . . make it."

"Did she die in the car or at the hospital?"

Butch blinked slowly, hating to remember that day. "She died in the car."

"Because of the truck."

"The semi, yes."

"Then what happened?" She was asking so matter-of-factly. It was like she was a reporter, digging for details, completely detached from the situation.

"I called your aunt Beth."

"Was Aunt Beth sad?"

"Yes, she was very sad. Everyone was very sad."

"Tippy, too?"

"Yes, Tippy. And Daphne. You know how much everyone loved your mom, right? I don't think there was a single person on earth who disliked her."

"Why did they like her so much?"

"She was very thoughtful. And she was always doing nice things for people, thinking of others besides herself. When someone was sick, she would take them a meal. When someone had a baby, she would bring them a present."

Ava looked to be processing all of this. She was frowning, not out of anger but out of deep concentration. "Did you ever get to see Mommy again? I never got to see her again, except in my dreams now. Sometimes I see her there."

Butch took a deep breath. "That's the best place to see her, you know."

"It is?"

"Yes."

"Do you see her in your dreams?"

"Sometimes."

"I wish I could see her every night. I used

to, right after she died, but now she only comes sometimes."

Butch put his hand to her heart. "But she's always here." He touched his own chest. "And here."

"And there," Ava said, pointing to the ceiling, though he knew she meant heaven.

"And there." He clasped his hands together on his lap. "Did I answer all of your questions?"

She nodded. "I just wondered about it, about you. Maybe nobody asked you those questions and maybe you thought nobody cared about your day. But I care."

He pulled her into a hug. "I know you care. You care just like your mommy cared."

Ava grinned as she lay back against her pillow.

CHAPTER 11
HELEN

It was after 8 P.M. when Helen sat down with two of her three children at their dinner table. She'd asked her husband, Charles, many times to remove the two leaves in the center of the table. They'd put them in for a dinner party four weeks ago, but the table was much too long for a family dinner, especially with Charles working late. The mood lighting she was normally fond of now made the vast dining room look like a cave.

"I thought Dad was going to be home tonight."

"Plans change, Cory," Helen said. She gestured toward him. "And please hold your fork correctly. Also, why isn't your hair fixed?"

"It is." Cory patted the top of his head. She was already sensing a rebellious spirit in him, at age eight.

"First," she said, "we pray. Madison, I believe it's your turn."

128

They all bowed their heads. Madison said, "Holy Father, thank You for the provision of food and home and opportunity. Amen."

"Amen. Go now, Cory. Comb it down. The table is no place to get slouchy. Do you know how many of your father's successful business deals have been brokered over a meal?"

Cory groaned. "Fine." He slid out of his seat, dropped his fork to the table, and left for the bathroom.

"Madison, please get his fork off the table. Put it on his plate."

As Madison did so, Helen looked at the clock on the wall. "Where *is* she?"

"She's with Sasha, Mom," Madison said with her mouth full. "You know that family can't get anywhere on time."

Helen groaned. "What kind of name is Sasha, anyway? I pray their influence doesn't rub off on Hannah. Theater is all fine and well, but it is not a career choice. Her parents can barely make a living running that ridiculous community theater. One can't be a wandering soul, directionless and shifting with the winds of desire. I want to take them by their slouchy knit shirts and tell them to attempt to thrive in the real world."

She turned her attention back to Madison, who was spinning her fork in the gravy meant for the pork loin. Helen worried about her oldest daughter. Though smarter than she and Charles combined, Madison had yet to make a career choice. "Speaking of careers, why not a business degree? An international business degree. It seems like such a natural choice for you, dear. You have your father's instincts."

Madison only shrugged. "Mom, you know what? I like what you do."

Helen set her silverware on her plate. "What do you mean by that?"

"You're a mom, and you take us places, and then you can have lunch with your friends. And you always get your nails done too. That's fun. Plus —"

"Madison, please. First of all, I'm not just 'a mom.' I support your father in ways that none of you can possibly comprehend. Chatting with strangers at business dinners is harder than it looks. Secondly, you need a degree in something lucrative, financially beneficial. You must be able to support yourself in this world."

"Can you get a degree in mom?" Cory asked as he sat back down, hair almost neatly in place.

Madison chuckled, but Helen didn't find the topic funny. Yet it wasn't Madison who kept her up at night. Hannah had always been the one she worried the most about, the true "free spirit" of the bunch. Helen knew there was nothing more detrimental to a life plan than a free spirit. She glanced at the door, hopeful to hear a car door shut, but it was quiet.

They kept eating, but Helen's thoughts soon turned to their mortgage and their bills. Charles had such a good job — and now a promotion — yet they were still stretched to the max with all the kids' activities and college expenses coming up. Madison had gotten a full scholarship, but there were many, many costs. Charles had questioned the children's activity level early on, but Helen knew it was their best chance at scholarships. Plus, there was nothing worse than a bored kid.

Madison and Cory finished their meals, dutifully taking their plates to the sink. Helen looked at the clock again. She'd specifically told Hannah to be home from the mall by 8 p.m. It was now five past nine. And Hannah had not left the house on good terms earlier in the day.

"Mom? Hello?" she had said to Helen, at the computer.

"What is it?"

"I've been saying your name for like ten

minutes."

"Don't exaggerate, Hannah. It's not flattering. Exaggeration signals desperation, and nobody likes a desperate person."

"I'm desperate for help with my computer." She crossed her arms, and her eyes twinkled in the way they always did when she was being sarcastic. "It keeps locking up when I save."

Helen sighed. She still had a dozen e-mails to return before dinner, mostly about the summer swim party the gymnastic team was planning, plus a pageant update. "Isn't there a help line or something? I thought I read something about that."

"They have live chat. But you've told me over and over not to talk to strangers on the Internet." Then came the smirk. Helen blew out a tense sigh, but Hannah was already backing away. "Forget it. I'll figure it out."

Helen had watched her shuffle to the stairs. When was that girl going to learn to pick up her feet? That sound caused the hairs on the back of Helen's neck to stand on end. "Hannah, pick up your . . ." But she'd already bounded up the stairs and out of earshot.

Now she was at the mall and late for her curfew.

Hannah was her dramatic one, the one

who never could seem to get her emotions in check. Helen had vowed to work on that over the summer. Hannah didn't know this yet, but emotions were a woman's worst enemy in the real world. One wrong outburst could be held against her for years.

Helen had learned that the hard way on a temp job in her early twenties. Men could scream all day long. Women could not even raise their voices.

As she cleaned the kitchen, she wished Hannah — and all her children, for that matter — better understood her intentions. She simply wanted to give them their best shot, afford them all the opportunities she didn't have. As she scrubbed the last pot, she lamented where those opportunities could've taken her, had she had them. Her life could've been different. She could've owned a business, she was sure. She'd had a lot of great ideas when she was younger. Her aunt once predicted she'd be an entrepreneur.

Now what was she? A station wagon in motion, according to Madison. A bakery on demand. A chef at everyone's service. She dressed as if she were of great importance, as if she were more than the source of her children's angst, but what was the point, really?

Helen slumped at the sink in the exact way she'd broken her children of. In the kitchen window, against the black night sky, she caught her reflection. She stared at herself for a long time, an expressionless face engulfed by darkness. The house, with five usually dwelling there, was quiet. The only sound was the faucet running into the sink.

They knew, didn't they? That she wanted to be left alone at night? It had become their ritual when Charles worked late. Sometimes she desperately needed the break, just a few quiet moments to herself.

"Don't be a bother," she'd told them when they were young. It was what her mother had told her, and her grandmother had told her mother. "Stay out of the way."

Helen turned off the water. Suddenly her feet hurt from the heels she'd worn all day, but she tried to make it a habit to greet Charles fully dressed. Next door she heard her neighbor Beth take out the trash. Beth seemed unable to break the jeans-and-sweats cycle, wearing one or the other, and a ponytail, virtually every day. Beth was everything that Helen didn't want to happen to her . . . to become lost in motherhood with no sense of who she used to be.

But she had to wonder if Beth felt the guilt

that cast a long shadow across Helen's heart. When the children were younger, she could be stern but then end the day with a hug and a kiss on the cheek and all was forgotten. Now, it seemed, nothing was forgotten, by any of them.

At the front window of the house, looking down the neighborhood street, Helen watched for car lights, though it was much more likely that she would hear Sasha's parents' car long before she would see it.

Of her three children, Hannah had looked the most angelic when she was born. Her face was completely symmetrical, with big blue eyes and hair as white as snow. But by the toddler years, she'd become the one who was more likely to embarrass them in public, with angry outbursts and a low threshold for obedience.

They had the most disagreements, and suddenly it exhausted Helen, a weighty burden at the bottom of her heart. She stood at the front door, one hand on the knob, wondering how to help this child. Maybe she should do something kind for her. Maybe that said more than words. Helen had never been particularly good with words, according to her high school English teacher. Of course, that never kept her from getting her point across.

She thought of prayer. It was not something she did regularly, but she'd felt the need to lately. Ever since Jenny Browning died. She wasn't extremely close to Jenny, though they scrapbooked together once a week. But Jenny was always asking about her kids, asking if there was anything she could pray for. It was such an odd request, Helen thought, that Jenny wanted to pray for other children. But every once in a while she would let Jenny know of a struggle in their home, and she knew it would be prayed for — and kept private.

It had been a Tuesday, on the way to take Hannah to a pageant activity, when Marlene called to let her know Jenny was dead. Helen dropped Hannah off and sat in the parking lot and cried, despite herself. She didn't even cry when her own mother had died. She couldn't explain the grief. It had subsided in the days that followed, but she did miss her.

A car rattled around the corner at the end of her street, its lights bouncing off the pavement as it headed for the Buckley home. It pulled into the drive as Helen stepped lightly onto the front porch, still holding the door handle. She pulled her cardigan closed as she gave a short wave to the mother, who she could see was wearing a tank top with her bra straps hanging out.

It was Charles who'd said to let Hannah hang out with Sasha. She was really the first good friend Hannah had found at school, and he'd described the family as harmless. They'd had quite a discussion about it.

"I don't like the influence they'll have over her," Helen had argued.

"Honey, it's not like she's going to drop out of school and go join the circus."

"She already writes so much poetry. The angst that spills out of that girl would make us rich if we were paid by the pound for it."

"She'll be fine," he'd said. He never worried as much as she did about the kids. He was hardest on Madison, but mostly just about her grades.

Hannah bolted toward the door, and Helen stepped aside to let her in, following her and closing the door behind them.

"You're late."

"Sorry, Mom." She grabbed the stair railing and started upward.

"Not so fast."

"Mom, I'm tired."

"We need to get some things straight about curfew."

"I'm sorry. Sasha's mom drives like a turtle. I told her eight. I promise. But she starts talking and telling stories and then she drives really slowly. I'm really tired. Can I get to bed?"

Something caused Helen to pause. That little hesitation in her heart saying something wasn't quite right. It was the way Hannah insisted on rushing upstairs. Nearly every time Hannah came home from anything at all, she went straight to the fridge.

"Stop right there."

Hannah froze midstep.

"Turn around, young lady."

She didn't.

"I said, turn around."

Slowly she did. She looked uncomfortable, scratching her nose, her eyes darting around. Yeah, Helen was definitely onto something.

"What is going on?" Helen crossed her arms.

"I just . . . think I have a nosebleed. I need to run upstairs and get some toilet paper or something. It's going to drip all over this white carpet."

Helen, startled, glanced down at the carpet. She knew how hard blood was to get out. Cory had proven that true four different times. "Let me see," she said, stepping forward. A little blood never bothered her.

"No! No . . . I'm fine. I just . . . don't

want to drip."

Helen grabbed her arm. "Is it pot? Is it? It's pot, isn't it? I knew those theater geeks weren't trustworthy."

Hannah's eyes, just seconds ago wide and frightened, narrowed quickly. "Pot? Really? They're nice people, Mom. They would never give me pot. I would never *smoke* pot. How could you think that about me?"

"Well, I can't trust you to be on time, so how can I trust you with anything else?"

Hannah's hands dropped to her sides and she only stared at Helen, right at her eyes, glaring.

"What? No nosebleed?" Helen spat.

"It did bleed. A little bit at first. Not much."

"What are you talking about?"

"This." Hannah pointed to her nose.

"Yes, I see your nose. It looks fine."

"It is. But look closer."

Helen leaned in. "You've got glitter on your . . ." And then it hit her. It felt physical and literal as the realization hit her. She stumbled backward, grasping at the handrail.

"Hannah!" she shouted, so loudly that Cory and Madison came running to the top of the stairs. "Go to your rooms!" The two turned and Hannah tried to leave with them. "*Not* you."

Hannah turned around, but there was no hint of fear in her eyes. "So what? I got my nose pierced."

Helen frantically searched her daughter's face, hoping not to see another piercing. She was secretly thankful the diamond was tiny. It looked like a speck. If Helen didn't know any better, she would've thought nothing of it, except to tell Hannah to go wash the piece of glitter off her face.

But it was what it represented. Hannah had gone and done something she knew she shouldn't, just to spite them, it seemed.

"Take that out this instant!" Helen said.

"No."

"No?"

"No."

"Your father cannot see this!"

"I don't think Dad is going to be as upset as you think." With that Hannah turned and raced upstairs, even as Helen protested.

At the bottom of the stairs, Helen stood completely alone and cold with shock.

Chapter 12
Larry

Because his office was on the east side of the building, daylight always faded far before the sky went dark. But at this late hour, it was pitch-black. Larry sat slumped at his desk, hovering over work that he no longer cared about, reading text that he was not absorbing, drinking coffee he didn't taste.

Was it just him or was time going by faster? It seemed like a week ago they were eagerly sending Nathan off to his first day as a senior. Then they were ordering his ring and his portraits. Then they were receiving acceptance letters to colleges.

And now he was a high school graduate.

And little Robin. He hadn't pegged her as a girl — young woman — who would rush off and get married. She was his steady Eddie, the kind of kid who "had her head on straight," as his father liked to say. She thought things through. She planned out her life, even as early as kindergarten, when she'd declared that she needed a file folder to organize her drawings from least well-drawn to most well-drawn. She was so kindhearted, too. The type of kid who played with the kids who had nobody to play with at recess. He'd thought she might go into the Peace Corps one day or do missionary work or something of that sort. Inner-city kids were great, but was that her vision for her life or Marvin's? Of all his children, it had seemed Robin had the most ambition and the highest calling to do well in her life.

Marvin didn't seem to fit into any part of that picture. He was a nice enough kid — young man — but how could he take care of Robin by delivering pizzas and spending his weekends jumping out of airplanes? He was dangerous, in more ways than one.

Larry set his pen aside, fell back into his chair, and stared at the floor in a lame attempt to pray something — anything — to get God to move a mountain named Marvin off their ranch and back where he belonged. He always knew he'd struggle with whatever man Robin chose to bring home, but this was testing his limits.

Still, he couldn't fall apart. Beth was doing enough of that for both of them.

If he thought about it, what he really wanted was simply to leave his mark on his kids' lives — to have impacted them and their memories. He wasn't an absent father by any stretch of the imagination. But he'd known college was coming and worked long hours sometimes in an attempt to move up in the company. It worked. He was now head of his department and could pay for two kids in college . . . except one had dropped out.

He bit his lip and closed his eyes, praying Scriptures that had nothing to do with the situation, but if taken out of context sounded like they could make things right in his life.

"You sleeping on the job?"

Larry looked up to find Carol standing in the doorway of his office.

"Awfully late for you to be up here," she said, her deep, craggy voice louder than usual since the hum of copiers and computers was nearly silenced this late.

"Hi, Carol. Just finishing some work." He sat up in his chair. "What are you doing here?"

"Making up for some work from a couple of weeks ago when I had to take that time off."

"For your dad's funeral."

"That's it. And thanks for the flowers, by the way."

"Sure. Hey, Carol?"

"Yeah?"

"How much vacation time do you have left?"

"I burned through it all taking care of Daddy in the last weeks of his life. Pancreatic cancer sure does take them fast. I don't have anything left."

"You know, I haven't taken a single vacation day this year. I just realized it. We haven't had the time, trying to get Nathan into college and working all that out."

"You got something like three weeks, don't you?"

"Plus sick time."

"You planning a trip or something?" She took a draw from the vapor cigarette hanging around her neck. Today it smelled like Dreamsicles.

"Not so much a trip as a . . ." Larry laughed a little. "A memory maker. Just *bam,* going home and making some memories with my kids."

"Doing what?"

"Don't have that really planned out yet, but I'm thinking it through. You got a kid, don't you, Carol?"

"A daughter. She's thirty-one now."

"You see her much?"

"No, not really." She picked something off her pant leg. "I'd love to see her more. She lives up in Michigan with her husband and two girls. She'll call sometimes on Mother's Day. I hope she comes to visit soon. I ask her every year to come visit us, but it seems like she's very busy with work and all that. You know how it goes."

Larry looked at Carol in a whole new way suddenly. Before, she was a cranky old woman who hated her job, her life, her boss. Now he saw the traces of a woman who had probably sacrificed everything to raise a little girl who never returned home to see her. Would that be Nathan? Off to his own life, too busy to even call? Would that be Robin? Would Marvin move them to some new town, a fourteen-hour drive away, and be unable to pay for a plane ticket to come home?

"You know what?" Larry began clearing his desk of paperwork.

"You're dying of cancer and leaving me your fortune?"

"I'm taking vacation starting today." He glanced up at Carol, who toyed with her cigarette, swinging it back and forth across her chest. "All three weeks of it, plus sick days."

Carol looked alarmed. "*Is* it cancer?"

"No, Carol, I'm not dying. I'm realizing time is . . . well, it's a cancer of sorts, I guess. It eats whatever is in its path and never stops. You have what you have and you better make good use of it. I'm taking time off and spending it with my boys and my daughter and my wife. We're going to have an amazing Summer of Intense Fun."

Carol's expressionless face managed a yawn. "Intense fun, eh? That's a step above ordinary, everyday fun?"

"It means," Larry said, grabbing his jacket and briefcase, "that I've got to pack a lot into a little time. There are things I always wanted to do with the kids. Now's the time. Right now. Wait. I can't. I have that proposal due tomorrow. Okay, well, the day after tomorrow. That's when it starts. I'll send Gerald an e-mail tonight about it."

"He's going to take that well," Carol said, stepping out of Larry's way.

"He'll understand. He's a family man."

Carol watched him walk to the elevator. "One time his wife was out of town and his kid was running like a 103-degree temperature. You know what he did? I saw it with my own eyes, right in his office." She pointed south. "He plugged that kid with two doses of Tylenol and sent him off to school." Carol moved toward her desk. "But good luck. Wishing you the best Summer of Intense Fun. I'll hold down the fort in case you survive it and come back."

Larry got on the elevator and pulled out his phone, calling Robin's cell.

"Hello?"

"Hey, spumpkin," he said. "Think you could work in a lunch date, next week or tomorrow or whenever, with your favorite dad?"

She laughed. "You bet, Daddy."

CHAPTER 13
TIPPY

"Hey, thanks for coming over." Butch stepped aside to let Tippy in while wiping his hands on his jeans. He closed the door with his elbow, like Daphne did now every time she germ-gelled herself.

Tippy held his toolbox at his side as he looked Butch up and down. "Are you baking or painting? I thought you said baking over the phone, but you look like you've been building something."

Butch sighed. "Follow me. But keep your voice down. Ava is asleep." He glanced over his shoulder. "Why'd you bring tools?"

"Never know when you'll need a tool."

When they arrived in the kitchen, Tippy stopped at the door. Batter clung to the side of the counter, dripping slowly to the floor.

"You *did* say baking." Tippy wiped something sticky off the doorframe with his grease rag. Maybe egg. The floor was covered in something that looked like flour.

148

"I know — don't say it," Butch said.

"Hey, I'm not judging here. Flour is volatile. One false move and *poof!* It doesn't play nice. Isn't Ava on summer break?"

"Almost. School ends Friday. Then it's day care starting Monday. I have to put her somewhere while I work. But for right now I need cupcakes." Butch moved to the island in the center of the kitchen, the last clear space to work on. "Obviously I would've started earlier had Ava not dropped this on me last minute." He shrugged. "I got the impression from her that this is a big deal. I gotta get it right. But I can't find that pan that has the circles, the one you make cupcakes with."

Tippy thought for a moment. "This isn't rocket science. I'll tell you what. Let's bake the cake first, then we'll worry about shaping them."

"Well, that's the exact opposite of how we'd approach a construction job, so that makes sense. Jenny used to bake a lot, you know. I should've paid attention but . . ."

Tippy slapped him on the back. "Kids don't care what it looks like, as long as it tastes good. It's the theory behind gummy worms."

Butch pointed to the mixing bowl in the corner. "Here's the thing. There were three

149

boxes of cake mix I found in the pantry. I ruined the first because apparently the measurements are supposed to be exact. Maybe it's more like construction than we thought."

"What happened to the second box?"

"I cracked the eggs in there and then smelled something funny . . . noticed the expiration date was four months ago. But the good news is I found a newer carton in the back of the fridge. I forgot I bought it for a science experiment Ava wanted to do."

"Oh, what experiment?"

"We never got around to it. But anyway, I precisely mixed it all up over there, and I know there's a cake pan somewhere." Butch rummaged around and emerged with a rectangular pan that seemed suitable in Tippy's opinion.

Tippy switched on the oven. "What do you think the temp should be?"

Butch studied the dial. "Should we broil it?"

"I don't think so."

"Where's the box?" Butch looked around. "It was sitting there like ten minutes ago, I swear."

"Okay, don't panic," Tippy said, opening the garbage and peering in.

"I feel like I should panic. It's ten o'clock.

Could we call Daphne?"

Tippy dropped the garbage lid closed. "Not a good idea."

"Too late?"

"No, it's not that. It's . . . She's . . ."

"What? Sick?"

"Not in the viral sense." Tippy cleared his throat. "It's just hard to take her out in public."

"I'm not public. I'm practically a hermit."

"We got this." Tippy poured the cake mix into the pan and put it in the oven. "I think four hundred is safe. Let's check on it in five minutes to see if it's done."

Butch leaned on the counter. "Talk to me. What's up?"

Tippy shrugged, staring blankly at the oven as he leaned on the counter opposite. "She's just been acting so *weird.* Weirder than normal. Not the kind of quirky that's adorable. She cries a lot. And she cleans all the time. Everywhere. Not just at home. If I lose track of her at a store, I almost always find her in the cleaning aisle."

Butch smiled. "It's called nesting."

"Is that the politically correct way of saying she's cuckoo?"

"Listen, Jenny did the same thing before Ava was born. She kept asking me to bring home the industrial-grade cleaning supplies

151

we use on-site."

Tippy looked relieved. "Did she also make you take written and oral exams every night?"

"No."

"Oh. So that's weird."

"Seems so. What are the quizzes about?"

"Baby stuff. I know a newborn has a lot of needs, but I think she's going overboard. I mean, we have to know the number of ounces the kid is eating. What? Like the kid won't stop when it's full? It's just going to gorge and explode?"

"Speaking of exploding, I should check the cake."

"It hasn't been five minutes."

"I know, but I don't want to overdo it accidentally. This is our last chance." Butch opened the oven door. "How do I know when it's done?"

"I think you're supposed to stab it with something. Here." Tippy handed him a screwdriver. "It's clean. I just bought it this afternoon after work."

"Thanks. Oops."

"What?"

"I dropped it in there. I don't think it's done because I can't even see the screwdriver now." Butch was folded over, trying to peer in, the heat practically baking both their faces.

"Here." Tippy handed him pliers. "See if you can fish it out."

"Got it!" Butch closed the door. "It definitely needs to cook longer."

Tippy rinsed the screwdriver off under the faucet. "So you're saying once the baby is born, life will return to normal?"

Butch leaned against the counter and smiled. "No, life will never be normal, not once you find yourself totally responsible for another human being. I was excited for Ava to be born, but when I thought of having to share Jenny . . . well, let's just say I liked having her all to myself. I never had any aspirations of being a father. Jenny, though, had seen herself as a mother since she was old enough to own a baby doll. It was the thing she lived for." Butch's gaze dropped to the floor and Tippy shifted, hoping he hadn't triggered a bad memory for him. "The thing was, until Ava was born, I hadn't even begun to see Jenny shine. When she became a mother, she propelled into sainthood. She seemed to know everything Ava needed. All Ava's cries sounded exactly the same to me, but Jenny knew if she was hungry or tired or even simply irritated. All before I got the hang of changing diapers." Butch turned away, wiping the counter behind him. "Somehow, this little baby who took so much time and effort made me love Jenny even more."

"Well, I hope something like that kicks in with Daphne," Tippy said. "Because right now I can barely get myself to go home."

"The first time I held Ava by myself, with no one around, was when she was two months old. There was a storm — loud and wicked — and Jenny had been sick. I heard Ava crying, so I got up by myself and went and got her out of her crib, and we sat there, her in my arms, just looking at each other. Every time there was lightning, we'd see each other's eyes. And I realized that I'd jump in front of a bus for this kid in a heartbeat. It wouldn't even be a choice." Butch sighed, tossing the rag in his hand into the sink. "Now I can't even make her a school snack. Or a proper dinner. Or shop for her. Or talk to her. Or . . . anything." Butch opened the oven door. "It looks like a cake!"

Tippy joined him, crouching down for a better view. "Yep."

"Okay, I think it's done." Butch grabbed an oven mitt and pulled the cake out carefully, setting it on the counter.

Tippy stepped away in case it was going to do something crazy, like bubble over or, worse, explode. But it just sat there, like a perfectly normal cake.

"So now how do we make it into cup-cakes?" Butch asked.

Tippy reached for his band saw. "I got this."

"Don't be ridiculous," Butch said. "We can't use power tools. Look, we'll just take a cup and I'll press it over the cake and plop them out. That's how my mom used to make biscuits."

"Makes sense," Tippy said, but thinking there was no way it would work. A band saw was reasonable. It was as precise as they were going to get. But when Butch had his mind made up, he had it made up. "Carry on."

Chapter 14
Charles

Beside him, Helen lay in bed, flipping aggressively through a home decorating magazine. It was later than he was accustomed to staying up, but he was finally done crunching the numbers.

"Randall was right. He was absolutely right."

Helen turned on her side to face him. "About?"

"Once this raise kicks in, if I could increase our income by 17 percent in the next twenty-four months, we'd hit our financial goals two and a half years early, which means we could invest more." Charles felt his temples dampen. They always did when he talked about money. "I told Randall we had to assume that not just Madison but all of our kids will attend Ivy League schools, and I was beginning to realize we were far from being able to do that, especially if Cory skips a grade as we expect him to."

Helen sighed. "His preschool teacher called him a genius, but the truth is, Charles, that when I observe him doing everyday things, I don't believe I completely agree with that assessment."

Charles now felt startled, the way he did when the Monday reports came in at the office. "What do you mean?"

"I mean, he picks his nose and he still plays with Hot Wheels cars. I tried to get him interested in the Rubik's Cube that Madison enjoyed at that age, and do you know what he did when I asked him to solve it? He peeled all the stickers off, put them on the correct sides, and called that 'solved.'"

Charles laughed. "Well, that *is* a way."

"I don't find it funny at all. Isn't that how deviant behavior starts? First you cheat on a puzzle and the next thing you know, you cheat on an entrance exam."

Charles set his laptop aside. "Sweetheart, you're overreacting. Cory does things his own way. He always has." He kissed her forehead, but she didn't look at peace.

"I'm assuming you haven't talked to Hannah about the piercing?"

"Honestly, it's so small that I can't even see it."

"That's not the point, Charles. She did it

out of rebellion."

"If that's the worst thing she ever does, we'll be okay. When you called, by the sound of your voice, I thought she'd been arrested for dealing drugs." Charles kicked his slippers off and slid under the sheets. He was about to turn out the light when Helen rose to her elbow, her blonde hair falling over her shoulder.

"What's the matter?" Charles asked.

"Do you think . . . ?"

"Yes?" It was odd. Helen didn't ask for his opinion much. She mostly just offered hers and offered it often.

"Never mind." She lay back down, her head sinking into one of the overly stuffed pillows she insisted they both sleep on.

"Helen, what is it?"

She turned her head toward him. Her eyes seemed deeply troubled. "Do you think our children . . . like me?"

Charles peered at her. Had he heard her right? "Like you? When have you ever cared if anyone liked you?" He laughed, but she didn't hint at it being a joke.

"Not anyone. Our children, Charles."

"How could they not like you? You give them everything they could want. A good education. Opportunity. Status. They're dressed well. Fed even better." He patted his stomach. "Sometimes a little too well."

"Charles, I'm not joking. I could see it in Hannah's eyes, even this evening."

"See what?"

Helen looked emotional. When was the last time he'd seen her emotional? He put his hand on her shoulder, but she maintained a steady expression.

"Hate," she whispered.

"Helen, come on. Hannah doesn't really hate you. She's fourteen. Doesn't every fourteen-year-old hate her mother?"

She sniffled, shrugged. A good, solid pout emerged. "I don't know. I don't understand it. I vowed that I would never raise my daughters the way that I was raised." Her hand moved to her heart, as it always did when she talked about her childhood, which wasn't often. But it was as if she were covering her heart's ears so it wouldn't have to hear about it all over again. "I remember sometimes my sister and I would go to bed hungry and if she fell asleep first, I wouldn't be able to because I could hear her tummy rumbling. It was like sleeping with a snorer. I told you we shared a bed, didn't I?"

"Yes."

"I wore the worst clothes. I never got my hair cut. I never had anything the other kids had, like radios and those electronic games

— not that I would have been interested, but you understand what I mean."

"Helen, I do. And someday the kids will too. They've yet to go out into the world and see how other people live. One day they'll appreciate all that we were able to provide for them."

Helen rolled to her back and stared at the ceiling, her eyes vacantly tracing memories or thoughts. "I worked so hard to pull my life together, to be better than what I came from."

"I know that."

"But I'm afraid it's not good enough." A tear dripped down her cheek.

Charles hated to see her like this. She was not an emotional woman. In fact, she was often accused of being the exact opposite. But Charles knew her, knew that behind the somewhat-starched exterior was a brave, driven woman who had a lot of talent she really hadn't been able to use much in her life.

"I'm tired. I should get to sleep." She reached for her light.

Charles turned his off too. "Hannah doesn't hate you. She's just at that awful age, you know?"

"Madison was never awful, at any age."

"I was awful at that age," Charles said.

"Then she must get it from you," she said, and he heard amusement in her tone.

The quiet darkness of the late night was now undone by noise. Not loud noise, but noise that was unusual at this hour.

Charles sat up in bed. "What is that?"

Helen groaned. "What it always is."

"The window is open." Charles rose, sliding his feet into his slippers and walking across the bedroom. He pushed the drapes aside. In the dark neighborhood, only one window was aglow.

"I'm right, aren't I?" Helen said, enveloped by complete darkness behind him.

How many days and nights had Helen stood at the very window where Charles now stood, undone by the neighbors they'd had for over a decade? From their vantage point, they could see right through the large window of the Anderson home, straight into their living room.

"What is happening over there?" Helen's voice was breathy and exasperated.

"It looks like they're playing . . . charades?"

"Playing. Figures. That's all that family does."

"Wait, no. Pictionary. I can see a big pad of paper on an easel."

"What's all the noise about? Pictionary

doesn't have to be some loud game like that awful . . . What was that called? With the naked man and the little tweezers?"

"Operation."

"Yes. I wanted to murder that man and his bulbous nose."

Charles squinted his eyes, trying to see more precisely. "There is also a food fight. Or maybe it's part of the game — I can't tell. I just see a lot of popcorn flying around."

"Shut the window. Come to bed."

Charles closed the window, locked it, and pulled the drapes. They could only hear the faintest sounds now of music and laughter. Charles crawled under the covers.

"When is Beth going to get a grip, get a handle on her family? I try at our scrapbooking meetings to give some helpful advice, you know? She nods and seems to understand, but then the very next day I'll see one of the kids leave in pajamas. Leave the house to go somewhere *public.* Half the time, I don't think Beth gets out of her pajamas before noon. If she would get up and get dressed, maybe she would find some motivation to tackle that awful weed problem she has in her front lawn."

"Well, their yard makes ours look twice as good." Charles laughed.

"Yes, well, glad to see you think this is funny. If we ever get a chance to move into our dream house, we'll have an uphill battle trying to sell this house with neighbors like that."

"They're not that bad. I know they don't keep their lawn up and their house needed paint about eight years ago, but they're good people." Charles had always liked Larry. He was a guy's guy, willing to stop what he was doing to talk sports over the fence between their properties.

"I'm going to sleep. I will see you in the morning."

Helen rolled away from him. The light snore she denied having came quickly as she drifted immediately into sleep.

But Charles, even at this late hour, was wide-awake.

On the heels of his promotion, something big had happened today at work. And as he stared through the darkness, he knew it had the potential to change their lives.

But he could not bring himself to tell Helen. Not yet.

Chapter 15
Butch

"Listen, I'm really sorry about the cup-cakes."

"Well, you gave it a good try. And they did taste good, even if they looked too awful to bring to class. Thanks for letting me have one for breakfast."

"I can't believe my cup idea didn't work. I should've just left it as a cake. I'm an idiot. I'm sorry. I'll make it up to you. The beef jerky wasn't a hit?"

"It was . . . interesting. The peanut butter with the M&M'S across the top almost made up for it, but some of the kids just licked the peanut butter and candy off, and Mrs. Murdock stopped that for bad manners, so . . ."

"Again, I'm really sorry." Butch opened the door of the mall and they walked in. "But here we are now. To get you a dress for your graduation, right?" Just a few feet in, Butch stopped in his tracks. "Oh . . .

wow . . ."

Ava, holding his hand, looked up. "What?"

"It's just that . . ." How long had it been since he'd been at the mall? He didn't remember it being this loud. And bright. Why were there so many blinking lights? In front of him, a large screen flipped through advertisements like a deck of cards being shuffled. People moved around them as if they were a jammed log in a fast-moving stream. Somebody bumped into Ava, almost knocking her down, and just kept walking, never looking back. "Are you okay?"

"I'm fine, Daddy. But I don't think you're supposed to stand still at the mall. It feels dangerous."

"Come on," Butch said, walking almost too briskly for Ava to keep up. Her feet were flying, but he didn't like crowds and didn't even know where he was going. His gaze darted to the larger-than-life lingerie store they passed, with all kinds of indecent pictures hanging in the windows. "Cover your eyes," he said to Ava, noticing she was gawking as they passed. The perfume alone coming out of that place was enough to knock him unconscious.

The very next store had pictures of near-naked teenagers hanging all over one another. Wasn't that illegal in some way?

"Cover your eyes."

"Dad . . ."

"Now."

"People are going to start talking about us."

"I don't care."

Her expression lacked any sort of amusement. "I'm eight, not four, you know."

"Okay, open." Butch looked around. "Where are we supposed to be going?"

"The dress store."

"Is that what it's called? The Dress Store?"

"I don't know."

Butch noticed a young woman standing behind a counter, trying to sell cookies the size of bicycle wheels.

"Excuse me," he said.

"Three for one."

"What?"

She pushed a greasy strand of hair out of her eyes. "Three cookies for the price of one cookie. These small ones." She pointed to the batch closest to her, each of which looked slightly bigger than a quarter. "Five dollars."

Butch laughed, but then he realized she wasn't joking.

"Daddy! Please? Look, they have M&M'S on them!"

"Ava, I don't think —"

"You owe me for the cupcakes." She crossed her arms. The girl at the counter didn't even wait. She just took three cookies and started putting them in a sack.

Grudgingly, Butch pulled out a wad of cash he'd stuck in his pocket at lunch and paid the girl. Ava looked very pleased with herself as they began to walk away. Butch stopped and turned back to Cookie Girl. "I need a dress store for girls her age," he said. "Nice dresses for a graduation."

The girl looked to be processing. Then she said, "Bella's Ball. It's down that way, up the escalator, past the Devil's Den and Grunge Masters."

"Thanks."

Ava ate her cookies as they walked. "Thanks, Dad. Mom wouldn't buy me cookies at the mall."

"Why didn't you tell me that?"

"Because then you wouldn't buy them for me."

"True. But why wouldn't she?"

"She said that I had to learn self-discipline. She said it's easy to get caught up in buying everything you see, but that you should go in and just get what you need and get out."

Butch smiled. That sounded like Jenny.

In the store, once again, the music was

loud, this time songs sung by kids who would end up on the covers of grocery store tabloids. Ava raced ahead, through the rows of clothes. He could barely hear himself calling her name. Finally he found her near the back, gawking at a wall of very fancy dresses. "Ava, don't ever —"

"Daddy! Ruffles!"

She looked like a pogo stick.

"Why are you shouting?" he shouted over the music.

"Please, Daddy. Let me at least try it on."

Like she'd appeared out of thin air, a willowy young woman was by his side, holding a long metal stick. "Size eight?"

"Uh . . . yes, I think so."

She hooked the dress and brought it down off the wall, handing it to Ava. "The dressing rooms are near the front."

"Um, how much is that dress?" Butch asked as Ava disappeared again.

"Eighty-five dollars."

"What? For a kid dress?"

"You're in luck, though." She smiled. "We're running a special. Half off."

"Oh, good."

"The second one."

"What?"

"Buy one at full price and get the second one half off."

"I don't need a second one."

"But think of all the money you'll save. Also," she said, whipping out what looked like a business card, "if you spend one hundred dollars today, you'll get 40 percent off."

"Well, that's something."

"Your next purchase. But you have to come in on Tuesday or Wednesday of the first week of the month." She whipped out another card. "Now, with each purchase, you get a hole punched. After twenty punches, you get five dollars off."

"That doesn't seem like a —"

"And don't forget she'll need shoes, a headband, and some jewelry. Let me know if you need any help." And she floated away.

Butch sighed, stuffed the cards in his pockets, and wandered to the front to find Ava. In one of the dressing rooms, shut by nothing more than a curtain, he could see her feet. "You doing okay?"

"Yes, fine. I'll be out in a second."

Butch walked to the very front of the store. He needed some air. And some clarity. He wished he could ask Jenny if eighty-five bucks was too much to spend on a dress. She would know these things. She always knew when something was important enough to spend money on. She knew which expecting couples needed gift cards and which would be offended by them. She could anticipate with amazing accuracy who needed what at Christmas. She had a budget for everything and, Butch realized, always used coupons. Every time they went out to eat, she produced some sort of coupon.

He leaned against the wall that led out of the store, watching shoppers walk this way and that. His attention landed across the way. Directly opposite Bella's Ball was Bob's Sporting Goods. It had been around since Butch was a kid, which was really the last time he remembered going to the mall.

And then he saw them. Larry and Chip. Chip had grabbed a football out of the bin, and they were playfully tossing it back and forth. Butch sighed loudly. He'd give anything to be over there and not here.

He checked his watch and was turning to go tell Ava to hurry up when he caught the tail end of her dress disappearing back into the dressing room. The curtain zipped shut.

"Ava?" Butch said, standing in front of the dressing room. "How does it look? Can I see?"

"It's fine, Dad. It fits. That's all that matters."

"You don't want to show me?"

He watched the dress drop to the ground,

puddling at her feet. In less than a minute, she was out, handing him the dress. "This one will work."

"You don't want to try more on?" He was sensing she was upset, but he didn't know why.

"Nope. It's fine."

"Okay . . ." Butch held up the dress. "You need shoes? Jewelry? Hair stuff?"

Ava looked like she was considering it, but then she shook her head. Butch went to the register at the back of the store and paid, after telling the lady that no, he didn't want to spend fifteen more dollars to make it to one hundred. He grabbed the bag and walked to the front of the store, where he found Ava standing at the railing, looking across the mall at Bob's Sporting Goods.

"Okay, are you ready to go?"

She was fixated on something. Studying it. Maybe she saw Larry and Chip, but he couldn't find them any longer. Now it was just a crowded store with lots of dads and sons.

"You wanna go over to — ?"

"We better go. It's a school night," Ava said. She took the sack and walked in front of him as they made their way back out to the car. Ava was awfully quiet. Maybe it was the sugar. It amped you up and then

171

dropped you like a sack of potatoes.

"You're sure there's nothing else you need?"

"Would you mind if I turned on the game?"

Butch glanced at the radio. Was this a trick question? But she reached for the knob, turned it on, and didn't need to change the station. He always kept it on sports talk. Butch found himself smiling. He had no idea Ava was interested in sports. Maybe this weekend he could teach her to throw a ball and even pitch, depending on her arm strength.

On the drive home, Butch would look over at her every once in a while and grin, and she would grin back and say something like "Good game, huh?" Actually it was a blowout, but she was only eight.

As they pulled into the drive of their home, the sun was already gone and the house was dark. *Man, time flies at the mall,* he thought. He checked his watch. They still had to order pizza and get her bath in.

"Dad?"

He looked at her. "Yes?"

"Do you think I could go with you to work sometime? Just to watch the construction?"

Butch ruffled her hair. "Definitely! I would love for you to come. I'll even get you a hard hat."

"Oh. Good." She smiled, got out, and walked to the house, dragging her dress bag behind her.

Chapter 16
Beth

Before kids, Beth had been superb. She dressed well. She multi-tasked well. She socialized well. Larry's family often said, "You're the best thing to ever happen to Larry." A lot of things had slipped after kids, namely her mind and sense of self, but she didn't regret any of it. She loved being a mom. And the one thing she still did well was cook. In fact, she was better now than when they got married. She'd started their marriage equally married to recipes. As her confidence grew in the kitchen, she began experimenting but returned to recipes after a few failed attempts at chicken dishes. Jenny was, and always would be, the creative cook. Still, Beth knew food would be in her children's fondest memories of her.

Yet in the midst of perfecting homemade mac and cheese and learning to quickly double a batch of fried chicken for unexpected guests, she'd forgotten to teach her gift to her children. She'd seen it as her duty to provide home-cooked meals to them as often as possible (which in certain sports seasons was almost never), but not once did it cross her mind that this might be a useful skill for her kids.

Now, though, she was trying to heed the advice of Dr. Reynolds, who encouraged her to seize the moments in the here and now. "Don't dwell in the past. Don't live in a future you're not promised. Just be present today."

She knew all too well about futures not promised. Of all the people in the world, Jenny Browning had deserved her future. She was the best there was — caring, thoughtful, loving, nonjudgmental. Everyone adored her. Even Helen.

Between gathering all she needed from the cabinets and the fridge, Beth listened for Robin upstairs. She'd made it to the shower. Then she heard her blow-drying her hair. Beth beat three eggs with half-and-half, her secret ingredient, and chopped up onion, bell peppers, ham, and tomatoes. In a small bowl nearby was a heap of Colby jack cheese.

She stepped back and smiled. The blow-dryer was off, which meant it wouldn't be long before Robin came downstairs. And

Robin was not one to skip breakfast, so Beth figured while she made her an omelet, she would teach her too. Just the basics first, and over the next few days she'd show her some fancier moves. By the end of the month, she'd practically be a pro. Later they'd move on to more challenging dishes, like chicken and pork. Dr. Reynolds had encouraged her to wait to be asked, but the Mustache wasn't a mom losing two of her children in one summer. Somehow she'd talk Robin out of marrying Marvin while simultaneously preparing her for the right man to come along.

Behind her came the noise of Robin rushing down the stairs. She knew what each of her children's footsteps on the stairs sounded like. Robin's were fast, staccato, and precise. With Nathan, there was usually a trip or stumble of some sort. And Chip took two at a time.

"Hey, Mom," Robin said. Her purse was thrown over her shoulder, and her keys were in her hand. She grabbed the last banana off the counter. "I gotta run."

"What? Wait. Where?"

"Mom, I'm planning a *wedding.* I've got a billion things to do."

"I know. Of course. But look." She gestured grandly at the counter full of food. "I was going to make you an omelet."

"Why?"

"To feed you, first and foremost. But also to teach you to make one."

Robin looked genuinely baffled. "Why?"

"Honey, you're about to be a wife." *Wife* came out sort of hoarse, not at all intentionally. "And motherhood will follow that. I'm afraid I've done a horrible job preparing you for this moment. Yesterday you were five, and now, here you are . . ." Her voice gave out because really, she wanted to talk her out of this marriage, not through it.

Robin's expression grew concerned. "Mom?"

"I'm fine. Sorry. It's the onion. Fumes that would rival Chernobyl."

"Cher-what?"

Beth began to speak fast and inconsistently, her tears spilling over. "I just want you to be able to cook. Eggs are a staple. Your dad and I lived on eggs when you kids were young and we were broke."

Robin's head was moving like she was trying to follow the start and stop of every sentence.

"And I'm also concerned you don't know what Chernobyl is, honey. Didn't they teach you that in school? And why didn't they have home ec at your school? What is going

177

to happen when a button falls off Marvin's pants — which always drag on the ground? And why aren't you going back to college?"

Robin set her keys down and walked to the side of the counter where Beth stood. "Of course this is important, Mom. Please, it's okay. Stop crying. Show me how to make this omelet."

Beth wiped her nose. "Chernobyl was the site of a nuclear meltdown."

Robin nodded vaguely. "This is one of those moments where you're trying to speak to me by metaphor, right?"

"No," Beth sighed.

Robin's phone dinged and she pulled it out of her pocket. "Oh no . . ."

"What?"

"Marvin's car broke down again. I have to go pick him up or he's going to be late for work."

"Who would order pizza in the morning?"

"He likes to get in early. He's very prompt. Haven't you noticed that?"

No, she hadn't noticed *that*. "I just don't know him well enough to —"

Robin grabbed her keys off the counter. "I'm so sorry, but we'll do this soon," she said, waving her hands in a circle toward the eggs. "Truly. I'll put it on my calendar, okay? Are you okay?" She began backing toward the door. "If you're not, tell me. Should I get Dad?"

Beth smiled wide enough to throw her cheeks out. "I'm fine."

"You're sure?"

"Totally fine. It was a spontaneous combustion of emotion — kind of like when people just burst into flames for no reason."

Robin reached for the door handle behind her. "What? People burst into flames?"

"No . . . I mean yes, sometimes. It's very rare. I'm just speaking metaphorically."

Robin blinked. "Can I go get Marvin?"

"Yes, of course. Have a good day. We'll talk egg soon."

Robin practically vanished behind the door just as Beth reached out to ask if she could pray for her, if they could pray together.

At the same time, Chip seemed to materialize in the room.

"What are you doing?"

Beth sighed, looking at all the food. "Making breakfast, like I do every morning. Your cereal is in the pantry."

"What are you making?"

"I was going to teach Robin how to make an omelet."

"Cool. Can I learn?"

"Honey, not now." Beth pushed her fingers

deep into her temples. A headache was coming on. "Where's your father? I think he's outside doing something with a kite, but he'll probably leave for work soon. Grab the cereal. You can eat it straight out of the box today. It's summer, right?"

"Are you okay?" Chip asked, walking to the pantry.

"I'm fine."

"Maybe I should pray for you today." Chip stood there and said a quiet little prayer for his mom. It made Beth want to cry harder, but she held it in.

Then Chip gave Beth a quick side hug and grabbed his cereal, taking it into the living room. Beth dropped to the counter, her head buried in her arms. Why couldn't she stop crying?

"Beth?" Her head popped up and there stood Daphne, her eyes wider than normal. Daphne was anxious by nature, so now she looked extra anxious. "What's the matter?"

"I didn't know you were coming."

"We were going to the scrapbooking shop today, remember? Larry said I should come on in. . . ." Her thumb was pitched over her shoulder but the rest of her was moving forward like she was about to consume Beth with a suffocating hug. Beth stood upright and went to the sink, pretending to need to wash her hands.

"What's the matter?" Daphne asked again.

Beth wiped her hands and turned, leaning against the sink. "I don't know. I'm crying a lot lately. It turns out that Robin is getting married and she doesn't even know how to make an omelet."

"Oh, congratulations." Daphne blinked. "Is that a requirement? The omelet?"

"She's not prepared for this world. I haven't done my job. Any decent mother shows her daughter how to cook. It's part of the deal. You teach them to shave their legs, pluck their eyebrows, and make an omelet."

Daphne looked frightened as her gaze roamed over the ingredients on the counter. "Well, Robin is really smart, you know. Savvy. You've taught her a lot of things. She goes to church, she helps at the food pantry . . ."

"I haven't done anything for her. She can't sew on a button. She can't iron a shirt." Beth covered her mouth. Another sob was about to escape. "She can't *hem,* Daphne! And I know it sounds like I just stepped out of 1950, but she has no idea what to do as a wife."

"Have you bought her the book *What to Expect Before You're Expecting*?"

Beth walked to Daphne, gently placing her hands on her belly. "Daphne, I know we're like two decades apart in age and you probably think of me as a dinosaur, but let me tell you something. The time goes by so fast. Don't take any of it for granted. One day they're wrapped in a blanket, held tightly in your arms, and you're singing them a lullaby. The next thing you know, they're unable to use a whisk. And they don't know how to get through hard times by themselves. It happens that fast." Beth sniffed and took a couple of steps back. "Listen, can we reschedule?"

"Sure, of course. I'm behind on bookkeeping for Tippy and Butch anyway." Daphne reached between them to pat Beth on the arm.

"The truth is, I'm seeing a therapist," Beth said. It felt like a confession that needed to happen.

"Oh."

"Yes, I know. Please believe me when I say this is the first time in my life. I'm not typically this toxically emotional."

"Honey, it's okay."

"Dr. Reynolds told me to live in the moment, and I'm trying, but . . . Robin isn't here with me. She's out there, living in her own moment without me. And we don't even know this boy."

"What was his name again?"

"Marvin. Marvin *Hood*!"

"Sorry, I mean that doctor you mentioned."

"Reynolds." Beth wiped her tears again. "It's such a sobering thing to realize you can't get time back. It's gone before you even know it came."

The two of them stood there for a moment, Beth staring into the bowl of whipped eggs, lightly dashed with pepper, Daphne just staring.

"Well, I'll see you at scrapbooking," Daphne said, her voice so heavy with forced cheer it sank the already-weighty atmosphere.

"Okay, see you then." For the third time this morning, Beth forced a smile. Then it dropped from her face when she realized that after finishing Nathan's graduation photos, her next scrapbook would be of the wedding. "Also, please don't mention the wedding . . . to anybody." She'd only told Butch, and through a text, not even a phone call. She told Butch because she would've told Jenny and he was the next closest thing . . . sort of.

"Okay."

She so desperately needed everything to

go back to where it had been, just for a few months, just for a little bit — Robin in school pursuing her degree, Nathan in his senior year, hoping for the college of his dreams, Chip, young and affable and still willing to hug his mom in public.

Out the window she saw Larry run across the lawn. What he was doing out there before work was anybody's guess, but he'd better get dressed or he'd be late. Larry, for now, was the only normal, steady thing in her life.

The front door opened and Larry walked in, sweaty and grinning and breathing hard. He went for a glass of water.

"I'd offer you breakfast," Beth sighed, "but it'd make you late for work."

"Yeah, listen, I wanted to talk to you about that."

"About what?"

And for the next ten minutes, he stood at the kitchen counter and explained why his Summer of Intense Fun idea meant that he needed to take all of his vacation time at once.

Like an unfortunate ending to a meringue pie, her life was collapsing, one overly beaten egg white at a time.

CHAPTER 17
HELEN

"It's so nice to see you, Helen. Your nose is looking wonderful."

"Thank you, Dr. Reynolds," Helen said, taking a seat in a chair so full of stuffing it was hard to keep her spine erect. "Once he realigned it after the first debacle, it was quite lovely."

"Much bruising?"

"Nothing a Sephora trip couldn't handle."

Dr. Reynolds pulled out his notepad. "It seems last time you were here, we left off talking about loving who we are and how God created us. And you mentioned you're planning a tummy tuck for next year?"

"I'm actually here on a different matter," Helen said.

"Oh? What brings you in?"

"It concerns my relationship with my children — in particular my middle child, Hannah, and the resentment she feels toward me for providing her with everything a child could possibly want or need. I've done a little research on the Internet, and I believe I'm dealing with full-blown narcissism, which, if not handled now, could lead to psychopathy."

Dr. Reynolds's eyes grew round. "Is she burning things down? Harassing small animals?"

"No, it's much more subtle than that. She's casting me looks, Dr. Reynolds, and let me assure you, my children were not raised to cast looks. They're proper children. I could take them to restaurants when they were young. They test near genius level in their vocabulary. My eldest was valedictorian of her high school and is going to Cornell this fall. Undecided, only because she has so many options."

"It sounds like you're raising perfectly wonderful children, Helen," he said.

"But Hannah . . . she resents me to the point that she's piercing herself."

"With knives?"

"With nose rings. Purely out of resentment."

"How do you know?"

"Resentment is not that difficult to spot, is it? Hannah is fourteen. She's got everything a child could want. What could she possibly be resentful of? I want you to be straight with me, Dr. Reynolds. Is she suffering from a personality disorder?"

Dr. Reynolds took off his glasses and set down his notepad. Under his mustache, Helen thought she saw a smile. "Helen, before we begin talking about what Hannah might be resentful of, let me ask you a pointed question. What are *you* resentful of?"

Helen's spine snapped straight, and her fingers dug into the kneecap they had so gently rested upon seconds before. "Why would that matter?"

"Humor me."

She sighed. "I suppose I'm resentful of my neighbors. The Andersons. I scrapbook with the wife, Beth, but I'm not fond of the way they're raising their children or keeping their house. And lately they've begun acting very strangely. Whipped cream fights in the front yard. I hear a lot of screaming at night. Loud music. Indecent behaviors for our neighborhood. All the while, they've got a weed collection the size of a cornfield growing near their front porch, which incidentally needs a coat of paint. Charles and I work hard to keep our home up. And our family. I'm afraid some of their influence is rubbing off on my children. Nothing I can't handle, but you asked about resentment, so that is my answer."

"You don't resent Hannah?"

Helen blinked. "Why would I . . . ?"

"For not appreciating what you've given her? Perhaps a life better than you yourself had?"

Helen's spine curved ever so slightly, and for the first time in a decade, she found herself slumping in public. "She has no idea how hard her father works to be able to give her all these astonishing opportunities. But do you know what she wants to do most of the time? Stay at home. I practically have to drag her to dance lessons and pageant events. Do you know what I would've given to take dance lessons?"

"You wanted to be a dancer?"

Helen nodded, remembering her mother's reaction when she'd asked. "I can't feed this family! How can I buy you dance lessons?" she'd screeched, and that was when Helen first realized how very desperate they were.

One night — a cold night in which she shivered under the covers because they couldn't afford proper heat — she said a prayer to the God her father had sworn off when he lost his job the first time.

God, I would like to dance.

A few days later, she'd been walking home from school. To get home, she had to cross the parking lot of a large dance studio. It was where she'd first seen dancing like that. Ballet dancing. Beautiful dancing. She stood, bundled in a coat three sizes too big for her, and watched them all through the glass, with their tutus floating around them like clouds and their hair in elegant buns, their bodies willowy and graceful, like delicate trees swayed by a warm, comforting wind.

Finally a stream of dancers piled out the door, eagerly racing to their parents' very shiny, very nice cars. The parking lot emptied and there, just fifty feet away, Helen saw something pink and small. Looking both ways, she stepped into the parking lot to see what it was.

A leotard. One of the girls had dropped it.

She picked it up gently. It was not new. It sort of looked like it might be on its last day. There was a small hole at the shoulder. It was chalky and smelled weird. Helen stood there for a long time, wondering if she should take it. Was that stealing? Or was God answering her prayer?

After deliberating, she took it. She figured that meant the little girl who lost it would get a new one, so it would all be okay. That night, after her parents retired to bed at seven, she put it on. It was too small. The leg holes cut into her skin, but she didn't care. She danced that night, using her window as a mirror, and she danced some more, anytime she could get away with it and not be caught.

Dr. Reynolds waited for her answer.

"Yes, I suppose I did. Hannah is naturally gifted, as was I. The problem with Hannah is that she's lazy. She just doesn't want to use the gifts that were given to her and the resources that were sacrificed for on her behalf."

"Helen, I want you to do something for me. I want you to go home tonight and write out all the disappointments in your life. Every one that you can remember, big or small. Nothing fancy, just a simple list."

"Why would I do that?" Helen said. "I'm not here about me. I'm here about Hannah, what to do about her, how to fix her."

Dr. Reynolds leaned forward in a fatherly way. "Unlike a crooked nose or being a size A, you can't fix other people. You can only fix how you view them, the lens by which you see them. You can pray for your children, guide them, live a good example in front of them. But you can't fix them."

Helen yanked her purse off the ground as she stood. "You, sir, should stick to counseling botched surgery victims. What you're saying is absolute nonsense. Of course I'm supposed to fix her! That's my job. You come out of the womb completely confused, and who is to set you straight if not your parent? Answer me that!"

And she stormed out of his office. She would've slammed the door, but it seemed it was particleboard, not wood, so it only swooshed.

Helen fumed all the way home. What a complete waste of time. If someone didn't knock some sense into Hannah, she was going to wander aimlessly in life, failing at everything that was important, including relationships. "It's called tough love!" Helen shouted to the stoplight as she waited for it to turn green.

She parked the car in the driveway because there was a scooter blocking the garage. As she opened the door, she spotted Cory watching the neighbors. She sighed heavily as she got out. Larry was in the front yard again. Didn't these people believe in backyards? He was sitting in the grass with Chip, doing something with a kite and a remote control car.

She approached Cory, trying not to draw attention to herself while simultaneously eavesdropping.

"Are you sure this is going to work?" Chip

asked, holding a small engine, presumably from the remote control car, which looked to have met an untimely death.

Larry punched a finger in the air. "Exactly what they asked Thomas Edison right before he invented the Easy-Bake Oven!"

Cory snorted a laugh.

Helen placed her hands gently on Cory's shoulders and whispered, "Sweetheart, it's not polite to gawk at people. I know it's hard because it's the Andersons and they do a lot of gawk-worthy things, but I've taught you better than that."

"But —"

"No buts. Move along."

Inside, she tried to lighten her mood by arranging flowers. It's what she did to stay calm. She had vases in every room, and she had to get the arrangement just right or it had the opposite effect of the one intended.

She was working a group of carnations to death when Charles came through the door. And not in any ordinary way. He hopped over the threshold. Closed the door with a gentleman's flair.

And he was carrying flowers.

"You're home early," she said, eyeing the flowers as he thrust them into her arms. She took a polite whiff. She did love flowers. But either Charles had done something wrong or there was cause for celebration. She'd never received flowers under any other circumstance.

"I've got some good news for you."

Cory was suddenly in the doorway. He didn't interrupt — he never did. But he did tend to linger, like he was doing now.

"Good news?"

"I'm telling you, this is our time in the sun, Helen. This is our time in the sun."

Helen felt her heart flutter with excitement. When was the last time her heart fluttered? "What is it?" she breathed.

"We've been invited to Franklin Hollingsworth's house for dinner tomorrow night!"

Helen touched his arm, looked into the air. "I know that name."

"Of course you do. Hollingsworth Homes."

"No! Him?" She was gasping, each word he spoke like a shiny gold coin.

"He's a billionaire. And we're going to his house."

Now she'd fully grabbed his arm. "Why?"

"All I know is that he heard about my promotion and now he wants to have me over. Maybe to share his wisdom . . . all Warren Buffett–like."

"That's remarkable," Helen whispered. "Yes."

"So he must think you're important."

"Franklin Hollingsworth thinks I'm important." Charles's hand glided through the air as if he were reading a large newspaper headline.

She touched his clean-shaven face. "Well, who are we to argue with that."

"We are no one." He grinned. "Well, we *were* no one. But then we had dinner with Franklin and Kristyn Hollingsworth!"

"I wonder what kind of china Kristyn owns."

"Oh yes," he said, taking her hands. "They definitely own China. And I'm talking about the country." Suddenly Charles's attention dropped. Cory was still standing there, waiting on them, quiet as a mouse but with an eager expression on his face. "Cory. Is there something you need?"

"Can we make a kite together?"

"Sure," Charles said but turned his attention back to Helen.

"Great!" And Cory whizzed past them toward the craft room.

"Wait! Wait!" Charles said. Shouted, really. Helen hated shouting. It caused her ears to ring. "Not right now, okay? Maybe after dinner."

"Oh. Okay." Cory smiled and bounded upstairs.

Charles led Helen to the kitchen, where he opened the cabinet for a glass. "I wonder if it would be tacky for me to take notes. Or bring my mini recorder?"

"Maybe I'll wear the diamond necklace," Helen said, filling his water for him. "She can't be the only person impressing at this dinner."

"I should get a picture with him. For my online profile."

"I should take a gift. What's something they wouldn't have?"

"Unpaid bills."

They both smiled at the idea. Then some horrible racket came through the back window. Outside, Larry Anderson was running around looking at the sky and making airplane noises.

Chapter 18
Daphne

"You're home late," Daphne said as Tippy took his work boots off at the door. "Outside, honey. We can't afford for even the smallest amount of dirt to come in. Just last night I read that tests are under way to determine if dust inhaled between three and six months of age contributes to early-onset asthma in children."

Tippy sighed like he always did when she tried to keep him informed.

"I sent you the link so you can read it."

"I'll just trust you on that." He shut the front door and came into the living room, where she had all her journals and books spread out. One was open on her lap, and she was immersed in it. Usually she would offer to tell him what she was reading. But she didn't this time.

Now he sounded curious. "What's that?"

She didn't look up. "It's a book Jenny gave me. I just found it. I forgot that she . . ."

Daphne trailed off, back to reading.

"It must be good."

"It's about praying."

"Praying?"

"For your child. It's got all these prayers in here, for everything. I mean everything, babe. She gave this to me when I found out I was pregnant. It's kind of . . . beautiful. Jenny's got dates written beside each prayer. I'm assuming they're the dates when she prayed each of these prayers for Ava. Some of the prayers have like ten dates beside them." He was about to sit down on the couch, but she put her hands out. "Don't even think about it!"

"Think about what?" Tippy asked, frozen midsit.

"Sitting down on our furniture, Tippy. Look at you. You're covered from head to toe in who knows what. Asbestos?"

"Sawdust, Daphne. We're building a brand-new house."

"I don't care. We can't have the filth in here."

Tippy stood there for a moment, his eyes narrowing with thoughts she couldn't read. "This *filth* is going to feed and diaper that baby."

Daphne sighed. These days it was like *he* was hormonal. "Tippy, please. You know what I mean. If you would read all the articles I give you, you'd understand."

"I understand that a baby who cannot even hold its head up is not going to be licking the couch."

"Don't be a smart aleck."

"I'm going to take a shower."

"Wait. I want to talk to you."

"About?"

"I'm worried."

Tippy slowly turned around. "Daphne, it's because you read too much. That's the problem. And you talked to the doctor, remember? She said not to worry about that strep B thingy."

It was all she thought about most days. But she tried to stay on point. "I'm preparing, Tippy. We have to be prepared. Which is why what I saw today really disturbed me."

"What did you see?"

"Beth."

"What about her?"

"She was standing in her kitchen and bawling. Talking about time and whisks, and it was hard to follow, but I think her point was that we're teaching our children too late. I'd planned on beginning cooking lessons with our child at five, but apparently Robin doesn't know how to cook and it's going to spell disaster in her life. Maybe I should replace our baby's Chinese lessons with cooking. What do you think?"

Daphne looked up just in time to see Tippy going pale. "Honey."

"I need to sit down."

"Wait . . . no . . . wait . . ."

"I need to sit down."

"Not on the couch! Go sit in the bathroom."

"I'm sitting."

"Don't sit!"

"I'm sitting!" Now Tippy's face was red and his eyes bulged with a dare to stop him. He looked like a lobster. An angry lobster. "I'm sitting! See? Contact! Now I'm leaning back. *Leaning!*"

"Stop it!" Daphne cried.

"I can sit on this couch if I want to sit on this couch!"

"You're being an idiot."

"Yeah? Well, I'm tired. Tired and hungry. But oh, that's right — there's no dinner tonight. Just like the night before. And the night before that. Why? Because you've decided to stop cooking. Because you're reading about nothing that concerns us!"

"Nothing that concerns us? We have a baby coming, Tippy!"

"I realize that. That's why I've been asking Butch for more overtime. And then you're mad at me for being late!"

Daphne was about to retort when suddenly, inexplicably, she burst into tears. Tippy, normally the kind of guy who rushed to her side when she cried, threw his hands up, stood from the couch, and walked out of the room, leaving a dusty shadow behind.

Daphne continued to cry, even as she heard the shower turn on in the bathroom. She didn't know why she was crying. But she'd felt anxious all day. She'd read a whole chapter about babies born with their spinal cords outside their bodies. That freaked her out. But then again, so did the online article about the deadly contaminants found in tap water. She'd already stopped dyeing her hair. Every time she looked in the mirror, she saw a crown of dishwater blonde growing into the Honey Harvest she'd paid over a hundred dollars for.

But that's what you did as a parent. You sacrificed. You *prepared.* You realized that love had costs, like water retention and cankles.

And all Tippy could think about was dinner? What was wrong with that man?

The bedroom door opened and Tippy returned to the living room, smelling of Dial and resentment. He'd changed into his favorite old jeans and a T-shirt he'd had since college. It had sweat stains under the armpits. He'd dug it out of the trash all four times she'd tried to sneak it out of his closet and bid it farewell.

He stood for a moment staring at the ground. Daphne stayed quiet. Sometimes it took him a while to find his words, especially when he was trying to apologize. She gently closed the book on her lap so it wouldn't be a distraction for either of them.

"Daphne?"

"Yes?"

"I'm going to get dinner. By myself."

"What?"

"I'm leaving the house, and I'm going to get three hot dogs."

Daphne's nostrils flared, a spontaneous reaction her body had when she tried to control her anger. She dropped the book to the coffee table and crossed her arms. "I can't have hot dogs. We've discussed this. They use preservatives in their —"

"I know."

Daphne blinked. Tippy was eerily calm.

"I know what's in them. I'm going out and getting three of them, all for me, and then I'm going to find someplace to watch the game while I eat them by myself."

Her nostrils were growing larger by the

second, and her chin hung an inch above her clavicle.

"I don't know when I'll be home. Good night."

Tippy grabbed his keys off the counter, walked so quietly to the door that she couldn't hear footsteps, and left.

CHAPTER 19
BUTCH

"Tippy? What are you doing here?"

Tippy held up a sack of fried chicken, grease seeping through the paper sack by the second. Butch couldn't see the chicken, but he would know that smell anywhere.

"I brought chicken. It was going to be hot dogs, but now I know too much about them and I couldn't bring myself to . . . so I just got fried chicken. Thought Ava might like that too."

"Why? You don't look good. What's the matter?" Butch stepped aside and Tippy walked in.

Ava, who was on the couch drawing, jumped up. "Tippy!"

"Hi, Ava. Have you eaten? I bought you guys some fried chicken."

Butch smiled, watching Ava's eyes grow large. That's exactly how he felt. Why had they been so stuck on pizza? Why hadn't he thought of fried chicken once in a while?

"Ava, grab some paper plates!" Butch said, ushering Tippy toward the couch.

But Ava just stood there, arms by her sides, her attention off the chicken and on Butch.

"What?"

"You're going to eat that?" Ava asked, one arm floppily gesturing toward the sack.

"Of course I'm going to eat it."

"We're not allowed to have fried chicken." Now her arms were crossed.

Tippy glanced at Butch. "Oh, uh . . . sorry . . . ?"

"What are you talking about?" Butch asked. He didn't like her tone.

"You know what I'm talking about."

"I don't know what we're talking about," Tippy said.

"Mom didn't let us have fried chicken," Ava said. "She said it was bad for our health. Very bad. Mom told me that she made you give it up when you two got married and she saw your cholesterol numbers."

Butch tried to halt the exasperated sigh that wanted to escape like a gale-force wind. "Look, Ava, Tippy was nice enough to bring this over. We're not going to be rude. Besides, what's the difference? We've been eating pizza every night."

"Pizza is different. Mom let us have pizza.

That's because it has vegetables and cheese." Her eyes narrowed like this was some kind of standoff.

Butch put his hands on his hips. "We're having fried chicken and that's the end of it."

Tears welled up in her eyes. Her mouth pinched closed just like Jenny's used to do when she was mad. "You're breaking all of Mommy's rules."

"That's not fair."

"Mommy hated paper plates. She hated eating in front of the TV. And now you're going to eat fried chicken?"

"I think Mommy would understand."

"No! You're doing everything wrong!"

"Ava . . ."

"You're doing everything wrong because you're mad at her for dying!"

"Ava, stop this right now."

"Ever since she died, you're breaking all the rules." Tears streamed down her face, and her cheeks brightened with rage.

"You're being irrational. Tippy just brought us dinner. What's so bad about that?"

"I hate you!"

"Ava!"

"I'm not eating that. And neither should you." Ava stomped down the hallway.

"Oh yeah? Well, I'm eating it! And yours, too! And you know what? I ate fried chicken every second Thursday of the month with the guys at the construction site. And your mom never knew about it. So how's that?"

Ava's bedroom door slammed.

Butch put his face in his hands, trying to keep from screaming even more ridiculous taunts at his eight-year-old.

"Dude, I'm sorry . . ." Tippy started for the door, clutching the bag of chicken.

"Tippy, no, please. Stay. It's fine. It was really nice of you. Ava's just having a moment. And to tell you the truth, I desperately need fried chicken. The thought of eating pizza again makes me want to barf."

Tippy walked to the couch and set the bag down. Butch handed him a paper plate, which felt heavy with the weight of guilt. It was true — Jenny hated paper plates. She never allowed dinner in front of the TV. Butch wasn't purposely being defiant. But he also didn't know how to make lasagna. And he hated washing dishes. And he couldn't carry a conversation with his daughter for an entire meal. So this was what it was.

"So . . . you just decided to bring us fried chicken?"

Tippy stared at the TV. "Daphne and I

had a fight. I guess there's something in the air tonight."

"Oh, man. Sorry. Want to talk about it?"

Tippy shrugged. "I knew having a kid would be hard, you know? I watched you, my other friends. But I didn't get that it was going to be hard before the kid ever got here." His fingertips shone with grease as he scratched his temple. "And I'm consumed with guilt in the weirdest of ways. I told Daphne I was going to get hot dogs. I knew she was mad about that. So what do I do? I pass the hot dog stand and go get fried chicken. Now I'm the one acting weird."

"What's wrong with hot dogs?"

"Preservatives. Plus I was a jerk about it, so I knew I wouldn't be able to enjoy them. But I'm telling you, Butch, Daphne is losing her mind. And I don't think I can take it anymore. We fit so well together until now." Tippy glanced at Butch. "I know you think I'm crazy, but next time you go by the office to drop off the books, just say the word *baby* and see what happens."

Butch stared at the chicken on his plate, trying not to be haunted by Jenny's explanation of how arteries begin clogging as early as childhood. "I wish I could say it gets better, but it doesn't. Not really. But it turns out you're going to love this kid and so it's okay." He looked up, trying to hold the tears at bay.

Tippy set his plate down. "Butch, I'm sorry. I'm such a moron. How could I talk to you about this? I wasn't thinking. I'm sorry."

"Just forget you saw that. You can talk to me."

The two were quiet for a moment, with Butch hating that grief never bothered to knock — it just barged its way in anytime it wanted to.

"I was thinking of talking to Jenny's sister," Tippy said after a few minutes.

"Beth?"

"Yeah. They all scrapbook together. I thought maybe she could talk to Daphne, get her straightened out."

"Uh, well . . ."

"What?"

"I don't know if Beth is in a position to help." Butch reached to the coffee table and picked up the business card Beth had dropped off an hour before Tippy arrived. "She gave me this," he said, handing it to Tippy. "Said I should think about it, and then she rambled about omelets and time passing by and pizza. I don't know. She didn't seem like she was in a good place, although she claims that I'm the one who isn't.''

Tippy held the card in the light. " 'Dr. Terry Reynolds, counselor.' " He laughed, grabbing a drumstick off his plate. "Really? She wants you to go see a counselor?"

"Yeah. I guess."

"Are you?"

"What good is that going to do me? Jenny's gone. That's not going to change."

Tippy was chewing on his chicken leg, still eyeing the card. He flipped it to its back, then to its front. "Wait a minute."

"What?"

"What if I sent Daphne to this guy?"

Butch gave him the sideways glance of all sideways glances. "Tippy. Really. Surely you've learned the death knell to a marriage is suggesting the other person needs help. I mean, what are you going to say? 'Daphne, you're whacked-out. Go get some help.' "

"I wouldn't say 'whacked-out.' I'd use a way more clinical word, like *psychotic.*"

"Oh yeah. That would really work."

Tippy still held the card as he finished the chicken, all the way to the bone. Butch did the same, listening for any signs that Ava had forgiven him and was coming out of her room. But the only sounds were the TV and Tippy licking his fingers, suddenly engrossed in the baking show that was on.

"I've got an idea," Tippy said finally.

"That's when things go really wrong."

"Hear me out." Tippy slapped the card down on the table. "We go see this guy."

"You think Daphne will agree to it?"

"Not me and Daphne. You and me."

"What?"

"Come on. It'll be cheaper. We'll split the difference. I don't need a whole hour and neither do you. We can just pick this guy's brain, you know? He can help us figure out how to fix the ladies in our lives." He glanced toward the hallway.

"Ava doesn't need fixing, Tippy. She's just grieving."

"Yeah, but do you know how to help her?"

Butch sighed. No, he didn't. He figured time would help. But then again, he couldn't have predicted a meltdown over fried chicken. "It would seem weird for both of us to go together."

"Look, we're in there, we've got each other's backs, right? If anything weird starts happening, we bolt."

"That's the thing. I think we're going to be the weird part."

"I'm desperate, man. Somebody's gotta help me figure out what to do with Daphne. She's got to get herself together before this baby comes."

Butch stared down at the greasy chicken thigh hovering over his lap. It had been so long since he'd smelled this much grease in one place. Maybe it was that brief euphoria that caused his common sense to lapse, but before he knew it, he'd agreed to accompany Tippy — only for "moral support." Tippy would make all the arrangements.

When Tippy left, Butch went in to make things right with Ava, but he realized as he cracked her bedroom door open that she'd gone to bed without saying good night.

He walked to the living room and sat down. On his knees, where the paper plate had been minutes before, was a large, circular grease stain.

CHAPTER 20
CHARLES

All things considered, Charles thought, the dinner had gone smoothly. Franklin Hollingsworth did not seem to be much of a talker. His wife, Kristyn, carried most of the conversation, though she would toss out a question for Franklin here and there. Franklin answered carefully, contemplating his words before he spoke. Charles took note of this. He liked how Franklin insisted on taking his time to answer. It gave him an air of authority, as if he knew everyone would simply sit and wait. Charles was a fast talker, he realized, jumping in to answer before a question was fully asked. It caused him to look too eager. This was to be the first thing he'd adjust.

They dined in a room that literally looked fit for a king, as if they'd risen to nobility on the drive over to the house. The walls were papered from top to bottom in scenes of days long gone. The flatware was silver.

The china, bone white. Everything sparkled under a chandelier so massive that if it suddenly dropped, the people on the other side of the world might see it come out of the ground.

Charles enjoyed watching Helen here. She observed everything, from how the flowers were arranged to the intricate detail of the plates they used. Helen had decided against the diamond necklace at the last minute and now touched her pearls often — he knew what they reminded her of, and it was sometimes a good way to tell if she was feeling insecure. He noticed it mostly when she accompanied him to important business dinners or banquets or whatnot. As Kristyn, who looked two decades younger than Franklin Hollingsworth, described the process she and her husband went through to build their home, Helen momentarily stopped fiddling with the pearls.

That left Charles free to engage Franklin in conversation. As he thought of another topic to bring up, Charles became distracted by his own reflection on the shiny, buffed table at which they ate. The butler, or whatever he was, had just cleared the dessert plates and Charles saw himself. What he wouldn't give to be able to have this kind of wealth and security, for himself, for

Helen, for their kids. How many business dinners could he have around a table like this? How much wealth could be acquired by serving a future business partner the kind of meal they'd been served tonight?

Charles had noticed as they made their way through the five-course meal that Franklin seemed particularly uninterested in his food. He'd take a few bites of this and that, but mostly his dinner remained untouched. Charles thought he must eat like this every night. It was just like any other meal.

"Everything was so lovely," Helen said, smiling at Kristyn. "The china is gorgeous. What kind is it?"

"It's from the Royal Doulton collection."

"Oh. I see." Helen's finger traced the rim of the plate. "I didn't realize it was a brand name. We have some handcrafted china that looks a bit like this."

Kristyn raised an eyebrow. "Yes, well, I didn't feel the need to bring out the priceless china for this particular occasion."

There was an awkward pause, Helen's eyes growing with each passing second. It seemed she was about to strangle herself with her pearls, so Charles jumped in to fill the silence.

"You know, Mr. Hollingsworth, I was a

bit surprised when you invited us over. It was quite an honor."

"I invite many up-and-comers to my house," Franklin said in a warbled voice that seemed too old for his age. "I've done my research on you. You have a brilliant mind."

Charles felt like he'd just been infused with hope and glee.

"And I decided long ago that I should never feel threatened by young talents like yourself. Instead I should work together with them. Putting aside competitiveness often leads to remarkable achievements." His finger was up, lecturing the air.

Charles nodded and smiled. "Oh, I agree. And I would be thrilled to work with you in any endeavor."

"Good to know," Franklin said, but his mind seemed to wander off again.

"Coffee?" Kristyn asked.

"I'd love some," Helen said.

Franklin, though, rose. "Charles and I are going to the study. You ladies occupy yourselves with whatever women do after dinner."

Kristyn's eyes flickered with the slightest bit of hurt, but she maintained a proper smile. "I'm going to show Helen around the house," she said.

Charles grinned as the ladies left. Helen

glanced over her shoulder, her eyes sparkling like the chandelier under which she passed.

"This way," Franklin said, leading the way out the opposite side of the dining room. Charles followed closely behind, noticing the slight hunch Franklin carried. He couldn't have been over sixty. His hair was like a seashell, white and fanned out over his skull. He didn't look all that aged in the face, except maybe his eyes, which appeared dull in even the most well-lit room.

Down a long hallway, dark even though it was lit, was Franklin's office. Charles marveled as they entered. A variety of clocks hung on each stately wall. There were clocks on his desk, too. Charles took a mental note of the collection. That would be a good Christmas gift.

The office was enormous, sporting its own library off to one side and a grand view of the pool and the golf course beyond. Charles stepped toward the window and felt the breath leave him as he imagined himself here, in this office, in that pool, after a day on that golf course. As he turned, he glimpsed a racket sitting in the corner, rather lonely-looking.

Franklin sat in his chair. It creaked like it suffered from old age.

Charles made his way toward the chair

opposite the desk. "Do you play racquetball, sir?"

"On occasion." He folded his hands over his belly and said nothing more.

"I love the game." It had been years, actually, but he could brush up on it. "Maybe we could play sometime." Charles widened his smile.

"That doesn't seem real likely, now does it?"

"Well, um . . . I . . ."

"Have a seat, Charles." Franklin's tone had lost any hint of warmth.

Charles dutifully sat, his knees pressed together, his back straight, his hands clutching the tops of his slacks.

"I didn't invite you here to be my friend. I have too many friends already."

"Okay." Charles felt like a small schoolboy at the principal's office.

"Most of them are just waiting for me to die to see if they're going to rank high enough to make the will."

"I see . . ." Charles didn't see, really. He couldn't imagine where this conversation was leading. He searched Franklin's face, his expression, his eyes, trying to figure out what he should say to the man.

Charles had come to admire Franklin Hollingsworth over the years, from a distance, of course. He was a legend around their town, their very own Warren Buffett. Charles had met him briefly at a few charity events and such. Although shorter than Charles, he always had a towering presence. Now, though, he looked shrunken in his leather chair, like it was eating him alive. And though he talked about friendship, there didn't seem to be a lonelier man around.

Franklin glanced out the window behind him. The sun was setting now, casting long shadows past the golf flags at both of the two holes that could be seen from this window.

"Imagine that. Someone plays a couple of rounds of golf with me and has the gall to think they'll share in my inheritance because of it."

Alarm prickled Charles's neck. "Sir, that wasn't my —"

Franklin waved his hand in the air. "I know it wasn't." With a long sigh that seemed to deflate him even more, Franklin placed his hands on his desk and forced the shortest and saddest of smiles. "Let's talk possibilities, Charles."

"I would love to." Charles's own smile had some trouble getting out. He didn't want to seem too eager. Too excited. Too greedy.

Although the word was right — *possibilities* — the mood didn't seem right.

Franklin continued. "If you're going to have power and wealth, Charles, you have to have a strategy and —"

His sentence was cut short by the shrill sound of his cell phone, muffled by the material on the front pocket of the vest he wore. He slid it out. Charles marveled that it was nothing more than a flip phone. It didn't appear he could do anything with it except take a phone call.

Franklin slipped his reading glasses on and looked at the number. "I need to take this."

"Sure."

Charles noticed that Franklin's face lit up as he answered the phone. Charles imagined that he was anticipating good news from a business partner or his accountant or someone else important. At least he hoped it was good news. Franklin seemed oddly temperamental, and Charles wanted to make sure he caught him on the upswing.

"Gregory. Hello." Franklin's tone was formal, but his eyes danced with excitement. "I'm so glad you called." And with that, Franklin Hollingsworth grinned wide enough to show silver caps on the teeth behind the incisors, the goofy kind of grin that a small kid might give when he caught a frog or got the BB gun he'd been wanting for Christmas. "We were just talking . . . Really?"

Charles tried not to stare, occupying his time gazing around at all the objects in the office. He noticed a red kite in the far corner, near some bookshelves. It looked delicate, hardly sturdy enough to endure a strong wind. He smiled, remembering the time his dad had taken him to the lake to fly his kite. The first gust of wind tore it out of Charles's small hands. It crashed a hundred yards away. Charles had burst into tears, but his dad was one step ahead of him. He'd brought an extra, just in case.

". . . Yes, that sounds like a good opportunity. . . . Oh, sure . . . You should do that. . . ."

Do what? Charles couldn't help but wonder what kind of big deal was going on behind that desk, that he was bearing witness to.

"Absolutely. We'll send you the money right away. Listen, your mother and I were thinking that maybe you could come home for a week or —"

Charles looked up. He was talking to his son?

"I see. Maybe later in the month. We could

go to the beach house. We'd love to see the kids. . . . Yes. Of course, I know you're busy. . . . Right . . . Maybe some other time then. . . ."

Franklin slumped toward his desk, the light in his eyes snuffed out by disappointment. The edges of his mouth turned down though he kept his tone the same. "Good, good . . . Yes, I'll send you the money right away. You tell Kara and Ricky that Grandpa said —"

Charles tried to glance away as Franklin slid the phone back into his pocket even as he seemed to slide away himself, somewhere distant and dark. Charles cleared his throat, unsure what to do. Franklin, again, seemed to forget Charles was even sitting there. He was staring across the room at a thought that Charles was not privy to.

"Are you all right, sir?" Charles asked after the silence strung on.

Franklin nodded vaguely.

"Would you like some time alone?" Charles pitched his thumb toward the door, offering to leave him to his thoughts.

But Franklin shook his head.

Charles waited for a moment, hoping they could pick up where they'd left off. But Franklin didn't speak and Charles was hardly breathing.

Finally Charles spoke up. "You were saying? I need to have a strategy?"

Franklin only stared, his old fingers threaded through one another, his chin dimpled with prickly sadness.

"Mr. Hollingsworth?"

Franklin looked up.

"You were talking about my having a strategy."

Franklin let out a long sigh, the kind that makes you feel like someone is releasing part of his soul. He stood, shakier than before. Charles noticed age spots dotting his temple and one cheek. The skin underneath his chin hung loosely, as if his head had shrunk bit by bit over the years.

"The nanny," he said, walking to the window to look out, "taught my son how to tie his shoes."

"Okay." Charles bit his lip. Maybe this was a test. He tried to stay alert and on task.

"That's sad, isn't it? That he didn't learn from me?"

"Is this . . . related to the strategy thing?"

"The what?"

"My business strategy."

Franklin turned from the window, shrugging one shoulder. "Business strategies are easy."

Excited they were back to talking business, Charles pulled his mini recorder out of his front pocket and hit the button. He was about to get some really great gems. He knew it.

"You know what's hard?"

"What, sir?"

"Being a father."

Charles felt his own sigh slip out. "Sir?"

"When you're rising high in the ranks, making more money than you can possibly spend, it's easy to leave your family behind."

"That's so true," Charles said and quietly hit the Stop button on his recorder. Getting to the point was going to take longer than he thought. He wondered what Helen was doing upstairs. "Really great advice," he said, "but I'm wondering if you could talk to me about —"

Franklin raised his hand, waved it with sharp irritation toward random objects around his office. A glass globe. An ivory statue. Pictures hanging on the wall. Charles looked closely. Was that Franklin with George Bush? *And* Bill Clinton? Near the end of the bookshelf there looked to be an actual bar of gold.

"Your kids," Franklin said, his lips a stiff line across his face, "are far more important than any of this. I figured that out too late. My son is almost thirty years old and I never once took him fishing. Or played chess with him." He looked toward a small table with two chairs that sat near the library side of the office. Charles noticed that the chessboard on the table appeared to be made totally from ivory. "I ignored him. And now I see my grandchildren twice a year. If I'm lucky."

Charles gripped the arms of the leather wingback in which he sat. He then tried to fold his hands in his lap, but everything felt awkward.

Franklin moved to the side of his desk, where a fishing pole leaned into a corner covered by shadows. "When your child is born, eighteen years seems like they'll last forever. But it goes by in a blink." His knobby finger traced the fishing line. "You have just eighteen summers to make memories together. You can't go back and rewind those days."

Charles nodded. And nodded again. He tried to nod at every point Hollingsworth made. By the time he prompted Charles to leave by going to the office door and opening it, Charles realized they had not talked business strategy at all. He remained polite, shaking hands with the man and thanking him for his time, but inside, he roiled with disappointment. Once they left the estate, he felt like he was leaving every opportunity behind.

Helen turned to him in the car with a pleasant smile. "Kristyn showed me the house. Gorgeous, honey. Absolutely gorgeous. Did you see the cathedral ceilings? And that winding staircase you liked when we arrived? There's an exact duplicate on the other side of the house! . . . Honey?"

Charles glanced at her. "I'm sorry. What?"

"It's okay," she said, patting his arm lightly. "You're distracted. Easy to become distracted around that kind of wealth."

Charles nodded and they drove home in silence.

CHAPTER 21
BETH

"So," Dr. Reynolds said, looking up and down his notepad as Beth finally took a breath from her description of yesterday morning. "Does Chernobyl represent the eggs? Or your heart? I'm still unclear on that."

"I think I was going for a general meltdown analogy." Beth sniffled even though she wasn't crying.

"I see." He clearly didn't. His twisted lips were practically wearing a question mark.

"I'm trying to live in the moment, like you said, but the moments are whizzing by, one after another, and I can't even grab them. This morning Chip and Nathan ran out of the house on their way to get kite supplies. They're building a kite with Larry, who has practically become a folk hero for taking three weeks off work. They're having so much fun, and I'm glad. But I can't build a kite. I wouldn't know the first thing to do.

Larry was going to launch the Summer of Intense Fun, and I was going to teach Robin domestic skills while talking her out of this marriage. That was the plan. The problem is, Robin doesn't have time to talk or cook. She's planning this wedding . . . without me."

Beth was equipped with a handkerchief today instead of a tissue. Tears were coming now and she dabbed her face, eyeing the wall of mugs. What would her mug say, if she brought one?

She focused her attention back to Dr. Reynolds. "They run out the door so fast. I tell them to be careful, always used to stop them and pray right there on the spot that they'd be safe, that they'd make good decisions. But is that enough?"

"Well, Beth, you know of course that there are no guarantees. You do what you can to equip them for what's out there."

"That's my whole point. I don't think I have done that. I thought I had years and now, suddenly, two of my kids are . . ." She pressed the handkerchief to her mouth even though there were no words to hold in.

"What did you pray for?"

"Well . . . I prayed for them to have the wisdom of God and the heart of Jesus and the feet of Paul and the hands of Samson and the blessing of . . . knowing they are loved and forgiven and free. I prayed they would find purpose and be kind, gracious, giving, extraordinary people."

"Those are beautiful things to pray over your children. You know," he said, setting down his tablet, "my mom told me when my first son was born that I would now have two clinging closely to me: my child and a new companion named Guilt."

Beth nodded. "Yes, yes. I feel so *guilty*. I wish someone would've told me to stop focusing on what didn't matter."

"Your prayers mattered. Very much. What didn't matter, do you think?"

"Whether their shirts were pressed. Whether their hair was fixed. Whether they were eating enough carrots. Whether they . . ." She broke down. "I don't know. It all seemed so important then, and now I just want to . . . to . . ."

"Keep them forever?"

"I know I can't."

"The hardest thing to realize is that from the day they are born, you're training them up to leave you."

Beth stared at Dr. Reynolds, pondering his words. It was so true, but she'd never thought of it that way.

"You train them to feed themselves. To

clothe themselves. To spend and save money. To work hard. To have character. And then it's time for them to leave the nest."

"I thought I'd be ready."

"Maybe your apprehension about Robin has nothing to do with omelets. Maybe it has to do with Marvin."

"*Marvin* is the omelet?"

"You believe that Robin's lack of kitchen skills is equated with her lack of judgment in a spouse."

"She can't cook; therefore she can't mate. . . ." Beth wasn't sure she'd even said that out loud. She mindlessly dabbed her eyes. "Yes. Possibly. But how will she listen to me now? She's a grown woman. She'll just think I'm meddling in her business."

Dr. Reynolds took off his glasses. "You are."

"Shouldn't I be?"

"Beth, you seem like a good mom. You've poured a lot of your life into your children. Eighteen-plus years with Robin and Nathan. Maybe you should trust that you've done enough."

"How could I possibly have done enough? There's not a lifetime long enough to learn how to live in this world."

"You say you're a praying woman. If you can't have faith in yourself, there is Someone you can have faith in."

"But didn't God entrust them to my care? He put me in charge of them." Beth looked down. "I'm trying to get a grip. I really am."

Dr. Reynolds leaned forward. "I've been doing this a long time. And do you know that almost everyone I see is dealing with the exact same thing?"

"What's that?"

"Regret."

Beth fell into the cushion behind her, resting her entire body and the burdens it carried inside on a single paisley pillow that didn't seem up to the task.

"And as you well know by now, time goes by faster the older you get."

"Isn't this the place where you give me some sort of encouragement?"

Dr. Reynolds gently smiled. "You've done all you can, Beth. It's time to let go."

"No! That's not . . . No, that's not true!"

"She's a grown woman. If she wants to learn to make an omelet, she'll watch a cooking show. If she wants to marry this Marvin fellow —"

"But *I'm* supposed to teach her that!" Beth meant to lightly tap herself, but instead her fist hit her chest as though a Tarzan howl might follow. "My mother taught me! Her mother taught her! It's just that I married a good man, and I assumed I had passed that natural talent along in my gene pool. I didn't realize I needed to teach her *that.* During the summers, when I insisted she enroll in the library program and make the top-ten list by reading a hundred books, I should've been taking her to the park and telling her to stay away from pizza delivery boys. That's it, isn't it? I wasted time, and now it's gone."

"I don't think it's as wasted as you think it is. But, Beth, I want to encourage you to continue trying to live in the moment. You can't force the moments. Just enjoy them. Remember how you used to delight in Robin? When she was little, weren't you mesmerized by every small thing? A smile. A wave. Why not be mesmerized now?"

Beth felt incredulous. "By what? The pepperoni smell that has replaced the baby powder smell?" She stood, not even meaning to. "I'm paying you for this? For you to tell me I'm suffering from regret and that I should be happy my daughter is marrying Marvin *Hood,* the pizza delivery boy? What if it was your kid? Would you be *mesmerized* by it?"

"Okay, Beth. Calm down."

"If I could *calm down,* Dr. Reynolds, I wouldn't be here!" She grabbed her purse off the couch. "I'm sorry. I have an appointment to get to."

"Just sit for a moment. Get yourself to —"

"Together? That's the problem. I'm not together. I never was together." She swept hair out of her face only to realize there was no hair in her face. What was tickling her nose, apparently, was rage. Or guilt. "Have a good day."

CHAPTER 22
BUTCH

Butch sat on a small retaining wall, mindlessly eating a bologna sandwich while looking over the schematics of the house. Next to him Ava sat eating her own sandwich, the big yellow construction hat he insisted she wear falling right above her eyes. She pushed it up with her forearm. She'd forgiven him for the fried chicken incident in exchange for letting her skip her first day of day care.

"Hey, thanks for making me lunch today," Butch said to her.

She beamed. "You're welcome. I should make you lunch every day. You shouldn't have to go to work without lunch."

"You don't have to do that. I should make my own lunch. Sometimes I just get a little lazy and forget."

"You never forget my lunch."

Butch smiled and looked down. That wasn't true, really. He'd forgotten a handful of times right after Jenny died, but Beth and Daphne and a few others had come alongside to help and taken a lunch to the school. But mostly he'd remembered. Maybe he was doing a little more right than he thought. But how could he take pride in small things like lunch? He should be doing far better than that.

"This sandwich is really good," he said to her, and it really was.

"Thanks! I put mayo on *both* slices of bread and used one and a half slices of cheese to make sure the bread was fully covered. I think I'm going to write Kraft and ask them why they don't make their cheese the same size as a piece of bread."

"Good idea."

"Hey, Daddy?"

"Yeah?"

"Can I try the nail gun?"

"No."

"How about the table saw?"

"Absolutely not." Butch was back to looking at the schematics, trying to find out if they were indeed short a shipment of two-by-fours as Tippy claimed.

"What are those guys doing?"

"What guys?"

"Them."

Butch looked to where Ava was pointing.

"My guys?" he asked. "Those are the guys that work for me."

"I know. But what are they doing?"

Butch squinted, pulling his hat down closer to his eyes to shield them from the sun. As far as he could tell, not much more than eating lunch together under a tree on the other side of the property. "They're on their lunch break."

"How come you're not eating with them?"

"I'm their boss. Nobody wants to eat with their boss."

"Why not?"

Butch wiped his wrist across his forehead, bumping his hat back up. "Well, it's just understood. They're not my friends. They're my employees."

"Tippy's your friend."

"True. But he's my foreman. He's kind of a boss too."

"But he's eating with them."

Butch sighed, glancing toward the tree, where Tippy was telling some funny story. He looked at Ava. "Go play with the nail gun."

"Yay!"

"I'm kidding."

"I know," she said, giving him a smile over her shoulder as she ran off.

Butch hurried to finish his sandwich. He

didn't really have time for a lunch break. His crew was required to take one, but he usually had fifteen hours of work to cram into each workday. He threw away his trash and walked up to the house. He loved the smell of pine and the way the wind blew through the frame of a house before the walls were up. He stepped across the concrete, dusty but still looking fresh and new.

He'd always promised Jenny that one day they'd build their dream house. She'd accumulated an entire binder full of ideas, from decor to floor plans. She wanted two stories, a craft room, and a playroom for Ava. Those were the three nonnegotiables, as she called them. She never knew it, but he'd worked for two years on plans, drawing up all her ideas, and his. He was going to surprise her with blueprints for their tenth anniversary, when he estimated they'd have enough money to begin construction.

Soon the walls on this house would be up, the roof would be on, the windows in, the carpet laid. It would be inhabited by Doug and Ruth Porter and their three kids. He was a dentist and she was a real estate agent.

Butch walked to the back of the house. For all the luxury it would contain, the view was horrible — just a ten-foot fence and the top of somebody else's luxurious home. If he were going to pay all this money for a house, he'd at least want to see some trees or a field or something.

"Hey, Ava."

That was Tippy's voice. Butch turned to see Ava walking toward the guys under the tree. She held a sack of break-and-bake cookies she'd insisted on making last night. All the laughter died down quickly as she approached. Good thing. It had probably been about something highly inappropriate for a young girl to hear. Butch realized he was well-hidden by the beam he stood by, so he peeked around to watch.

"Whatcha guys doing?"

They glanced at each other. A few shrugged. What? Nobody knew how to talk to a little girl?

"Anybody want a cookie?"

The guys stared at her and Butch sighed. Ava didn't fit in his world. It was becoming clearer by the second.

Then Steven sheepishly raised his hand. "I'll take one."

Ava smiled and handed it over. The next thing he knew, all the guys were raising their hands, and Ava was proudly passing the cookies out one by one.

Ava pushed her hat out of her eyes again. "Can I hang out with you guys? My dad's kind of boring today."

"Really?" Jack asked. "Your dad's not laughing it up? Imagine that."

Butch slid behind the beam, completely out of sight, and closed his eyes. He remembered the days, long ago, when he was just one of the guys. But when he started his own company, married Jenny, and had Ava, suddenly work was more than work. Everything rested on his shoulders. He had a family to support, and the pressure got to him sometimes. The first time he had to fire one of his guys was the last time he ever ate lunch with the rest of them.

From behind the beam he heard Ava ask, "Anybody wanna play I Spy?"

Chapter 23
Beth

Beth pulled into her driveway and parked the car. Next door at Helen's house, everyone had already arrived for their weekly scrapbooking session. She pulled herself taller to look in her rearview mirror. Evidence that she had been crying was clear by the ring of black mascara under the bottom lid of each bloodshot eye. She quickly licked her fingers and tugged at the skin, trying to get the marks off. Were her eyes really that red? She couldn't tell with the sunlight. She had to look normal. Women were very in tune with other women not looking as they normally did. She didn't even feel like scrapbooking, but she had to go. Not showing up would raise more questions, and Daphne had already witnessed her meltdown. She could only pray she wouldn't mention it to the other women, but that was the key: Beth had to show up. If she didn't, Daphne would almost be obligated to share what she'd witnessed in the kitchen.

Beth pulled her giant scrapbook off the seat and got out of the car, breathing in the air and trying to refresh herself enough to look presentable. She smoothed her shirt, her hair, and her anguish as she casually walked over to Helen's house.

"Sorry I'm late!" She breezed in, smiling and patting backs, taking the free chair at the end of the table. Daphne and Helen smiled and went about their scrapbooking. Marlene Waters was busy trying to get her six-month-old son to calm down in the car seat while their other friend, Jackie Mendez, attempted to help. Jackie pushed the pacifier into the baby's mouth and Ethan pushed it right back out. Only Jackie's gaze hovered a bit as Beth sat down.

The problem with Jackie was that she was older and wiser, which meant she was less self-absorbed and could sense things the others could not. Not only that, she cared a lot, which was awesome in most cases but not today. Beth didn't want to be cared for. She'd been stricken with the incurable disease of somewhat-undefined regret and there was nothing anybody could do about it.

"Fresh-squeezed limeade?" Helen asked, pushing a silver tray toward Beth. "I used agave nectar to sweeten it." Red cherries bobbed just underneath the ice. There was also the faintest smell of mint.

"Lovely," Beth said, reaching for the pitcher. She only said words like *lovely* when Helen was around. Admittedly, Helen's pearls intimidated her. Something about those white, iridescent beads strung tightly around her neck made Beth feel inadequate. And today, in particular, they seemed to mock her with a choking motion. Helen was rarely seen without them.

Beth poured her drink, set it aside, and leaned toward Jackie, who was still watching her. "Oh, Jackie, that one's beautiful," Beth said, touching the photograph in the middle of the page, hoping to distract her. "Where was that taken?"

"Yellowstone," Jackie said, handing the cutter to Marlene, who was still trying to get Ethan to take the pacifier.

Beth opened her book. "We really have to take a trip there one of these days."

Helen reached for the paper. "You've never been?"

"No."

"What a shame."

Shame. Was *that* what was suffocating her? Yes, it must be. Shame was the punishment for regret.

Jackie touched Beth's book with her fingertips. "This isn't yours, Beth."

Beth looked down and then smiled to herself. No, it wasn't. It was something even better, at least for today. She closed it, picked it up, and turned it around for everyone to see.

Everyone grabbed their hearts except Helen, who grabbed her pearls.

"Yeah, I decided I'm taking over Jenny's album. I thought I'd finish it for her and give it to Ava for her next birthday."

"That's so nice of you," Daphne said.

"I figured it was the least I could do." She hated herself for even uttering that sentiment. Jenny had been struck down in the prime of life and it was like Beth was doing her a favor. Except she knew, as she turned the book back around, that this was exactly what Jenny would want done. Her love for scrapbooking was the reason they were all together in this group. She'd started it and invited everyone. And when Jenny was a part of it, all the pieces of the machine worked. Without her, the wheels barely turned. Nobody wanted to say it, but they knew — Jenny was the strand that had strung them all together.

Also, this book was a good excuse not to do Nathan's and Robin's. Maybe if Beth stopped scrapbooking their lives, time would stand still.

"How is Butch doing?" Jackie asked.

"I noticed at graduation he needs a little help in the dressing department," Helen said.

"I know." Daphne shook her head. "I thought that poor girl was going to drown in her own sweat."

"I meant his undying attraction to plaid," Helen said, sipping her drink, "but yes, the sweater in May was disastrous on many levels."

Beth sighed, opening the book and looking over the pictures of Jenny, Ava, and Butch when they went to SeaWorld, just a month before the accident. "He's not very good at asking for help."

Jackie took the scissors. "What would he do if I just showed up at his door with a pan of lasagna and a box of laundry detergent? Because we all know that's what Jenny would do for any of us."

"I think he's coming out of the grief a little bit," Daphne said. "Tippy has managed to talk him into going to do something fun. I'm babysitting Ava tonight."

They all looked up from what they were doing. "You are?" Beth asked. "Butch hasn't gone out since Jenny died, other than to go to work."

"I know. I was shocked too. But Tippy asked me and I said yes."

Beth nodded cheerfully, though she was a little hurt Butch hadn't asked her. But then again, she was on the emotional roller coaster that put all other coasters to shame. She cut her eyes to Daphne. Maybe Daphne had let that story about the kitchen meltdown slip out in conversation with Tippy somehow.

Beth's nose tingled, which was alarming because that was always the first sign she was about to cry. She sniffled under the guise that an allergy attack was coming on — ridiculous because Helen's home was so clean, there wasn't an allergen that could live through it. She pretended to search for Benadryl in her purse.

"So, Marlene," Daphne said, "how often does Ethan use a pacifier?"

Beth sighed in relief. All attention would now be on Marlene because there was no doubt Daphne was about to quote a statistic on how toxic rubber nipples were or something to that effect. It didn't matter as long as nobody was looking at Beth.

Baby Ethan finally cooed into a quiet sleep and Marlene returned to her scrapbook. "Oh, he loves it. Can barely fall asleep without it."

"Oh?" Daphne clipped the top of the contact paper she was holding. "You probably ought to have some money saved for orthodontia, then. And by money, I mean thousands of dollars."

Beth bit her lip as Marlene's expression turned sour — like she was sipping the version of limeade without the agave nectar.

"Hm" was all Marlene said, her eyes narrow as she pretended to be consumed with the stars-and-stripes stickers Jackie had brought.

"It's true," Daphne said. "In the book I'm reading right now, they also say that you should never use a pacifier to calm a baby down. They become reliant on it, when they're supposed to be able to calm themselves."

Marlene raised her hand, scissors pointing toward Daphne, who was bent over retrieving something out of her bag. Beth calmly helped her lower the scissors and gave her a knowing, reassuring smile.

When Daphne popped back up with her stamps, Marlene excused herself to the bathroom and Beth blew out a relieved sigh. These days Daphne was getting on everyone's nerves. She had been a know-it-all ever since Beth met her, but she was so sweet nobody cared. But since she'd gotten pregnant, her "child expertise" made everyone in the group feel like utter failures in every aspect of parenting, from not checking the number on the bottom of plastic cups to the simple act of microwaving green beans. Somehow, some way, everyone was doing it wrong.

Beth tried to divert the conversation by leaning over to Helen's book. The picture she was working on showed Madison, her oldest, holding a trophy.

"What is this one, Helen?" she asked, tapping the picture.

"Oh, that was in December. Madison won an essay contest."

Beth glanced around the table with hopes that jets were cooling. "I remember you telling us about that."

Helen pulled a stack of paper from her bag. "Here's the essay. I was going to put it into the scrapbook too." She handed it to Beth, who offered the obligatory smile.

"Oh. Yeah. Long, huh?" She glanced over the first three pages, pretending to be interested while only catching random words.

"Twenty-five pages," Helen gushed. "It's a formula for peace, based on the history of the world."

"Ambitious," Marlene growled as she returned. She picked up her scissors and snipped the corner of some ribbon.

"The history of the world." Jackie didn't even force a smile. "Suddenly twenty-five pages doesn't seem as long."

Well, at least everyone's attention was off Daphne, but Beth was starting to come to an understanding — parenthood made the most normal of people turn into freaks. And currently the freak show was wearing pearls.

". . . and then the school administrators sent it to Washington, and Madison received a handwritten message from Senator Polk, thanking her for the ideas. I can't confirm this for sure, but page 14 sounds a lot like part of the president's State of the Union address this past January."

Everyone stared at Helen as if their eyelids were trying to keep the words in their heads from popping out their eyeballs. Jenny, Beth knew, would've had something funny to say right at this moment. She always knew what to say, when to say it, how to say it.

Marlene smirked. "You think he ripped her off?"

"I wouldn't put it that way," Helen said. " 'Borrowed heavily,' perhaps." She used air quotes.

"That's amazing," Beth said, resisting the

temptation to say *amazing* also with air quotes.

Silence ensued for a moment, each of them pasting and cutting and arranging. Then Helen cleared her throat. "So, Beth, what about your kids? They've been *quite* active lately out in the yard. What are they up to?"

Beth looked up, looked around, looked down. She didn't want to talk about Robin right now. She couldn't. Yet it came flying out of her mouth. "Robin's getting married."

That brought a rush of silence right over the table, swallowing up even the soft sound of Ethan sucking on his pacifier.

Beth stretched that smile again, a smile that seemed unable to come out without a good deal of beckoning. "We're just so blessed. So happy."

"What good news!" Jackie said. "Robin is such a wonderful young lady. Any young man is lucky to have her."

"Thank you, Jackie," Beth said.

"I hadn't even realized she was dating someone," Daphne said.

"A college, um, sweetheart." He wasn't in college, but proximally close enough.

"Tell us all about him," Marlene said. "You must be so excited!"

"Oh yes. I can hardly sleep at night. He's a fun young man. A lot of, um, drive and passion for . . . what he does."

"What does he do?" Marlene asked.

"He's in the food service industry. Anyway, we're just so delighted."

"What's this precious boy's name?" Jackie asked.

Beth gulped her limeade. She didn't want to say his name. Either of his names. She set her glass down. "Marvin Hood."

"Marvin?" Helen snorted. "He's not a cradle robber, is he?"

"No, he's . . . he's her age. And yes, Robin will be Robin Hood. Isn't that great? Larry and I laughed for hours."

The women chuckled and the conversation diverted to all their maiden names and their married names and, thankfully, left Beth sitting and pretending to be the happiest mom on earth.

She looked down at the scrapbook, Jenny's smiling face gleaming brighter than the sunshine she stood under. "I miss you," she whispered.

Chapter 24
Butch

"Bob, look, I need to get that order in by the end of the day. Do whatever you have to do, okay? Call me back." Butch slid his phone into his work vest and finished walking the perimeter of the house, noticing the guys hadn't done the job he normally required for cleaning up before going home for the day.

Through the slats, he saw they were all gathered around something. When Jack stepped out of the way, Ava appeared, sitting on a pile of wood. Butch checked his watch. He was going to have to get Ava home. She'd been out here with him all day, and he'd realized around noon, when her cheeks began glowing like hot steel, that he hadn't put any sunscreen on her.

He pulled out his notepad and was jotting some to-do notes when he suddenly heard a catcall. He sighed. As a general rule, the guys didn't catcall when Butch was around

— they knew he hated it — so he imagined this must've been one hot woman walking by.

Except to his amazement, it turned out not to be. Hot. Or a girl. It was a boy, about Ava's age, riding by on his bike. Butch gripped the beam next to him as he realized the catcall had come from Ava.

The guys were high-fiving and knuckle-bumping her as Butch rushed over, trying not to be in a rage but basically in a rage. "What's going on here?"

The smile dropped off Jack's face. "Nothing, Butch. We're just having some fun."

Half of them stuffed their hands in their pockets while the other half found something interesting to look at in the sky.

"Ava," Butch said sternly, "why don't you leave these guys alone? They've got to get back to work."

"Fine," Ava groaned and walked next to him, dragging her feet and falling a little behind. She took off her yellow hat and threw it to the side, then said over her shoulder, "Steven, let me know what happens this weekend."

Steven gave her a thumbs-up.

"Did you know that Steven's proposing to his girlfriend on Saturday?" Ava asked.

Butch took off his belt and put it in the

bed of his truck as he glanced toward Steven. "No. That's cool."

"Right?" She grinned, then spit, except it only drooled down her chin. "I'm working on that."

"Ava, stop that," Butch groaned. Tippy was walking toward them, so Butch opened the passenger side of the truck. "Hop in. I'll be there in a minute."

He went to the other side, stuck the keys in, and turned on the air, in hopes of keeping Ava from rolling down the window and eavesdropping as she liked to do. "Here," he said, handing over his cell phone. "You can play on this for a second."

"Thanks!"

Butch took a few steps from the truck, peering around to see if any other guys were nearby. Tippy was doing the same thing. It looked like a drug deal was about to go down.

"Did you make all the arrangements?" Butch asked.

"Yeah," Tippy whispered. "Daphne is going to watch Ava. You and I are going to go get hot wings. Our appointment is at six thirty."

"I'll be at your house by six."

"Okay, see you then. And, dude, we have to play this so calm and cool, okay? We can't even hint there's something going on besides hot wings."

Butch nodded and got in his truck. The blast of cold air felt good, and Ava seemed to be totally immersed in Angry Birds on his phone. *Ka-kaw!*

"So, fun news," Butch said.

"What?" She didn't look up.

"You're going over to Daphne's house tonight while Tippy and I go get some hot wings."

"Oh, I love chicken wings! They're so cute!"

Butch glanced sideways at her as he pulled from the curb. "You hate chicken wings. They're spicy and there's gristle and preservatives and stuff."

"Those cute wings and drumsticks? I like to pretend they're people and put on a little play with them."

"Well, I'm sure Daphne has something far more fun in mind. She's babysitting you, and babysitters are always fun."

"That's true. But why can't I go?"

Butch suppressed a sigh, which made his stomach start hurting. Why did kids ask so many questions? It was like she knew something was up. But the more he tried to play it cool, the more he looked like a raging liar.

"Just . . . You can't, okay? It's just . . .

We're talking business. You'd be bored and then you'd get whiny."

"I get whiny when I'm tired, not bored."

"Ava, you're going over to Daphne's and that's the end of it."

She threw the phone aside and folded her arms. "Fine."

"And you're going to behave yourself. Daphne is doing us a favor."

"She's doing *you* a favor."

Suddenly Butch felt very much like an angry bird.

CHAPTER 25
BETH

After scrapbooking and before beginning to prepare dinner, Beth went to her room and prayed, kneeling at the foot of the bed. Normally when the weather was nice, she sat on her back porch and prayed for her children while sipping her coffee. This, though — this anguish she felt deep in her gut — required more than nice morning air. God *had* to move. God *had* to do something. The more she thought about Marvin, the more she understood that Robin was wrecking her life. What kind of mother would she be if she didn't try to save her from herself?

Her prayers for her kids had never been pretty but had always been earnest. Many were in the middle of a crisis. Lots of bad breakups of friendships and love interests. There was the year nobody showed up for Robin's birthday party. There was the year it looked like Chip was going to fail fourth grade because of his handwriting. Lots of hospital visits for croup and stitches and broken bones.

When there was no moment of crisis, she rested in the Lord, except for the daily prayers of protection over her children. She was sleep deprived most of the time — so exhausted she would fall asleep when her head hit the pillow but then startle awake in the early morning hours, remembering she had to wash a jersey or make cupcakes or sign a detention slip. How had she survived? By the grace of God, she believed, and now she had another hill to climb. When would it end? When would she be able to rest and watch her children simply live?

The more she thought about Robin marrying Marvin, the more her heart raced and her mind crumbled into despair. Robin was so smart. How could she really think Marvin was a good match for her? Something had blinded her. Maybe it was true love, but true love didn't pay the bills. Beth knew from experience that it was possible to find love and practicality all in one guy. Robin needed to marry a guy like her father. Why wasn't she out looking for that guy?

That ended her prayer time. It was mostly questions and worries, tossed up and handed off to the one she always trusted would hear her.

Downstairs she began preparing dinner — probably an overly ambitious undertaking, considering her emotional state, but Marvin was coming over. And Robin needed to clue in to what would be expected of her as a wife. They couldn't order pizza every night. She needed to think about her future — the future of her meals, at the very least.

Beth roasted asparagus, baked Italian chicken, and opened a bag of salad, but she'd sprung for the fancy salad dressings — the kind that were refrigerated in the produce section — and picked up a cheesecake from the bakery. Now she took off all the labels, putting it on the glass cake holder she'd gotten as a wedding present from her mother-in-law but had never used. Not legitimately, anyway.

She put out the nice dishes and lit the candles and moved the dinner off the stove to platters on the table. Marvin arrived right on time, just like Robin said he would, and Robin greeted him excitedly at the door. They kissed and hugged, and Beth had to turn away.

"Did you bring them?" Robin asked Marvin.

"Bring what?" Beth asked.

Marvin held up a paper bag. "The wedding invitations!"

"Chip! Nathan! Dinner!" Beth caught herself and her words. The anger that had curtsied in front of Dr. Reynolds was now showing up for the dinner call, which sounded more like a cattle call. Regardless, Chip and Nathan rumbled down the stairs and gawked at the table as they passed by.

"What's the occasion?" Nathan asked.

"There's no occasion. Just dinner as usual," Beth tried. But even Larry looked confused. Mostly they ate in front of the TV these days.

"So, invitations! How . . ." Her words hung in the air, partly because she couldn't get herself to say *wonderful.* She'd thought the invitations were something she and Robin might do together. "Let's sit down before the food gets cold," Beth finished.

At the word *food,* everyone swarmed. Beth sat lost in her own paradox. She didn't want Robin to marry this fellow, yet she was devastated by being left out of the planning. Of course Robin had to start now. The wedding was planned for August. Why was that surprising? Because she'd always dreamed of Robin's wedding day, and she'd been in that dream, shopping and giggling and having memorable moments with her daughter.

"Beth, this looks amazing," Marvin said,

scanning the table.

"Thank you, Marvin."

"Maybe one day I'll share my secret family recipe for pizza dough."

"Oh. How thoughtful of you." Beth smiled like it was punctuation, but nobody seemed to notice the emphasis. Marvin had already forked a chicken breast and was now sawing at the poor bird as if they were in medieval times.

"Why don't we say a prayer?" Beth said smoothly, warmly, like Blythe Danner in *Meet the Parents.* She'd always wanted to be Blythe Danner. Wispy and wise and thin. She made pot holders look elegant.

Chip cocked an eyebrow. "We never pray at dinner."

"That's not true," Beth snapped. "We always pray when we eat at the table." Which was never these days, thanks to the invention of DVR and TV trays.

Larry tried to break the tension. "We pray, just not always on a schedule. We bless the food, we don't bless the food. But we always feel blessed."

Marvin chuckled. "I understand. I like that about you people."

You people? Larry led the blessing while Beth stewed. She excused herself to the kitchen for salt so she could compose herself. Losing her temper wasn't going to help. She grabbed the counter, breathing deeply, trying to let her little girl go. She imagined herself putting Robin in God's hands, and then God working it all out — driving some kind of wedge between Robin and Marvin. Yes, she was just going to have to trust God and be available to help Him whenever possible.

She smoothed her hair for the seventh time and returned to the table, forgetting the salt.

"Mom," Robin said, her eyes shining, "come look! Tell me what you think!"

Beth's heart melted. *"Tell me what you think."* She'd stopped hearing that when Robin turned thirteen and, that she could recall, hadn't heard it since.

Beth slid into the seat next to Robin and put her hand on her shoulder. "Look at what?"

"Our wedding invitations!" Robin slid a stack out of the bag Marvin had brought in. Beth, admittedly, felt a tiny shudder of excitement. Even more than her own wedding day, Beth had dreamed of Robin's wedding day and all that she hoped it would be.

She held one of the envelopes up into the light. Her first thought was that the color scheme seemed . . . different. "Orange and, um, what is that? Aqua?"

"That's the new rage — putting colors together that don't match at all!" *All* came out with a squeal after it.

Beth felt her teeth clamping together in the exact way that her dentist had warned would cause TMJ problems. She lifted the flap and there it was, so official-looking, with the invitation formally coming from Larry and her, but in a font that looked like it came from a horror movie.

"Oh, how . . . how nice. And looks like everything is spelled correctly," Beth said, pressing her resolve into whatever positive element she could. She looked at Marvin's parents' names. Dan and Judy Hood. They seemed so normal, except where did the name Marvin come from? She'd almost expected to see a Marvin Senior. Maybe it was Dan's middle name or something.

She had noticed that Marvin had the self-confidence of a kid with a much more age-appropriate name. Maybe she should just get over the name. She had other, bigger things to worry about.

The conversation continued around the table without Beth until there was an audible gasp from Nathan.

"What's wrong?" Larry asked him.

261

Nathan was reading the invitation. "Marvin's last name is Hood . . ."

Chip said, "You'll be Robin Hood!"

"Isn't it cute?" Robin clapped. Marvin grinned. Chip snorted. Nathan cackled. Beth rose to get the salt for the second time.

From the kitchen, she heard the conversation continue. "That's cool!" Chip said.

"That should be your wedding theme," Nathan said. "Your groomsmen could be the merry men!"

"Hilarious," Larry said, and Beth felt herself grow angry. Again. Not Larry too. Surely he could see what a joke this *wasn't*.

"Oh no, we already have a wedding theme," Robin said, and Beth felt a wash of relief as she picked up the saltshaker. Maybe there was common sense left in her daughter after all.

"What is it?" Beth asked, returning to the table.

"It's a surprise," Robin said, grabbing for the salt.

"It would be cool to have, like, a bow and arrow with my tux," Marvin said. Knuckle bumps ensued.

"We've already decided this," Robin said, pinching his cheek. "Babe, you're going to look so handsome!" She set her fork down. "Mom, Dad, listen. We know weddings are expensive. Marvin and I are going to take care of the whole thing."

Beth said, "But, honey, it's tradition to . . . The groom's parents do the rehearsal dinner, and the bride's parents do the wedding. I mean, we can't fly you to Hawaii for a beach wedding, but your father and I can help out." With a loan they were going to have to get at the bank. College was doing a number on their finances. "Right, Larry?"

"Well, what were you thinking in terms of cost?" Larry asked.

"We've already decided," Robin said authoritatively. "We're paying for it all. We just want you to come and enjoy yourselves." She put her arm around Marvin. "I have to brag on Marvin a little. He's been working two jobs to help pay for the wedding."

Larry looked impressed, and Beth felt a surge of hope. She remembered what Dr. Reynolds had said, that nobody had ambitions to be a pizza delivery boy forever. It was a step toward something else. And if Marvin was willing to work two jobs, it meant he had fortitude. He was a sweet guy, always polite, and seemed to adore Robin, but until now Beth had not sensed fortitude.

Larry helped himself to more asparagus as he asked, "Another job? Really? What's your second job?"

"Pizza delivery."

"We know about that one," Beth said. "What's your new job?"

"Pizza delivery."

"He works for *two* different pizza places," Robin gushed.

"Oh," Beth and Larry said together, though Larry's sounded like he'd been informed and Beth's sounded like a dream had met a sudden and violent death.

"I figure it's what I know, you know?" Marvin said. "It's what I'm good at. I got all the ins and outs of pizza delivery."

"It's way more complicated than you think," Robin said.

"It's like the other night," Marvin said, stretching his arm around Robin's shoulders. "I had a supreme and a half-sausage, half-mushroom to deliver to Parker Avenue, but I also had a pepperoni and hot wings to deliver to Maple. Buck, this slightly incompetent guy I work with, he forgets to put the peppers on the supreme, so I have to go back, and by this time, I've only got twelve minutes until they get the pepperoni and wings for free. And you can't get to Parker and back to Maple in twelve minutes."

"No, there's no way," Nathan said, and Beth was momentarily distracted by the fact that both Chip and Nathan seemed to be listening in utter hero worship.

"What did you do?" Chip asked.

"It gets worse," Marvin said.

Doubtful, Beth lamented.

"I start down MacArthur, and . . ." He paused dramatically. "Construction. There's a line of cars a quarter mile long."

"Oh, that's it. You're toast," Nathan said.

Suddenly Marvin took on an air of authority, his eyebrows raised as if he were about to impart philosophical wisdom. Beth shifted her attention from Robin to Larry. Yep, it was confirmed. All were enamored.

"In the pizza business," Marvin said, "never say never."

Beth tuned out the rest of the conversation about how Marvin somehow got to where he needed to go with all the pizzas still hot. That same irrational feeling that had lurked over her at Dr. Reynolds's office, that made her yell at a man she hardly knew, caused her to grip the edge of the table. She could not lose it. Not here, not now. If she lost it, Robin might not ever listen to her again. She tried to focus on what Dr. Reynolds had been telling her. *Be present, focus on the moment, do what you can now, don't live in the past — and also, yes . . . Remember, Beth? Remember? He told you nobody wants to deliver pizza for the rest of their lives.*

She turned and smiled at Marvin. "It's great that you take it so seriously," she said. "It really is. Not that many people would've cared so much."

Robin looked delighted. She leaned over and gave Marvin a hug and then hugged Beth, too.

"Boy, Marvin, you've really impressed us tonight. I'd like to hear more about your future plans," Beth said.

Larry nodded. "Yeah, definitely. What are you going to do once you've moved on from the pizza business?"

Beth nodded, glad Larry was connecting back to reality.

"Well, that's what I want to do." Marvin looked unsure even as he said it.

"You have no post-pizza plans?" This was the first time all evening that Larry seemed concerned. He'd been living out the Summer of Intense Fun so much that he'd forgotten some essentials.

"Pizza *is* the future," Marvin said. "It's still the number one food in America. It's the only recession-proof meal. You know what they feed troops overseas?"

"Pizza," Robin chimed in with a smile.

"You know what four of the last seven

death row inmates chose as their last meal?"

"Pizza," Robin said again.

There was no questioning Marvin's passion for the product. His face lit up every time he mentioned it. But wasn't that a problem? A Chernobyl kind of problem?

"Last month," Marvin continued, "you know those miners who were trapped for three days? You know what they asked for when they got out?"

Nathan, Chip, and Robin answered in unison: "Pizza."

Beth realized her hand was over her mouth like she'd just witnessed a pedestrian accident. But no, it was her daughter's future being slammed by an overrated American staple.

"He does eventually want to manage his own pizza place," Robin said, placing her fork upside down on her plate, then folding her napkin over it, just like Beth had taught her when she was little. She still remembered that, and Beth felt emotion surging up her throat. She'd taught her daughter manners. How could she have failed to teach her the dangers of falling in love with a pizza delivery boy?

"That's right. I do," Marvin said.

"That sounds good. Nothing wrong with

that," Larry said, casting Beth a hopeful glance.

Robin turned to her, grasping her hand. "Mom, did you ever hear how he proposed?"

Beth shook her head. "No. We know so little. I would love to hear . . ."

"We were having pizza, and when I opened the box, *Marry me* was spelled out in pepperonis."

"Oh, that's so . . . original."

"And," Robin said, plunging her hand into her purse and emerging with a miniature pizza box, "this is where the ring was."

"So . . . cute . . ."

"She freaked." Marvin smiled.

"Tell us another delivery story!" Chip said.

With that, Beth touched Larry's knee. It was a soft touch with a scorching undertone, the kind that needed no explanation. "We'll get dessert!" Beth said, her voice high with desperation disguised as excitement.

As Larry followed her into the kitchen, Beth collapsed against the counter.

"Oh, cheesecake!" Larry said.

"Larry!" Beth said. "Don't you see what's happening here?"

Larry put a hand on her back. "Sweetie, I know this is a little terrifying, but —"

"A little terrifying? Larry!"

"Listen, Robin is going to be fine."

"No, she's not. . . . She's really not. . . ." Beth fought back a sob that wanted to escape. "Why isn't she being smarter about this? Making Marvin understand he's got to have a more stable job?"

"Well, he does make a good case for the stability of the pizza business."

"This isn't a joke," Beth said, standing fully erect, turning to scrub her hands under the faucet water for no reason.

Larry rubbed her shoulders. "I want to tell you a story."

"This is no time for one of your stupid stories."

"This is a good one."

Beth rolled her eyes.

"The day after I asked you to marry me, your father paid me a visit at work."

Beth turned and looked at him. "No, he didn't."

"Yes, he did. I never told you."

"My dad? That doesn't sound like him."

"I know. He's typically a laid-back, easygoing guy. When I asked for your hand, he simply said yes. But he wanted me to know something that day — that I better move heaven and earth to take care of you."

"I had no idea." Beth wiped her hands and ran her fingers through her hair. "But you're that kind of guy, Larry. You've always held a steady job, always had ambitions."

"Listen, it's all going to work out."

Beth shook her head, moving into his arms. "I don't think it will. We always say that, but I don't think it's going to work out." She leaned her head against Larry's shoulder. "Above all else in this world, I want our kids to be happy."

"Beth, Robin is happy."

"It's the kind of happiness that a pizza oven is going to burn to a crisp." She stepped back from him, sniffling. "You've got it easy. Flying kites. Whipped cream fights. The boys are loving it. They seem like they're having so much fun."

"I'm going to have to go back to work in a couple of weeks, and then what?"

"You and the boys, you're living in the moment. That's the way it should be, even if it's only five minutes." She sighed. "Maybe I should do more stuff with you guys. With all this Robin drama, maybe I'm not paying enough attention to the boys — though if I feed them and do their laundry, they always seem perfectly content with me."

Larry smiled. "I'll give some more thought to things we can do as a family. We have to make this summer count."

Chapter 26
Daphne

The doorbell rang just as Daphne finished organizing her diapers from smallest to largest in the nursery.

"Honey, can you get that?" Daphne called, but she didn't hear Tippy answer, so she went to the door. Opening it, she was greeted by Ava, who walked right in without being invited. But Daphne only smiled.

"Hi, Butch," Daphne said. She gave him a hug. "I'm looking forward to spending some time with Ava."

"Oh, good. Very good. She is too. Been talking about it all day."

Tippy rounded the corner, smoothing his shirt as he walked down the hallway.

"I'm glad you and Tippy can spend some time together outside work."

For some reason Daphne thought Butch looked alarmed by that statement, but she didn't dwell on it. It was obvious the man was having a hard time. Without Jenny, he

271

probably didn't know which way was up.

"Hey, Butch," Tippy said and slapped him so hard on the back that Butch stumbled. "Oh, sorry. I'm just so excited to go eat *hot wings*."

"Yeah, and watch that game you've been so excited about," Butch said.

"So excited about," Tippy said, his head bobbing up and down.

They both looked at Daphne and smiled.

"Well, don't stay too long," Daphne said. "I can't stay up late anymore." She looked at Butch. "My back's been killing me. I'm getting no rest."

Butch smiled. "Just wait until the baby gets here."

"We're doing the Baby Sleep Wave method. It's where you sync your baby's sleep waves to your own so she doesn't wake up unless you do. It's tried and true. Apparently it's how the cavemen did it."

Butch smirked. "How do they know *that*?"

Tippy stepped forward, actually between the two of them, and said, "She knows what she's talking about. She's done hours of research and also bought the podcasts and the book. Well, listen, we better get going. We'll be home soon."

"Thanks again for watching Ava," Butch said, and they were out the door.

Daphne turned to Ava. "So it's just us girls! How fun, huh?"

Ava was glancing around the room. "What's with the pool noodles?"

"They're not pool noodles. Well, they are. They're pool noodles repurposed as corner protectors. It's an inexpensive way to keep the baby safe. If she falls, she'll be totally protected. Every corner is covered. Every ledge." Daphne made a sweeping motion across the room.

"See this scar here?" Ava asked, pointing to her forehead. Daphne leaned in. "I fell when I was one and a half and split my forehead open."

"Hitting a ledge?" Daphne asked with a small smile.

"Nope. Just the carpet. Came down so hard it ripped 'er right open."

Daphne's heart skipped a beat. She glanced down at the carpet. "Was it Berber?"

"No idea."

Was her carpet plush enough? She hadn't even thought of that.

Ava had her hands clasped behind her back. "So you're having a girl?"

"Well," Daphne said, guiding her into the kitchen, "we won't know for sure until she's born. Tippy really wanted to be surprised.

But . . ." She lowered her voice even though Tippy was nowhere in the house. "Just between us, there is a 98 percent chance she's a girl."

"How do you know that?"

"There's a complex calculation you can do concerning body temperature, the moon cycles, and your consumption of soy the week the baby is conceived. According to Pinterest, it's extremely accurate."

"Oh, cool."

"So what would you like for dinner? I can stir-fry some organic bok choy with grass-fed beef."

"Oh. That sounds awful. I don't want that."

Daphne gently put her hands on the counter. "I don't want that, *please,* is what I believe you were trying to say."

Ava's eyes widened. "I don't have a mommy to teach me manners."

Daphne's hand moved over her mouth and her throat swelled with regret. "Oh, Ava, I'm so, so sorry. I didn't mean to . . . I'm just an advocate for manners in young people and I . . . I'm so sorry."

Ava looked down and shook her head. When she looked up, her cheeks were wet. "No, Daphne, I'm sorry."

"For what?"

"It's kind of mean of me."

"It wasn't mean. It was just bad manners not to say 'please' or 'no thank you.' "

"No . . . it was mean of me to say I don't have a mommy. I say that a lot when I'm in trouble at school because it gets me out of things. I shouldn't do that, I know. Sometimes I do it to make my mommy mad because I know she wouldn't approve, but she's not here to tell me that and so I do it just to make her wish she were here."

Daphne reached for Ava's hand. "Oh, honey, your mom wishes she were here. Don't you know that?"

"People aren't supposed to want to come back from heaven. She's probably happy there."

"Yes. I think so. But she wants to be with you too." Daphne bit her lip. She was no theologian and was not sure she was answering it right.

Ava shrugged. "What's bok choy?"

"Will you trust me to make you something fabulous?"

"I usually eat pizza."

"So aren't you ready for something a little different?"

"Is this like cooking-show different?"

Daphne nodded, hoping Ava wouldn't ask for boxed mac and cheese instead.

"Okay. I'll try it. But if I don't like it, can I not eat it if I'm polite about not eating it?"

Daphne laughed. "Deal." She began getting the ingredients out of the fridge.

"Are you scared to have a baby?" Ava asked.

"Why do you ask?"

"My mom said my dad had his first anxiety attack the day I was born."

Daphne chuckled. "There's nothing to fear if you're prepared. I've done a lot of reading, taken a lot of classes. That's the key to it all. If you're prepared, you'll know what to do when something happens. I even took an eight-week online course. I feel very assured that nothing is going to go wrong." She tried to say it with confidence as she pulled her stir-fry pan out of the cabinet, took the knife out of the triple-locked drawer, and began thinly slicing the sirloin.

"So . . . how do you know that knife isn't going to slip and cut your finger off?" Ava asked, resting her chin in her hand.

At that very moment, the knife did slip, but only because it was such a shocking question to come from such a little girl. "Well, because I know how to use a knife. I know where to put my fingers and how to hold it so I'm safe."

Ava nodded. "You really do seem very safe. My dad's not safe. You should see him walk across a room with scissors. It'll make you shiver."

Daphne tossed the beef in the oiled pan. "You'll have to see the crib. No covers, no bumpers, nothing in there that can harm the baby. That's just one of dozens of things Tippy and I have done to prepare."

"Well," Ava said, "you're probably going to need to take those handles off the cabinets and drawers."

"Why?"

"When I was two, I walked straight into one and tore the top of my ear off." Ava lifted her hair. "See? Where that chunk is missing?"

Daphne peered at it. "Really? From a handle?"

"Yep. And also, I should tell you about the toilet."

Daphne moved the meat and bok choy around in the pan. "I'm on top of that. We have locks on all the toilets."

"When I was four, my mom came into the bathroom and I had the plunger stuck to my cheek."

Daphne almost dropped her wooden spoon. "What? On your face?"

"Yeah. I thought it was funny. Obviously

my mom freaked out."

Daphne felt a little sick to her stomach.

"And listen, I have to tell you about something else, and it's really disturbing. But you should know about it." Ava leaned in and spoke very quietly. "I only heard about it from Carson in my class, who heard about it from Joey. And maybe I shouldn't tell you because I don't know if there's anything you can do about it, really."

Daphne braced herself against the counter, staring at Ava. "I should know. I have to know. There's always *something* you can do. I have eighteen books to prove it."

"Well, apparently head lice is more contagious than the flu. Those little suckers can jump from kid to kid at school, and before you know it, the whole class has them. Then your whole family gets them. It could probably wipe out a neighborhood in a week. Carson said there's nothing you can do except boil everything in your house."

Daphne felt the first stages of hyperventilation. She waved her hand like she understood and dumped the food onto a plate before the vegetables were tender. "Excuse me for a moment. I have to go check on something." She swiped her phone from the counter.

"But the thing is," Ava said, resting her

chin on her hand again as she watched the steam rise from the plate, "you can do everything to protect someone. Everything in the world, you know? But then a truck runs a stop sign and they're gone. My dad says there was nothing Mommy could've done. She never saw it coming. So sometimes things just happen that you can't stop. Can I watch TV while I eat?"

Daphne nodded, clutched the phone, hurried to the bathroom, and locked herself inside.

CHAPTER 27
TIPPY

Butch and Tippy ate their hot wings in Dr. Reynolds's small office. When they'd offered him some, he'd looked heartbroken but said he was pretty sure there was something in some oath he took about not eating while counseling.

"The wings were a guise, really," Butch said. "We told our girls we were going for wings. Then Tippy got paranoid and said we better really get wings because his wife could find out, that she has ways of knowing things that sort of blow the mind. So we were trying to cover all of our bases."

"We needed to smell like hot wings," Tippy said. "Plus, we're kind of nervous about being here, and nothing calms a dude down like third-degree burns on the tongue."

"Exactly," Dr. Reynolds said, gazing at the wing in Tippy's hand like it was a long-lost lover. "So what can I do for you gentlemen?

Are we having relationship problems?"

"Yes," they both said.

"I mean, not with . . . He's my boss," Tippy said. "We came together because we're both having trouble with the women in our lives, and we also thought it would be cheaper to do a two-for-one deal."

Dr. Reynolds smiled. "I see. You're both married?"

"I was," Butch said. "My wife died recently, leaving me with our eight-year-old daughter. Tippy is married and about to have a child."

"The thing is, Doc, they're all crazy. Totally crazy. We have no idea what to do," Tippy said.

"My daughter baffles me. I'm trying to connect with her, but we don't speak the same language," Butch said. Tippy noticed Butch twisting the wedding ring he knew he would never manage to remove.

"And my wife has gone off her rocker. She used to be so normal. I loved coming home after work to see her, and now I feel like driving around the block a hundred times before I go home."

Dr. Reynolds nodded and pulled out a notebook, which made both of them flinch. Tippy didn't like the idea of someone writing down thoughts about him.

The counselor looked up at Butch. "Butch, give me an example of a baffling conversation between you and your daughter."

Butch didn't think long. "Just this afternoon I was taking her home from my job site. I'm in construction. And she starts talking about church and how we have to get back into it, and there's no way she's not going this Sunday. It has to be *this* Sunday. When I told her I'd think about it, she burst into tears. When I told her fine, I'd go, she yelled at me for changing my mind and said that I was putting her on 'an emotional roller coaster.' She's also recently scolded me for eating fried chicken. Sometimes she's this perfect angel, and then other times she gets locked onto something and I can't get her distracted, not even with candy. Before Jenny died, Ava was just this easygoing kid. We never had any trouble with her. Now that Jenny's gone, I feel like I'm losing control of her. The thing is, Jenny would know what to do. But I don't."

Tippy looked down. He hated to see the pain his friend was in. He hated to hear Jenny's name in the past tense.

Dr. Reynolds nodded. "I understand. And the truth is, you're probably dealing with a lot of different aspects here. Ava is getting older, and the older kids get, the more attitude they start displaying. But she is also testing you, Butch. She's testing you to see what kind of parent you're going to be, how you're going to raise her."

"I'm lucky to get her dressed in the morning."

"But you get her dressed, nevertheless. You get her fed. You get her to school, right?"

"I guess. It's not pretty, but I guess."

Dr. Reynolds turned to Tippy. "What about your wife? Give me an example of what's going on."

"Well, she's pregnant. And that was good news until she flipped out."

Dr. Reynolds smiled knowingly. "Oh yes. I've seen a few pregnant women over the course of my career. In fact, just got a new client this week."

"Do they all freak out or am I just lucky?" At that moment Tippy's cell phone dinged with several text messages right in a row. He sighed and rolled his eyes, collapsing into the pillows behind him. "Perfect example, right now." He held up his phone. " 'We have to take the handles off the lower cabinets. We can no longer keep the plunger in the house. Tonight I'm going to check you for head lice. Also, our carpet is too hard.' See what I mean? It's like this every day."

Dr. Reynolds chuckled.

"Somehow, most likely on the Internet, she read about all this and now she's freaking. You know, I've actually thought about sabotaging our Wi-Fi just to keep her from finding crazy stuff like this. Except then she'd go buy another book on it. And when you try to make a commonsense statement, like 'Our carpet isn't too hard,' she accuses you of being uninformed or misguided or ignorant of the demands of parenthood. The kid's not even here yet and apparently I'm an utter failure."

"Your wife means well. But women typically begin worrying about parenthood before men do, simply because they're carrying the baby. It usually hits men later, when the baby is born."

Tippy looked at Butch. "Is that true?"

Butch shrugged. "Yeah, I mean, I had a brief moment of hesitation after Ava was born. . . . Fine, more like a seizure of panic." He sighed. "I was so overcome with dread and fear that out in the hallway I insisted to the maternity ward nurse I was having a heart attack."

Tippy cracked up. "Are you serious?"

"Yeah. She was like, 'Honey, you're just

nervous.' And I'm like 'My chest literally feels like it's going to explode. I'm seeing two of you.' I was drenched in sweat and felt like I was floating."

Dr. Reynolds laughed too. They were all three laughing, and Tippy was glad. It was rare these days to see Butch do more than smile.

"So she sat me down and brought me this tiny box of apple juice with a straw so small it looked made for a baby doll."

"Wow," Tippy said.

"You get ready, buddy," Butch said, pointing at him. "You have no idea. It's nothing like you imagine. Jenny was . . . she was pushing and squeezing my hand and screaming. And then suddenly the baby was out. A little blue. Then bright red. Then the doctor held up scissors and asked me if I wanted to cut the umbilical cord — this slimy thing that looks like an alien tentacle. And the baby's wailing and the nurses are clapping and Jenny is on the bed in a pool of sweat, looking prettier than I ever saw her. . . ."

"It is a lot to take in," Dr. Reynolds said. He looked at Tippy. "When did your wife begin acting this way?"

Tippy raised his eyes to the ceiling, calculating. His gaze dropped to Butch, then to the floor. "It doesn't matter."

"It might."

"I don't want to talk about it."

There was an awkward silence in the room as Butch looked between Tippy and Dr. Reynolds. "Tippy, what is it? That's why we're here."

"Just . . . No, it doesn't matter."

"It obviously matters," Dr. Reynolds said.

Tippy sighed loudly, his hands clasped together, his elbows on his knees. "I just put it together."

"Put what together?" Butch asked.

With a reluctant look at Butch, he said, "Daphne began acting this way shortly after Jenny died." Tippy closed his eyes, regret filling his heart.

Dr. Reynolds asked, "They were friends, your wives?"

"Yes," Butch said softly.

"It makes sense," Dr. Reynolds said.

"What does?" Tippy asked.

"How did your wife die?"

Tippy watched Butch take several deep breaths before the simple explanation. "Car accident."

"Daphne's actions are rooted in fear," Dr. Reynolds said. "She realizes how unpredictable life is. She is trying to control her world so that nothing bad happens. We all know this is futile, but she feels completely responsible for the welfare of the child."

"I guess we are completely responsible," Tippy said.

"Tippy," Dr. Reynolds said, leaning forward, his full attention on him. "What do you fear in this situation?"

Tippy tried to give it serious thought. Maybe there was so much to fear that he didn't know how to choose just one thing. "Look, I trust God with our baby. I think I fear that I may not ever see my wife again. The wife I knew and fell in love with. I'm afraid she's going to disappear into this new person that I dread seeing every day."

Dr. Reynolds nodded, jotting down notes. "I can understand why you'd be concerned and fearful," he said in a way that made it seem okay. His focus shifted to Butch. "What about you? What do you fear?"

Butch leaned back, then forward, then sideways. The man who'd once severed his thumb without shedding a tear — when it happened or when they sewed it back on — looked to be on the verge of an emotional collapse. Tippy wasn't sure he could watch. He slapped his friend on the back in encouragement. At least he hoped Butch took it that way.

Still, Butch refused to speak for a little bit.

"Take your time," Dr. Reynolds said.

"I guess I'm afraid," Butch finally said, "that Ava is going to grow up and turn out to be . . ." He swallowed, his voice starting to give out.

"Be rebellious?" Tippy asked, trying to finish for him.

"No," Butch said. "I'm afraid she's going to grow up and look and sound and talk and act just like Jenny, and I don't know if I can face that every single day for the rest of my life."

Then Butch put his hand over his face and cried.

CHAPTER 28
BUTCH

"So if Tippy and I were to need — want — to go out again, you wouldn't mind staying with Daphne?"

"She was cool."

"You're sure you were good for her?"

"Of course, Daddy."

"Because last time, when I came to get you, she looked startled."

"She looks like that all the time."

"More startled than usual."

"I was just giving her some tips on how to raise a kid, that's all."

Butch laughed as he pulled into the parking lot. "You're an expert on that, are you?"

"Well, I've had to raise you on how to raise me." She grinned, loving her joke. Butch tried to smile too, but it was the saddest thing to think about and so awfully true.

And with that innocent statement, Butch had a change of heart. He pulled to the curb in front of the church.

"You know, you're probably old enough to go to church by yourself now. I can just meet you out here after you're done." Already the tweed jacket he was wearing was feeling uncomfortable and tight and a decade too old.

Ava's eyes widened with guilt-inducing shock. "You don't want to go to church with me? You said last night you would."

"Look at me, Ava. I'm going to stick out like a sore thumb. I haven't been here in six years. These people don't even know me."

"They know you," she said, cutting her gaze away from him and folding her arms.

"How?"

"They pray for you all the time." She grabbed her purse — one of Jenny's that looked big enough for her to fit inside. Her shoes were too small, they'd realized this morning, so she limped a little as she stomped away from his truck, not bothering to shut the door.

Butch undid his seat belt and reached for the handle, trying to close the door. On the third grab, he shut it, but not well. He gripped the steering wheel, closed his eyes, tried to figure out what the right thing to do was. The last place he wanted to be was church. He'd known the day he became a

290

parent that his will was going to be the last one considered, and with Jenny by his side, he learned to make the sacrifices. But now . . .

He caught a glimpse of Ava trying to open the church door by herself. It was heavy and she was fighting a stiff breeze. A man about Butch's age came to the rescue, greeting Ava and chatting with her as they both went inside.

Butch found a parking place, turned off the truck, and stalked toward the church. He pulled open the door and there Ava stood, clutching her purse, waiting on him.

She grinned. "I knew you'd come."

The next thing Butch knew, a crowd was gathering around him, shaking his hand, even hugging him. He wasn't sure he'd ever felt more welcomed in his life. He definitely didn't feel any animosity, which he figured he'd get as soon as he walked in the door. Why shouldn't he? He'd stopped coming with Jenny and Ava long ago, citing too much work, which was the case early on in his business when he was still trying to gain clients and underbid competitors. By the time the business got on track, they'd gotten into a routine of going without him, even though they invited him every week. Still, he felt like a third wheel. And about the time he decided he should go, Jenny died and Butch realized there was no use in praying — it was too late for that, and he wasn't the kind of guy whose prayers would be listened to anyway. Why would they be? He'd been MIA from church for years.

Since then, Beth had been taking Ava, and Butch had continued to stay at home. Until Ava got the funny idea that they should go together.

They went to sit by Beth and her family. Butch removed his jacket and loosened up a bit. Nobody seemed overly concerned with dress. He saw everything from jeans to dress slacks, so he didn't stick out at all. A few people turned and smiled and waved at him. He smiled back, pretending to know them. He didn't recognize a soul. Ava, however, seemed to know everyone and was busy hugging necks and shaking hands.

After a nice organ prelude, Beth rose and went to the front.

"What's she doing?" Butch whispered to Ava.

"She's in charge of announcements."

Beth pleasantly welcomed the congregation and introduced herself for visitors. "If you'd open your bulletin, you'll see that the Fourth of July picnic will be at Evans Park, starting at ten thirty. Sign-ups for the softball game, tennis tournament, and flag football will be in the foyer after the service." She glanced at the notes in her hand. "Also, on the twenty-third of this month, we're having a potluck for the homeless. Do we have an update on that?"

Ava suddenly stood, causing Butch to startle. "Everything is still on track," Ava said loudly and almost theatrically. "We need more vegetables if anyone can volunteer to bring those. The sign-up sheet is in the foyer, or you can e-mail me."

She sat back down and glanced at Butch. "What?"

"You're in charge of the homeless ministry?" Butch whispered.

"Mom was," she whispered back. "They let me take over a few of the little things." Ava smiled and returned her attention to the front, but Butch couldn't stop looking at her.

CHAPTER 29
BETH

Beth stood on the porch, sipping Sunday afternoon coffee she'd once enjoyed very much. These days everything had a bitter taste.

She checked her watch. Robin was supposed to come home and they were supposed to look at a dress catalog together, but once again she was MIA.

Beth set her coffee down, deciding to grab her rose clippers and do something about the bushes along the fence line she shared with the Buckleys. She knew they hated overgrowth. She did too, yet somehow she'd learned to live with it. But being a good and reliable neighbor was one thing among many others she should've been doing over the years.

At the fence line she stood and watched Larry, Chip, and Nathan try to get that silly kite off the ground. For the boys, it truly was the Summer of Intense Fun, and though

Beth could admit it to no one, she was jealous of how boys remedied their troubles. It seemed so *easy.* Just get a ridiculous, fun project and memories were made forever.

"Do we really have enough room to launch it here?" Chip called from the front lawn.

Larry was over by the garage fiddling with something. "It's a soft launch. Just to test it."

"Hi, Beth."

Beth turned to find Charles getting into his car. He was wearing slacks, a button-down shirt, and a tie. She rarely saw him dressed any other way.

"Hi, Charles. Looks like you're off to someplace important."

"Just work. I have a deadline, so I have to push through the weekend."

Cory was trailing Charles out the door, bounding down the steps of their front porch. "Dad! Wait! Can we make a kite later?"

Charles's gaze shifted to Larry and Nathan and Chip in the front yard.

"All right, start the engine!" Larry said.

Cory's face was awash in awe. Like she said, boys were so easily entertained.

"Um . . . I'll probably be home too late, buddy. I've got lots of —" Charles glanced at his watch — "lots of work, but maybe

Monday after school."

It was summer break. What school?

Charles tried a smile Beth's direction. "He's taking some classes this summer, aren't you, Cory? To get ahead."

Cory nodded, though not very enthusiastically.

"Oh. How nice." Should she have been doing that too? Sending the kids to summer school to stay ahead of the pack?

"So how about that? Monday afternoon? And listen, stay inside till your mom gets home from taking Hannah to that pageant thingy, okay?"

Cory nodded vaguely, but his attention was on Chip, who was running across the front lawn with the kite, about to launch it into the stratosphere. Larry followed with a remote control of some sort in his hand. She glanced around. Where was Nathan?

As Charles backed out of the driveway, Beth heard the faint whir of an engine, and to all of their surprise, the kite launched into the sky.

"Awesome!" Cory said, leaning against the fence.

Chip and Larry had their arms lifted in the air.

"Uh-oh . . ." Cory pointed to the string beginning to collapse in front of Chip.

"This isn't good," Chip said, and they all looked up.

Suddenly the kite dive-bombed. Beth shrieked and covered her head as the kite dipped low and then screamed skyward.

"Can you control it?" Larry yelled.

"I don't think so!" Chip yelled back, just as the string broke.

Beth peeked out from behind a hand to see the kite narrowly miss the Buckleys' roof. "Cory, you should probably —"

The kite whizzed past, and Cory's head whipped right, following its every move.

Then they all saw it at the same time. An unsuspecting mom pushing a purple stroller. The kite was headed straight for them.

"Watch out!" everyone screamed.

The mom turned just in time to duck.

The kite shot upward again, but this time straight into the Buckleys' tree. It lodged below a large branch.

Beth brushed the hair out of her face as Chip and Larry ran to check on the woman and the baby.

"That was soooo cool," Cory said.

"Sorry about the tree. I'll have one of the boys get it, okay? Tell your parents not to worry," Beth said.

Larry walked back to the house, closely

followed by Chip as they discussed whether or not they should try it with bottle rockets. "Hey, buddy, run inside and get us some drinks, okay?"

"Sure, Dad!"

"Can't believe that thing flew," Beth said.

"Where is Nathan?" Larry threw his arms up. "He just disappeared. He missed the whole thing."

Beth had spotted him seconds ago. She pointed toward the end of the porch, almost around the corner. Nathan was texting something on his phone.

Larry looked dejected. "I can't believe a motorized kite couldn't keep him off that thing. A *motorized kite* that we built ourselves."

"Honey, you're doing a great job."

"This is going to take drastic measures," Larry mumbled and then strode into the house.

Just then Robin's car pulled into the drive.

"Hi — sorry I'm late, Mom." She smiled as she got out of the car. "I brought the book! Come on."

Beth grinned genuinely. She couldn't resist when Robin got excited about something.

"How about on the porch? It's a nice day." Beth pointed to the two wicker chairs that were in decent shape. She'd set out some lemonade. This time it was from a mix, but whatever.

They sat down and Robin placed the wedding dress catalog on her lap and turned to a bookmarked page.

"Before you show me," Beth said, touching her arm, "I want to tell you something. Your dad and I aren't poor, sweetie. I mean, we have bills. But we can pay for the wedding."

"I know," Robin said. "I know that, Mom. It's just . . . Marvin and I want to do it our way, you know? We want to spend money where it's important to us and skip the things we don't care about."

Beth nodded, understanding the insinuation with a great deal of pain. What Robin was trying to say so delicately was that if Beth were in charge of the budget, she'd be controlling.

"Besides, Mom, Marvin is really good with money. He's amazing."

"He is amazing. I really . . . admire his passion for what he does. I'm sure one day he'll find something even more exciting that he can be passionate about."

Robin glanced at her, uncertainty flickering quickly across her face, but it was gone as soon as she looked at the bridal gown book.

"Okay, I'm so excited to show you this one." She opened it up, and Beth leaned in for a look.

"It's gorgeous," she said, but she couldn't keep her attention on the dress. Ever so slowly, her gaze dropped to the price at the bottom. "Kind of expensive, though, don't you think?"

"I know," Robin said.

"The less expensive ones are usually in the back."

"I already looked. I don't like any of those."

Beth tried to steady herself for a somewhat-difficult conversation. "Sure, but . . . you may have to make some sacrifices."

"I'm only getting married once. My dress is *not* being sacrificed. It's the thing I've most looked forward to about my wedding. I want to look beautiful for Marvin."

Beth leaned away and nodded, trying to seem compliant. "Okay. Of course. But you may have to cut corners somewhere else."

"I know."

"That photographer you mentioned last night that you hired is a little pricey."

"What do you mean? He cut us a deal."

"Still, Nathan could take pictures. He's very good —"

Robin's eyes cut sideways, glaring at Beth. "Why do you care so much? Marvin and I are paying for this."

Beth moved to the edge of the wicker chair. "I'm not just talking about the wedding. Believe it or not, there are things to pay for after the wedding. Like rent. And car payments."

"We got it covered," Robin said, whipping through one page after another.

"Have you made out a budget?"

"We got it," she said, still flipping, but this time toward the very high-end side of the catalog.

It started out as a small, niggling feeling, almost like a hiccup that wasn't quite ready to launch. But Beth knew better — this was no hiccup coming. It had a lot more heartburn behind it.

"What do you mean, *you got it*? How do you know *you got it*? Have you considered unexpected expenses?"

"We have some in savings. I told you Marvin's good with —"

"How much? A couple hundred? He delivers pizza."

Robin didn't even look up.

"Have you weighed the fact that Marvin's

301

a good saver against the fact that you're a very good *spender*?"

"What, so I'm just like some silly teenager who is gonna blow her life savings on cotton candy and lip gloss?"

"You have *two hundred and twenty-three* Beanie Babies! You tell me!"

Robin shot to her feet, the catalog falling to the dusty porch. Beth rose too. Robin leaned in, hands on her hips. Inside her memory, Beth found herself looking at Robin, eight years old, hands on her hips in the exact same way, trying to convince Beth and Larry that she was old enough to walk to the 7-Eleven by herself — a mile away.

Now Robin was a good two inches taller than she. "You don't think I'm mature enough to get married."

"I didn't say that," Beth said, though she desperately, desperately wanted to. It was all she could do *not* to say it. Robin said it. Why couldn't she?

"You think we're gonna end up broke."

"No, I don't. . . ." *Yes. Yes, I do!* And when had *gonna* replaced *going to* in her vocabulary?

Robin stepped closer, so close that Beth could smell the bubble gum in her mouth. "So you haven't had that conversation with Dad? The one where you're worried that

Marvin and I are gonna have to move into your basement?"

Beth blinked. Had they? Maybe Beth was just remembering that they should've had it. Maybe they were going to have it before Larry began his Summer of Intense Fun.

Beth lifted her chin a bit, trying to show how a mature person argues. She put on the tone she often used with Larry — no matter what pitch the other person used, they still sounded whiny comparatively. "Every parent worries about their children."

"Well, stop. I'm not a child."

Robin's cheeks were bright as if she were sunburned. "I knew you would do this. I knew it. That's why I told Marvin we should just elope. But no, he wanted —"

They heard the most bloodcurdling scream.

Robin grabbed her arm. "Mom, look! It's Cory!"

Beth spun around. Cory lay on the sidewalk on the other side of the fence, a pool of blood spreading out from underneath him as he grasped the kite that had been stuck in the tree.

CHAPTER 30
HELEN

Helen walked so fast that the automatic sliding doors of the ER caught the toe of her shoe, barely opening in time. "Hannah, hurry! Hurry!"

"I am! I've got these stupid heels on!" Hannah barked from behind her.

Helen's large purse swung and hit her leg with each stride, but she didn't care. She had to get to Cory.

A nurse sat behind an ugly blue desk. Helen raced to it, trying to catch her breath.

"I'm here to see my son. He was brought here. My neighbors, they brought him."

The nurse looked like nuclear war couldn't frazzle her. She slowly blinked, finally looked up at Helen as if just now noticing someone was speaking to her. She took a long sip of a Big Gulp and said, "Name?"

"Helen."

"His name, Mom," Hannah said, taking

off her shoes as she stood next to her.

Helen glanced down. "Hannah! Put your shoes back on this instant! Do you know how disgusting this place is?"

The nurse's facial expression didn't change a bit. Hannah kept her shoes off. They dangled from her fingers, taunting Helen.

"Cory. Cory Buckley. He's eight."

The nurse typed his name into the computer at a pace that seemed indicative of no prior computer experience. Hannah was smirking. Why was she smirking?

"You can go on back. Room nine."

Helen rushed toward the large doors that were opened with a buzz from the nurses' station. "Hannah, come on!"

She hurriedly glanced up at the numbers above the tiny ER rooms. Nine seemed to be nowhere in sight. But Hannah pointed and began leading the way.

They got to the room and Helen ripped back the curtain around the bed. Cory raised his head and smiled a sad smile when he saw her. Blood looked to be soaking through a large bandage across his forehead. His leg was propped up with pillows.

Charles stood by his side, hands in his pockets.

"My leg hurts," Cory moaned.

"The doc is coming back and he'll get you something for the pain," Charles said.

"How bad is it?" Helen asked, sitting on the edge of the bed, gently squeezing Cory's toes.

"We don't really know yet. Doc says he'll need stitches on the forehead and the side of his head, and they're doing X-rays on his leg, but he thinks it's just a deep bruise. I got here two minutes ago, so I'm still catching up." Charles ruffled Cory's hair.

"What happened, Cory?" Helen asked.

"I fell out of the tree."

Helen glanced at Charles. "Our tree? You were climbing it? Why?"

Cory winced in pain, but only for a second. "The Andersons built a kamikaze kite. It got stuck up in our tree. I just wanted it."

Helen felt her blood boil. Of *course* it was the Andersons' fault! But when she looked at Charles for confirmation of her rage, he looked unusually . . . burdened. Guilty, even.

"Oh," Charles said and paused. "I'm sorry, Cory. I know I told you we'd make that kite, but I had to get things done at . . ." Helen watched as Charles's words and thoughts seemed to ride off into a hazy sunset together. "I'll tell you what. Forget my deadline."

Helen's gaze cut back and forth between the two. "Forget your deadline? You can't just —"

But Charles held up a hand. "I'll stay home tomorrow and we'll make one, okay?"

Cory sat up in bed, perched on his elbows. "Really?"

Charles glanced at his watch but then seemed to regret it. "We need to get you better first, though."

"Right," Cory said, staring at his leg.

Helen felt herself growing slightly hysterical. Her husband was suddenly more interested in kites than work? And her son, who knew better than to climb anything over three feet high, had broken two rules: going outside the house while she and Charles were gone *and* climbing the tree. Then there was the unspoken rule of not engaging with the Andersons or their stupid activities.

Speaking of . . . The curtain opened and Larry and Beth entered, Larry holding a blue snow cone.

"Hey! There he is! Looks like they're whipping you back into shape!" Larry said. "Here you go, bud."

But Helen intercepted the snow cone just as Cory reached for it. "I'm sorry, Larry, but we don't let our kids have anything with corn syrup in it. It causes . . ." She paused, glancing at Nathan and Chip, who stood behind their dad. "Hyperactivity."

Charles took it from her. "Helen, he's had an ordeal. This is what you do when you have an ordeal. It's universal kid-in-the-ER protocol." He flashed a smile and Beth and Larry laughed. Charles handed the snow cone over to Cory and then shook Larry's hand. "Thanks so much for driving him to the ER and calling us and all that."

"Oh, it was no problem," Beth said. "I'm just glad he's okay."

"Obviously he should've been wearing his tree helmet," Charles said.

Helen's gaze cut toward Charles. "What's a tree helmet?"

"Isn't that a thing?"

"No."

"I could've sworn that was a thing."

Helen smiled in a way that let Charles know he should shut it. Then she turned toward Larry and Beth. "Can I talk to you two for a moment?"

Helen followed them out, jerking the curtain closed.

Larry handed Nathan the keys. "Why don't you bring the car around, okay, bud?"

Chip and Nathan walked off, and Helen was glad. This would be a tough enough conversation as it was.

"Beth. Larry. I'm just not happy about this at all."

"I wouldn't be either, Helen," Larry said. "It's scary when a kid has an accident. Chip's knocked himself unconscious three times. Nathan once broke his pelvis. And even Robin —"

"I'm not happy about the influence your children have had over mine."

"What do you mean?" Beth asked.

"I mean, Cory is not the kind of kid who would wander out of the house and climb a tree for some stupid motorized kite. That's what I mean."

"You're saying this is our fault?" Beth asked.

"I'm saying that ever since summer arrived, your family has been acting very strangely, running all over the yard, whooping and hollering and doing all kinds of nonsensical things. Cory's been watching all this, hardly able to concentrate a lick on the summer classes he's taking. And so who do you think planted this grand idea in his head about making a kite? Before this, Cory never once in his life mentioned anything about making a kite."

"Of course he hasn't," Beth said. "That's because he's been too busy taking tap, speech, baseball, fencing, chess club, diving lessons, scuba classes —"

"We're molding a well-rounded kid," Helen snapped.

"Yeah? Well, any eight-year-old should be able to climb a tree. They don't have a class for that. They usually learn it on a family camping trip or in the backyard while playing cowboys and Indians or dreaming about building a fort."

Larry patted his wife's back. "Beth, okay, let's just —"

"What is *that* supposed to mean?" Helen folded her arms.

"I see you over there, on your manicured lawn with your manicured nails, *judging us,*" Beth said, her face tight. "Well, I'll have you know that this man right here —" she pointed to Larry, almost jabbing him in the eye — "this man right here is a good man. His kids love him! And yeah, maybe he looks like a fool running around with whipped cream and cherries and kites and who knows what else, but he's creating memories, Helen. *Memories.* And maybe all of us could stand to take a lesson from his playbook."

Helen glanced around self-consciously. People were starting to stare. The security guard in the corner stood up.

"Maybe if I had spent a little bit of time

tearing my bathing suit up on our home-made Slip 'N Slide, my daughter would be more prepared for life. But instead, I always felt like something more important needed to be done. And now look at her! She's about to leave the house and . . ."

And then, suddenly, Beth began to cry.

"Oh, Beth, honey . . ." Larry took her arm.

"She messes with my family, she messes with me." Beth swiped at her tears and pointed at Helen as Larry redirected her toward the door. "You better listen to me. Or Cory is going to grow up and have no idea what to do with an egg. And don't think I didn't notice Hannah's nose piercing!"

They disappeared through the large-frame automatic doors. Helen could still hear Beth crying. She looked around, her hands tapping against her pearl necklace, and offered a short smile to the gawkers. Soon everyone went back to their business, but Helen felt rattled. What had gotten into Beth?

Composing herself, Helen returned behind the curtain. "How are you feeling?" she asked calmly, signaling that everyone should just pretend they didn't hear any of that.

"I'm okay."

Helen gasped and glanced at her watch.

"Oh, boy. Okay, listen, I've got to run and get Hannah from her pageant training class. I'll drop her off and then come back to —"

"Mom, I'm right here."

Helen glanced to the corner. Hannah sat, slumping just like Helen had taught her not to, iPod in hand.

"Oh. Yes. Of course you're here. I'm sorry, honey. It's been a stressful . . . I just didn't see you there. . . ."

Hannah rose. "That's the thing. You don't see, do you?"

"Where are you going?" Helen asked as Hannah slid sideways and out the curtain.

"Why do you care? I'm not really here anyway."

Helen started to open the curtain and go after her but Charles said, "Stop."

Helen glared at him. "You're not suggesting we let her get away with behavior like that."

"I'm suggesting that it may be time you and I adjust our parenting strategy."

Helen felt herself breathing hard even as their little curtained room grew very still.

The only sound was Cory slurping his blue drink.

CHAPTER 31
BUTCH

Once again, using thinly veiled guilt, Ava had convinced Butch to let her come to work with him. He kept a decent eye on her as he sipped his morning thermos of coffee. Mostly she stayed out of the way, except at one point he noticed Jack pass by with a hot-pink glitterfied hammer proudly bouncing against his hip as it hung from his utility belt.

Around ten, when the guys took a fifteen-minute break, he walked by them near the water cooler. Ava stood right in the middle of the group.

"C-a-r-e-f-u-l. Careful," Ava said to some cheers.

"The spelling bee is all yours," Jack said, knuckle-bumping her.

Butch stopped. "What spelling bee?"

"It's the summer one they put on for kids at the library," Ava said.

"Oh. Nice. Maybe we can practice at home."

Ava shrugged and turned her attention back to the guys until they returned to work.

Around noon, Butch began to wonder who was running this construction site when he looked up from his toolbox in the back of his truck to find Marvin walking toward him. Carrying four pizza boxes.

"Marvin, what are you doing here?"

"Just bringing you your order."

"What order?"

"Your lunch order. Two pepperonis, one Canadian bacon, and one half-olive, half-anchovy."

"I don't think —"

"Marvin, hi!" Ava said, waving as she skipped toward them. "Right on time."

"I always am." Marvin grinned.

Butch turned to his daughter. "Ava, what's this about?"

"The guys were hungry. Day after day they have to eat lame bologna sandwiches. Sometimes they even forget their lunch. They said you don't give them enough time to really go anywhere, so I thought I'd bring lunch to them."

Tippy walked by, grabbing the pizza boxes. "Thanks, Ava!"

"Ava! You can't just . . ."

Her smile dropped.

Butch sighed, turning to Marvin. "I'm sorry . . . Um, here, let me pay you. What do I owe you?"

"No, we're good. Ava already paid. See you soon!" And Marvin was gone.

Butch looked at Ava. "Paid for too?"

Ava shrugged. "Your wallet was in the truck, just like Mom told you not to do. I got your credit card and it was done."

"Why would you do something like this? Without asking me? Four large pizzas? Do you know how much that's going to cost me?"

Her pupils seemed to grow into orbs of innocence. "I thought it would help."

"Help what?"

"The guys like you better."

Butch glanced up. They were under a tree, enjoying their pizza. "It's that bad?"

"They said they miss the old you."

"Who said that?"

"I'm reading between the lines."

Butch smirked. "Are you. Well, listen, Ava, after today, you have to go back to day care."

"That's not fair!"

"What's not fair is you ordering pizza without my permission."

"You're being mean!"

"I'm being reasonable, which is something

315

I'm going to have to teach you, I guess."

"*R-e-a-s-o-n-a-b-l!*"

"*E!* You left off the *e!*"

"Who's the child now?" Ava said and stomped off.

The guys stared, most of them midchew, but Butch ignored them. A long breath dragged through his lips. He just needed to get through this day without any more incidents.

By later afternoon, he was happy with the progress they'd made. He had a lot to sort through, including what to do about Ava. Dr. Reynolds had been helpful, but Butch didn't see himself going to therapy regularly. He didn't have time. Maybe he should send Ava. Or call Beth. He didn't know. He just needed time to think. And to have a lengthy talk with Ava about her behavior.

Then he saw Tippy rushing toward him. And though Tippy was long legged, he was a slow walker and never hurried for anything. So as Tippy got closer, a feeling of alarm shot through Butch. Was someone hurt? He once had a guy shoot a nail through his foot. Nailed it to the board he was standing on.

"What's wrong?" Butch asked.

Tippy was nearly out of breath. "I just need to warn you." He glanced over his shoulder. "Before she gets here."

"Before who gets here?"

"Ava."

Butch tugged his gloves off. "What now? She promised steak dinners to the crew after work?"

"Not exactly."

"Then what?"

"Don't tell her I told you."

"What is this, second grade?"

Tippy shrugged. "I like Ava. I don't want her mad at me. I've seen her mad at you. It's not pretty."

"Just tell me what's going on."

"I was standing at the water cooler — I was legitimately thirsty this time — when I heard Ava talking to someone. So I kind of moved toward the fence so I could hear better. Just watching out for her, you know?"

"Who was she talking to?"

"A girl named Bryn. Said she was six. Said she was just watching us build a house, and then Ava warned it was dangerous and she shouldn't be so close or she was going to have to wear a hard hat, which I thought was cute —"

"Get to the point, Tippy."

"Anyway, Ava struck up a conversation with her and it came out that she lives with her dad and that they live there." Tippy pointed over his shoulder, toward the end of the block. "That church. It has a homeless shelter."

Butch scratched his head. "So what's the big deal?"

"Well, then she . . ." Tippy glanced up. "Uh-oh, here she comes."

"Just tell me."

"I gotta go."

"Tippy!"

But he was racing the other way, trying to seem inconspicuous but doing a horrible job of it. Butch turned to face Ava, who was moving as innocently as a shark. Once again Butch found his hands on his hips. What was it with that posture? It wasn't like it did any good or gave him superpowers. He guessed he had to stake his ground while he could.

Ava walked up. "What?"

"What have you been up to?" Butch asked.

"Good things, Daddy. I promise. I've been staying out of trouble. I thought about trying out the handsaw earlier when no one was looking, but I didn't. I swear."

Butch's hands dropped to his sides. "Good. Well, listen, we've got about another hour and then —"

"But I *do* have good news!" Ava said.

Butch pulled his gloves back on. "Oh

yeah? What's that? I need some good news today."

"I met a girl named Bryn. She's six. And she's homeless."

"Oh, wow. That's too bad. Were you nice to her?"

"I told her my dad builds houses."

Suddenly the alarm returned. "And . . . ?"

"And I told her you'd build her and her dad one! I said you make them really fast!"

"You *what*?"

"It doesn't have to be a big house. I think it's just the two of them."

"Ava!" Butch pulled his gloves off again, this time throwing them to the ground. "You can't go around making big promises like that! I can't build them a house!"

"Why not?"

"We're not using LEGOs here, Ava. This kind of thing requires land and materials and people who are willing to work on the house. They obviously don't have any money to pay for it. How am I supposed to do it?"

Ava looked disappointed, but then her eyes brightened. "We could get money from the church. The church helps homeless people all the time."

"It's not that simple."

"Why not?"

Butch's eye muscle twitched. He was losing his patience. "It's impossible, okay? Please tell me you didn't already say something to the dad."

"No."

"Good."

"But Bryn is going to."

Butch turned away from his daughter, scooping up his gloves and throwing a box of nails into the truck bed. Why would she do such a thing? He didn't look at her. "You've put me in a very awkward position."

"Look! There they are!"

Butch turned. A rail-thin guy walked toward them, wearing a dirty white shirt, or more like it wore him. His jeans were baggy and ripped, not in a stylish sort of way. He held his little girl's hand as they stepped onto the sidewalk.

"I have to disappoint them now," Butch said out of the side of his mouth as he tried to stretch out a smile he hoped would erase the embarrassment he was already feeling.

As the two approached, he stepped forward and offered his hand. "Hi. I'm Butch."

"Keith. This is my daughter, Bryn."

Butch glanced down at the little girl, whose unkempt hair reflected their obvious desperation. "Hello. Listen, I don't know what all your daughter told you —"

Keith smiled a little and waved his hand. "It's okay. I figured there was some mistake. No such thing as a free house."

"No, there really isn't. If I could, I'd . . ." Butch's words trailed off because they seemed so inadequate, so ridiculous. "I'm sorry" fell out of his mouth like a crumb.

"It's fine. Thanks. Come on, Bryn," Keith said and began turning back toward the homeless shelter.

"Do you guys need anything? Money?" Butch thought he might have a twenty in his truck somewhere.

"No, we're okay."

"We've got some lunch over here. Pizza." It was cold and he felt bad for offering it, but Bryn's eyes lit with excitement. She looked up at her dad.

Reluctantly he nodded, then looked at Butch. "It's been a while since she's had pizza."

"It's probably cold. . . ."

"It won't matter," Keith laughed.

Butch watched Ava trail Bryn, skipping along behind her. "Yeah, it doesn't matter to me, either. I lived on cold pizza before I got married." He glanced at Keith. "I didn't eat lunch. You hungry?"

Keith nodded.

"Come on, let's grab some."

They sat on the woodpile with the kids. Behind them, Bryn was telling Ava how much she liked unicorns. Butch smiled. Perfect. Ava was a unicorn expert.

"So," Butch said, unsure how he should broach the subject, "landed on tough times?"

Keith slowly ate his pizza. "Yeah. It's just been me and Bryn for about four months now."

"Where's your wife?" Ava suddenly inserted herself into the conversation.

Butch scowled at her. "Ava . . ."

"No, that's okay," Keith said, smiling gently at her. "She died. Cancer." Butch looked away while Keith kept talking. "She had the good job, and I got laid off about a year ago. So we lost the house pretty quick."

Butch nodded. How easily, he realized, the tables could've turned on him like that. He noticed Ava's shoes . . . brand-new. Her socks, white. Her hair, brushed. She was bathed and her teeth were clean. What would he have done if they'd become homeless? What if it had been Jenny who'd made more money?

"I'm sorry," Butch said, but it came out more as a mumble because the words sort of stuck in his throat.

"I'm working at a body shop part-time now," Keith said. "Hoping that'll turn into something bigger. Of course, it'll be tough to go full-time. I got nobody to watch Bryn."

A pause swelled between them, Butch finding it hard to know what to say next. Finally he took a cue from Ava's chatty side and said, "Listen, are you going to be around here in the next couple of weeks?"

"Yeah, looks like it. We're staying at the shelter until we can find someplace else."

"I'd like to talk with you again sometime."

"About what?"

Butch laughed a little. "I don't know yet, but I feel like we're supposed to talk again."

Keith smiled. "Okay. Sure." He took Bryn's hand. She grabbed for another piece of pizza as they walked away and happily ate as Butch and Ava watched them.

Ava crawled down to where Butch sat. "What are you going to do?"

"This is crazy . . ."

Ava squealed and clapped. "You're going to build him a house!"

Butch shook his head. "There's no way. I need money and materials and people who'll work for free."

"No problem on that one." Ava jumped from the woodpile and whistled to the workers, the exact way they'd shown her last week. Everyone stopped what they were doing. "Hey! Would you guys work a couple of weekends for free if we could give a house to a homeless family?"

"Sure!" Tippy yelled back.

"Absolutely!" Jack said.

And the rest followed with thumbs-ups and claps even though they knew full well it would be more than a couple of weekends.

"Great! Thanks!" Ava turned back to Butch. "I got your workers. Now I'll get your money and your materials."

Butch wanted to protest. Normally he would protest. But something in him said that this tiny bundle of enthusiasm could actually pull it off.

"This is nuts," he whispered.

"This is fun!" Ava said. Then her face turned serious. "But I'm going to need to use your phone. I need to call the church." He slowly handed it over. "I promise I won't download Fruit Ninja." She bounded off.

"Fruit Ninja is the least of my concerns." Butch sat on the woodpile, slumped by the burden he'd just taken on, but in awe of Ava. He didn't know how this was even possible. Was his crew really going to come on weekends? For free?

He closed the pizza box and looked toward the homeless shelter. Keith and Bryn were gone now. Some trash blew down the street and he watched it go, but he was thinking about Jenny.

He'd heard people say they still felt close to their loved ones after death, that "their spirit lives on," but Butch thought it was just a way to cope with death. Once Jenny was gone, he'd never felt her nearby. Not really. Not in a tangible way.

But as he sat on that woodpile and considered building a house for a homeless man, it was as if Jenny stood beside him, smiling at him, proud of his unusual moment of selflessness. It wasn't his strongest suit, for sure. Jenny was the unselfish one in the relationship. He mostly just tagged along.

Ava stood near his truck, chatting and using her free hand to talk, like Jenny used to. Butch smiled.

"Okay, Jenny. I'll do this. I'll do it for you."

CHAPTER 32
BETH

It had been almost a full day since her meltdown. The hospital meltdown. She'd had so many she was starting to have to name them.

The family quietly went about their business. Larry pretended she'd never yelled about eggs in the ER. That was one thing she loved about Larry. He didn't judge. Although sometimes she wished he would. They might have more in common.

Beth leaned against the kitchen counter like she was stretching her calves for a long run. She hadn't exercised in four years; she was mostly just trying to keep herself from collapsing.

Robin came bounding downstairs. Beth stood upright, smiled broadly. "I was just about to start dinner. Want to help?"

Robin didn't look amused. "Have to go. Wedding plans."

"Maybe later we can look through the —"

"Probably not."

She breezed out the door without another word.

"Don't . . . don't . . ." Beth swallowed back the hysteria that was creeping up her throat, the same feeling she got at the thought of seeing Helen again.

Outside, she heard Larry arrive home from getting supplies for some fun project he had planned. He swung open the door and smiled at her, greeting her with a warm hug. "Hi. How's your day going?"

She shrugged. "Okay. Not great. How was yours?"

"It's getting ready to get *real* exciting." He turned toward the staircase. "Nathan! Chip! Come down here!"

Beth listened to their feet beat against the ceiling and then tumble down the stairs.

"Where's Robin?"

"Gone," Beth mumbled.

Larry sighed. "By the way, you need to call Butch. Or Ava. Not sure who's in charge, but they're undertaking a big project, building a home for someone. I didn't quite understand — Ava was talking fast. But we're signed up to volunteer for something."

In a matter of seconds Nathan and Chip were by Larry's side.

"What's going on?" Chip asked.

"Look out there," Larry said, pointing to the front window.

The boys hurried to the window. Beth did too, without the hurry. It was hard to get excited about much, but she tried.

"Dad!" Chip gasped. "What *is* that?"

Beth wiggled her way in between them. Sitting right in the middle of the driveway was an old Cutlass Ciera.

"That is our new project!"

The boys poured out the front door and Beth followed. Nathan circled it. It was the most hideous car Beth had ever seen.

"It's a piece of junk!" Chip said, but it came out as if they'd just purchased a Jaguar.

"Exactly. Our project is to make it *not* a piece of junk." Larry smiled.

"We're going to restore it?"

"Yep!"

There was a pause, and for a moment Beth thought Larry's idea had bombed, but suddenly Nathan slapped his hands together and Chip flung himself over the hood of the car.

"You're kidding!" Chip laughed.

"Do you have any idea how to do this?" Nathan asked. Beth was thinking the same thing.

"Absolutely none." Larry pulled a book from his back pocket. "But I got this."

Beth glanced at it. *Restoring Cars for Dummies.*

Nathan gave Larry a playful shove. "This is going to be a complete disaster."

"An utter waste of time!" Larry laughed.

"I love this family!" Chip said.

Larry rubbed his hands together. "All right, boys, why don't you go into the garage and see if we have any tools."

"What tools do we need?" Chip asked.

"I have no idea." They all burst into laughter again.

As the boys went into the garage, Larry turned to Beth. She wasn't sure what expression she was wearing, but whatever it was, it murdered Larry's smile. "What's the matter?" he asked.

"How can you do this to me?"

"Honey, this car was like five hundred bucks. Totally in our budget for our Summer of Intense Fun."

"I'm not talking about the money," Beth said, and despite her best intentions, her voice rose with every word, causing *money* to sound like it was being sung. Badly.

"What's the matter?"

"What's the matter? You're doing the stupidest things, Larry. Building kites. Playing with whipped cream. Now bringing this literal piece of junk into our driveway. And they love it! They're eating it up!"

Larry stood there shrugging and staring and kicking the toe of his shoe into the concrete. "I'm sorry. I didn't —"

"It's just not fair! It's not fair, Larry!"

Larry looked genuinely confused.

"You pull these stupid stunts and the boys adore you! But the more I pine after Robin, the more she pulls away. Apparently the only way I can win her heart is to buy her a log of pepperoni!"

Larry reached out for Beth, but she turned away. "I wanted a summer of fun too. I wanted to spend some time with my daughter, and now she won't even eat breakfast anymore because that would mean she'd have to eat it with me."

Larry was behind her, she could feel, but he didn't touch her. "Look, Beth, here's the deal. And I'm telling you the truth. Guys bond over stupid. That's just how it is. We're shallow, you know? Put a Mento into a diet soda and shoot carbonation fountains and you're friends for life."

Beth turned to him. "Did you do that, too?"

"I had that planned for next week, except I thought . . ." He glanced at her, waving his hands like he was trying to erase every-thing. "Doesn't matter. Listen," he said, his hands on her shoulders. They felt like they weighed a ton each. "It's not what you think here, with you and Robin. She's on her own now. She's flexing her independent muscle. The more you want her to think one way, the more she will think the other. That's just what kids do."

Beth rubbed her thumbs under her eyes, hoping to save her mascara. She took a deep breath and looked at the car. It was a beat-up old thing, on its last leg. It looked like she felt. She hadn't even fully raised her children. Nathan would be gone soon too, but there was still Chip.

She watched her two boys pop the hood of the car. It creaked open like it hadn't been lifted in a decade. They laughed and peered in. They would miss each other. This was *their* last summer together. She hadn't really thought of that. And here she was, about to ruin a moment because of her selfishness.

She touched Larry's arm. "I'm sorry."

"Honey," he said, pulling her close. "It's okay. I understand. I promise. And I also promise that you and Robin will get through this."

"But will she be okay, Larry? Marrying

331

Marvin? *Marvin?*"

Larry paused. "I don't know, to tell you the truth. It kind of has disaster written all over it. But it's her life. We have to let her live it. We have to let God take care of her."

Beth nodded but didn't want to. "The day she was born, I held her in that beautiful pink blanket your mom made her, and I promised *I* would always take care of her. I kept that promise. I just didn't realize, I guess, that there would come a time when she wouldn't want to be taken care of."

"She will always need her mom," Larry said.

"I've prayed her whole life for her soul mate. Marvin has to be a mistake, right? He has to be."

Larry shrugged. "I mean . . . the more I'm around Marvin, the more I like —"

Then they both heard the most awful noise, the kind of noise that sends a chill down the spine and a burst of nausea through the stomach.

Helen.

"Oh, my," she was saying, standing behind her little fence, tapping her finger against her little pearls, looking at the car. "What do we have here?" It wasn't a question born out of curiosity. It was the kind of condemning statement that tries to disguise itself behind a question mark. Her eyes cut to Beth. "Beth, how nice to see you. Are you feeling better?"

Larry put his hand out, but Beth broke through it, marching to the fence line. "I'm feeling fine, Helen. Just fine. As fine as I've ever felt."

Helen shifted her eyes back to the car. "What is this? A car for Nathan for college? How . . . excited . . . he must be."

"It's a project," Beth said, though she thought it might've actually come out with a growl.

Larry hurried over. "It's something we're doing for fun. Restoring an old car. Charles is welcome to come over with Cory."

Helen smiled, but it was not warm. It wasn't even cool. It was filled with . . . pity. Beth's chest tightened so drastically that she might've otherwise thought she was having a heart attack if she didn't perceive the knife right in front of her, stabbing her in the chest.

"Well," Helen said, "it is quite the monstrosity you've parked here. How long will this restoration take?"

Nathan and Chip simultaneously jumped back and yelled, "Whoa!" Inky black oil slowly drained out from underneath the car.

"That's going to leave a stain!" Nathan

laughed. The boys stuck their heads under the hood again.

"It may take a while," Larry said.

"Well, I'm sorry to break this to you, but the homeowners' association has strict rules about parking nondrivable vehicles in driveways."

Larry glanced back. "Oh, I wouldn't worry too much about that. The HOA is kind of lax on that kind of stuff."

Helen crossed her arms. "I wouldn't count on them being lax on this one."

"Not to worry," Larry hollered as he walked to the car. "We'll have this thing up and running in no time."

"I certainly hope so," Helen said. Her attention shifted back to Beth. "Will you be at scrapbooking this week?"

Beth held on to the fence post so tightly that she knew if she slid her hand down just a fraction, her palm would be riddled with splinters. But she was having a hard time holding her own. What she really wanted to do was shove Helen. Shove her right at her pearl line. She pictured the pearls breaking apart, rolling down the driveway one by one.

"Beth?"

Beth blinked. "What?"

"Scrapbooking? Are you coming this week?"

Beth drew in a breath through her nostrils and realized she knew Helen's Achilles' heel. It was her own as well. "Yes. Well, probably, though Robin and I are planning on doing some errands together. We like — love — to spend time with each other, you know."

It was fleeting, but Beth saw it. Jealousy colored Helen's expression.

"I'm sorry — I have to leave. Appointments." Helen stepped away from the fence and walked toward her house, one arm wrapped around herself while the other hand fingered her pearls, all the way inside.

For the first time in days, Beth didn't have to fake her smile. But then she felt guilty about it because she always had the thought *What would Jenny do?* WWJD — she should get that bracelet. Jenny, she knew, would give Helen the benefit of the doubt.

She called, "I'll get some soda" and bounded up the porch steps. They didn't even creak. She opened the door and floated inside, heading for the pantry to find an unopened bottle. The boys liked their soda fizzy.

She found two and turned to put them on the counter. Then she startled because sitting at the breakfast bar was Nathan, slumped over and looking a little weary.

"Nathan? Are you okay?" She slipped up beside him, felt his forehead. He wasn't running a fever.

"I'm fine," he said, gently swatting her hand away.

"What's the matter?"

He glanced out the window, watching his dad and Chip for a moment. He looked reluctant to speak.

"It's okay, honey. What's wrong?"

"Getting an old car and fixing it up, that was my idea."

"Oh, Nathan, it's fine. I'm not mad about the —"

"I had that idea when I was ten."

Beth searched his expression.

"And again at twelve. It sounded fun then."

Beth wasn't sure she was following.

"But I'm eighteen now. It's too little, too late."

"You seemed like you loved the idea."

"I know," Nathan said, resting his cheek on the arm that was propped up on the bar. "I'm trying to. I mean, the whipped cream was kind of fun, I guess. More fun than the board game idea. I've tried to get into Pictionary and charades every night. The motorized kite was . . . a waste of time." He looked sideways at her. "I don't want to hurt Dad's feelings, but there's a thousand things I'd rather be doing this summer."

Beth couldn't hide her astonishment. "Oh, Nathan . . . I . . ."

"But Dad is so into this. I mean, he took *vacation time* and is spending all this money. He told me yesterday that he has plans to buy us all metal detectors and we're going to hunt for treasure." They both glanced out the window as Larry clapped at something. "I would've loved this stuff when I was younger. Even Chip's age." He shrugged. "But now it's just sort of . . ."

Beth touched his shoulder. "It's okay. Maybe you should talk to your dad about this."

He smiled a little. "You're easier to talk to than Dad."

"I am?"

"Yeah. We get each other. I know that you're getting what I'm saying."

She nodded, though secretly she was astonished by everything he was saying.

"Well, I better go back out there. I told Dad I was running upstairs to try to find a tool."

"Nathan," Beth said as he slid off the stool, "you don't have to go back out there if you don't want to."

"I know," Nathan said, and in his small

smile was a manly type of wisdom she had never seen before. "But Dad needs this."

And with that he was gone.

Beth stood watching him out the window, realizing she'd just seen a character trait in her son that she had prayed for ever since he was little, every time he left the house, every time she could — that he would put others first.

She'd just witnessed it firsthand.

Chapter 33
Charles

Charles found himself whistling. Helen had an aversion to sounds louder than a whisper, so he'd stopped whistling around her long ago. But when he was alone, he didn't whistle much either. Most of the time he was too busy worrying about something or on the phone for the entire car ride home. Today, though, even as he was stuck in traffic, Charles found himself whistling. He glanced back and smiled at the supplies he'd had his secretary gather at lunch. All for Cory. All to build a kite. He had no idea how to build a kite, but Cory assured him they'd figure it out together.

Cory never called him at work, but at lunch he'd called, whispering so his mother couldn't hear him. "Dad! Are we still on?"

"We're on, buddy!" Charles laughed. "Hey, maybe your sisters will want to do this too?"

"Aw, Dad. Come on. Do they *have* to?"

Charles smiled to himself. "No, buddy. This'll be our deal." But he made a mental note to find something to do with the girls soon too. If he wasn't careful, having fun with his kids might become a habit.

His cell phone rang and the caller came up on the display screen in his car. He sighed. He specifically didn't want to talk to anyone at the office. He'd told his secretary to hold all his calls until tomorrow. Everything could wait.

Charles pushed the answer button. "What is it? I said no phone calls."

"Charles, it's Bill."

"Look, Bill, whatever this is, let's deal with it in the morning. I'm headed home, and I'm not coming back until tomorrow." Charles glanced at his watch.

"You're going to want to hear this."

"Bill, I promised Cory I would make a kite with him and —"

"Dean called Grant and offered him the whole sum."

Charles's foot pressed on the brake, even though there was nothing to stop for. "What? I didn't authorize him to make that deal."

"I always thought he was a loose cannon."

"You and I already discussed that this wasn't the deal we wanted to make."

"I know. That's why I called you."

"Well, get him back in there."

"I can't. He's on his way to London right now."

"What? You've got to be kidding me!"

Charles gripped the steering wheel. Dean going rogue could mess everything up. A thin layer of perspiration rose out of his skin like morning dew.

"Charles?"

"All right. All right. Let me think." He looked at his watch again. "I'll figure this out."

Charles took the first exit off the highway and pulled into an empty parking lot. What was he supposed to do? If this deal sank, rumors would get started and his reputation could be ruined. Helen was hoping for a new semicovered sundeck this summer. Madison had a scholarship, but there would be expenses, especially if she wanted to get her master's. His head spun as he methodically traced all the lines sprouting out into the future.

He loosened his tie and rolled up his sleeves. He had to think. He couldn't let Cory down again. It was all the kid had been talking about since he fell out of that stupid tree.

Then an idea sprang to mind. A good

idea, the more he thought about it. A really good idea.

Charles took his phone off the dock and scrolled through his contacts. Unusual first name, Tippy. He was married to one of the ladies Helen scrapbooked with. And good friends with their neighbor Beth's deceased sister's husband, Butch — his foreman, if he remembered right. Charles had actually talked to Tippy about the possibility of building his sundeck this summer.

Charles high-fived the air as he found the contact. He quickly dialed the number.

Chapter 34
Tippy

Tippy pulled into his driveway. Hank Williams's "Cold, Cold Heart" blared from his radio, and he rolled his window down so Daphne might hear a bit of it if she was home. He sat for a moment, watching the window. Then he saw her, her profile lit against the sheer drapes. She was so cute with that belly. But these days, it felt more like she was a sleeping dragon.

He swallowed down some of the bile that kept rising in his throat every time he thought there might be a confrontation between the two of them, which was pretty much every minute he was home.

From a Tums roll, he popped two tablets out and chewed through the chalky grit as he got out of the truck, leaving it running. Josh Turner was now singing "Punching Bag." He walked to the front door and hesitated, gaining his courage. He started to open the door, but it swung open before he even touched the knob.

"You're late." She was both teary and furious. Great.

He spread his feet into a wide stance. "I'm home at all different times. You know that."

"I sit on that couch and think, *What if something happened to you? What if you've been in a car wreck? What if I have to raise this baby all . . . ?* Why is your truck still running?"

"That's what I was coming in to tell you. I won't be home tonight because I got a one-night job."

"A what?"

"Just some extra work, you know."

She stared at him, holding her belly up like a ball.

"We can use all the extra income I can bring in," he said. "It's nothing big, but every little thing helps, right?"

"It didn't sound small to me."

"What didn't?"

"Ava called today. Said you volunteered to help build a house. For free. A whole house."

"Oh . . . yeah. That. I was going to talk to you about that. But this is different. It's a paying job."

"How much?"

"A hundred bucks."

Her bottom lip quivered. "You don't want to be around me because I'm fat. Look at me. I'm so fat and grotesque."

Tippy bit his knuckle as he plugged his fist into his mouth. It was true. He didn't want to be around her, but not because she was fat. She wasn't anything close to fat. In fact, he thought she'd never looked more beautiful in her life.

"You're not fat," he said. "But . . ."

He tried to remember what Dr. Reynolds had said about speaking gently to her, trying to explain his position. He said there was nothing worse than passive-aggressive behavior. Tippy needed to be forthright.

"Daphne, it's just that . . ."

"Yes?" The look on her face was exactly the same as the day he asked her to marry him. He realized he'd been silly not to express his feelings over this. She wasn't some kind of monster. She was probably just scared, like he was, of all that was in front of them as parents.

He smiled at her.

"Why are you smiling?"

"Because, Daphne, you look beautiful."

"You're just saying that."

"No. You do."

She gazed coyly at him. Gave him the first smile he'd seen in days.

Maybe he should call Charles, tell him he couldn't make it. Maybe things were getting back to normal.

Then Daphne took a step back, presumably to let him in, but said, "Are you having an affair?"

Tippy stumbled just standing still. "What?"

"You heard me." Her eyes were narrow and mean.

"You've lost your mind."

"Have I? I see it in your eyes. You don't want to be here, with me!"

She started to slam the door in his face, but he held out his hand and stopped it. "The *reason* I don't want to be with you, *Daphne,* is because you're acting like a freak. A freak of a freak of a freak!"

She gasped, her mouth a wide, black, gravity-sucking hole.

Tippy regretted it immediately and stepped off the porch because she looked like she was about to slug him. "I'm sorry. I didn't mean it."

But the door slammed, the sound so loud the neighborhood dogs started barking. Tippy stuck his hands in his pockets and walked back to his truck, where Johnny Cash was singing "Ring of Fire."

"Fine," he mumbled as he climbed into

his truck. "I didn't want to be home any-way."

He drove the ten minutes to Charles Buckley's home. Next to him was a sack of supplies he'd picked up at the hardware store. He pulled to the curb and got out, grabbing the sack and trying to shake the Daphne scene off him. Nothing pulled him out of depression like building something.

As he came around the back of his truck, he saw Larry Anderson and his boys work-ing under the hood of a very old-looking car.

Larry glanced up and waved. "Hey, Tippy! What are you doing here?"

"Just helping Charles with something. What's going on?"

Larry handed Nathan a wrench and met Tippy at the end of the driveway. "Just do-ing some fun things with the boys this sum-mer." He gestured over his shoulder. "Re-storing a car. Or at least trying to." He chuckled. "We're not having much luck. We don't know what we're doing."

Tippy watched the boys. "They seem to be having fun."

"You're in for a treat, Tippy. I guess that baby's about to be here, huh? Boy, let me tell you, it's going to seem like an eternity before your kids can wipe their own noses, but then the next thing you know, they're leaving for college or getting married. It happens that fast."

Tippy smiled, but from what he could tell, he wasn't sure he could endure anything slower. The kid wasn't even here yet and look where they were.

"Larry, can I ask you something? . . . Get your advice, maybe?"

"Sure," Larry said, wiping his hands on the rag sticking out of his pocket.

"Did your kids ever injure themselves on your carpet?"

"What?"

"I know. But I have to ask."

Larry scratched his head. "Well, not that I can recall. Chip once ate potting soil. But he was our third kid, so we weren't watching him as closely. We once left him at the grocery store too. You'd think the kid would be scarred, but ironically he's the most well-adjusted." They turned to find Chip with a stick, beating the grass for no identifiable reason. "Why do you ask?"

"Just, um, trying to assess the risk factors. Do all we can to prevent catastrophe."

Larry laughed. "Listen, Tippy, I don't want to be the bearer of bad news here, but kids can manage to hurt themselves with anything. Robin once got a Q-tip stuck in her ear canal. Chip knocked his tooth out with a Monopoly game piece." He laughed. "We still don't know how he did that. When Nathan was ten, he decided to see what would happen if he ran an eraser up and down his arm really fast. Second-degree burns. Then it got infected. Had to have a skin graft." Larry glanced at Tippy and bit his lip. "Sorry. I'm just saying that kids are kids. They do stupid things."

"How am I supposed to protect him or her?" Tippy asked.

"You do the best you can. I've been trying to tell Beth that. You've got to let go and trust God. You raise them the best way you know how, but at some point you have to let 'em go." He looked at his boys. "This is going to be a great summer, but then Nathan's leaving and things are going to be different. That's the thing about parenthood. You finally get it, pull it all together, understand, and then something changes. You get comfortable, but then they grow. You buy eight pounds of chicken nuggets because that's all your kid will eat, and then they decide they're not into chicken anymore. It's just the way it is. You gotta stay flexible."

Tippy smiled. "You seem like you've done a really good job with your kids."

"That's Beth's doing, really," Larry said. "She's the one who stayed home with them, taught them all the tough lessons. I worked a lot when they were younger, trying to afford this house in this school district. I guess I'm lucky enough now to reap the benefits. But as with everything in life, there are no guarantees. You do what you can while you have them." He gazed toward the driveway. "In the blink of an eye, time has passed and you missed half the things you intended to do."

Tippy spotted Cory bounding out of the Buckley house. "Well, I better get going." He offered his hand. "Thanks, Larry. Oh, by the way, did Ava call you?"

"Yep! We're on it. Don't know exactly what we're doing, but you know we can't say no to Ava. She selling chocolate or wrapping paper or something?"

Tippy smiled. "Something like that." He returned to his truck to grab a couple of tools, including his table saw. He opened the back end just as Cory came down the driveway.

"Hi, Tippy."

"Cory, my man. It's been a while since I've seen you. How are you?"

"Good. What are you doing here?"

"Well," Tippy said, dangling the bag of

supplies in the air, "we're gonna build a kite."

Cory looked at the bag, then back at Tippy. "We are?"

"Yep. And not just any kite. A rock-your-world kind of kite that'll make your friends really jealous." Tippy handed him the extension cord. "Your dad asked me to come by and help you."

"Oh."

"It's going to be awesome. The best kite you've ever seen. This thing'll probably fly to the moon." Tippy handed him the sack and reached into the bed of his truck, trying to grab the wood. "The secret is the wood strength. A lot of people don't know that but . . ." He looked up to hand Cory the duct tape. But Cory had dropped the sack and cord on the sidewalk and was walking toward the house. It was a sad, slow walk.

Tippy watched him until he went inside. He was beginning to realize something. Yes, it was true, kids could hurt themselves on nearly anything. But it seemed adults had the potential to hurt them more.

CHAPTER 35
BUTCH

"Man, Butch, I can't believe we've gotten this much done in just a couple of weekends," Tippy said, standing next to the truck.

Butch leaned against it, lighting up the calculator. "I know." He glanced up to where the guys were on break. He laughed, watching Bryn and Ava show the guys how to have a proper tea party. They all sat in a circle, legs crossed, each holding a plastic princess teacup. Ava looked to be taking this pretty seriously.

"Hey, Eddie," Ava said to the biggest, burliest guy on the crew. She wiggled her pinkie. "Go full pinkie or go home."

The guys roared as Eddie's pinkie went obediently erect. He sipped carefully and daintily.

Butch took a break from the calculator and looked at the house. Ava had garnered forty thousand dollars in donations from church members alone. Then another twenty thousand in donations from various home improvement stores. Butch had pitched in the rest. Every moment he was here, doing this for Keith and Bryn, he felt like Jenny was with him. He couldn't wait to get to the project every weekend. It gave them something to do. Since Jenny died, weekends had typically been spent at home, working on the house or lounging in front of the TV. They'd become virtual recluses unless they absolutely had to get out.

He loved hearing her laugh. And seeing her play.

"Tippy, let me ask you something."

"I've got something to ask you too," Tippy said, leaning against the truck next to Butch.

"Oh." Butch glanced at him. "Well, you go first."

"Um . . ."

"What's the matter?"

"It's just . . . awkward."

"Why?"

Tippy glanced at him. "It's about marriage. Again."

"Oh."

"And it's awkward because of what happened to Jenny and now you're not married, and I know I keep dwelling on this, but . . ." Tippy sighed and tried to gather his strength. "What happens to a marriage once your kid arrives? I mean, is it awful? Tell me the truth. Is it really awful?"

Butch chuckled.

"It is, isn't it? It messes everything up." Tippy shook his head, staring at the ground. "I don't know if I can be a good dad. Kids seem to get disappointed pretty easily, you know? What if I can't make a birthday party? What if I totally wreck this kid's life? What if — ?"

"Tippy, hold on. What's got you so riled up?"

Tippy threw his hands up. "Daphne and I are hardly speaking. We fight every time we see each other. One of the books said she might be hormonal, but I thought that meant crying over accidentally breaking a dish. I didn't know it meant that she was going to turn into Medusa."

"You're right," Butch said, gazing over at Ava. "Everything changes. And it's the hardest work you'll ever do. Remember that Harrington home we built a couple of years back?"

"The one where we found Eddie crying behind the house because he was so tired?"

"Yeah. That's the one. Well, it's like a thousand times worse than that."

Like an implosion, Tippy's resolve collapsed in front of Butch's eyes.

"But it's worth it."

"How can it be worth it?"

"Because you don't know it yet, but you'll love in a way you didn't think you were capable of."

"I'm not sure Daphne and I are going to make it."

"You'll make it."

"What can I do to make it better? I can't even stand to be around her."

"Just take all the kindness you have in you and pour it out on her."

"I've already read a half-dozen books."

"Then read a dozen."

Tippy folded his arms. After a little bit he asked, "What were you going to ask me?"

Butch nodded toward Keith, who was still hammering away while everyone else took a break. He was the first one here and the last one to go. "What do you think of Keith?"

"Great guy. Like him a lot. Sorry he has fallen on hard times."

"Yeah. I like him a lot too."

"What are you thinking?"

"I'm thinking I can't afford to hire him."

Tippy dragged his steel-toed boot against the concrete. "Probably not. Work hasn't exactly been chasing us down. Plus this house is going to cost us a pretty penny."

"But I don't think I can afford not to."

"What do you mean?"

"I mean," Butch said, turning away and gripping the side of his truck, "if Jenny were here, she would tell me to hire Keith. I've been crunching numbers, and it makes no sense. Daphne would tell us it makes no sense. No sense whatsoever. But I feel like I should."

Tippy nodded. "Then you should do it."

"You're supposed to be my voice of reason."

"You're your own voice of reason, and if even *you* are saying to do it, then it's gotta be done."

Butch blew out a breath, the breath that always told his gut to be sensible. The breath that always told him to be cautious. Then he turned.

"Hey, Keith, come here a sec."

Keith dropped what he was doing and hurried over. "Yeah?"

"You're a great worker."

"Oh, uh, thanks." He wiped the sweat from his brow with his sleeve.

"You want a job?"

"What kind?"

"Chief justice of the Supreme Court."

Tippy chuckled, and even some of the guys nearby laughed. Butch hadn't realized they were listening.

"What do you think?" he said, smiling at Keith. "Working for me. Construction."

Keith blinked, his typically docile expression frozen in shock. "Really?"

"Yeah. Absolutely. Ava and Bryn can spend the rest of the summer together. We'll figure out something to do with them."

Keith shook Butch's hand, nodding his thanks. Butch remembered what Jenny had said once about giving. *"Once you understand you've changed somebody's life, no gift you'll ever receive will stack up. Nothing can compare to what you feel the day you look someone in the eye and show them they were worth all your effort, that they were worthy of everything you could give."*

A UPS truck rumbled up. The driver put it in park right next to Butch's truck and hopped out, holding a package. "Butch Browning?"

"Yep," Butch said.

"Sign here."

The driver left, and Butch waved Ava over. "I need your help with something."

"What, Daddy? The nail gun?"

"*Nooo,* not the nail gun. Open this box."

Ava put it on the ground and stooped.

"Pull that tab there," Butch said.

She pulled it and tried to peer inside.

"What is it?"

Butch helped her pull out the tarp-like roll. It was heavy, so he helped her lift it. "Come on over here," he said, walking toward the house. "Boys, come here. We have a presentation to make!"

Ava gazed up at him. "A presentation?"

"Yep."

The guys followed them.

"Now, you stand here and hold it like this," he said, showing her, "and I'm going to walk over here and open it."

"Okay," Ava said.

Butch walked sideways, unrolling the material with the corners folded together. When he was four feet away, he let go of one of the corners. A sign fell open.

Still holding her corner, Ava stepped in front of the banner to get a good look. *This House Is Part of the Jenny Browning Project.* Her face was so bright with delight it was as if she'd been offered a year's supply of cotton candy. "Dad, it's perfect."

Butch smiled. "Okay. Let's get it hung."

Chapter 36
Charles

Charles checked his watch as he whipped into the driveway. It couldn't have been worse timing. Next door, the tow truck had arrived on the Anderson property, and the driver was climbing back into the cab. He started it up and began pulling down the drive, the sore sight creaking and groaning as it was dragged away.

Charles hurriedly exited his car, but again, the timing couldn't have been worse. Larry, trailed by his two boys, came running out of the house, chasing the truck and car down the street before giving up. Larry threw his hands up. Chip kicked his foot and hung his head.

Charles swallowed. He hadn't exactly agreed to the idea that it should be towed. Helen was the one who'd insisted on it. But he hadn't disagreed either. It was an awfully ugly thing, and who knew what crazy plan they had for it once they finished. Lawn ornament? Playhouse?

Grabbing his briefcase and a plastic shopping bag out of the car, he gave one more glance toward the Andersons and moved toward his house. Larry, though, called Charles's name. Larry was a guy who always smiled and waved. Tonight he was not smiling, nor was he waving. Charles wanted to bolt for the door, but that would definitely make him look even guiltier.

"Hi, um, Larry," Charles said with a brief wave. "Nice day. Real nice day. Well, better get inside."

"Hold up," Larry said. "Boys, go inside." Chip and Nathan skulked toward the front porch, throwing Charles a couple of nasty glances but not saying a word. Larry approached the fence between them.

Charles stood a good distance back. "What do you need?"

"I don't need anything, Charles. But why would you do a thing like that? Have our car towed?"

Charles sighed. He was caught. He dropped his briefcase to the ground and slowly walked to the fence. "I'm sorry, Larry. I really am. It was driving Helen up a wall. You know how she likes things neat and tidy. She'd get up every morning, stare

360

out the window, and it'd put her in a bad mood."

"I see," Larry said.

"Look, I didn't mind it. But it is in our HOA rules, you know. . . ."

"Okay. It's just that . . ." Larry looked at the empty spot in the driveway. The only thing left was a black oil stain. "We were having a lot of fun."

Charles nodded. "I have to admit, it looked like you were." He cleared his throat. "What's been going on over there, anyway? We've noticed a lot of activity. Even during the week. You get laid off?"

"Nah. Just taking some time off to spend with the kids. Nathan graduated. You know how it feels, with Madison graduating and off to college soon. Robin's getting married in a couple of weeks." Larry sighed, gazing up at the sky. "Man, time goes fast, doesn't it? I mean, it goes really fast. I can't believe they're moving out. I'm glad for all the time we had with them, but boy, do I wish I had more."

Charles looked at his feet. "Larry, we've been neighbors for years now. You're home almost every night for dinner."

"I guess. I tried. Maybe I should've stayed for breakfast, too, instead of running out the door, trying to get to work on time. I could've stayed up reading them a book instead of reading reports. I don't know — maybe I'm just realizing time is running out."

Charles nodded. "Me too, me too. I just got back from a business trip. Brought the kids some stuff."

"Oh. That's nice." Larry took a step away from the fence. "Better go. Listen, I won't tell Beth that Helen was the one who called. Scrapbooking is Beth's only activity during the week where she gets to go do something for herself. I'd hate for it to be awkward, because Beth can hold a grudge. See you later."

Charles watched Larry walk to his house. He checked his watch, a habit he couldn't break if someone held a gun to his head, and rushed inside.

Helen stood in the kitchen. "Hi, honey. Want me to heat some dinner up for you?"

"No thanks. Are the kids upstairs?"

"Yes, they're . . ."

Charles darted to the stairs.

"What's the hurry?" Helen called, but Charles didn't have time to explain.

Upstairs he noticed Cory's door open. He was in bed, reading a comic book. "Hey, buddy!"

Cory didn't glance up.

Charles pushed the door open and walked in. He sat on the edge of the bed, remembering the days when Cory wanted to be tucked in and sung to. Charles didn't have time for long bedtime routines back then. A kiss and a hug and that was it. Maybe a story if he didn't have to be at work too early.

Since the kite incident, Cory had been distant, though.

"Hey, listen, I wanted to —"

"I'm tired. I better get to bed."

"But I brought you something from my trip." Charles pulled a remote-control helicopter from the white sack. "It actually flies. You can even fly it indoors. It's so cool. I played with one at the store where I got it."

"Neat."

"It cost a hundred bucks or something."

"Thanks." Cory went back to reading his comic book.

"You don't seem very excited," Charles said.

"It's fine."

"Look, buddy, I'm sorry I couldn't make the kite-building night. Something really crazy came up at work. A guy authorized a deal that he shouldn't have, and it was a big mess."

"Okay."

"Didn't your mother explain all this?"

"Yes."

"I know it's hard for you to understand, but I've got some important opportunities coming up at work. Opportunities that a lot of guys only dream of. And if they come true, it could mean some amazing things for our family."

"What kinds of things?" Cory asked.

"I don't know, like maybe a house."

"We have a house."

"But a really cool house."

"I like our house."

"What about a pool?"

Cory shrugged. "It'd get boring swimming by myself."

It struck him then: Cory felt alone. How? With all the activities? All the opportunities they were giving their kids? He glanced around Cory's room at the souvenirs he'd brought back from business trips. There was an elephant carved out of ivory from Africa. A boomerang from Australia. A wooden train set from China. The list went on and on.

"Cory," Charles said, "I want to make sure you have a stable future. Do you understand? That you can go to any university you want. Those kinds of things. Give you a good, reliable car when you turn sixteen."

"Maybe we can get an old car and fix it up?" Cory's eyes brightened as he looked at Charles. "That would be fun, wouldn't it?"

Suddenly Helen was in the room, her arms crossed and her eyebrows raised high. "Cory, you're supposed to be studying for your spelling bee. You're not going to achieve anything with your nose stuck in those *stupid* comics."

Cory looked at Charles, who tried a faint smile, but Cory might not have even seen it. He tossed the comic aside and grabbed his sheet of spelling words off the bedside table. Helen left the room but Charles lingered, unsure what to say or do. Cory didn't bother acknowledging he was there.

Charles was still holding the helicopter. He had been so excited to give it to Cory. Just a couple of years ago, the smallest of gifts caused him such happiness. Now, it was as if this box were totally empty, totally void of any intent of kindness.

Charles gently set it on the edge of the bed and walked to the door.

"Dad?"

He turned. "Yes, Cory?"

"Maybe you can help me study my spelling words tonight?"

Charles smiled. "Sure, I would love to."

But at that moment his phone vibrated in his pocket, and he didn't have to look. It was a reminder that he had an international conference call in thirty minutes.

Cory's eyes shifted from Charles back to his paper. He knew what that sound meant.

"I'm sorry, buddy. Maybe next time."

"Shut the door on your way out."

Charles did, closing the door gently and standing in the hallway for a moment, still clutching the white shopping bag. "I'll make it up to you, buddy," he whispered. "I promise." He had to look at his schedule, clear a large frame of time. It had to be a priority. First thing in the morning when he got to the office. After the team meeting, anyway, but before his lunch with Don Willis.

Across the hall he heard Madison and Hannah in the bathroom, giggling the way girls do. He smiled, remembering the first time he heard Madison giggle. Helen had recorded it for him, and he'd watched it late one night. It was pure joy to hear a baby giggle. It was pure joy to hear them now.

He knocked on the door.

"Yes?"

"It's Dad."

The door opened. Hannah stood there with foam around her lips like a rabid dog, grinning like a Cheshire cat. She had a goofy side that Helen didn't approve of but that Charles thought she got from him, back in his younger years when he could afford to be goofy. Helen didn't really know that side of him, but he wished the girls did.

"Hey, Dad," they said in unison. Madison put her toothbrush away.

"Hey. Sorry I'm home so late."

"We had lasagna, your favorite," Hannah said. "Mom saved you some."

"Awesome. Listen, Madison, I got something for you."

"Me?" Madison slipped by Hannah and stood in the doorway. Hannah peeked over her shoulder. "Why?"

"I'm sorry, but I . . ." Charles looked at the carpet. Why was this so hard to say? "It turns out I have a business trip coming up and I might not be able to make it to your birthday party." He hoped the *might* could soften the blow, but he knew there was no *might.* His gaze lingered on Madison, who was nodding like she understood, smiling like it didn't bother her. He'd seen her do this a thousand times, but suddenly he knew she was faking it. There was pain in her eyes, and he'd never seen it before. Maybe he'd been too busy making excuses to see this for what it was.

Charles clutched the bag. "If I don't get back, we'll go out later. Okay? Just the two of us, maybe to that Thai place you like so much."

"Okay."

"So I thought I'd give you your present — one of your presents — now."

Used to be, when she was a little girl, she'd hop up and down at the sight of a sack, knowing there was something special for her inside. And he'd smile and tease her, pretending to take it out, but then teasing her again. She would almost faint with anticipation.

He reached inside the sack and pulled out an eight-by-ten head shot that he'd even found a frame for at the airport gift shop. He turned it toward his chest so she couldn't see it. "You know how I was in California? Well, while I was there, I met with a guy who knows someone you'd love to meet."

"Channing Tatum?" Madison asked, her face almost expressing some excitement.

"No," Charles said. "Not her."

"Him," Hannah said.

"Oh. Well, think singer."

"Taylor Swift?" Hannah asked.

"No . . . think singer/actress with her own TV show."

Both girls looked perplexed and Charles smiled. He turned the picture around. "Ashley Tarleton!"

Both girls stared at the picture.

"From your favorite show, *This Life of Mine.*"

Madison reached for it. Hannah, he noticed, had stepped back into the bathroom and was finishing her teeth.

"I had her sign it to you. Look, it says, *Madison, best wishes.*"

"Oh, wow! This is great!" She pulled the frame to her chest. "Thank you."

"You can show that off to all your friends," Charles said with a wink.

"Yeah. They'll be so jealous."

"I thought you'd like that."

"Well, good night, Dad. Thanks for the picture."

"You're welcome."

Madison shut the door to the bathroom, and Charles stood in the hallway smiling, glad that he'd gone to the extra trouble to get that arranged and signed. He turned and looked at Cory's door, then checked his watch. Maybe he could help Cory at least for a few minutes before the conference call.

He tapped lightly on the door and opened it when there was no answer.

Cory lay asleep on top of his covers, the

sheet of paper on his chest, still held by one of his hands. Charles sighed. Why couldn't he get the timing right with this kid? He walked in and took the spelling paper, laying it gently on the bedside table. He started to move Cory's legs to get him under his covers, but he was heavy. When had this kid gotten so heavy?

Cory rolled to his side and groaned, and Charles realized that short of waking him up, he couldn't get him under the covers. He grabbed a blanket folded at the end of the bed and pulled it to Cory's shoulders.

He clicked off the lamp and walked down the hallway. He had to get downstairs to his office for the call. But as he passed Madison and Hannah's room, he heard them giggling again. The door was cracked open and he could see them on Madison's bed, talking. He stopped to eavesdrop a little, to share in their joy and excitement. Maybe they were talking about where to hang the picture.

He put his ear closer to the crack.

"How long has it been since I liked Ashley Tarleton?" Madison laughed.

"I don't know. Like four years?" Hannah answered.

Charles turned to peer at them.

"Here," Hannah said, taking the lid off a

370

Sharpie. "Let me help it."

Charles watched through the small crack as Madison handed the picture over and Hannah scribbled something on the girl's face. He couldn't tell what, but they both laughed.

Charles walked down the rest of the hallway, descending the newly carpeted stairs, and went around the corner to his lavishly furnished office. He sat in his chair and turned his computer on, barely recognizing that he had only five minutes until his conference call.

Was he that bad of a parent? He'd been reduced to a permanent-marker joke. Tears stung his eyes and he blotted them with the back of his hand. He had to get himself together. He was an important man about to take an important call.

His cell phone dinged with a text message. It was his assistant, Mark.

Conference call canceled. They will reschedule. Family emergency.

For a long time, Charles sat in his leather chair, staring into the bleak and underlit office, wondering if he was in a family emergency. Wondering what kind of emergency it would take for him to cancel a phone call like this.

It was like he had blinked and Madison

was a young woman with Hannah not far behind. And Cory, well, he no longer fell for the gimmicks that had worked so well for all those years.

What was he to do now?

He trudged upstairs as slowly as he'd come down. He stopped and listened at Madison and Hannah's door, but it was quiet now and the door was shut. Reaching Cory's room, he nudged the door open. At some point he had awoken and moved beneath his covers.

Or perhaps, Charles thought, he was never really asleep in the first place.

He was not a crying man, but for the second time this evening he was on the verge of tears. There was a lump in his throat, a lump the size of a kite. He silently went to the bathroom, passing Helen, who was propped up in bed reading a book. He changed into the silk pajamas that Helen had already put out and pushed his feet into his slippers. He didn't bother brushing his teeth or taking his vitamins. He simply came to bed.

Helen glanced up. "What's wrong with you?"

"I missed it, didn't I?"

Helen went back to reading her book. "The present? Don't worry about it. Kids go through phases. It's hard to keep up with what they're into."

"I'm not talking about the present." Charles pulled the covers to his neck. "I'm talking about everything. I missed everything."

Helen removed her reading glasses and put her book on her lap. "What is that supposed to mean?"

"Our kids are . . ."

"Are what, Charles? They're fed. They're clothed. They've got more opportunity in front of them than any of our friends' kids. Look at Madison! Look at the scholarship she received! And it's not because I ran around our front yard throwing whipped cream in her face. It's because I made her study. She comes from hardworking parents." Helen crossed her arms. "I don't think these kids have any idea how hard we've worked for them."

Charles glanced at her. "And Hannah? Has that gotten any better?"

Helen sighed, sinking into the pillow behind her. "Besides being in danger of getting picked up by a metal detector, she just seems to be determined to make me feel bad, all the time. What does she want from me?" She sighed and slid her glasses back on. "Maybe it's a phase. I mean, Madison never acted like this, but then again, Madison was valedictorian."

"We can't compare our children. Hannah has always been more of a free spirit."

"Free spirit or not, things are expected of her in this family."

Charles slid down into the bed, now staring at the ceiling. "What if we failed, Helen? What if we've done everything wrong?"

Helen ripped back the covers and threw her glasses down. "Now you're being dramatic. Our kids have a perfectly good life. What more could they want?" She stood and grabbed her robe off the end of the bed.

"Where are you going?"

"Downstairs. I need some space. Some air. I'm not going to be made to feel guilty."

"Helen, wait. Maybe we should listen for once. Maybe we should think about how we're doing some things, make some adjustments."

"Like what, Charles? You deciding to come home in the middle of the day to play with the water hose?" She gripped the doorknob so hard her knuckles turned white. "Let me tell you something! I grew up wondering where my next meal might come from. Sometimes I didn't even get a meal. I certainly never got new clothes. Or lived in a house without a draft. They should be *thanking* us for what they have."

"But maybe that's the point. They have everything . . . but us."

Helen stood at the door, glaring at him, her chest heaving. Without another word, she turned and left. He heard her stomp all the way down the stairs.

Charles didn't move for a while. Then he sat on the edge of his bed and grabbed his cell phone. Maybe he couldn't make things right for his family, but tonight he could make things right for someone else's.

As he looked up the number, he heard the bedroom door creak open. He braced himself for a hard conversation. He was going to have that car towed back to the Andersons', no matter what Helen said.

"Look, Helen, I — Hannah, honey, what's going on?"

She stood biting her nail, grasping the doorframe with her other hand. In her pajamas, she looked small again. She'd always been petite, but right now she looked like the little girl he'd known her to be just a few months ago, it seemed.

She thrust her chin into the air and let her arms fall to her sides, but she looked no more confident than she had before. "I am here to tell you something."

"Okay. Do you want to sit down?"

"No."

Charles stood, his limbs shaking with sudden alarm. He was on the other side of the bed from her. It was a large gulf for two people trying to have a conversation, but he sensed he shouldn't move.

"What's on your mind?"

"First of all, I get Madison's gift, as a peace offering for potentially missing her birthday. Cory, though, gets a hundred-dollar helicopter?"

"I got that for Cory because we had this kite thing, and I —"

"I'm just here to tell you that I am not, and never will be, what you want me to be. I don't want to be that, okay? I'm glad you're an important man, but I don't want that. I'm not that person."

Charles took a small step around the bed. Hannah held out her hands, so he stopped. "Hannah, what person are you talking about? We just want the best for you, whatever that is. We're not telling you that you have to be this or that."

"I might want to be a barista. They're cool. They're around people, and I like people."

Charles swallowed. "Okay, well, we'd want a slightly higher goal, like perhaps owning a coffee shop or a chain of coffee . . ." His words trailed off into his own regret.

She folded her arms. "You just can't help it. You and Mom. Mom's the worst. The absolute worst."

"Hannah, she just wants the best for you."

"You want the best for *you.*"

Charles frowned. "Everything I do, I do for you. For your future."

"What if I don't have a future?"

"What is that supposed to mean?"

"Like Beth's sister. She's dead, so why am I planning on something I might not have?"

Charles was stunned. He hadn't realized Hannah even thought of Jenny. Helen had attended the funeral, but the kids stayed in school and Charles had to work. "You can't live like that, Hannah. You have to assume you have a future. You have to plan for it."

"Well, that's not me. I'm going to live day by day. I'm going to get up in the morning and just see what the day is about. That's what I'm going to do."

Charles sighed. "Okay. I mean, that's not how I tackle life, but . . ."

"Also," Hannah said, "I'm depressed."

"What?"

"Clinically."

"What are you talking about?"

"There's an app where you type in your medical symptoms, so . . ." She paused only

377

to take a deep breath. "You should do something about that. I probably need medication. We'll keep it on the down low. I don't want to embarrass the family. But I have nine out of the ten symptoms."

Charles couldn't think of a thing to say. Hannah wasn't depressed, was she? And by definition, weren't all fourteen-year-old girls depressed?

Hannah turned and left. Charles stood by the bed, a heavy numbness coursing through his body.

CHAPTER 37
BETH

Even before the sun rose, Beth was up. Not fixing breakfast. Not fretting over details. She only got up to pray. She sat on her back porch, at first in the cool, lingering shadows of the house, then in the warming light of the sun as it cleared the roof and spread over their almost-green grass. She didn't lament over the fertilizer they didn't get laid this year or the paint that was peeling from the deck railing.

From her porch, she had the perfect view of the Buckleys' backyard. It was meticulously manicured. The grass looked like velvet. The flowers were bright, like they'd been personally blessed by the sun. Luxurious porch furniture, complete with a wide umbrella, had taunted her for years. They even had a small toolshed, where they stored the lawn equipment that they never used because they had a professional do it. She'd always wanted a toolshed.

But today was about something different.

Beth took a deep breath, asking the Lord for strength. She hated how things were between Robin and her. But she also hated the idea of Robin being in a marriage she would soon regret. Marvin was charming, all right. That had been evident the first time they'd met him. But charm, she knew, only took a woman so far in marriage. Larry was the man she'd always known he would be, but Marvin . . . it was hard to see where his loyalty was really going to lie, considering his fond affection for all things pizza.

Robin didn't even like pizza until she got to high school.

Between the thoughts that rose and fell every few seconds, she asked God for help. She wasn't specific because by now she knew that her plans were not what was important. God's plan needed to prevail.

But the issue was clear. Insist Marvin wasn't right for Robin and risk pushing her away forever, or keep her mouth shut and watch her daughter make the worst mistake of her life.

After an hour, Beth went inside, unsure of the answer to her prayers. Sometimes, she knew, God said no. But what was He saying no to?

This nervous energy and many other

things prompted her to fix one of her world-class buffets, the kind of meal that stopped all the kids, Larry included, in their tracks. It had pancakes, eggs, waffles, crepes, and muffins. And of course, the all-star of the whole thing — bacon.

Finally Beth finished an hour's worth of cooking and baking, timing everything so that it all landed on the table at precisely 7:45 a.m., just as Larry was making his way down the stairs. Whether he went to work or not, he always woke at the same time.

Larry paused on the bottom step. Sniffed the air. Then looked toward the dining area. "Is that breakfast?"

Beth smiled. "It is."

"Is that bacon? The real kind? Not the turkey bacon?"

She nodded. Larry glanced at his watch.

"What's the matter?" she asked.

Larry looked conflicted. "Shoot. I was going to go look into metal detectors first thing this morning. . . ." He laughed. "What the hay! I'm going for it!" Larry sat down and dug in. "Maybe we shouldn't tell the kids," he joked.

Beth joined him at the table, bringing the syrup. "I was hoping we might have a meal together, you know? Dinner doesn't seem to be working out very much." Since the day they'd had Marvin over, they hadn't all been together for dinner a single time.

"Sure, yeah," he said, shoveling eggs onto his plate.

Chip and Nathan came down. "It *is* bacon!" Nathan said. "Told you!"

"What's the occasion?" Chip asked.

"Well, I know the car being towed was a big disappointment. Thought you could use some cheering up."

Nathan groaned and gave his father a desperate look. "Yeah. *Big* disappointment."

"My money is on Helen," Beth said, glaring out the window toward the Buckleys' house.

"That woman is where fun goes to die," Nathan said.

Beth cringed. Nathan had obviously picked up a few things from her over the past several weeks, not the least of which being a biting sarcasm against all things Helen.

"Look," Larry said, "let's not make assumptions. Besides, we'll find something else."

"Not like that," Chip said.

"We'll figure something out."

Beth joined them at the table. "Was, um, Robin awake?"

"Yeah," Chip said, grabbing more eggs.

382

"Hogging the bathroom as usual."

"Easy on the eggs," Beth said. "Leave some for Robin."

Beth had decided to just give her a clean start. Smile like nothing was wrong, and maybe when tempers cooled, they could talk. Of all her children, Chip was always the one who could move on quickly from things and not hold a grudge. Robin was more like Beth herself.

And she'd prayed this morning, prayed that things would be resolved and relationships would be mended. She'd prayed for God's favor and blessing on this day, for her and for her little girl who'd suddenly grown up — the girl who couldn't fall asleep for years unless she was kissed on the forehead by her mother before bed.

Then Robin was at the bottom of the stairs, gazing at them all.

"Hey, sweetie," Larry said. "Look at this breakfast your mom made. Chip, pass the syrup."

Robin walked slowly, looking it over, but then kept walking to the door.

Beth quickly rose from her seat. "You want some breakfast?" She didn't mean it to be so light and airy, but trying to take the strain out of her voice resulted in her sounding like she was delivering lines from a Disney musical.

"No time," Robin said, grabbing her keys from the cubby.

Beth rushed around the table. "How about some juice?"

"I gotta go."

"Pray with me?" Beth smiled, holding out her hand across the breakfast bar. There hadn't been a day of her little girl's life that she hadn't stopped to let her mother pray for her when asked.

Robin reached for the doorknob. "Got wedding stuff."

And then she was gone.

Beth rounded the kitchen bar and hurried to the door, but by the time she got there, all she could do was watch Robin back out of the driveway.

Soon, Larry was behind her. He smelled like bacon and syrup as he wrapped his arm around her shoulder. "It's going to be okay."

"Easy for you to say. You're the superhero this summer. I'm the Kryptonite."

He laughed and pecked her on the cheek. "Hey, ours isn't going great either. Our fun got towed off."

She looked at him and tried a smile so he wouldn't worry so much about her. She hadn't told a soul she was going to see a therapist, but she had another appointment later this morning — an appointment she would've gladly canceled had Robin asked for her help planning the wedding.

Larry turned her and gave her a hug. She let him hold her. She needed comfort from somewhere or something.

"Hey! Look at that!" Chip shouted.

They found Chip pointing out the front window. Nathan rose from his seat just as the clunker of a car was being towed toward their driveway.

"What is going on?" Larry asked nobody in particular as he let go of Beth and opened the front door. Chip followed him out. Nathan and Beth stepped outside and watched from the front porch. The car was backed into their driveway, a loud alarm sounding as a warning. A burly tow truck driver climbed out, clipboard in hand. Larry went to meet him on the front lawn.

"Here you are, sir. Got your car for you," the driver said, handing Larry the clipboard. "Just sign here."

"What? How?"

"You didn't ask for this?" the driver asked.

"No, uh . . ."

The driver took the clipboard back, scanning it quickly with his finger. "Let's see . . . I got a signature here. It's been paid for by a Charles Buckley."

"Charles Buckley?" Larry glanced at Beth, who glanced over at the Buckley house. All seemed quiet over there, but it usually did.

"Yep. You know him?" the driver asked.

"Our neighbor."

"Seems like a nice guy." He handed the clipboard back to Larry. "Just sign here."

As Larry signed, Nathan gave Beth a forlorn look. She smiled at him, and they had a funny, private moment where they both understood each other. Why couldn't it be this easy with Robin?

Chip and Larry hurried toward the garage, chatting about tools and parts and nothing Beth understood. Larry punched his hands in the air and waved at Nathan to join them.

Nathan stretched a smile across his face. "How long is Dad's vacation again?"

She swatted him on the back, and he hopped off the porch to join them in the garage.

Beth leaned against the post, gazing over the fence, realizing she'd just witnessed a minor miracle — the Buckleys showing some kindness and compassion. But she couldn't help wondering where her miracle was. Larry got all the breaks.

Beth, apparently, got the breakups.

She walked inside, grabbed her purse and car keys. The table, spread from one side to the other with food, sat empty. Nobody had even finished their meal.

When she came outside, Larry looked up. They'd already popped the hood. "Where you going?"

"Out. Just an errand. Milk. Butter."

"You're in your pajamas."

"These are sweats."

"You slept in them."

"I sleep in sweats sometimes."

Larry stood fully, facing her. "Your shirt says *good night* on it."

"I'll be back. Just out of stuff." She got in her car and backed up, waving enthusiastically and pitching her thumb up as she drove away. Honk, honk. Happy, happy. Fun, fun.

As soon as she got out of sight, she cried so hard she could barely see the road.

CHAPTER 38
BUTCH

Onstage, Ava sat properly, and Butch marveled at that because not once in their lives together had he ever shown her how to sit straight and cross her legs at the ankles. Her hands were folded gently on top of the purple flowered dress that she'd picked out in a frantic rush to the mall last night when she realized she had "nothing to wear for a spelling bee! I can't wear jeans! I can't wear shorts!" Butch had managed to calm them both down and get them to the mall fifteen minutes before it closed.

Jenny must've taught her how to sit. As he shifted in one of the uncomfortable plastic chairs set out for the parents, he wondered what kinds of things Ava would miss out on learning from him. It would never, ever have occurred to him to teach her the proper way to sit. It seemed that if she hadn't learned it before the age of eight, there would be no hope for her to learn it now. Maybe, he thought, he could ask Beth to help with those things. Beth, from all he could tell, was a great mom to her kids. They adored her, and if he had to admit it, that's all he wanted in life — for that little girl in the purple dress to adore him, even when he was old and worthless.

While Ava glanced away, waiting for her next turn, Butch sneaked a peek at his watch. The guys were probably wondering where he was. He hadn't figured a summer spelling bee at the library would be such a big event. He figured a few kids would show up, but he counted fifty to start with. Now they were down to three, including Beth's neighbor's kid, the one Tippy was supposed to go build a kite for.

"*Playful,*" the judge said.

"*P-l-a-y-f-u-l. Playful,*" Cory said.

The crowd clapped politely. Butch felt uncomfortable making any noise at all. It was the library spelling bee — there might be special rules in place.

The other girl stood and spelled *clever.*

This went on until Butch realized that Ava was one of the last two standing. The other was Cory. Butch glanced around to find the Buckleys. Helen wasn't hard to spot. She sat near the front, clapping what he could only assume was the correct clap for the circumstance as Cory neared the microphone. But the dad wasn't there.

Ava's face was hard and determined, and suddenly Butch realized how much this meant to her. His heart caught in his throat when he pictured her disappointment if she lost. He realized why she'd been working so hard and why the guys at the site had been helping her.

Cory clasped his hands behind his back. *"R-e-c-y-c-l-e. Recycle."*

"Correct," the judge said.

Ava walked to the microphone. Normally she was so sure of herself, but now she looked timid. She had to strain to put her mouth by the microphone.

"Preview," the judge said.

"Preview," Ava repeated. She took a deep breath. Then another. Her attention moved to the back of the room, and instantly she stood up straighter. She unclenched her fists. She even smiled. Butch wondered if she was imagining her mom back there. He was about to turn around to see what she was looking at when her gaze shifted to him. She smiled and blinked, and he held up his hand in a fist, showing her she could be strong. She nodded resolutely, and he was astounded at their moment. They'd had a moment. He knew she could do this.

"*P-r-e-v-i-e-w.* Preview."

"Correct."

Butch was about to mimic Helen's clap when all of a sudden a huge, rushing, boisterous wave of applause roared past him, causing everyone, including him, to turn around.

In the very back stood all his guys, covered in sawdust and dirt and still dripping sweat. They were clapping and cheering and chanting Ava's name like it was NASCAR. Butch grinned and turned back, joining their cheer, much to the surprise of the judges, the other parents, and most of all Helen.

Cory stepped up next.

"Invisible," the judge said.

Cory looked away from his mom toward the back, where the guys stood, seemingly wishful that he might get a whoop and a holler. But all was still and silent. His chest rose and fell, and behind him Ava bit her nails.

"Invisible. I-n . . ." He paused, doubting. *". . . v-i-s-i-b-l-e. Invisible."*

"Correct."

The room was silent but for airy clapping as Cory sat down. Butch kind of felt bad for the kid. Maybe somebody would whistle for him. But it stayed quiet.

Ava approached.

"Unbelievable," the judge said.

Butch watched panic seize Ava's small face. Her fingers twitched as they hung by her sides. She shifted her weight from one foot to the other.

Butch tried smiling and nodding in encouragement, trying to convey the message *Do your best* with the other message *It's not the end of the world if you lose.* He wasn't sure any of that was coming through, but Ava kept her eyes on him nevertheless.

"Unbelievable. U-n-b-e-l-i-e-v-e-a-b-l-e. Unbelievable."

Behind him, Ava's cheering section erupted in applause.

But the judge's voice reverberated over it all. *"In*correct."

The room settled into an awkward silence. Butch watched as Ava stepped away from the microphone and graciously smiled at Cory. She was such a class act, just like her mom.

The spelling bee ended with Cory accepting a large trophy.

Ava stepped offstage and ran to Butch. She gazed up at his face. Sure enough, her expression was filled with the kind of disappointment that he'd never wanted her to have to handle.

"You did great," Butch said, pulling her into a hug.

Soon the whole lot of guys had gathered around.

Ava looked at all of them. "I'm sorry. I feel like I let you guys down."

"Forget that!" Tippy said.

"You were amazing!" Eddie said.

Jack agreed. "Smarter than me, I'll tell you that."

Ava smiled, but her attention had drifted to Cory, who was onstage holding his trophy, smiling dutifully for the camera. "Look how big that trophy is," she said.

Butch knelt by her side and took her hand. "That big trophy would be very cool. I get that. But what matters to me is what kind of person you are, and you're an awesome person. The best I know. I'm proud to know you, and I'm really proud of you."

Across that tiny face spread the biggest smile he'd ever seen on a little girl.

Butch shook hands with the guys and thanked them for coming. "Take the rest of the day off," he told them.

They looked bewildered.

"Really?" Jack asked. "Time is money, you always say. We used our break to come, but we can get back pretty quickly."

"No. It's fine. I promise."

Ava grinned. "Told you he's a good boss," she said and high-fived them all.

Today he felt like a good boss. And a good dad, too.

Chapter 39
Beth

Dr. Reynolds smiled as he opened his office door. His mustache, as always, cleverly hid his real expression, but nevertheless it stared her down like a cat on a windowsill.

Very lightly and slowly, Beth sat on the couch. She didn't want to make any sudden moves or seem like she was capable of another episode.

"I brought you this," she said, handing him a yellow paper sack with tissue paper stuffed in the top.

"Oh . . . you didn't have to do that."

"I know. But I wanted you to remember me by something other than . . . the other day."

Dr. Reynolds pulled out the tissue paper and reached in, his hand emerging with a yellow mug. Its handle was a mustache. He laughed.

"Read the other side," Beth said.

He turned it around. " 'I mustache you a

question, but I'll shave it for later.' " He grinned. She could actually see his teeth. They were nice and white. "Clever." He stood and placed the mug on the shelf with all the others.

"I want you to remember me for that mug and not for a mug shot," she laughed.

Dr. Reynolds cleared his throat. "You're planning on going to jail for something?"

Beth sighed. "Sorry, poorly timed joke. No. I'm just . . . distraught."

"About your daughter. Robin, right?"

"She's going to marry this boy. In a matter of days. And now I wonder if she's doing it just to spite me."

"I learned something recently that I would like to share with you," Dr. Reynolds said.

"Sure."

"It's been hectic around here. Typically I have a nice flow of clients in and out, but lately I've had an influx of people, and many of them are having similar problems — parenting problems. An unlikely food source showed me something significant. You see, I was very stressed because I'd been focusing on my work so much and wondering if I could keep up the pace that I was suddenly thrown into. And then one night two clients brought hot wings during their session. Not for me. But it was a true gift. It made me realize something."

Beth was trying desperately to follow. Now that he mentioned it, she did think she could detect the faintest smell of hot sauce . . .

"I realized that I needed something outside work. Something to look forward to, if you will. Something that had nothing to do with anything or anyone here. So now I've decided that once a week I am going to treat myself to hot wings."

Beth nodded, trying to glean clues from his mustache. Was he saying she should start eating hot wings?

He smiled gently at her. "Let me put it another way. Sometimes we get absorbed in things, and it's hard for us to step back. And we can't help but be absorbed by our children. It's what we do. But as they grow and leave the nest, we have to realize that our lives can no longer be consumed by them. Your children are grown people now, and you have done all you can to help them make the right choices. Be assured they won't always. But in the meantime, as you begin to watch from a distance, find something to do with your life. Find something that's separate from your kids, a gift God has given you that you can enjoy using."

"I scrapbook. I have a whole group of

ladies I scrapbook with."

Something strange flickered across his face, but it was gone in a flash. "That's good. Definitely a start. But I imagine you're scrapbooking using pictures of your family. I'm talking something totally different."

"Hot wing different."

Dr. Reynolds chuckled. "I'm not advocating using food to replace your children. But for me, I realized that I don't take time for myself. So now I go have hot wings and watch sports once a week, and it's nice."

Beth looked at her hands, folded limply on her lap. That familiar sadness, the emptiness that ballooned in her heart, kept her from talking for what seemed like forever. Dr. Reynolds waited patiently, and finally she looked up.

"Every day, her whole life, I prayed for her before she left the house. For all my children. But I started the tradition with Robin. It seemed inadequate at times but always necessary. I guess I knew, deep down inside, that I couldn't be responsible for another human being all by myself. I knew I needed God's help. And He has helped us. He's been there in so many moments. But somehow, in all those prayers I tossed up in the morning — launched at Him, really, like my boys throw rolls across the table — I never imagined it would come to this. Robin marrying a man named Marvin who will probably never be able to fully support her."

"Does Robin want to be fully supported?"

Beth shrugged. "I guess I wanted a more secure future for her. There are enough troubles in life without having to worry so much about money."

"Securing futures causes half the trouble in our lives," Dr. Reynolds said with a smile.

Beth nodded, though she didn't want to believe it. "I think I've done some damage," she said quietly, "by pushing the idea that she wasn't ready for marriage because she couldn't make an omelet, when all along what I really wanted to say was that she wasn't ready for marriage, period. She's not. She hasn't lived. She doesn't know what's out there." She started to cry despite her best intentions not to. "What if she gets a divorce? What if she hates her marriage and is so miserable she can't even eat pizza anymore?"

Dr. Reynolds set his pad of paper aside and leaned forward. For the first time, Beth was drawn to his eyes, not his mustache.

"Beth, can I ask you a personal question?"

Beth clutched the pillow she'd grabbed

just moments before. "That's kind of your job, isn't it?"

"Yes. But it's a very personal question."

"Oh. Well, okay."

"What's the hardest thing you've ever been through?"

"This."

"No . . . this is not."

"Jenny dying."

"Look further back. What was the hardest time in your past? Something you didn't think you'd make it through?"

Beth sat there, twisting the edge of the pillow, trying to remember. When did she have time to think about her own life? She was too busy thinking about all of theirs, worrying about all of theirs.

"I . . . I don't know . . ."

"You've sort of lost yourself, haven't you?"

Beth nodded.

"But think about it. What was it?"

Beth took a long breath. Deep inside she knew. It had taken a piece of her. It was a part of her life that she couldn't shake. Not really. Not ever. "When Larry and I were first married, about six months into it, I got pregnant. At first I was devastated. I had plans for my life, and they didn't include getting pregnant that early. I was going for my real estate license, and I had to put that on hold."

Dr. Reynolds picked up his notebook again.

"That's not the hard part." Beth swiped her nose with her hand. "As the weeks passed and I could feel the baby growing in me, I got more and more excited. We started planning the nursery. I was buying maternity clothes. It was so fun and amazing."

Dr. Reynolds nodded, still taking notes.

"At five months, I began bleeding. By that evening — it was a Tuesday — I had miscarried. Our daughter was stillborn." Beth hardly realized it, but she was trembling as she thought of that day. They'd wrapped her baby up, bundled her just like she was a healthy, thriving newborn girl, and let Beth hold her for a little bit. She'd been beautiful. It was obvious she had Larry's nose and Beth's chin. A photographer came in and took pictures.

"That's a horrible thing to have to go through," Dr. Reynolds said. A moment settled between them. Beth didn't know what kind of moment, but it felt peaceful. Then he asked, "So what do you think that did for your life? What kind of mark did it leave, good or bad?"

Beth stopped twisting the pillow. She was going to twist the corner right off if she didn't stop. "About a year later, I got pregnant again. With Robin. And I was fearful, sure. But we made it through, and I remember thinking that I would never take for granted a single moment of motherhood. I really tried, you know? I was always thankful for my kids, even if I got sidetracked by unimportant things." Her eyes filled again. "I got so sidetracked . . . so often. Stupid things that I see now didn't matter."

Dr. Reynolds held up his hands. "Beth, I don't want you to go *there.*"

"Where?"

"To Guiltville."

"I practically vacation there."

"I noticed. What I want you to see is what kind of mother you became because of your hardest moment. You cherished your children. And that's what you have to believe for your own kids. They'll face tough times. Heartbreaking moments, sometimes due to their own decisions and sometimes due to someone else's bad decision. But you've told me you're a woman of faith, right?"

"Yes."

"Then remember what God did in you when you faced tragedy and difficulty, and trust He'll do that for your kids, too."

In her mind, Beth stepped away from the

room, into a memory. She saw a beach. She and Robin were walking on it. It had been one of the few vacations they took, years ago. Nathan was just a baby. Chip wasn't born yet.

Beth held Robin's hand, swinging and jumping and skipping. Laughing. The sun was setting, its warmth hitting their faces and its colors splaying out before them. It was bulbous and orange and easy to look at. The sand tickled the bottoms of their feet.

Then, in her imagination, it went from a memory to something else. Beth saw herself stop, her feet sinking into the sand. She let go of Robin's little hand and watched her continue to walk alone, her feet washed in the foamy water of the sea as the waves rolled in and out.

She looked so vulnerable, so tiny, by herself. Beth wanted to run and catch up with her, grab her hand, warn her about the riptides and the undertow and the sharks.

But as the water retreated into the sea, Beth noticed it. Another set of footprints walking alongside Robin, pressing into the sand, in unison with her short stride.

Beth smiled through her tears. Just like that famous poem said, she knew there would come a day when only one set of footprints would be in the sand. Robin would need to be carried through something. No one knew what, but she would need it. Just as Beth had been carried when she lost her baby. When she lost Jenny. Just as she was being carried now.

Before her, little Robin disappeared into the washed, hazy light of the day's end.

CHAPTER 40
LARRY

Larry gazed into the long mirror on the back of their bathroom door. Behind him, Beth smoothed her hand over his shoulders as he adjusted the jacket. He filled out this suit more than the last time he'd worn it. The buttons tugged against the holes that barely held them.

"I'm thankful I don't have to wear a tux, if I'm being honest," he said.

Beth shrugged. "I think you look handsome in a tux." She walked around him and straightened the tie he'd been fiddling with. "I can see you so clearly the day of our wedding."

"I bet I look just about the same, don't I?" he asked her with a wink. "Minus the thirty extra pounds and the gray."

"You look great, honey." She smiled at him, but in her eyes he could still sense sadness. He felt it too but didn't let himself go there. He couldn't. Today was a celebration, and dads were expected to celebrate. "I can't believe this day is already here."

"*You* look amazing," he said, twirling her around. "Prettier than the day we got married!"

"*Please,*" she sighed. "I don't even know what the mother of the groom is wearing. Maybe we should've invited them over for dinner. Why didn't I do that? I mean, I figured we'd meet them at the rehearsal dinner, but then there wasn't one. . . ." Beth looked at her feet. "I picked blue, you know, just because it's kind of neutral. But what if *she's* wearing blue?"

"I don't think anyone will care. Robin and Marvin don't seem to care either, so why should we?"

Beth sat on the end of the bed, shaking her head. "This morning I asked Robin what time she wanted me at the church and she looked shocked, like she hadn't thought about it. I'm not sure she even wants me there. Maybe I should just sit in the pew like everyone else."

"Beth, of course she wants you there. How could you think otherwise?"

"I know it seems . . ." Beth stared at the ground, her hands limply open in her lap. "I know it seems like I haven't come to terms with this. But I have. I really have."

Larry sat next to her on the bed. "I've accepted it. Last night I couldn't sleep. I went downstairs and got down on my knees in the middle of the living room floor, and I . . . I cried."

"Oh, sweetie." He pulled her into a hug.

"And I think all the tears were for . . . were . . . I realized all these years I've prayed and I've prayed and I've prayed, but I never really trusted. I never trusted God because sometimes — most of the time — it felt like I didn't have to. I had full control. They were under our roof. They were dependent on our money. The things that were hard in their lives, I could make easier by doing something special for them. I think at the end of the day I trusted in . . . me. And God's called me on it, you know? I'm spinning out of control because I trust in me: to be a good mom, to keep them safe and fed, to raise them as productive human beings. But you know what? It wasn't me. It wasn't ever me. They're the people they are because of God's grace in our lives. God's *mercy* in my life, to be the parent I was to them. If I did anything good at all, it was because of Him."

She took Larry's hand, held it tightly. "You're such a rock to our family, Larry. I'm sorry I've been such a basket case. I'm okay now. I don't know what's going to happen with Robin and Marvin, whether it's the worst idea for a marriage ever or what, but I'm letting go. I'm putting our baby girl right into God's hands." Beth made a motion like she was putting a little bird back in its nest. She smiled at him through tears. "You seem to be doing pretty good today."

Larry shrugged. "Nobody likes to see a big guy blubber at a wedding."

"Are we old enough to have a daughter getting married? I still feel twenty. Except when I get out of bed."

"Me too, except when I get off the couch. Luckily I don't do that much, so I usually feel pretty good."

Beth laughed and checked her watch. "Well, I still don't know what I should do."

"You should go. Be with her, Beth. I promise that's what she wants."

Beth nodded. "All right. I'll just try to push aside all my thoughts about what I imagined this day would be. I'll be honest — in my head it looked a lot like a Hallmark commercial. There was soft, glowy light, and everything was in slow motion."

Larry chuckled. "Come on, let's pray." Just as they grabbed hands, they heard the doorbell ring.

"You expecting anyone?" Larry asked.

"No."

They went downstairs, and Larry opened the door. Standing on the porch, with his hands in his pockets and his jeans dragging on the ground, was Marvin.

"Hi, um . . . hey. Larry and Beth. Can I . . . ?" He pointed beyond them. "In?"

Larry glanced at Beth, then back at Marvin, who didn't look so good. "Marvin, is everything okay?"

"Well, yes . . . I just need to . . ."

Larry and Beth stepped aside, mostly because the kid couldn't seem to finish a sentence and didn't look steady on his feet. He seemed pretty short on breath and courage, too. They trailed behind him to the dining room, where he sat down at the empty table. The house was so quiet. Robin was already at the church, getting ready with her bridesmaids. Nathan and Chip had gone to get haircuts before the wedding. Beth hadn't fixed a breakfast because nobody was going to be around.

"Marvin, what's wrong?" Larry asked.

He looked up from the table. "Nothing is wrong. I just feel like I need to tell you something. Confess . . . *Confess* isn't the right word."

Larry swallowed down the rising fear that was burning his esophagus.

409

"It's more like . . ."

Beth slipped out of her seat next to Larry and into the seat next to Marvin. She put her hand on his shoulder and said, "It's okay, Marvin. You can tell us anything. We're here for you."

That seemed to ease Marvin up a bit, but Larry still couldn't imagine what this was all about. What in the world could he be so upset about? On his wedding day? Larry remembered his own wedding day. He wasn't nervous about marrying Beth. He couldn't wait. It was just the ceremony of it all that made him cringe. But as far as he could tell, there was hardly any ceremony planned for this wedding.

"I don't really know where to start," Marvin said to Beth.

"Just from the beginning," she said.

"Okay. Well, I was born in Wichita, Kansas, to —"

"Maybe not that early." Larry smiled.

"Well, it has to do with that."

"Oh. Go ahead, sorry."

"I was born to Marvin and Janelle Rawlings. I was named after my biological dad."

Larry glanced at Beth. *Biological?*

"On my first birthday, they decided they didn't want me anymore. I spent twelve years in orphanages, boys' homes, and foster homes. I just wasn't the kid that — I never caught anyone's eye, I guess you could say. I wasn't cute or funny or, you know, the kind of kid you'd want to bring home."

Larry couldn't help it. He was stunned. He tried not to show it.

"Anyway, when I was thirteen, a couple came to the boys' home that I was living in at the time and said, 'We want to adopt the oldest kid here.' And that was me. So I went home with Mr. and Mrs. Hood. And, man, did I give them trouble at first. But they got me through all that, and then they became Mom and Pops Hood. The adoption officially went through when I was seventeen. And that's when I changed my name to Marvin Hood. I'm named after a man I'll never know, but I took the name of the man who taught me how to be one."

Larry noticed tears running down Beth's face. She didn't even swipe at them as she usually did. She was locked onto everything Marvin was saying.

Marvin picked at a fingernail, seemingly trying to compose himself, find the right words. "I know . . . I know I'm not every parent's dream for their daughter. I get that. And I'm sorry this wedding has been so . . . weird. It's my fault. Robin was trying to protect me. Sometimes I get embarrassed by who I am, who I was. I was abandoned, you know. And there's not really a lifetime long enough to get over the fact that you weren't liked well enough by your own parents for them to keep you. But Robin, when I met her, she didn't judge me. And she loved me, the way Mom and Pops loved me. She didn't care that I don't have much money and all that. She knew I love God like she loves God, and all the other stuff didn't seem to matter to her. But it mattered to me. I wanted to make a good impression." He looked up, first at Beth, then at Larry. "I wanted you to be happy for Robin. But I realized by trying to hide who I am, I was just . . . being disingenuous."

Larry looked down. Wow, he'd judged this kid hard. They both had.

"I know it must seem like a nightmare for your daughter to marry a pizza delivery boy. But Mom and Pops Hood, they own a little pizza place over on the east side, and my hope is that I can take over the business for them when they're ready to retire. They have four other grown kids of their own, and they've all got their careers. I'm the only one who has any interest in it." He laughed a little. "Because I like pizza so much, I guess. And because I'm proud to be a Hood."

Larry reached out his hand and shook Marvin's. "Marvin, I'm glad you told us. I wish we'd been . . . maybe been the kind of people who would've been easier to talk to. I'm sorry we weren't."

Beth put her head on Marvin's shoulder. "We love you, Marvin."

Marvin grinned. "And I want you both to know, I fully intend to take care of Robin in every way. Mom and Pop brought me up right. I know what is expected of me." He checked his watch. "I better get to the church." They all stood. "I'm really excited for you to meet Mom and Pops. Dan and Judy, I guess."

"So are we," Beth said, rubbing his shoulder.

Marvin turned straight to Beth, putting a hand on each of her shoulders. "Beth, I want you to know the kind of daughter you have. She knew that Mom and Pop don't have a lot of money, and she didn't want to burden them with traditional roles that come with traditional weddings, like the groom's family paying for the rehearsal dinner and all that. She decided we could do a lot of the wedding for pretty cheap. All she wanted was her perfect wedding dress. Everything else, she said, we could do on our own. But she knew I was . . ." His toe traced a line on the floor. "I was embarrassed, so that's why she's been acting so weird. She was just trying to protect me. But I realized it was hurting you, so I decided that I should come tell you the whole truth."

Beth, Larry knew, was going to have to redo her makeup. And Larry couldn't lie — this was more than a grown man could handle. He gave Marvin another firm handshake. "Welcome to the family."

"Thanks," Marvin said. "I'll see you in a couple of hours."

Marvin walked to his car. Larry and Beth stood on their porch and waved good-bye to him.

Larry whispered, "You've just had your Hallmark moment."

Beth turned to him, tears shining in her eyes. "You know what I just realized?"

"What?"

"Marvin is the answer to all my prayers for Robin, since the day she was born."

Chapter 41
Beth

Beth stood quietly in the corner of the Sunday school classroom, now transformed for the bridesmaids and the bride with a mirror, makeup table, and rack for clothes. The bridesmaids, two high school friends, rushed here and there, doing this and that. Framed by the mirror, Robin checked her dress and her hair and her dress again. The gown was gorgeous, a trumpet style with organza flowing down the back like a foamy waterfall. Beth would've never guessed a design like that would fit Robin well, but it was absolutely perfect.

Yet the truth was, even though she was present in the room, she still didn't know where she stood . . . therefore she didn't know where to stand. She didn't want to bother Robin now with what Marvin had told them, with a bunch of gushing apologies and all that.

Instead she found a memory of Robin trying on an evening gown from Beth's closet. She couldn't have been more than six. It hung off her like a sack, but there had been no doubt she felt beautiful in it. She twirled and danced, tripping over the fabric. Beth had a busy day, as she remembered it, but at Robin's request, she stopped everything she was doing and put some makeup on Robin and fixed her hair like a princess's.

Now here she was, all grown-up, a real princess, looking remarkably like Jenny did at that age. Across the room, Robin fiddled with her hair. Beth noticed she was smiling at all the right times, but something seemed to be bothering her. Should she go ask? She didn't know anymore. She didn't know a lot, truthfully. But she knew this — it was out of her hands now, fully and completely.

So she tried, just like Dr. Reynolds suggested, to live in this moment, taking in all the joy and fun of the day, even though she was essentially relegated to the sidelines, admittedly for good reason. All she could do was let go of Robin's hand and hope she didn't get washed away by the sea of life. No, not hope. *Trust.*

She took a deep breath, smiled, and watched. There would be time later to say she was sorry. Today was Robin's day, and she needed to let her have it. All of it.

Robin's friend Amy leaned over her from behind, looking into the mirror with her, and Beth tried not to feel the sting in her heart. In the Hallmark commercials, it was always the mom.

Robin pushed her bangs one way, then the other. "It's not working," she said. "I'm sorry, Amy. Where's my mom?"

At the word *mom,* Beth stood up straighter. She did a little wave from the corner.

"Mom, can you do my hair?"

Beth tried not to cross the room in a single bound. "Sure," she said as nonchalantly as possible, casting her purse to the side. She couldn't seem overeager. That's what had scared Robin away in the first place. That and a few other things.

Beth stepped behind her, and there they were in that mirror, both gazing at the prettiest girl Beth knew.

"Do it like you always used to," Robin said, talking with her hands. "How you'd twist it up and then the little pieces fell to the sides."

"Yep, I remember." She took her daughter's hair between her hands — it was thicker now that she was older. She hadn't put Robin's hair up for years. Beth twisted it and reached for some bobby pins, pushing them in this way or that, trying not to linger on Robin's expression, which was both tense and hopeful.

She got it just right . . . at least what she hoped was just right. She let go, and the curls fell delicately against Robin's cheek. Robin smiled warmly at Beth, at which point Beth probably would've burst into tears except there was a knock at the door.

"It's Marvin," came the muffled voice.

"Hang on," Robin said and slid off the stool on which she sat.

"What? He can't see you before the wedding." It was out of Beth's mouth before she even understood that this was yet another disapproving statement her daughter had to hear from her. She slapped her hand over her mouth. It was tradition, of course, the groom not seeing the bride. The most deeply rooted of traditions, dating back probably hundreds — or was it thousands? — of years, but who was she to argue with bucking tradition?

She'd turned to give Robin an apologetic expression when Robin said, "I've already got this worked out. Okay, girls, form the wall."

The bridesmaids, both of whom were almost six feet tall, stood shoulder to shoulder, creating a human wall. Robin stepped close to them. "Come in!"

Chewing on a fingernail to keep from speaking, Beth watched as the door opened. She could barely see the top of Marvin's head. She actually thought she got a whiff of cologne, not pepperoni.

"What is this? What are you doing?" Beth asked, wide-eyed with wonder.

"We're praying together. We do it every day. Can't very well miss this one. It's kind of important." Robin gave her a knowing smile.

Marvin poked his hand between the two bridesmaids and Robin took it. They bowed their heads. So did the bridesmaids. The only one who wasn't praying was Beth, who couldn't stop gawking. They had, she realized, an easy, comfortable, warm relationship.

"Dear God, thank You for such a wonderful day to have our wedding. Thank You for such a wonderful, godly man to start this new life with," Robin prayed.

Then Marvin said, "Help us to start this marriage off right. Give us a good wedding. And thanks for Robin. I really love her, and I can't believe You gave her to me. Amen."

Their hands slipped away from one another.

"See you up front," Robin said.

"See you up front."

Robin glanced at Beth as Marvin left the room. "Mom, what's wrong?"

"How did you . . . ?" She gestured to where they'd just prayed. "Where did you learn that?"

Robin looked confused. "From you, of course. I can't go a day without praying because you always prayed for us. And now I do it with Marvin, like you and Dad do." She faced the mirror. "My hair looks perfect. Thank you!"

Beth nodded, her throat swelling faster than she could talk. "I'm going to go put on some lipstick. I'll be right back."

A hand touched her shoulder as she turned. "Mom?"

"Yes?"

"I know this has been . . . a hard year. Aunt Jenny died. Nathan graduated. Now I'm getting married. But I want you to know you're not losing me. Not like you lost Jenny. You're gaining Marvin. He's going to be a great addition to the family."

Beth put a finger to her tingling nose. "I'm sorry about all of this. It seemed so sudden, and I was afraid that you were . . ." She shook her head. "It doesn't matter. I'm not afraid anymore."

"When Jenny died, I realized how quickly

life can be taken away, and I decided that I would live every day with purpose. Jenny told me once, when I was little, that I should try to live like every day was my last. I know marrying Marvin isn't the most cautious of decisions, but in my gut I know it's right. I know he's right." Robin pulled Beth into a hug, the kind of hug that made you realize your kid was in a more mature place than you were. She gently patted Beth's cheek. "You've been the best mom a girl could hope for." And then she turned to join her bridesmaids.

In the bathroom, Beth gazed into the mirror. It had a slight film over it, making the reflection foggy. Even with the blur, Beth knew it was going to take more than lipstick to fix this face. She started crying, but for the first time in a long time, they were tears of joy. By living her life fully every day, Jenny had reached into a future that wouldn't be her own and impacted a young woman who wasn't hers.

Beth knew that it was her turn to do the same, every single day, with her kids home or not.

She still had purpose on this earth. And it turned out she was a good mom too.

CHAPTER 42
DAPHNE

She was as uncomfortable as she could ever remember being. Her ribs felt like they were going to explode — actually burst out the sides of her body. Her bladder now had the capacity of a walnut. Her hips, for no reason she could identify, hurt. And there wasn't a single shoe in her closet that could make her ankles look human. She tried her best to sit erect in the metal-frame chair, but it creaked with the slightest of movements.

Robin and Marvin said their vows, and Daphne watched Beth, who seemed lighter and happier than she had in weeks. Beth dabbed her eyes and nodded with every proclamation of love and commitment the two made to each other. Daphne loved the sheer happiness of weddings, but she couldn't relax enough to enjoy this moment.

As soon as Marvin and Robin dashed down the aisle, Daphne dashed to the bathroom, which was at the end of a small, dark hallway, like it was some kind of shameful secret. She told Tippy to walk on over to the reception hall. She'd be fine.

But she didn't feel fine. She felt like a whale in a skirt. What she wouldn't give for her maternity sweats right now.

It took her so long in the bathroom that by the time she walked out, the crowd noise had died down and there was hardly a person in sight. A slight pain shooting through her side caused her to pause and grab the wall, and as she did, she thought she heard the faintest sound of weeping. She glanced around, but there was nobody in sight. Still, she heard crying. The boards creaked as she walked toward the sound. As she got closer, she noticed a shadow emerging from the corner, dark against the afternoon sun shimmering through the window.

She paused. Maybe she should just turn around. Someone was having a private moment. She should let them have it. But even as doubt filled her mind, she kept walking forward until the hallway turned. There, slumped against the wall, was a man with his face in his hands.

Daphne tried to step backward, but the floor creaked, and as the man looked up, Daphne recognized him.

"Oh, Larry, I'm sorry. I . . ." It was the

most awkward thing, to see a strong man crying, tears streaking weathered skin. But it would be more awkward to walk away at this point, she knew. "Are you, um, okay?"

He smiled, his bloodshot eyes squinty. "I'm okay. Just trying to . . . process my reality."

"Is something wrong? Should I go get Beth?"

Larry glanced at her belly, which she was holding with both hands like it needed help staying where it was. "I bet you're excited. Any day now, right?"

"Two more weeks."

"I can remember every detail of the day Robin was born. The first time I held her. I was terrified about being a father, and then she opened her eyes and looked at me . . ." He choked through a few words she couldn't understand. "The thing is, you think they're going to stay small forever, and then suddenly they're wearing lip gloss. You think they're going to stay young, and then they're driving. It just happens so fast. There are days you think the hardship of parenting will never be over, and then it is . . . and the next thing you know, God has put another man in charge of your little girl. I've lost my job today, in a sense. Maybe even to a better man." A tear dripped right over his cheek and onto his jacket.

Daphne didn't know what to say. "Larry, nobody can replace you as her daddy."

"Did you know that she always wanted to go camping with me? She begged and begged me to take her, but I had things to do, and you know, it sort of passes away without you even realizing it." He stood taller. "By the grace of God, she has turned out to be the kind of woman that any man would be lucky to have."

Daphne reached out to touch his shoulder. "You and Beth are amazing parents. Truly. If Tippy and I can do half the job you've done . . ." She looked down. "We can't even seem to get through the pregnancy. I don't know what we'll do when the baby gets here."

Larry wiped his eyes and stuffed his hands in his pockets. "You'll be amazed at what you're capable of when your baby arrives. It's like you get superpowers or something." He straightened his tie. "Listen, you go ahead. I'm fine. There's cake and punch and all that. Rumor has it there are pizza bites, too. You don't want to miss it."

Another pang shot through her, this time on the other side. She smiled through a grimace. "Okay, if you're sure."

"I gotta get myself together. Tippy and

425

Butch would never let me live this down. Our secret?"

She laughed. "Sure."

Daphne made her way out of the building and across the most challenging gravel drive of her life toward the building where the reception was being held. She walked in unnoticed — the attention was on the bride and groom, taking pictures by their cake. In the back of the room she spotted an empty table.

She tried not to groan as she lowered herself into the chair. Nobody wanted to hear a big, fat pregnant woman groan. But it seemed like it would make her feel better. Just one loud, long groan.

Shifting in yet another metal fold-out seat, she tried to distract herself by watching Robin and Marvin dance, but nothing was working. And it kind of made her sad that she and Tippy were long past the days when they gazed into each other's faces.

Tippy spotted her from across the room and wove around the tables toward her. "There you are."

"Babe?"

"Yeah?"

"I need some punch."

"Punch? You don't drink punch. It has red food dye in it."

"I just need some. Now."

"But the book says you shouldn't —"

"Let's just roll with it this once," she said, pressing her fingers into her temples.

"Oh, okay." Tippy wandered off just as Helen approached her table, dropping into a chair with a disapproving sigh.

"Can you believe it?" Helen's gaze darted over the crowd. "I assumed we'd find Beth in a heaping puddle of nerves and sorrow somewhere near the grocery store punch. But she seems fine."

Daphne tried a pleasant smile, but she didn't think it ultimately landed on her expression.

Helen was now staring at her ankles. "Sweetheart, your electrolytes must be off. Are you drinking enough liquids?"

Daphne tucked her ankles underneath her chair. "It's a balancing act because I have my bladder to consider."

"I see." Helen sighed loudly, which meant she was about to disapprove of something else. "This decor," she whispered. "I mean, Pizza Hut tablecloths. Sure, I think they were going for gingham, but with a groom's cake that looks like a giant supreme pizza, who isn't going to make the pizza chain association? Who *was* their wedding planner? And if you think about it, the groom's

427

mother's dress is the color of marinara sauce. Beth must be dying a thousand deaths."

Suddenly Helen looked startled, her gaze fixed on something across the room. "Is that Dr. . . . ?"

Daphne turned to see what was so atrocious. A small gasp escaped. It *was* Dr. Reynolds! Why was *he* here? Daphne shrank in her seat while simultaneously looking sideways at Helen. "Do you know him or something?"

Helen shook her head. "No. I've just seen his face on billboards around town. He's a horse whisperer or therapist or something." Helen fixed her attention on her punch.

"Oh . . . hmm." Daphne put a hand near her face, hoping he wouldn't recognize her. She'd gone to him once after Beth mentioned his name. He'd offered good counsel about trying not to stress. She hadn't exactly heeded his advice.

"Hey, Mom," Hannah, Helen's middle daughter, said as she came up to the table. "Can I — ?"

"Not now," Helen snapped. "Go play with the other kids."

"The kids? But I —"

"*Go,*" Helen said, and Hannah skulked away. "Just wait," Helen said as Daphne watched her. "The teenage years. Awful. You've given them everything in life, and they still hate your guts." Helen glanced toward Dr. Reynolds and smirked as she watched Beth talk to him.

Tippy, thankfully, returned with the punch. "Here you go."

"No."

"You said punch."

"No . . ."

"You didn't say punch?"

"Tippy?"

"I'm sorry. I thought you said punch."

"Something's happening."

Tippy turned to look out at the wedding party. "What?"

"To me. My . . ." She looked at Helen's face to confirm. Yep, something was happening, because Helen was choking herself with her pearls. ". . . water broke." And then, suddenly, Daphne couldn't breathe. Pain the likes of which she'd never felt gripped her belly as if it were in a vise.

"This isn't the plan. . . . This isn't supposed to happen for . . ." Each word was like pushing a beach ball through a keyhole. "Fourteen. More. Days." Why couldn't she breathe? "I'm not getting air!"

Tippy was both frozen and frantic. He started scratching his head, his fingers the only thing moving on his whole body. "Um . . . um . . . how many minutes apart are the contractions?"

"I don't know!"

"I'm supposed to get that information. You said to get that information!"

"I don't know!" She realized she was yelling because now everyone was staring. The only thing that could be heard was the slightest trickle of water down the side of the metal chair and Italian pizzeria music playing in the background.

"Okay, um . . ." Tippy reached into her large bag and pulled out a book. A small crowd had gathered, mostly those they knew. Beth and Larry rushed over. Butch and Ava too.

Daphne tried a small, appreciative smile even as she barked at Tippy, "Page 56!"

Tippy was flying through the pages. He stopped. "It says I've got to get you to the hospital!"

"What's going on?" Beth asked.

But Daphne couldn't speak. She couldn't breathe. The room was spinning. She'd been practicing and practicing the breathing. Why was nothing working right?

"I'm having the . . ." She could only point to her belly. "I wasn't expecting this tonight. It wasn't supposed to happen . . ."

Beth put a hand on her shoulder. "It's okay. Breathe. Breathe."

Larry had a hand on Tippy's shoulder. "Breathe, Tippy. Where are you parked?"

But Tippy was still flipping through the book. "Ice chips! I need ice chips!"

"Tippy," Beth said. "You don't have time. Go get the truck."

"The truck, the truck."

Larry said, "I'll go with him. Let's get Daphne to the door."

Beth and now Butch helped Daphne stand. In any other circumstance, it seemed she should be totally embarrassed that it looked as if she'd wet herself, but she didn't care at the moment. She had a baby to protect, and she couldn't let her come early. She was responsible now . . . completely responsible. Her chest seared with pain as she tried to breathe and grasp the magnitude of it all. Was she failing? Was this failing? She'd tried to do everything right. Eat all the right foods. Get all the right sleep.

Butch and Beth, with an arm around each of hers, slowly walked her to the back doors of the hall, Beth assuring her and reminding her to breathe, Butch supporting most of her weight.

"The book says . . ."

"Daphne, honey," Beth said as they stood

431

waiting for Tippy to bring the truck around, "books are great. Nothing wrong with books. But this is a human life, and both life and humanity are unpredictable. There are no guarantees, nothing beyond this time right now. All the books in the world won't help you live in the moment, so don't miss a second of it. You're going to be fine. God has a plan and a purpose for this little child, and He's letting you be a part of it, so don't worry. God is not surprised."

Daphne nodded, sweat trickling down her temple. Wow, it was hurting. That chapter on contractions was not doing this justice.

"Daphne?"

Daphne looked down and noticed Ava standing there. "Yes?"

"Remember what I told you?"

"Drawer handles are dangerous."

"The other thing. I told you that night before I left."

"To love my baby."

"Yes, that's it. Love your baby. That's what parents are supposed to do. My dad's really good at it. And my mom was too."

Daphne touched her bright-pink cheek. In the few years that God allowed Jenny to be in Ava's life, she'd done an amazing job with this little girl.

As she clung to Butch for support,

Daphne realized she would need to cling to Jesus just as tightly. There would be days of pain and sorrow and fear, just like now. She had no more control over this child's life than she had over this day.

Tippy hopped out of the truck. "Okay, let's get you in."

"Wait," Daphne said. Everyone froze. Daphne tried to talk through the pain. "Tippy, I need you to go get the book out of my bag."

"I have the book. It's in the truck."

"Not that book. The other book."

"You're going to have to be more —"

Robin suddenly ran outside, hiking her dress up with one hand and carrying Daphne's bag in the other. "You forgot this."

Daphne let go of Beth and took a moment to rummage around until she found what she was looking for. Her hand emerged with another book. She looked at Ava. "Your mom gave me this book."

"She did?"

"It's a prayer book, with all the prayers she prayed over you when you were little."

Ava looked up at Butch. "That's cool."

"Maybe after our baby is born, you can come over to my house, and I can show it to you."

"I would like that."

Another piercing pain shot through her belly and she winced. They helped her to the truck, where Larry opened the door and Butch boosted her into the seat. Tippy was soaked in sweat. She waved a thank-you, and Tippy tore out of the parking lot, tires squealing.

"Honey, you've got to calm down," Daphne said, touching his arm.

"But we're not on the plan. The plan!"

"The plan's out the window."

"It is?" She felt the truck slow a bit.

"Yes. We're getting ready to meet our little angel."

"Is that what we're naming her?"

"I'm speaking metaphorically."

"Oh. Because it could be a boy."

"Trust me — it's a girl."

Tippy gazed at her more than the road. "You're back," he said with a grin.

"Was I gone?"

"Kind of." He drove with fierce but cautious determination toward the hospital, smiling all the way.

CHAPTER 43
HELEN

On the drive home, Helen mentally went through the rest of her day. Madison's family birthday celebration had been pushed to this evening because of the wedding, and Charles was flying back from his trip. Cory had a mound of homework. She hoped he was getting it done. She still needed to go get the cake, maybe pick up another small gift. Helen turned off the radio that Hannah had turned on a few minutes ago. She couldn't stand the noise, and it wasn't helping to get that silly pizzeria music out of her head anyway.

"I was listening to that," Hannah said.

"My head," Helen groaned, rubbing her right temple. "There was so much wrong with that wedding, I don't know where to start."

"I met Marvin. He was nice."

Helen shrugged. "I suppose. It's just that it was campy, you know? Pizza cake. Pizza music. The tablecloths." She glanced at Hannah, touched her arm. "I promise you, sweetie, you will never have to have a wedding like that. Yours will be classy and beautiful and the envy of everyone there."

There was silence for a while. Helen was lost in her thoughts about what in the world she was going to say to Beth the next time they saw each other. Admittedly, Beth and Larry had looked very happy, but she was bound to ask what Helen thought, and Helen figured she'd see through any lie she would attempt to tell about how wonderful the wedding was.

"Mom?"

"What?"

When Hannah didn't answer, Helen glanced over to see what the delay was about. Hannah tended to get distracted, leading Helen to often wonder if she should get her tested for ADHD.

"Hannah?"

Tears fell down her daughter's face.

"Mom . . ." She wiped each eye with a hand. "I don't like life very much."

Helen gripped the steering wheel while trying to stay in the lines on the highway and look at her daughter. "Hannah, how can you say that? You have —"

"I know, I know," she said, nodding, her

chest hiccuping with one sob after another. "I have a lot. I know that. I really do know that."

Helen patted her shoulder. "Sweetheart, I think what we're dealing with here are hormones. It happens at your age. Sometimes you start crying and you don't know why."

"It's not that."

"I know it seems that it's not, but it is."

"No. I'm sad."

"Why on earth are you sad?"

"Because, Mom, I don't fit in anywhere. But I especially don't fit in with this family."

Helen's foot slipped off the accelerator, and the car slowed. Semis zoomed by her, shaking the car. She quickly accelerated, trying to stay with traffic.

"How can you say that?"

"Because I see it. I mean, I have to go to pageant classes so I can fit in better with us."

Helen drew a deep breath. "I enrolled you in pageant classes because you're beautiful. When you were little, people would stop and gawk and tell me how pretty you were. It happened all the time. Every time we went out in public. You had this snow-white hair and those big eyes."

Hannah was staring at her kneecaps. "Yeah, well, that was then. Nobody thinks I'm pretty anymore."

Helen could hardly keep her eyes on the road. "Hannah, what are you talking about?"

"Guys don't even look at me. It's like I'm invisible. Like I'm not even standing there."

"Sweetie, you're just being self-conscious."

"When you and I go to the mall, guys my age are . . . looking at you."

Helen couldn't help the gasp that escaped. She was now in a full-blown stare at her daughter. Hannah wiped her eyes over and over. Helen couldn't get a single word to come out of her mouth.

"And even with these pageant classes and stuff, I just can't . . . I can't be like you. I don't look that good. I never will. I mean, I'm not pretty like you and like Madison. I'm just sort of plain, you know? And Sasha says that's okay, that it's more about who I am, not what I look like."

Helen couldn't even process what she was hearing. How could Hannah think that about herself? Of all her children, she'd always thought Hannah was the most naturally beautiful.

Without warning, Helen jerked the car to the right and flew down an exit ramp.

Hannah held on, glancing at her mom. "What are you doing? This isn't our exit."

The tires squealed as Helen turned in at the parking lot of a closed bank. Hers was the only car there, but she pulled fully into a parking space and shut off the car. Hannah's eyes were wide, and her back was pressed against the passenger-side door.

"Hannah Lauraine, you listen to me right now."

"I'm sorry, Mama. That's just how I feel."

"You are the most beautiful, most amazing person."

Hannah paused. "Huh?"

"I mean that. You're stunning. In every way. In your heart. In your mind, the way you think. Your ideas are creative. Your eyes are mesmerizing."

"They are?" Hannah said as tears streamed from them.

"Yes! Yes. You belong in those pageants. I think you could win Miss America someday."

Hannah looked down. "I hate that stuff. I hate wearing dresses and tiaras and, like, making little speeches."

"But you're so good at it. . . ."

"Not really." She wiped her nose with the back of her hand. "But I'm glad you think I am. I thought you were trying to . . . I just thought I . . ."

"What?"

"I've been feeling bad because I realized that no matter what, I would never be . . ." She looked at Helen. "As good as you."

Helen stared out the front window. "As good as me?"

"You and Dad, you guys are like really important. I mean, look at you . . ." Hannah gestured toward Helen.

A thousand things tumbled through Helen's mind, a thousand things she wanted to say, but she realized at this very moment she had to make whatever words came out of her mouth count. She might not have this time again. It was now that mattered. In the leather bucket seat next to her, Helen saw herself, many years ago. And she wondered, what would she say to herself then, to help her now? What had Helen needed to hear that her mother never said? What did Hannah need to hear that would change the course of her life?

"Hannah," she said carefully, slowly. "I dress this way because . . . because I'm not important." She felt physical pain just saying it, but it was the truth.

"What?"

"I'm not. I'm nothing special, and so I dress very nicely to make people think that

440

I am important. I dress like this because I'm insecure. I don't go out without makeup because I'm afraid people will . . . well, they'll see the real me."

"The real you?" Hannah asked.

Helen let go of the steering wheel and glanced away from her daughter, hardly believing she was about to speak of days long ago that she'd sworn she wouldn't mention again. "When I was your age, a little younger, I guess, I sometimes had to wear the same outfit three times in a week. Sometimes I didn't take baths because we couldn't afford to heat the water in our home and it was too cold. My hair was always —" she touched it, remembering the feel of grease — "very oily. It sort of shined, and I couldn't do anything about it."

"I . . . I knew you didn't have much money when you were growing up, but I didn't, like, realize . . ."

"I managed my way into the world, got a job, got some college education, and met your dad, and well, the rest is history, I guess." Helen felt heavy tears sitting at the edges of her eyes. "I was embarrassed a lot when I was a kid. I never knew manners or poise or social skills, so I was always doing the wrong thing and being corrected. Being told over and over to sit up straight and not smack and those sorts of things. It was humiliating, and I never wanted any of my kids to be . . . humiliated."

"Mom . . . I'm sorry. I didn't know."

"Of course you didn't know. How could you? I never told you. And now, with all my good intentions, I've hurt you." Helen reached for Hannah's hand, and for once Hannah let her grab it. "I think sometimes parents hurt their kids the most when they're trying to keep them from getting hurt. We make a lot of decisions, say a lot of things, because we remember a hurt in our own life and we don't want to . . ." Helen shook her head, engulfed in her regrets. She held Hannah's hand against her heart. "And we end up hurting you more."

"It's okay, Mom."

"No. No, it's not okay." Helen put a hand over her mouth because sobs were about to escape. But then she decided to let them. "I'm sorry I've hurt you, Hannah."

Hannah reached over the console between them and pulled her mom into a hug. "I thought I wouldn't ever, like, be able to live up to you. But now I hope that someday I do."

Helen let go of her a little, pushing the hair out of Hannah's eyes and wiping the tears from her cheeks. "What a brave thing you've done today."

"Brave?" Hannah asked.

"I am not the easiest woman to talk to, am I?"

Hannah shrugged. "I guess not."

"But you did it anyway. You have many qualities, but above all you are courageous."

Hannah pulled her back into a hug. "Maybe sometime you can tell me about your life when you were a kid."

"That would be fine."

"I love you, Mom."

Helen pulled her tighter. Children, she suddenly understood, had an enormous capacity for forgiveness and mercy.

"I love you too," she whispered.

CHAPTER 44
CHARLES

At the Denver airport, Charles Buckley sat by a cold window, though it was warm outside. The dark night, inky and void of much more than man-made lights glowing along distant runways, swallowed the gloss of all its reflections. Voices crackled over the intercoms, but he hardly heard them. What he needed to know he already knew.

He thought he'd planned it so well, to come to the meeting and fly home early. He could get there in time for the party if Helen waited until seven.

Charles had not counted on this thunderstorm. It wasn't in any weather report he saw.

He watched for a moment, but not the business travelers or the pilots walking by, pulling their luggage and trying to make it to their destinations. No, he watched the families. A mother sat nearby, holding an infant while helping a toddler draw with crayons. Across from her a dad sat talking with his son, both of them looking at an iPad and laughing.

Near them was an old man, hunched over a cane and wearing a cardigan with as many holes as buttons. He stood with great effort, wobbly in every way imaginable.

Soon, sliding up beside him was a woman, lovely and gentle, taking his elbow and steadying him. "Dad, what are you doing? I told you I would bring you a coffee."

"Did you? I'm sorry. I thought I was supposed to go get it."

"You —" she grinned, helping him back to his seat — "are supposed to sit and relax."

"You're too kind," he said, smiling at her. "Thank you."

"Are you hungry? Do you want something to eat?"

"Those cinnamon rolls smell good."

"Your doctor says no sugar."

"What do doctors know? Please?"

She laughed. "Well, you are ninety-one. I guess you've done pretty well, haven't you?"

He nodded eagerly.

"Okay, I'll go get it."

"I love you, Denise."

"Love you too, Daddy."

Charles watched her walk away and then checked his watch. He loathed this watch now, the one he'd checked impatiently over the years, certain that it would give him all the time he wanted, eager and greedy for it, not realizing that it was a taker, too.

Slowly he slid his cell phone out of the front pocket of his blazer. He pushed speed dial, and Helen answered. "Where are you, honey? I've put off the candle lighting as long as possible."

"Let me talk to Madison."

"Well, hurry up, okay?" Helen said, and he could hear her call Madison's name.

Then she was on the phone. "Hello?"

"It's Dad."

"Hi. Where are you? We're starving for this cake!"

The words were harder than he'd imagined. "I'm not going to make it."

"But . . . but you said you would." And he had. He'd arranged to leave the meeting early so he could get home in time for cake.

"There was this storm that came into Denver, and I'm stuck at the . . ." The words didn't matter. They both knew it. Words, Charles realized, mattered not at all. "I'm sorry."

"It's fine. I gotta go."

"Madison, wait."

"What?"

"Tell Mom I said to give you a hundred

— no, two hundred bucks. That's for missing your birthday, okay? I'll take you shopping when I get home, and we'll spend it on
whatever you want."

"Okay. Bye, Dad."

"Bye, Madison. And happy eighteenth
birthday."

But she was already gone.

CHAPTER 45
DAPHNE

Daphne reached out for Tippy's hand. Sweat streamed down her temples and puddled in the hollow of her neck. In a few seconds, the pain would return with a vengeance.

"I'm here, baby. I'm here." Tippy sat on a stool right by her bed, brushing the hair out of her face, unconcerned with the sweaty mess she'd become in the last twelve hours. "What can I get you?"

"A baby out of my body." She smiled weakly at him, but her heart was filled with love, even through the pain. Here he was, right by her side. He hadn't left for even a second since they arrived.

The baby had not come as they had expected — quickly, easily. At midnight Daphne's blood pressure had dropped. Doctors and nurses buzzed around her as she passed in and out of consciousness. Once they got her pressure back up, the doctor said a C-section might be in order, but Daphne begged to do it only if absolutely necessary.

She rolled her head to the side and looked at Tippy. "Why didn't I do the epidural?"

"Because you read that book."

"Yeah . . ." She sighed, then took a deep breath and exhaled, ready for the next round of contractions. A nurse was by her side, and then the doctor came in to check her. Dr. Petree had been in and out of the room no less than ten times, and it was always the same — not yet.

He checked her once again, but this time he beckoned the nurse over, leaned into her and said something, then looked at Daphne. "It's time."

"Push?" she asked, her voice frail and reedy.

"Yes."

Daphne gripped Tippy's hand and pulled herself up. She'd been to three different classes and had read all the books, but she couldn't have imagined all of this in her wildest dreams. It was so painful, yet she felt a strength in her that she couldn't explain.

"Push!" the doctor urged.

She thought she was. "I'm trying," she said, looking tearfully at Tippy.

"You're doing great. Keep going," he said.

"Push harder," the doctor said.

Daphne clenched her teeth, and that long groan that had been waiting to be released finally made its way out.

"Harder, Daphne."

"I'm pushing! I'm pushing!" Tears or sweat — she couldn't tell which — rolled down her face. Every limb on her body shook, almost to the point of a convulsion.

And then a cry. The tiniest, weakest of cries, otherworldly and vulnerable. Daphne couldn't see anything, but Tippy's face said it all. The baby was here. He wiped rare tears off his face, the only time he let go of her hand.

"It's a boy!" the doctor said.

Tippy broke down, covering his face, and Daphne was so moved she couldn't speak. She watched as the umbilical cord was cut. She was just getting quick glimpses of the baby as he was cleaned and wrapped. Then the nurse brought the little bundle to Daphne and placed him in her arms. Tippy leaned in and hovered over them, and it was the most comforting of moments — their family together in one small space.

"He's so pretty," Tippy said, his voice cracking. "Can I say that about a boy?"

"Look, he has your nose!" Daphne

touched the baby's cheek and he stopped crying, his wide eyes searching like he recognized them, their voices, their touch. "He knows us, Tippy. I can't believe . . . I have a son."

"That's your mama holding you." Tippy's voice was so soft, so sweet. She had never heard him speak with such kindness and gentleness. "I'm your daddy. We're going to take care of you. You have nothing to worry about."

Daphne pulled her son closer, stroking the top of his head. *Worry.* It was all she'd done over the past nine months — worried about everything that might go wrong, planned for all the scenarios that she might encounter. Yet with his — *his* — arrival, there also came a sense of peace, and it wasn't from the books or the classes or the advice she'd sought from every source she could find.

Oddly, the peace came with the sense that the task before her — motherhood — was too big and daunting to do alone. Or even with Tippy — they weren't fully equipped to do all that was before them.

Daphne reached up and touched Tippy's face.

He smiled and took her hand. "We should name him."

Daphne nodded. "But first, we have to

give him away."

Tippy frowned. "Not following."

"To God. We have to give him back to God. Our baby is His, after all, when it comes down to it. He knows him top to bottom, inside and out, and already . . ." Her voice cracked. "He knows the number of his days and the journey that is set out for him. We have to trust Him because we can't do this by ourselves."

Tippy stood upright and looked at the ceiling for a brief moment. Then he placed his strong hand over his son's little head, and before he even had a name, he had a purpose and an identity and an everlasting hope that only came from above.

CHAPTER 46
CHARLES

It was 4:49 a.m. and Charles sat alone in his office without a single lamp on. Sometimes when he was a child, he'd sat in the darkness after he'd done something wrong, as if he could hide from himself. But even now, as he attempted to do the same thing, he knew the soul could fool itself but it couldn't hide.

He thought of Franklin Hollingsworth and wondered now if he, too, had sat alone in his office and realized what time had stolen. How could he not have seen what a thief time was? How, as a grown man, had he not understood that he was now reaping what he'd sown?

Just outside his office on the kitchen table sat a single piece of birthday cake, saved, he presumed, for him. Around it lay eighteen candles, their wicks burned to ashes, their lights blown out, never to be lit again. What did the birthday cake mean if he was not part of the celebration?

He slid his phone out of his pocket and easily found the contact he needed. It was at the top of his list of "important" people. As it rang in his ear, he slumped at his desk, weary from travel and life and regret.

A groggy voice answered the phone. "What is it?"

"Randall, it's Charles."

"Did something happen?" Covers rustled in the background. His voice became more alert. "You said everything went as planned."

"Listen, Randall, what I'm about to tell you is going to make no sense to you, but . . ." He turned toward the window of his office, though it was black outside and he could only see the faintest reflection of himself from a small night-light on the wall. "I'm resigning."

"What?"

"I've got to make some changes. Time is running out."

"What are you talking about?"

"It's one of those things you learn after it might be too late. I hope it's not. But it might be."

"I don't understand. Have you been drinking? I haven't known you to drink, but I know the last couple of weeks have been stressful."

"My resignation is effective immediately. I really appreciate all the opportunities you've given me, Randall."

Charles ended the call, holding the phone to his heart and realizing a heavy weight that he had dragged behind him for years was cut loose, the chains no longer rattling behind him.

Suddenly a light clicked on. Helen stood in her nightgown at the door, her eyes wide in a way that made Charles understand she'd been there a long time.

"Charles," she whispered, not like it was the middle of the night, but like it was shameful. "What have you done?"

"I've done what I needed to do." He rose from his desk and walked toward her. "I've been all over the world and met powerful people and made good money. I know I have the potential to make much more money. But what good is it all if my kids hate me in the end? If they're left to navigate this whole world by themselves?"

The blood had drained from her face. "They're . . . they're kids, Charles. They don't know what's good for them."

"But I do." He took her hands. They were frigid, as usual. "I thought I was doing what was right for our family, but I now see. I see, Helen."

"But how will we . . . ?"

He smiled a little. He didn't know the how-will-we. He just knew the why. He figured the how would work itself out. "I'll get another job, a job that fits us well in the ways we need it to."

Helen stood still for a long time, glancing distantly behind him at nothing but doubt. Then she reached for him in a way she had not in many years. She held his arm, and her eyes shone with a strange, soft resilience that he wasn't sure he'd ever seen.

She dipped her hand into the pocket of her nightgown and pulled out the string of pearls she wore almost constantly. She opened his hand up, put them in, and closed his fingers around them.

"My mother, as you know, gave me these pearls."

"Yes."

"She had received a small inheritance from an uncle. She barely made ends meet, even at the end of her life, but she bought these for me."

"It was such a kind thing for her to do."

"It was less sentiment," Helen said, "and more like insurance. She told me if I was ever destitute, to sell them for food or whatever I needed." Her hand was warming on top of his. "And I've worn them around my neck ever since, as a reminder of a place I never wanted to return to." She looked down. "But even with all this around us, I feel destitute. I have for a long time. I didn't understand why. I thought I needed more . . . more assurance that we'd be okay. But we're not okay. Not at all, are we?"

"We've sown into the wrong garden, I believe."

She touched his face. "I believe so." Then she stepped away from him. "Tomorrow I will get up and fix us pancakes, and you can make your announcement to the children, and we can . . . celebrate." She smiled at him, more genuinely than he'd ever known her to smile, and moved into the darkness of the hallway and out of sight.

CHAPTER 47
BUTCH

Butch stood on the front lawn of newly laid sod, marveling that a house could be built on such short notice and that people who didn't even know Keith and Bryn would donate their time and money and resources to build it. But here it was, humble and unassuming but standing and sturdy and built with the kind of sustaining materials you couldn't find at a home improvement store.

As Ava led Keith and Bryn from behind a building, blindfolded, and as the crowd gathered for the big unveiling, Butch prayed despite himself. He suddenly understood all that Jenny had been trying to tell him, all the urgings she'd given for him to step outside himself and find a cause worth fighting for. He'd fought for his family, sure, to keep them fed and sheltered. But he understood now what she meant, that there was life even beyond a family — that humanity was in need and they were his family too, and he should do what he could to help them.

Even as he stood there, he began to appreciate what God had sown into his life despite the tragedy and loss he'd endured. He saw a bigger picture. For much of his life, he'd only seen the two-by-fours and the nails and the sawdust and the concrete. He'd never stopped to step back and see the house — God's house — that served a bigger purpose and sheltered a lot of souls.

The crowd of about fifty began cheering, and Butch turned to see Ava leading Keith and Bryn, still blindfolded, to the center of the street. Both were laughing and holding on to each other. Of course, they already knew what the house looked like, but Butch and his helpers had managed to put some last-minute landscaping in, and some people from the church had donated furniture and decor. They'd even stocked the refrigerator with food.

Butch remembered when he brought Jenny by the small but cozy home he'd found right after they were married. They'd rented an apartment and planned to stay awhile, but Butch saw a home on an auction list and thought they could afford it. He picked her up from work, blindfolded her, and brought her to the house. She joked all the way there that people were going to think she was being kidnapped. He led her carefully to the front lawn and removed the blindfold.

To this day, he could still see the look on her face. It was like first love. Her eyes had tried to take it all in at once. Her hands grasped him, and her laugh was filled with delight.

"Really?" she'd asked him.

"Yeah. We need a place to build our lives."

Jenny had started crying.

"Bring the bus!"

Butch blinked at the sound of Tippy's voice, instructing the volunteers to bring the butcher paper. Everyone laughed as they unrolled it. The crowd's view was now blocked by a large crayon drawing of a bus. Ava went to Keith and Bryn and removed their blindfolds.

Tippy smiled at Keith and said, "Sorry. Couldn't get a real bus." Then he turned to the crowd and, like a conductor, led them in a roar of voices.

"Move. That. Picture of a bus!"

The crowd went wild, and Keith and Bryn laughed and clapped as they walked toward the house. Bryn ran inside, but Keith stopped by Butch's side and shook his hand.

"I don't know how I'll ever be able to thank you enough."

Butch looked at the house so he didn't have to see the emotion in Keith's face. These days, he knew, he could cry at the drop of a hat — for all the right reasons. "You're welcome. You know, my wife used to tell me that any one of us could find ourselves homeless or in need at any time in our lives, that it just takes one bad thing happening." He looked at his shoes now, trying to get out all the words he wanted to say. "If I'd died instead of Jenny . . ." He looked over at Ava, who was chatting with Daphne and Tippy and admiring their new baby, Quinton Marshal. "I'd just . . . I'd want someone to help them. My wife always told me that sometimes we humans have to suffer ourselves before we find compassion to help others."

Keith slapped him on the back. "Well, I promise to pay it forward as much as I can."

"Go! Enjoy!" Butch said. "Just make sure you're at work on Monday."

Keith laughed and ran inside to join Bryn. The crowd started to disperse, but Tippy was waving the hand that wasn't holding his son.

"Okay, everyone! Hang on, hang on. Don't leave yet. I have another presentation." The crowd quieted down at Tippy's voice. "For the one who made this happen, we have a little something. Ava Browning, why don't you step over here."

Ava smiled, looking at Butch, who could only shrug. He had no idea what was going on.

Ava stood proudly next to Tippy, and Tippy, bouncing the baby in one arm, waved to the crew of guys Butch worked with — a crew he respected more than ever for what they'd done for a dad and his little girl . . . and he wasn't referring to Keith and Bryn.

The guys walked over, carrying something draped with a tarp. It was huge and seemed difficult to carry. Was it a bench?

They set it upright, still covered. Ava looked like she was about to burst with anticipation. Tippy grabbed the tarp and, with the flair of a stage performer, ripped it off to reveal . . . the biggest wooden trophy Butch had ever seen.

"Dad! Look!" Ava was jumping up and down, and even jumping, she wasn't as tall as the trophy. She gazed up at it, truly stunned. And now he knew there was no way to stop the tears. He was overwhelmed with gratitude and joy, and to see Ava smile like that — the pure delight in her face — it was just like the day he'd brought Jenny to the house.

Tippy handed Quinton to Daphne and walked over to Butch, hands in his pockets. "Choked up with pride?"

"Yeah." Butch nodded, trying to swallow his emotions. "And regret."

"Regret?"

Butch looked at his daughter, who was hugging the trophy now while the guys laughed. "For wasting the last eight years when I could've been getting to know the best person I've ever met."

"Well, man, you're the best person I've ever met, and if I'm half the dad you are, I think I'm going to do pretty good."

"You're already a pro."

"Won't lie to you. The diapers are challenging."

"Wait till you have to eat creamed peas and pretend they're good." He spotted Beth nearby, watching all the activity. "Excuse me. I gotta go talk to someone."

Beth smiled through tears as he approached. "Butch, Jenny would be so proud. Of you and Ava." She smiled through tears.

"I wish I could've been better when she was here."

"She would tell you not to look back, to just be here. Now. Cherish this moment."

"Yes, she would." Butch glanced at her. "When do you take Nathan?"

"About a week. I just can't believe time has passed so fast. Robin and Marvin had a great honeymoon. I'm going over tonight to see a slide show they put together." She looked at the sky, shaking her head. "And God help me, but I'm already dreaming of grandchildren."

Butch laughed and watched the house, all the people milling about. "I've decided time is not good or bad. It is only neutral. It gives back what you put into it."

"You know what I've found to be amazing?"

"What?"

"That God is not at all restrained by time. What I've perhaps wasted, He can multiply miraculously."

"That is good news, isn't it?"

"It is. . . . Hey, Butch?"

"Yes?"

"Can I take Ava shopping tomorrow?"

"Why?"

They both glanced over to watch Ava. "Those pants you have on her? They're not supposed to hit two inches above the ankle."

"They're not?"

"It would be my pleasure if I could."

"You got it." Butch pulled her into a

sideways hug. "I know I've got a lot to learn. Thanks for your help."

"Sometimes the days will feel really long, Butch," Beth said, pulling him tighter, "but just remember, the years are really short."

A NOTE FROM MICHELLE COX

During a Sunday church service, my pastor prayed with a couple who were dedicating their infant son to God. As they turned to walk off the platform, Reverend Sexton said these words: "Don't forget — you have just eighteen summers. Take time to make some memories."

Whew! The poignancy of those words moved me to tears. I was at the end of my eighteen summers with my youngest son, and I knew how quickly each of them had zoomed by. Even though we had made an effort as a family to have fun and make memories, I found myself wishing that we had taken even more time to enjoy those precious fleeting moments with our sons.

Most parents can relate to that. Sometimes we're so busy with the responsibilities and tasks of parenting that we forget to enjoy the journey. We're busy. So are our children. Activity fills every space in the daily schedule. Before we know it, that newborn in pink is zipping around the cul-de-sac on her bike. That tiny boy is yanking at his collar as he poses for graduation pictures. We've heard it before — so many times: "Enjoy these days now. Time passes quickly."

Believe it.

Eighteen years sounds like a long time. The fact that we have just eighteen summers really brings it home. Enjoy those days with your child now because someday you'll wish you could . . . Just ask any mother as she watches her child leave for college.

That's the message behind the Just 18 Summers brand. Our novel is the first piece of the brand to release and we're excited about that. We are in the process of raising the funds for a feature-length film and have plans for additional books, music, and other Just 18 Summers products.

Be sure to check out our blog at just18summers.com. I think you'll love our staff of amazing contributors! We will feature eighteen categories each month, ranging from home decor and hospitality, recipes and meal ideas, to fun things to do with your kids, parenting and relationship tips, inspiring stories, and much more.

Moms and dads, you have just eighteen summers with your children. Please don't miss the moments! Take it from a mom who would give a million dollars if she could walk down the hall and tuck her little boys into bed just one more time.

How many summers do *you* have left? What you do with your children now will determine whether you look back someday with regrets or sweet memories.

I'll close with the words of the elderly lady who stopped me at the mall when my son was just a little guy: "Enjoy that sweet little one. The time goes by so fast and he'll be grown before you know it." Turns out she was right.

Blessings to you and your family,
Michelle

ACKNOWLEDGMENTS

Rene Gutteridge:

One afternoon a very nice lady was driving me to the airport after I finished teaching at a writers' conference. We were chatting and I asked her about what she wrote, so she told me. She mentioned an idea she was working on called *Just 18 Summers*. As she explained the premise to me, and the motivation behind the concept, it struck me as such a wonderful idea that I thought about it for many days afterward and began looking at the time I was spending with my children quite differently.

Fast-forward a couple of years. That nice lady, Michelle Cox, called to tell me she'd written, along with two other screenwriters, the screenplay for the concept she'd told me about and she wondered if I'd be interested in writing the novelization. As soon as I read the script, I knew it was not only something I'd be interested in, but something that many parents all over the world would love too. Every moment that I invested in this project was a moment that I also invested in my kids, because with every page I learned something about them, something about me, or something about my family. I saw myself as a mom through the eyes of each of the characters — my strengths, my flaws, my good intentions gone bad, and my deep love for my kids.

I'd like to thank Michelle Cox, along with Marshal Younger and Torry Martin, for the fabulous script that led me to this novelization. There were so many poignant, funny, and heartwarming moments in the script, and the characters were a lot of fun to play with. Thanks for trusting me with your vision!

I'd also like to thank the fabulous team at Tyndale, including Jan Stob, Sarah Mason, and Karen Watson, along with Cheryl Kerwin, Shaina Turner, and Christy Stroud. Thanks for putting in so much time and effort to bring this book to life in a way that will touch many hearts and lives.

Special thanks also goes to my agent, Janet Grant, and my family, Sean, John, and Cate, for supporting me on every project and loving me in a way that makes our eighteen summers together fly by way too fast. John and Cate, would you please stop growing? Well, I know that's not possible, but I'm so proud of the people you are and the character you show every day of your lives. Thank you, Sean, for being the perfect dad for our kids, and thank you for all the effort you put into raising them and loving them.

Thank You, Father, for the blessing of being a parent, for the wisdom to do it with strength and love, and for the grace given when I fail. Thanks for being the perfect parent to my family and me.

Michelle Cox:

A book like this doesn't happen without the effort and support of many people, and I'd like to thank some of those special folks who have been part of the Just 18 Summers journey with me.

Thank you to my pastor at Trinity Baptist Church, Reverend Ralph Sexton, for making the comment that led to the idea for the Just 18 Summers project and for being a wonderful pastor, friend, and neighbor.

A huge thank-you goes to my agent, Jonathan Clements of Wheelhouse Literary, for believing in me and for all his hard work and support in making this Just 18 Summers dream become a reality. Also thanks go to Rene's awesome agent, Janet Grant of

Books & Such Literary, for all her help.

Thank you to Dave Moody of Elevating Entertainment and Lamon Records for being the first to catch the vision with me. I'm grateful to have you as my business partner for the Just 18 Summers brand.

Thank you to Marshal Younger and Torry Martin for working on the script for *Just 18 Summers* with me. It was fun! I am in awe of your brilliance, comedy, and writing skills. The script provided a wonderful base for the novel, and I can't wait to see the movie!

Thank you to Rene Gutteridge for coming on board to be my coauthor for this book. God has given you an amazing gift with words, my friend. Your stellar writing skills and your ability to see between the lines in such awesome detail have been a blessing.

The team at Tyndale has been tremendous, and I thank all of you for your help on this project. Of special note, thank you to Jan Stob for catching the vision for *Just 18 Summers,* for being our cheerleader, and for pushing us to make this book the best it could be. Thanks to our wonderful editor, Sarah Mason, for all your help, and to the promotion and marketing team of Cheryl Kerwin, Christy Stroud, and Shaina Turner, who've worked so hard to get the word out about *Just 18 Summers.*

Thank you to my dear friend Irma Torre for your gracious offer to draw our logo. I am stunned by your talent and see why Disney animation valued your work so highly.

Thank you to the friends and colleagues who took time out of your busy schedules to read and endorse the book. You're the best!

I've been blessed by some special friends who have been my brainstorming pals and my constant encouragers as I've worked to put the Just 18 Summers brand and book together. Thank you to Margaret Skiles, Jenny Cote, and Lori Marett for always being there.

One of my biggest blessings has been to have a team of people who have prayed faithfully for me and for the Just 18 Summers concept. There are not enough words to thank you adequately for what your prayers have meant to me and to this project. God bless you all!

Thank you to my husband, Paul, who is my biggest cheerleader. Our boys couldn't have had a better dad! Thanks for loving me and encouraging me to chase God's dreams for my life.

And last — but definitely not least —

thank You to God for allowing me to be part of this Just 18 Summers journey, for the precious gift of those eighteen summers with each of my three sons, and for the blessing of watching as my sons and daughters-in-law enjoy their eighteen summers with my sweet grandbabies: Anna, Jack, Ava, Eden, Ethan, and the new little one who will arrive in a few months.

Thank you so much for reading *Just 18 Summers*. Rene and I hope that you'll enjoy it and that you'll make time to enjoy each of those priceless summers with your children.

DISCUSSION QUESTIONS

1. Jenny Browning's death had a big impact on the people in her life. Have you experienced the loss of a family member or close friend? How did you get through that time, and how did that experience change you?

2. Jenny's prayers and daily example touched her daughter's life in many ways. What examples of Jenny's influence do you see in Ava throughout the story? What things can you do to be a good example to the children in your life as you go about your day?

3. When Larry and Beth Anderson receive the news that their daughter is getting married, they are stunned to realize that two of their children will leave home at the same time. How do you think parents can best prepare their children — and

themselves — for this kind of transition? If you're a parent who has reached the empty nest stage, what would you say to parents of young children?

4. Larry and Beth have very different reactions to their children leaving home: Larry decides to have fun with the kids and make memories, and Beth worries that she hasn't taught them enough to be prepared for adult life. Whose approach do you relate to most? During times of major change, how do you respond?

5. Like most expectant parents, Daphne and Tippy are nervous about the birth of their first child, and Daphne's fears easily run away with her. When have you found yourself overwhelmed by worries, whether about parenting or another area of your life? Looking back, did God teach you anything during this time?

6. Charles and Helen Buckley have put their focus on providing monetary things for their children — and yet what the children really want is to have time with their parents and to feel like they are important. How do you see this family — both the parents and the children — struggling to

understand one another? Have you ever faced a similar struggle to balance priorities?

7. Butch wasn't involved much with Ava before Jenny's death but now has to learn all the necessary skills to care for his daughter. How do you see him growing as a dad throughout the story? What can we learn from this father and daughter as they work to build a close relationship?

8. Franklin Hollingsworth is extremely wealthy and successful in the business world, but he realized — too late — that he had missed the important moments with his son. Looking at your life now, are there areas where you're not fully present or living the way you want to? What steps could you take to avoid regrets later on?

9. Inspired by his wife, Butch starts the Jenny Browning Project to build a house for a homeless dad and his daughter. How does this project impact other lives, too? What skills do you have that could be used to help others? How can you inspire your family, friends, or church to help someone else?

10. If you're a parent, how many summers do you have left with your children at home? What are you going to do to make the most of them?

ABOUT THE AUTHORS

Rene Gutteridge is the award-winning and bestselling author of twenty-two novels, including her latest releases, *Misery Loves Company* (suspense), *Greetings from the Flipside* (comedy), and *Heart of the Country* (drama). Her recent suspense titles also include *Listen, Possession,* and *Escapement.* She has novelized six screenplays, including the upcoming release *Old Fashioned. Never the Bride,* a romantic comedy with screenwriter Cheryl McKay, won the Carol Award in 2010 for best women's fiction.

Her indie film — the comedy *Skid,* based on her novel — is in postproduction and due to release in 2014. Rene is a creative consultant on *Boo,* a film based on her beloved novel series, which is in development at Sodium Entertainment with Cory Edwards attached as director and Andrea

Nasfell as screenwriter. Rene is also a co-writer in a collaborative comedy project called *The Last Resort* with screenwriters Torry Martin and Marshal Younger.

Find Rene on Facebook, Twitter, or at renegutteridge.com.

Michelle Cox is the author of seven books with content ranging from inspirational nonfiction to cookbooks to humor books. *Just 18 Summers* (with coauthor Rene Gutteridge) is her first novel.

Michelle is the food blogger for Fox News personality Todd Starnes (toddstarnes.com) and a contributing writer for *WHOAwomen* magazine, and she has been published on FoxNews.com. She has done interviews and written movie reviews for ChristianCinema .com and has written for multiple publications at Focus on the Family. She has been a guest on numerous radio and television programs, including *Hannity, The Harvest Show,* and *Focus on the Family,* and is a speaker at many events. Michelle is on faculty for a number of Christian writing and media conferences. She has also taught webinars for the Jerry B. Jenkins Christian Writers Guild and written scripts and designed book trailers as associate producer Book Preview, a division of Tentmakers

Entertainment. Whew, she'll figure out what she wants to do eventually.

Michelle and her husband, Paul, are the parents of three sons and grandparents to five perfect grandchildren (with one more on the way). They've owned Cox Masonry for the past thirty-nine years and have spent thirty-five years working with teens and single young adults at Trinity Baptist Church.

Join Michelle for "Encouragement with a Southern Drawl" on Facebook (MichelleCox Inspirations), Twitter (@michelleinspire), and her blog (michellecoxinspirations.com). And visit the Just 18 Summers page on Facebook or just18summers.com for Michelle's family and parenting blog.